Circus

JM Dragon

Affinity E-Book Press NZ LTD

Circus

Affinity E-Book Press NZ LTD
Canterbury, New Zealand

ISBN: 13: 978-0615622255
ISBN: 10: 0615622259

This is a work of fiction. Names, characters, places, and incidents are the product of the author's imagination or used fictitiously and any resemblance to actual persons, living or dead, businesses, companies, events, or locales is entirely coincidental.

Editor: Gail Robinson
Editor: Dawn Belistreri
Editor: Kathie Solie
Cover Design: Helen Hayes

Acknowledgments

I'd like to thank those who have read Circus and have given me their honest assessment of the story good or bad. In particular, I'd like to thank Nancy and Mel for their support of my story.

I would also like to thank Gail for taking my raw story and making it readable. Thank you also to Dawn and Kathy for finding all those typos that always seems to crop up unseen.

Dedication

This story is for all those who take a chance on love.

Chapter One

The employment list amounted to a tiny column in the *Rochester Bugle*. In a small town like Rochester, it was *whom* you knew, not *what* you knew, that often secured employment. The woman casting her eye over the newspaper glanced at the available jobs and found two clerical administrative posts at the lowest pay possible and a gardener needed part-time, probably for old man Beaufort, who thought it beneath him to cut his own lawn. That left a motor mechanic and a part-time cinema attendant.

Rita Collins bit her bottom lip as she circled the clerical posts and wondered how ends would meet if she had to take a cut in salary. Not that she had any choice. Watson's Mill, where she had worked, filed for bankruptcy. With no chance that a new buyer would bail it out at the last minute, Rita was desperate to find work. She wasn't the only one in trouble. The mill had employed over thirty people, and they were all looking for work. It was going to be tough to secure any administrative post, especially because she'd be overqualified for most.

The door to the small, three-bedroom house opened and her younger sister, Angel, breezed in. "I've got the ideal position for you, Ri, but you'd best be quick if you want it, since the interviews are tomorrow. Take a look." Her sister threw her a flyer and left the room.

Rita's gaze traveled to her pretty sister, now disappearing down the hall. At twenty-five, Angel had blonde hair, usually in a pony tail, and thick lashes that covered light blue eyes. Her slim figure never seemed to put on weight no matter what Angel ate—it wasn't fair. At an early age, Angel decided that all she wanted to do was settle down, get married, and have a hundred kids—a decent education wasn't on her list. From Rita's point of view, their parents were over indulgent and didn't insist that Angel attend college. She at least attended college and had a career to fall back on—except in Rochester.

Rita and Angela's father, who owned the local hardware store, had been rather stingy with money, but he had decided it would be a good thing if Rita learned a useful skill. . Dutifully, she'd done her stint at college, obtaining a degree in accounting before she went to work for her father. He didn't pay much, so she decided that someday she'd venture out on her own when Rochester became a more affluent town. Then she'd make pots of money—but that never happened. Their parents died in a freak accident when the only bridge over the Jansen River flooded as they crossed it in an unexpected storm. Rita had been twenty-five and Angel seventeen. They couldn't afford to keep up the store and the mortgage on their house, so their only option was to sell the business to the highest bidder. Fortunately, the profits from the sale made it possible for them to live mortgage-free, but they still had to live. From then on, Rita had taken over the care of her sister. After the death of their parents, Angel went a bit wayward and that resulted in Charlie, Angel's seven-year-old son.

Angel refused to tell Rita who the father was, but it didn't matter. Rita loved Charlie.

How could you not love a tousle-haired boy with an impish grin and sea green eyes that looked in wonder at all he saw? He questioned everything and announced to anyone who would listen that he was the man of the house. The sisters had brought up a wonderful, loving child. Just thinking about little Charles Collins made Rita smile.

Her smile lingered as she looked at the flyer clutched in her left hand. *Hmm,* she thought, puzzled. *I wonder why the job's posting is in a flyer and not in the local paper.* She read the flyer with curiosity.

Wanted Immediately: Accountant- must be experienced - to work for half a year from May to October, with the possibility of a full-time position. Excellent compensation for the right candidate. Call L Garmancelli at 888 213-8898.

Rita read it again. *How strange. I've never heard of a Garmancelli in Rochester.* With her brown hair swinging from side to side, Rita contemplated the flyer still in her hand. She walked over to the bathroom door and shouted, "Angel, where did you get this flyer?"

There was no immediate answer.

"Angel, turn down the radio and speak to me, please."

A few moments later, the radio muted.

"What did you say, Ri?" Angel's blonde head, with a cheerful smile, peeked out the door.

Rita looked at her sister and shook her head. *How can someone look so good with their hair all wet? I always look like a drowned rat.* "I asked where you got this. Do you know someone in town named Garmancelli?"

Angel said, "No. Whoever Garmancelli is, he must be new in town. You should go, Ri. Who knows? It could be just what you're looking for."

Rita considered her sister's suggestion. Angel often told her that she had a tendency to think about things too much and too seriously. Perhaps this time spontaneity would win the day. *Yeah, right, one night of spontaneity for Angel resulted in Charlie.* Still, something about the position intrigued her. "Okay, I suppose it won't do any harm to inquire." While her sister was deftly applying make-up, Rita asked, "Are you planning on a late night tonight?"

Angel smiled. "Is that okay? The girls and I are going over to Johnstown, where a new band, *The Grunge* is wowing the locals. We thought we'd check it out," she said with a shrug.

"You're making a habit of going to Johnstown every Friday." Rita heard a note of irritation creeping into her voice. "Oh, go ahead and enjoy the band. I promised Charlie a trip to get ice cream."

Angel asked, "Did you hook up with Dan? He was asking about you again."

Rita considered how she and her sister were complete opposites. Her looks were nothing special. Her brown eyes matched hair that hung just over her shoulders. Her figure wasn't the best either. Wide hips, from their mother's side of the family, would never help in the quest for the perfect figure. She also was cautious, which might have had more to do with her career path than her personality. However, whatever she lacked in looks and daring, she more than made up for in compassion and love. She loved her sister and Charlie fiercely.

"No. I did not *hook up* with Dan. Now finish getting ready."

Once back into the kitchen, Rita gazed intently at the phone on the wall before she made a decision. Her hand trembling, she picked up the receiver and called the number on the flyer. Within two minutes, her name was on the list, and she received a time and place for the interview the next day.

"Well, that was painless. I guess I should call about the other positions, too." She found that one job already hired someone but she obtained an interview for the other at six that evening. "I guess it will be good practice for tomorrow. It's been a while since I've had an interview."

After the calls, Rita sank down on one of the kitchen chairs. She had no choice but to accept the evening appointment. Though it would disappoint Charlie, she would make it up to him.

†

Rita quietly opened the door to her house and smiled at their neighbor, Lory Parker, a motherly soul who had been able to babysit for the two hours that Rita took for the interview. Although Angel had volunteered to give up her big night out, the disappointment that flooded her sister's face, even for a few seconds, had Rita declining the offer. They could afford the few dollars that they insisted Lory take.

"Hi, was he okay?" Rita asked in a hushed tone.

Lory Parker grinned, her wrinkled skin creasing even more as her eyes moved to the sleeping child. She gently moved him off her lap, placing him on the sofa as she got up. "As good as gold. He's never any trouble, Rita. You and your sister are doing a grand job of bringing him up."

Rita looked down tenderly at the boy. Although she and Angel shared parental responsibility, Rita took the lion's share of raising him. Her sister's job as a waitress at Mel's diner had long hours. "I promised him a visit to Hopkins for ice cream and he didn't even make a face at not going. Instead, he said another time was okay."

Lory smiled. "That's Charlie for you, considerate to a tee. Are you sure he isn't yours?"

Rita frowned. *Is Lory being critical of Angel? If so...* "Thanks for taking care of him, Lory." She opened her purse to pay the older woman. "Here's the money I owe you."

"I don't want your money, Rita. I enjoyed watching Charlie. Now that all my boys are away, it feels good to be needed again." Lory began to put on her coat.

Rita insisted "Please, Lory. You know I like for us to pay our own way."

The older woman scowled and shook her head. "I know, Rita, but if that job doesn't come your way, you're going to need every cent. How did the interview go?"

Rita considered for a few minutes exactly how it had gone. "I have more than enough qualifications, probably too many. It was clerical work for Riley Cropper's supermarket with minor cashier work at night. They knew people are desperate for work and offered the lowest wage they legally could."

Lory scrunched up her face. "Why, Rita, if you take that job, what about Charlie?"

Yes, what about Charlie? "I know. I'll have to talk with Angel tomorrow. Seems I can have the job if I give my answer by Sunday," Rita quietly replied. *Cropper wants cheap labor from the desperate, and he knows our family circumstance. He's such a cruel mongrel.*

"It will all work out as it should, Rita. The good Lord will come to your rescue, I'm sure." Lory pocketed the money with a shake of her head. "Good night, Rita."

Rita gazed at the little boy, now curled into a ball on the sofa. He was the reason they would be in trouble if she didn't get a job quickly. His needs were most important. Working for Cropper, however, was about the worst possible scenario she could think of. "I hope that interview tomorrow works out. It might be our only chance to keep things as they are."

Moving to the sofa, she picked up the child, a featherweight, and hugged him to her. "I love you, Charlie, and we will just have to hope that Lory is right and the Lord will make things okay."

Chapter Two

Lorenzo Garmancelli resented his elder sister. He loved her dearly, yet he felt that vexing emotion associated with a close brother-sister relationship most siblings have at some time in their lives. His main irritation: she loved the circus environment, but he had never felt that magical attachment. Their parents, third generation performers of the high trapeze were feted the world over in their early days, particularly in Europe. Today they paraded their talents in hick towns and out in the boonies, hoping to make decent money during the six-month season that would keep them through the winter. The one good thing that had come out of the last twenty years, since his sister had taken over the reins, was that she'd replaced the animals with people. They now employed high-wire acts, clowns, jugglers, and fire-eaters, along with a variety of performers from all over the world. Lorenzo was glad the cruelty of keeping the animals caged was outdated, along with the expense of caring for them during the winter.

It wasn't that they didn't make a good living; his sister wouldn't have it any other way. However, he detested their constant moving from one town to another, never allowing enough time for him to make friends with anyone other than circus performers.

"I'm thirty-eight and I want to settle down," he announced to the empty room. Lorenzo cast his eyes heavenward, sighed, and then looked at the folder with the name of the next person he had to interview.

†

"I'm sorry. Is this the right place? Are you Mr. Garmancelli?"

Lorenzo gave the woman a once over, as his deep-set eyes crinkled at the corner. "Sorry. Yes, I am. And you must be—" he looked at his notes. "Ah, yes, Ms. Collins."

Rita smiled slightly and sat down at the seat he pointed for her to take. "Yes, that's right."

Lorenzo, steepling his fingers, gave her a bright smile. "Do you have your work references?"

Rita nodded and opened the plastic folder that held her resume and handed it to the man. Watching him read, she looked at his features. He was younger than she expected with curly black hair cut relatively short. His features gave the appearance that he was strong and kind. Deep-set blue eyes moved rapidly as he read. His body looked wiry, but not frail, and she noted his long, tapering fingers as he turned the page of her document.

He looked up unexpectedly and gave her a smile. "This seems to be in order, Ms. Collins. Now, I'll tell you a little bit about the job and what we expect."

Rita listened intently. When he'd finished, she was certain there wasn't anything about the job that she couldn't do, except for quirky systems differences, which she'd learn with experience. *Bean counting is bean counting, right*?

"Do you have any questions?"

Rita reflected on the job he'd described. *It all sounds too good to be true...the job, the salary, the hours.* "Only one." Rita looked at the man seated across from her. "Exactly where is the operation based?"

Lorenzo chuckled, his eyes shifting downward to his own papers. "Sorry, a pertinent point that I forgot to mention." He looked up, directly at her. "Have you ever heard of the Garmancelli Circus?"

Rita shook her head.

"Well, if you love traveling, then this is the job for you. You see," he paused for just a moment, "The job is with our traveling circus."

Rita felt her jaw drop. *Crap, I'm going to have to take the Cropper job.*

Lorenzo folded his papers and smiled again. "I'll be in touch by tomorrow, Ms. Collins. Thank you for your time."

Rita got up automatically, shook the offered hand, and left the room in a daze. *A circus? Oh, my! No wonder I've never heard the name before.*

Still in a daze, Rita walked along the main street until she was jolted out of her thoughts. "Rita, wait up," a man shouted. "I want to ask you something." Rita recognized the voice as that of Dan Flounder, a thick-set man with bushy eyebrows and a dark complexion, which most said was from long hours in the sun as the owner of the local garage. In a long, quick stride, he was beside her before she could feign not hearing him and duck out of sight.

"Hi, Dan. How's business?" Rita smiled, hoping he wouldn't keep her long.

Dan replied. "I must say, I'm doing mighty well. Sorry to hear about you being laid off. However, it could change overnight if you let me help."

It was an almost generous offer, but she knew there were strings attached. She and Dan. No way. She liked Dan; he was a good man. However, the thought of spending the rest of her days waking up beside him was something that she couldn't bear. Thankfully, she now had other options, even if it might have to be at Croppers. "Yeah, I can't understand why the other towns around are thriving, but we've been left behind."

Dan stroked his unkempt beard speckled with grey and nodded. "Well, you know, Rita, it's that darned Council of ours. Why they think they need to apply so many ordinances to anyone starting up business here is beyond me. Thank God, my daddy bought the garage when he did."

It was true. The Town Council was rather hard on business. They had taken a stand to focus on protecting the environment and, in the middle of timber and mining country, that wasn't attractive to the big companies that would sink millions into the local economy. What they needed was an attraction three hundred and sixty-five days of the year or at least through the winter. *Although who has the money or inclination to invest in Rochester, is beyond me.*

"I was going to ask if you want to come to the circus with me tonight," Dan said. "Charlie would enjoy it."

Rita had only half heard Dan, but she did notice one word—*circus*. "There's a circus in town?" Her attention now focused on Dan.

"Sure. It's the Garmancelli Circus. Larry Westlake rented them one of his empty lots, the one that has easy access to the main road out of town. I heard the Council is offering free transportation from four to eleven this evening."

"Well, that's a good thing, I suppose. At least they're trying to do something other than annoy prospective businesses." Rita's reply sounded bitter but she couldn't help herself. At least now, she understood why the circus had circulated flyers in their town.

Dan nodded his head. As he did, Rita considered his face. *Yep, definitely Neanderthal. High forehead and big cheek bones*. Another reason Rita wasn't keen on him. Not that she was much of a picture portrait herself. "I'll call for you and Charlie at six then?"

Rita nodded reluctantly.

Dan grinned and headed back across the road to his garage.

Rita groaned. She didn't want to go with Dan. But, it would serve several purposes that had nothing to do with Dan. She would see the circus in action, Charlie would love it, and it would make up for not taking him for ice cream last night "Might as well go, what harm can it do?" She headed home.

†

Music filled the air, and the light show, which spelled out the name of the circus and the town, startled the growing crowd. As Rita looked up, she smiled. *At last, Rochester in lights. Maybe we need a circus in town all the time.*

"This is awesome, Auntie Ri. I wish I could join a circus." Charlie's eyes were wide as he held her hand and walked alongside her and Dan.

Dan laughed with a volume so high that it was drawing the attention of several people. Most knew Dan personally and smiled at him.

"Joining the circus isn't for everyone, Charlie. It looks great on the surface, but I bet it's hard work…really hard work." A tall woman leaning against the side of the ticket office and looking intently at her had caught her attention. It made Rita uncomfortable, and she didn't know why and quickly looked away.

Dan lifted the boy up on his shoulders. "Here you go, Charlie. Now you can see what I see."

Rita glanced back at the dimly lit profile of the woman, who was still watching them with an odd expression. Then Rita looked up at the giggling Charlie. "Dan, he might fall."

"He won't fall. I keep telling you that I'll look after him and you. You only need to say the word, Rita." Dan wove his way through the crowd to provide Charlie an unobstructed view of the parade that heralded the arrival of the main event in the big top.

Rita frowned. "Shouldn't we go inside? It's about to begin."

Dan and Charlie's eyes met. They both grinned. "Spoilsport, Rita. Okay, young Charlie." Dan placed Charlie lightly on the ground. "We have to go inside."

Rita watched Dan buy their tickets from a woman with her face covered in heavy makeup. A few moments later, clutching their tickets, they walked inside the big top.

A cacophony of music, crowd noise, and clowns' bicycle horns accosted them immediately.

"It's so big, Auntie Ri, look, look!" Charlie pointed to the high wire and the trapeze atop the rafters supporting the canvas.

A midget dressed as a clown stepped forward. "Tickets, please."

Dan relinquished the tickets. The little clown looked at the tickets and leaped from one foot to the other.

Charlie grinned from ear to ear at his antics.

"VIP, whoopee!" The clown pointed up to box seats that overlooked every possible angle.

When they settled, Rita turned to Dan. "You didn't have to buy such extravagant tickets, Dan. We would have been happy anywhere."

Dan shrugged. "Hey, you and Charlie are worth it."

Rita considered his remark, her thoughts unsettled. *Maybe I've been too harsh on him.*

"Ladies and Gentlemen, children of all ages," the ringmaster bellowed. "Welcome to the Garmancelli Circus."

For the rest of the evening, Rita and Charlie shared the same transfixed expression.

†

From a distance, Lorenzo gazed at his sister. Occasionally, she chose a family, for whatever reason, and issued the instruction to give them the best seats in the house. She claimed it was a tradition, but he knew differently. It was something else. In some strange way, he felt, his sister was reaching out to those she believed looked *normal*. With a steady stride, he reached his sister. "Hey, it's a good crowd tonight."

"Yes, it's rather remarkable. I understand there have been heavy job losses here recently."

"I did what you asked, and there are two candidates."

An impenetrable gaze caught his. "Two. That's good. Do you have a favorite?"

Lorenzo shrugged. "Not really, both are qualified, but I suspect that one will fall by the wayside."

"Really, why do you say that?"

"When I mentioned the circus, she looked—" He stopped, fumbling for the right word. "She looked confounded. Stunned."

"Confounded? That doesn't sound too promising."

"Yeah, well, who knows? The guy seemed willing though." Lorenzo looked around at the crowd who'd already begun enjoying the final performance of the night. "I have to go. The Carmines want me to make sure that their equipment is one hundred percent." He waved and headed in the opposite direction.

†

Lorenzo's sister moved from her position lounging at the side of the ticket office and muttered. "Willing? Doesn't everyone want to run away and join the circus? Some of us would rather it be the other way around so we could leave the circus behind us." She then walked over to a side opening of the big top and walked inside. From her vantage point, she could see almost everything. She surveyed the many customers and she nodded. Almost a full house.

Her focus took in the box seats she'd authorized for the large man, the attractive woman, and their darling son. *Happy families, exactly what my circus is all about*. Her gaze was resting on the rapt face of the young boy.

A voice from outside called her name and she disappeared into the darkness.

†

By the time they arrived home, Charlie was asleep. Dan had carried him the few hundred yards from the bus stop to Rita's house. The porch light glowed invitingly as they approached the front door. Angel was working a late shift and, with the circus in town, probably would work until at least one in the morning.

"We enjoyed the evening, Dan." Rita opened the door, turned, and reached out her arms. "I'll take him now."

Dan handed her the sleeping child and waited.

Rita drew in a breath. He wanted a kiss. She was sure that he probably expected more, after spending so much money on the tickets. With Charlie wrapped safely in her arms, she smiled warmly at Dan. "Maybe we can have coffee together on Monday. Call me."

Fortune was on her side, as he appeared to accept her *thank you* in words rather than deeds. He nodded, grinned widely, and turned to leave. After two steps, he turned and waved goodnight.

Rita entered the dark house and deftly switched on the hall light. *These are nothing like the big top lights at the end of the performance.*

Ten minutes later, Charlie was sleeping soundly in his bed. Rita switched on the television, sank into her old sofa, and contemplated her options. Given her current circumstances, only one had any merit. .She had to take the Cropper job and hope that Riley Cropper would have compassion if Charlie ever became sick.

Chapter Three

Angel paced the kitchen floor as she waited for Rita to wake up. Normally, her sister was up at dawn but not today. Maybe she had finally accepted that Dan was her chance to have a family life of her own and she had spoken with him about their future. *In one way. I hope so*, Angel though. *In another, Ri can do so much better—she deserves better.*

As if on cue, Rita walked into the kitchen, yawning. "What are you doing up? It usually takes my bacon and eggs to open your eyes on a Sunday."

"Yeah, well, some of us can get up at a reasonable time. Besides, Charlie wanted to go play with James next door," Angel glanced at the clock—it was nine-thirty. "How did it go with Dan?"

Rita scratched the top of her head. "Okay, I guess. It must have cost him a fortune to get the tickets. We could see everything and we had a clown as a permanent companion. Charlie was enthralled."

"Yeah, I've heard *the circus this* and *the circus that* since he woke up. Dan must really think a great deal about you, Rita, to pay for those kinds of seats." She paused for a moment. "What do you think about him after last night?" Angel smiled.

"He didn't expect anything much. I said we could get together Monday for coffee," Rita replied.

Angel grinned. "Wonderful. Now I don't feel so bad about what I have to tell you."

Rita gazed at her sister. "Do I need to sit?"

Angel smiled gently. "It probably won't hurt if we both do."

Once seated, Rita turned an expectant face to her sister.

"You know we never discussed Charlie's father, at least not in detail. You've always been so good not bugging me about that." Angel toyed with the salt and pepper shakers on the table.

"I figured that one day, when the time was right, you'd tell Charlie. After all, it's about him, not me," Rita replied.

Angel nodded. "I met up with his father again six months ago. That's the reason I've been going to Johnstown every week."

Rita's eyes flew open as wide as possible in surprise. "What do you mean?"

"Charlie's father's name is Trevor…Trevor Arnold. He's a doctor and works at Johnstown General Hospital. We met when he was in med school. You remember I used to work in Johnstown Friday and Saturday's at Rocky's diner…" Rita nodded, "He'd study for hours at the diner, drinking coffee. Occasionally I'd slip him a piece of pie, and we just got to talking, and…" She stopped abruptly and in a rush she blurted, "We, that is Charlie and I.... Trevor's asked me to marry him, Rita, and I love him."

A stunned atmosphere took over the room, imitating the aftermath of an exploded bomb. Rita said nothing as she stood, walked over to the kitchen sink, ran the water, and filled the kettle.

"Aren't you going to say something…anything? I'd like your blessing." Angel asked her voice trembling slightly. She'd never before seen her sister go so pale.

In a low voice, her lips in a tight line, Rita faced Angel. "Why? It seems to me you have everything worked out."

Angel pushed a few strands of blonde hair behind her ears. "It wasn't planned that we would meet. I thought he'd left the state. He came back for me, Rita." She looked at her sister. "Can't you be happy that I've met him again? If not for me, then for Charlie."

A cloud passed over Rita's face. "All I want to know is why you've never told me. You could have said something months ago. I would have understood." Rita softened her tone. "If you and Charlie are happy, that makes me happy. Don't you know that by now?"

"It's because you love us so much that I didn't," Angel replied. Her voice faltered. "I was afraid."

"Afraid? Of me? Why?" Rita asked.

Angel stood up and placed a hand on Rita's arm. "Because you have no one, especially if Charlie and I leave. I wanted you to be happy with someone, too. Does that make me a bad sister?"

Rita drew in a shaky breath. "Has Trevor met his son?"

Angel shook her head. "No, I wanted to make sure that things would work out with him first. I didn't want him to come into Charlie's life and then leave him high and dry."

"You think he would do that? Didn't he know you were pregnant?"

"No," Angel explained, "I broke it off before he guessed. It was the hardest thing for me to do. I loved him, but he had his career to think about. He was about to begin his residency."

Rita schooled her features. "Over the years since Charlie's birth, I expected you to meet someone and marry someday. To be frank, I was surprised you only flirted with men but didn't actually take them seriously." Rita shook her head. "You've loved this Trevor all the time, haven't you, Angel? You always lived in hope that he'd come looking for you?"

Angel gave Rita a wry smile. "Yes, I guess I'm just a dreamer. I was hoping that it all would work out."

After a momentary silence, Rita spoke again, her tone bright. "Then, I guess you'd best bring him over to meet us." Rita pulled her sister close and hugged her tight.

"Oh, Rita, I do love you. I asked him to come over for breakfast. He's in the car outside, across the street. I'll go and get him." Angel kissed her sister's cheek and rushed out of the house.

Rita chuckled. *Typical Angel!* Her thoughts quickly changed direction. "Well, I never saw that coming." Her bravado crumbled for a moment and her face took on a hurt expression. *Not only am I going to lose Angel, but Charlie too. He's the son I'm never likely to have, unless I consider taking on Dan.* The very idea made her shudder. Rita squared her shoulders and said aloud, "Darn it, no. I want what Angel has and don't want to compromise. Maybe one day I'll find it."

Watching from the window, Rita saw Angel walking hand in hand with a tall fellow who had the same coloring as Charlie, along with his curly hair—a tell-tale sign. When Trevor Arnold shyly walked into the house to meet her, Rita saw Charlie's sea green eyes look at her with a serious expression. This definitely was Charlie's father, and she could envision him as a doctor. His expression seemed compassionate.

"Welcome to the family, Trevor." Rita stretched out her hand.

Trevor ignored the hand and his strong arms engulfed Rita in a warm hug. "Thank you, Rita, for a great many things. Most of all, thank you for loving Angel and Charlie so much."

Rita, uncomfortable with the praise, nodded. "You're welcome." She turned and headed into the kitchen. "Right, let's have some breakfast, shall we? I make a decent one. Besides, Charlie will be here any moment, wondering why it isn't on the table."

While Rita reached into the refrigerator for eggs and bacon, she fought back tears. Yes, she was genuinely happy for Angel and Charlie. She couldn't help but wonder what it would be like without them. Just as Rita set the breakfast ingredients on the counter, the phone rang. She reached for it automatically.

"Yes, this is she," she said. After talking for a few minutes, she hung up with a surprised look.

"Who was that?" Angel asked.

Rita didn't answer immediately. She let a half smile curved her lips. "You don't need to worry about me being alone here, Angel."

"I don't? Was that Dan?"

"No, it wasn't Dan. I've just accepted a job." She paused. "I'm going to join the circus."

Rita found the words strange as they rolled out of her mouth. When she glanced at her sister and Trevor, she saw shock and astonishment.

After accepting their surprised congratulations, Rita leaned against the counter. *Oh, my God, what have I done?*

†

Lorenzo tucked his left leg under his right thigh as he lounged on the sofa in his sister's trailer. He lazily glanced around at the minimalist decor within the luxurious motor home. A compact kitchen area boasted every convenience including comfortable seating. His sister's one indulgence was a curving blue-black leather sofa on which he now lounged. The monster couch enclosed him in its pliable material, and he enjoyed the feeling of being in a comfortable cocoon. He continued surveying the trailer. A study area at the rear of the trailer housed a laptop and all the usual paraphernalia associated with running a business. There were three generously sized bedrooms one was a mini-gym complete with a shower and commode. He noted the absence of photos, knick-knacks, or any personal touches.

His sister glanced at him, and then turned back to the computer screen that captured her complete attention. "I take it from your smug expression you've hired us a bookkeeper?" she asked in a low, smoky voice.

Lorenzo gazed at the back of his sister. She sat on the swivel chair with almost perfect posture. Dark black hair reached her wide muscular shoulders. "Yes, I did."

"Good, when do they start?"

"You don't want to know which one is coming to work for us, only when?" Lorenzo craned his neck at the disturbance he heard outside the trailer. *Jacamar is in a tantrum again.*

His sister's chair swung around.

Lorenzo grinned boyishly at his sibling, noting the three deep frown lines across her high forehead. Her cobalt eyes narrowed as she looked at him.

"Okay, I'll ask. Was it the *willing* or the *confounded* candidate?"

The younger man laughed. "Would you believe, Ms. Confounded? I must say she was the best qualified, but I really didn't think we had a chance." He stood up and stretched. "I guess I must be losing my talent for figuring people out."

"I doubt that. You're one of the best judges of character I've ever met, which is why I trusted you with the hiring process." She arched one eyebrow. "When does Ms. Confounded arrive?"

Lorenzo beamed at his sister's kind words. It was a rare occurrence. "I said we needed her at Mateo City a week from today, around noon." The sound of the escalating argument had Lorenzo moving toward the door. "Jacamar is causing merry hell again," he observed, peering through the window. "I bet he went drinking in town last night. He's always grouchy after a heavy session." He opened the door. "I'll catch up with you later, sis."

†

Neve watched her brother disappear. She stood up, stretching her lean, five-foot ten-inch frame. Her eyes tracked to the window and she watched her brother ably diffusing the situation. "I don't know what I'd do without you, little brother."

With a sigh, she returned to her computer and the headache of working out the numbers. She hated bookkeeping.

Her thoughts turned to her Uncle Silvestre, a trapeze catcher until that terrible freak accident in which Neve's mother died. After that, Silvestre never went back up. In fact, he left the circus, went to college, and studied accounting. When he returned to the circus several years later, he kept the books.

Well, thank God, Lorenzo settled that annoyance. Neve's thoughts returned to the present and the new hire. "Lorenzo never even told me the name of this woman. He surely doesn't expect me to call her Ms. Confounded," She snorted. "Then again—" Her smile vanished as she stared at the numerous columns of figures she was trying to understand. *Next week can't come fast enough.*

Chapter Four

Mateo City was considerably larger than Rochester, and, even at eight-thirty on a Sunday morning, the bus station was busy. Rita stood on the station's platform, surveying the bustling environment. Men dressed in business suits, harried mothers pushing strollers with one hand while clutching at a toddler with the other, and college students with hefty backpacks plugged into iPods. A booming voice announced three greyhound buses were about to leave for various destinations.

Rita thoughts turned to the trip that got her to Mateo City...

Because of the distance, she'd had little option but to begin her journey from Rochester late in the afternoon the day before. The trip was more tedious than arduous. The bus seemed to stop at every small town in its path. One town had a twenty-four hour café, which was where the bus driver had taken his thirty-minute break and the passengers stretched their legs and had a snack. Then it was back on the bus stopping at more small towns until finally arriving in Mateo City.

The journey had been a time for her to take stock of what she had done. Her joining the circus amused the few people she had told. Some laughed in a teasing way. Others—like Dan—not so much. He'd taken the news badly, which had irked her. They were hardly a couple. Lory, her next door neighbor, had been surprised at first but then wished her good luck. It was, she said, *time for a change, Rita.*

Angel was basking in her rekindled romance with Charlie's father. And Charlie —well, Charlie had made her cry. Of all the people she was leaving behind, he was the one she would miss the most. Yet, it had to be that way. She'd always known deep down that one day Angel would make a life for herself and Charlie that wouldn't include her. Now that it had happened, she had her own journey of discovery to undertake. At first, Charlie couldn't understand why his Auntie Ri was leaving. Eventually, however, he was excited for her, especially when she said that if the circus came back to town, he'd have a personal guided tour.

The sound of a horn, indicating a bus was leaving, drew Rita out of her musings. She looked down at the notes she'd scribbled during her last conversation with Mr. Garmancelli two days before. The circus was currently encamped at Riley Industrial Park. Her gaze sought out someone who might know what bus to catch to get there. Once she spied the only open window, she strode purposefully with her suitcase in hand and then stood patiently in line until she came face-to-face with the man behind the information counter.

"Hi, I'd like to know which bus I need to catch to reach Riley Industrial Park, please."

The counter operator, a thin, balding man with a long face, shook his head. "Sorry, not today. The nearest you can get is ten blocks away on the number twelve or seventeen. They're on row 'A'." He pointed in the vague direction of several platforms.

Rita muttered a sarcastic *thank you* before walking away.

The morning was cool, and a soft breeze ruffled her hair. Her breath, though not visible, felt warm when she exhaled. As tired as she was, Rita dreaded the thought of walking ten blocks lugging her heavy suitcase. There was only one thing to do—take a taxi. She normally loathed spending her money on such an extravagance, but under the current circumstances, she could justify it. Besides, she was weary of waiting and traveling. The sooner her journey was complete the better. Then she could put her feet up and relax with a hot cup of lemon tea.

Fortunately, there was a taxi stand at the bus station. Two cabbies chatting amiably looked up expectantly as Rita moved closer. The smaller of the two men nodded his head in the direction of the cab at the front of the line and directed her forward with a toothy grin.

Rita climbed inside still clutching her suitcase, which made the maneuver difficult. She didn't want to relinquish it—it held the sum of her personal life.

"Where to, lady?"

"I need to go to Riley Industrial Park, please."

The taxi driver gave her a second look then nodded before speeding off into the mainstream of traffic.

Rita, who was feeling wearier than before, hoped that whatever accommodation there was available to her she could have it immediately. *A short nap should do the trick.*

The kaleidoscope of buildings and streets that had no meaning for Rita whizzed by, as she was tempted to take a few short winks. However, she'd seen the movie *Bone Collector* and decided that napping in a strange town in the company of a stranger—even if it was a cab driver—wasn't a smart move.

In what seemed like an age, the taxi began to slow and the driver spoke again. "Exactly where do you want to go, Miss? Riley Park's a large place, filled mostly with derelicts." He looked at her reflection in the rear-view mirror. "Are you sure this is the right place? You don't look like you come from around here."

"Well, actually I'm looking for the circus…Garmancelli's Circus."

The driver chuckled. "Now, I wouldn't peg you for running away to join the circus type. No offense."

Rita half smiled. "Me either, but here I am."

The driver didn't say any more as they turned a corner. A beehive of activity came into view. Several people crowded busily around the main tent. People of all ages and ethnicities scurried about, occasionally barking an order to unseen others, and folks zipped in and out of trailers, cars and eighteen wheelers that were scattered haphazardly across the lot. Above everything was the noise of boom boxes blasting music, hammers pounding, drills buzzing, and people shouting above the din of moving equipment.

The difference from her previous job at the mill astounded her. At the mill, the actual physical part of the work was undertaken a few miles into the forest and far from the quiet of the administrative offices.

The driver pulled his cab to a stop. "Here you are."

Still overcome by the sights and sounds, Rita nodded. *Yes, here I am.*

After climbing out of the cab, Rita gave the driver his fare, along with a decent tip, before collecting her suitcase.

The driver tipped his hat, wished her good luck, and left her standing on the road opposite the frenzied hustle.

"I wonder where I go," Rita mused aloud. "Guess the only way to find out is to ask." Taking a deep breath, she crossed the road and walked toward the first set of people she saw. It looked like to her that they were heaving on ropes to pull down the main tent.

Rita watched in fascination as people suddenly came from out of nowhere and began to help. The contrast in physiques indicated they weren't the usual manual laborers.

"Can I help you?" A squeaky voice interrupted Rita's speculation. She looked at eye level and saw nothing. Dropping her gaze, she realized the voice had come from a little person who stood next to her.

"Hi. Yes, I hope so. I'm looking for Mr. Garmancelli." Rita gave the man a slight smile.

The dwarf gave her a long look with his Roman nose jutting out as he nodded. "I'll take you to him."

"Thank you." Rita virtually ran to keep up with the small man who led her around large truck cabs, some hooked up to trailers and others empty. They wove through a maze of recreational vehicles in various shapes and sizes, many mobile, others the type that needed to be towed. They stopped outside the largest motor home Rita had ever seen. It was beautiful, with crimson paintwork and meticulously polished chrome that traveled the length of the vehicle. Rita estimated it to be the same size as the bus she'd traveled on to get here.

"He's inside," her escort said.

When Rita turned to thank the man, she saw him disappearing around the corner of the RV before she could say a word.

Rita climbed the three short steps of the trailer about to knock on the door when she heard raised voices. To her great surprise, she heard her name. She knew that eavesdroppers rarely hear anything good about themselves, but the temptation was too great.

"I keep telling you, Neve, her name is *Collins* not Confounded. She'll be here at lunch time. Please don't call her that to her face."

"Well, then you never should have described her as that in the first place," a woman's voice responded. "She does know she starts work tomorrow morning at six, right?"

"Well, I didn't go into the finer details, Neve. I figured we'd go through all the issues this afternoon."

"Hrmphf, if you say so. That's your job, not mine."

Rita heard some drawers opening and banging closed. "That brings me to the other reason I wanted to see you."

Rita stood transfixed to the spot. *They call me 'confounded'"* Why had Mr. Garmancelli called her that? It wasn't very nice. And, if he thought that, why did he hire her in the first place? Before she could knock on the door, it opened wide and two pairs of eyes looked at her, one in amusement, and the other with suspicion.

"Is there something I can do for you?"

Rita stared at the woman who was glaring at her as if she were an auditor from the IRS. "I…that is I…"

Lorenzo moved, slid past his sister, and held out his hand. "Why, Ms. Collins, you're early."

Rita politely shook his hand, still not happy about what he'd called her. However, at least his smile was warm unlike the frosty expression she was receiving from the woman he called Neve. "I had to take an overnight Greyhound to get here today. It feels like I've been traveling forever."

"You'll get used to that." The words came as a hiss from the woman who still looked at Rita in the most unfriendly manner.

Lorenzo moved to stand in the doorway, effectively blocking out the unfriendly woman. "Why don't I show you your trailer and then maybe you might want breakfast…"

"Breakfast is over, Lorenzo," Neve interrupted. "As you well know. If Miss Con…if Miss Collins requires sustenance, she will have to wait until lunch."

The words were so formal that Rita wondered if they were attached to a clipboard.

Lorenzo smiled at Rita. "Ah, yes, but I can manage to rustle up toast if you like."

"No, I'm fine, thanks," replied Rita. "Actually, I'd love some tea, if that's possible." She shot a quick look at the woman in the trailer who was still glaring at her.

Lorenzo chuckled and reached for her suitcase before hooking his arm in Rita's arm. "Ms. Collins, you've now joined the ranks of the gypsies. Tea is an essential rite of passage."

"I guess I'll be okay then." Rita moved away from the brooding woman who was still standing the doorway. *Gee, I hope I don't have to see much of her. I swear that she doesn't like me.*

Lorenzo steered Rita toward a beautiful bright blue motor home with silver and chrome flashings. She watched in surprise as Lorenzo opened the door and passed her the key. "Here you go. Home sweet home." He stepped aside to allow her to enter first.

When she did, she put a hand to her mouth. The interior was virtually new, and the place was pristine. Hardly used, as far as she could tell. Her eyes took in the kitchen galley with oak cabinets, microwave, stove, and every imaginable modern convenience. A lounge area with a curved seat faced a recessed TV and entertainment unit. Rita blinked in amazement. It looked better than the house that she owned with Angel.

"What do you think? Your first impression, that is. There's a bedroom with a double bed and a small bedroom with a bunk-bed, shower, flushing toilet—the works." Lorenzo grinned. "Oh, and in the far corner behind the television wall there's a small alcove that has a computer, etcetera. Call it the miniature office."

"It's beautiful." Rita whispered. "Thank you for this opportunity."

"Thank you for accepting, Rita. I can vouch for the bedding being clean. We aired and changed everything yesterday. Why don't you go take a shower, maybe a short nap and I'll call at," he looked down at his watch, "at, say, one. That will give you a little time to settle in. We'll have lunch, and I'll tell you a little more of what is expected from the accountant here."

Rita nodded. "That sounds great to me."

"Excellent." Lorenzo deposited the suitcase near the door and left with a wave, shutting the door behind him.

Rita could not believe this was hers. It was different from a house, sure, but it had all the comforts of home. The furnishings put her comfortable but well-worn furniture and ancient electronics to shame. Her fingertips trailed the work surfaces and she moved to the living area, sinking onto a bench covered in what she would call oatmeal fabric. Rita noted with approval the attractive square pattern and smoothed her hand over the cushion appreciatively. She picked up the remote, pressed the *on* button and the TV came to life. "Wow," she exclaimed. "Satellite."

†

Neve stood for a few moments, simply staring at the wasteland in front of her. *How odd is it that someone I'd given preferential tickets to is actually going to work for us? It makes a damn mockery of my theory about happy families. Maybe she's left the family behind.* She shook her head in disbelief. *Who'd do that to a kid?* Her name, that someone in the distance was calling, caught her attention and, discarding the thought, she strode off in that direction.

With the final folding of the tent, there was a tradition that she, the boss, should fold the final corner. A superstition, some might say, but fables and mystic omens of good and bad luck were the norm for circuses.

"I've got it, Jacamar." Neve smiled at the small man, who gave her a warm, toothless grin.

Half an hour later, the tent, the foundation of the circus, encased in its cover, was ready for shipment to the next town.

Jacamar tied the final strap before crossing his arms. "How are we doing, boss?"

Neve hesitated then shrugged. "I'm no bookkeeper, but the figures look okay to me."

"Yeah, but will we all be coming back next year? Silvestre was always complaining that we didn't make enough to make ends meet." The small man looked at his boss's trying to discern what was behind her bland expression.

"Jacamar, please, haven't we always come back? Things aren't that bad." Neve tried to sound reassuring. "Silvestre should've retired five years ago, but he insisted he wanted to stay until he couldn't work anymore. He was my uncle, so what could I do?" she shrugged. "Anyway, we'll know soon enough since we've hired a new accountant.

Jacamar narrowed his eyes. "Was that the woman who wanted to see Lorenzo?"

Neve nodded. "How did you know?"

Jacamar winked. "She asked for directions."

"Yes, Rita Con…Collins. Hopefully, she'll catch on quick, so I can go back to doing what I do best."

"What would that be, boss? You don't do the high trapeze anymore, well not for money anyways."

Neve flashed the small man a harsh stare then relaxed a little. "Don't be facetious, Jacamar. What I can do is kick butt. Yours is looking mighty welcoming since you're gossiping instead of working."

Jacamar laughed as he did a double somersault and gave her a wave before heading away.

He was one of the older troupers and she'd known him all her life. He was her godfather and looked the least likely to give her advice; however, he did so pragmatically and only when asked. She understood Jacamar's concern.

Her father bought the circus when she was three years old and soon after that, her mother died. They hadn't much money—the nature of the business meant lean times —but they were happy ones, especially in the old days. In the last twenty years, Neve had to work through winter to keep the hounds from the door just to keep the business marginally afloat. Winter holidays for her usually meant working as a trainer of young talent wherever she could. She'd do anything to add to the business's dwindling funds. The death of her uncle from a heart attack three months earlier had been a hard blow, and she should have had someone in the wings waiting to take over. That would have been the ideal, but she couldn't afford to have anyone on the bankroll who wasn't contributing.

Her thoughts drifted to the newcomer. *She won't stay. I'd bet my next pay check on it...if I ever get one that is.*

"Boss," one of the clowns said. "The Carmines are going crazy because they want Jed to drive them."

Neve rolled her eyes and nodded. "Okay, leave it with me. I'll handle the Carmines." She placed her fingertips to her lips and kissed them, then placed them on the cover of the main tent. "Safe journey."

Chapter Five

The sound of someone knocking on the metal door jarred Rita into consciousness. Peeking out of one eye, she attempted to work out where she was. From her comfortable queen-sized bed, her slightly glazed eyes took in a dressing table with an enormous mirror and oak paneled walls.

Another hearty knock.

"Oh, crap…my new boss!" Rita jumped off the bed and grabbing a robe, ran to the door.

She opened the door and came face-to-face with Neve. Her heart pounded and she wished she'd taken a few extra seconds to put on some decent clothes. She clutched her flimsy robe tightly around her middle. Rita felt dark blue eyes with flecks of what Rita decided could only be termed flakes of frost, assessing her like a bug under a microscope. The tiny movement of thin lips clearly indicated disapproval.

"Lorenzo was otherwise engaged and he asked me to take you to the tent for lunch."

Rita bit her bottom lip. She surveyed the woman's sturdy black boots, long denim-clad legs, and a red and blue plaid shirt. Rita normally would associate that apparel with the lumberjacks at the mill. She sucked in a short breath of courage and caught Neve's unusually colored eyes, virtually kaleidoscopic. They were the bluest she'd ever seen, mingled in with flecks of ice and an almost purple haze. She also noticed the bland expression "I'm sorry. I fell asleep. If you point me in the right direction, I'll dress and catch up with you."

Neve nodded slightly. "I'll wait." She crossed her arms and leaned against the door frame.

Rita was unsure what to make of this standoffish woman. "Do you want to come in while I dress?"

Rita moved away from the door, and the woman entered. She seemed to make the room tiny and yet she wasn't that big. *She holds herself in a way that makes her look bigger.* Rita felt an overwhelming need to make small talk. "Are you a performer?"

"Once. A long time ago."

Rita felt the woman's eyes assessing her.

"Are you going to get dressed?"

Rita almost could feel the chill that accompanied Neve's words.

"Sure, I'll be just a few minutes." True to her word, Rita was back in less than five minutes. She wore a pair of black slacks and a soft woolen sweater, pink, that accentuated her generous breasts and hips. She hoped she looked presentable but didn't have time to worry about her appearance.

When Rita walked back into the main living area surprised to see the woman had moved. For some reason, she expected the woman to remain a statue, solidly planted in the place she'd left her. Instead, she was in the far corner bending over the computer. "I'm ready."

Neve turned her head. "Good, let's go."

Rita's anger was simmering at the woman's arrogance. *Who does she think she is? She comes marching in here as if she owns the place. I hope this isn't a community vehicle. I'll have to ask Mr. Garmancelli.* "Yes, let's," she replied, equally cold.

Once she closed the door behind her, she fumbled in her pocket for the key before locking it.

Neve said nothing but raised her eyebrows.

They headed for the tent in silence. Even though Neve didn't speak, Rita was glad for the escort. A myriad of vehicles of all shapes and sizes made their route complicated.

Eventually, they reached the tent. Once inside, a cascade of sights, sounds, and smells washed over her. Rita was amazed at the wealth of skin colors, ethnicities, accents, and above it all, the aroma of delicious-smelling food. At the center of the circular tent was a buffet table laden with a variety and abundance of food.

"Eat as much as you want," Neve said.

Rita stood transfixed when she heard someone shout out Neve's name from a darkened corner and the woman with an absent, *excuse me*, left her standing alone. Rita allowed her stomach to dictate her next step. She filled her plate with salad and a small piece of smoked chicken, and then turned to find an unobtrusive place to eat.

Just then, Lorenzo arrived, smiling warmly. "Rita—I take it that I can call you that? *Ms. Collins* seems so formal, and around here it just doesn't fit." He chuckled.

The sound made Rita relax. "Better than *Confounded*?"

"You heard that. I'm sorry."

Rita sensed his discomfort but said nothing.

"I didn't mean it to be derogatory, Rita. It described your expression when I told you where you'd be working. Usually people don't react as interestingly as you did." He looked at her imploringly. "Can you forgive me?"

"You're forgiven, Lorenzo." Rita gave him a small smile.

Lorenzo grinned widely. "Thank you, Rita. Okay, now it's time to meet some of the old-timers. You'll find in a few days that you'll have met just about everyone and they're all friendly." He winked. "If they aren't, you just let me know and I'll growl right back at them for you." He led her toward a crowded table.

"Ladies and gentlemen, I'd like you to meet our new accountant, Rita Collins." He motioned for Rita to sit on the bench and he sat next to her.

A chorus of "Welcome, Rita" and "Glad to have you on board" greeted her.

Lorenzo reached over the table and retrieved a pitcher of lemonade. "Want some lemonade, Rita? I can vouch that it's the best, right, Clara?" He grinned at the large woman to his left.

Rita smiled at Clara, who looked as though she had just stepped out of a storybook. Her round cheeks were rosy, her lips shaped like a bow, and wisps of silver hair escaped the bun on a head that seemed far too small for such a rotund body.

"Yah." She nodded, several chins wobbling. "You can *mein liebchen.* I've been making it for the last thirty-five years. Clara turned toward Rita and smiled broadly. "You'll love it here, Rita. We are like family. When I arrived from Germany many years ago to join this troupe, they became my family." She beamed at the others seated at the table.

Rita learned that three brothers, Leo, Caspian, and Tony Marley, was the most acclaimed high wire act in the sixties. A very thin woman named Mary Lou was an ex-contortionist and Clara was on the bill as *The Fat Lady*. Her heart went out to Clara whose hands were so arthritic making her barely able to hold the fork she used to take tiny morsels of food.

As they ate lunch, Rita relaxed while Lorenzo gave her some insight into the workings of the circus. By the end of her meager meal, Rita's head was spinning. Maybe she'd been too frugal with her selections for lunch. The meats smelled delicious, and her eyes moved to the food table. Lorenzo nudged her gently. "Go ahead. We expect everyone to go for seconds. Neve hates waste. Besides, I doubt that the tiny chicken and salad you had touched the sides." He grinned. "Call it the appetizer."

With an effort, Clara stood up. "Come with me, Rita, I'll get you a plate and show you all the goodies." She waddled off, and Rita followed obediently.

At the table, they joined a small line. "Dessert," Clara explained. "Philippe made it today—a French chocolate concoction. It's wunderbar, marvelous. But Philippe, he don't give the recipe to no one."

"Oh, I don't eat much chocolate," Rita responded. "I'm more of an apple pie person."

At that remark, the person in front of them, obscured because of Clara's girth, leaned around the large woman and piercing eyes caught Rita's eyes.

Rita swallowed hard. *Oh, no, not her again!*

"Neve, liebchen, you know you shouldn't eat the dessert first. It's not good for you."

To Rita, the German term for darling didn't quite fit the brooding features of the woman Clara warmly chastised. Then she recalled Lorenzo's remark that Neve hated waste. *Ah, perhaps that explains it. Neve is in charge of catering.*

"If I don't get a piece of Philippe's truffle torte now, I never will."

Rita noted that Neve's reply was less cold than any verbal exchange she'd had with her. But what she heard couldn't be called warm.

She turned her attention to Rita. "I see you've met the old troupers, Ms. Collins." She nodded at the large woman who was busily filling a plate with an assortment of meats and vegetables. "Clara will certainly ensure that you don't go without food or friendship."

Rita was unsure of how to respond. "She's being very helpful."

Neve nodded. "Good. We can't have you saying the circus starves people on their first day. It would be a terrible impression to give to an outsider."

Rita watched as Neve moved to the front of the line where Phillippe, cutting what looked like a heavenly chocolate delight, greeted her warmly. *Charlie would love it*. The thought of her nephew brought a sudden rush of tears to Rita's eyes, and she wiped them away self-consciously.

"Here you go, Rita." Clara handed her a plate piled high with food. "Take that back with you and enjoy. I'm going to get myself some of Philippe's creation." She giggled like a schoolgirl and lumbered to the head of the dessert line.

Rita's eyes popped at the enormous plate of food, but dutifully she took it back to the table where everyone chuckled.

"Don't worry, Rita, we won't expect you to eat all that. Clara gets carried away sometimes. In case you hadn't noticed, she loves her food." Lorenzo smiled.

Rita laughed. "Thanks, this would last me a week at home." She'd just dug into a savory piece of roast beef when Neve arrived and sat at the end of the table. Rita nearly choked.

Lorenzo smiled at Neve with a look so tender it reminded Rita of one she might give Charlie.

Lorenzo turned to face Rita. "I know you've kind of met Neve, but I was remiss in not introducing her properly to you. Rita, the woman at the head of the table is Neve, Neve Garmancelli, my sister, and the owner of the circus. Rita, meet our boss and now your new boss and who pays your salary."

At that news, Rita coughed, sputtered, and that saved her from having to reply.

"I think someone should give Ms. Collins a slap on the back and a drink of water." Neve announced.

Several people obliged.

When Rita finally stopped coughing, she felt like an idiot. She knew her face was red, and she cringed at the sight of scattered food morsels. *Darn, how to make a good impression and influence people.* Rita leaned closer to Lorenzo. "I thought *you* were my boss."

Lorenzo shook his head and smiled. "Sorry, Rita, I'm just the fix-it guy around here." He patted Rita's hand. "Neve is okay. You just have to give her a little time to get to know you."

Rita's appetite had flown out of the window and her stomach lurched. "Do you mind if I go back to my RV and sort out a few things?" She was unable to make eye contact with Neve Garmancelli. She was certain that the woman would probably be laughing at her gauche behavior.

Lorenzo smiled. “Sure, go ahead. We need to go over a few things. I’ll come around in a couple of hours. Will that give you enough time?”

“Yes, thanks.” Rita smiled at everyone, even her new boss, who appeared to have no interest in her sudden departure. Neve didn’t even look up.

With what she hoped look like confident steps, Rita headed out of the tent praying she’d find her way back to her RV. She needed to mull over how she felt about working directly for Neve Garmancelli.

†

Lorenzo watched Rita leave, then stood up and walked over to his sister and dropped down on the bench close to her. “You could have been civil, Neve. We need her, or, rather you do. Isn’t that what you said? If she’s half as good as her résumé, we’re darn lucky to have her.”

Neve about to begin her dessert looked up. “I was civil. Did anyone hear me be otherwise?” She looked at the faces around the table and they all shook their heads.

“Yeah, right.” Lorenzo frowned in frustration. “Our friends here are hardly going to say otherwise. You’re their meal ticket. Remember, they don’t bite the hand that feeds them.” He looked directly into Neve’s eyes. “Look, just try to be slightly warmer than an Eskimo in winter. Do you think you can do that, for me, if not for Rita?” Lorenzo gave her a rascally smile.

Neve gave her brother a hard stare before she smiled. “For you, Renzo, I can be slightly warmer. Just don’t ask me to be best buddies, okay?”

Lorenzo impulsively kissed her cheek before standing “You got it. Unless you want to be, that is.” He winked and headed to the table for coffee.

†

Neve shook her head as she watched him leave. She was about to begin her chocolate extravaganza when Clara spoke.

"Neve, is everything okay? I mean, if we're a burden, and the circus is in trouble, you know we can always go to that home on the coast."

Neve groaned softly, before lifting her gaze to face the interested parties seated at the table. "Guys, we're a family, remember? I don't want any talk of a home on the coast. Unless you really want to go, that is. While I'm still running the circus, I wouldn't hear of any of you going anywhere. I want you traveling with us.

"Hell, what would we do without your lemonade, Clara? And, Mary-Lou, your sherry trifles are the best in the country, not to mention your talent for reading the tea leaves." She winked at the women, one large and one tiny, and then shifted her gaze to the three brothers. The youngest was seventy and they waited expectantly for what she was about to say regarding them. "My favorite adopted uncles, what would the kids do without you giving them tips on how to be the best performers out there?" There were smiles all around. "Now, may I eat this before someone thinks I don't want it and they steal it right from under my nose."

"Ach! No one would dare," Clara said loudly.

The others laughed.

†

Rita and Lorenzo had been talking for over an hour. He had explained the general daily routine of a circus on the move, and its typical schedule when stopped in one place. He also assured her that the young man assigned to drive her RV was a safe and careful driver. She could either stay in the back when it was on the move or sit up front, whichever she chose.

Rita noted every detail. "Will you be showing me the actual accounting work, or will your sister?"

"Neve will," answered Lorenzo. "She's taken care of the books since Uncle Silvestre died of a heart attack three months ago. Just between you and me, she hates doing the books. So, if you can tolerate her less than friendly manner for a few days while you take the reins, she'll pretty much leave you to it."

"Is it *me* she doesn't like, or is it new people in general?"

Lorenzo chuckled. "Oh, she doesn't *dislike* you. She's not the friendliest woman on the planet. Neve's like that with everyone, even those she knows well. I guess the pressure of running the circus and keeping it all together takes its toll." Lorenzo shifted in his chair. "Remember one important thing about my sister…she's fiercely loyal to the business and to the people who rely on the business. Since she stopped performing herself, she has dedicated her life to this enterprise."

"What did Neve do as a performer?" Rita watched a huge grin appear on Lorenzo's face before he replied.

"We come from a long line of trapeze artists. Neve was a catcher, with excellent skills, and would have been one of the greats of her time, if she hadn't retired early." He stopped speaking abruptly and the smile disappeared. "Anyway, I can fill you in on the history another time. We start on the road at six tomorrow morning. A few will be leaving shortly so they can get the tent in place. Our next show is Tuesday afternoon in Kildare. It'll be fun." Lorenzo stood up and began to leave.

"I know you do the personnel thing around here, but do you perform, too?"

Lorenzo shot her a quick look then rubbed his face with his hand. "Not exactly perform, but I make all the mechanics happen. Call me a Jack of All Trades.

He turned to go. "Oh, if you want to join us, dinner is in Jacamar's Fifth Wheel."

Rita's eyes had widened at the offer. "He must have an enormous vehicle."

Lorenzo laughed. "No, not everyone will be there. Just the family, everyone you met at lunch excluding Jacamar, who rarely eats lunch. If you want, I'll come by at six and pick you up."

"Oh, if it's family I wouldn't want to intrude…"

"Rita, before you know it, you will be family. It's the nature of the business. Besides, it would be good for you to come along. You can meet Jacamar's grandson, your driver." He grinned. "See you at six."

Rita barely nodded agreement before he was out the door. The soft ping of the metal door closing had Rita wondering what would be next. She was grateful that so far, there'd been time to pine for home or think of her family.

Family.

Her thoughts traveled to the enigmatic Neve. *How can siblings be so different?* She smiled before softly chuckling. "Yeah, right. Like Angel and I are two peas in a pod."

Chapter Six

Rita frowned as she rebooted the computer in the steel box she now had to think of as home. "Darn thing won't let me pass go." She wondered how to decipher the password. It was still early, and she hoped she could work on the computer after the relatively brief evening meal with the Jacamar family.

Jacamar, her host, had been pleasantly polite but left early without a word. Larry, his grandson and her RV driver, had stayed a bit longer. Probably in his mid-twenties, Larry had the build of a jockey with spiky bleached blonde hair. Rita thought he'd looked out of place among the older people gathered around the table. Although not that old herself, Rita had more in common with the older generation than with the younger Larry. *It's probably because I catapulted from childhood to being a responsible adult with no in-between. No sowing of wild oats? No nightclubs or rowdy parties?* The more she thought about it, the more depressing it became.

Larry's low voice had interrupted her thoughts. "I'll be round yer trailer to hook up the cab 'bout five-thirty," he mumbled. With that, he was gone, much like his grandfather. Other than a remote smile from Lorenzo, no one commented about *his* abrupt exit, either. Rita wondered if these sudden comings and goings was a natural thing with circus folk.

When she returned to her new home, it was eight-thirty. Somewhere along the line, her body had defeated the earlier fatigue and taking advantage of her the unexpected adrenalin rush, Rita thought she'd use the computer to write a quick note to Angel and Charlie. After trying several possible passwords, the screen filled with laughing clowns and shut down.

Disappointed, Rita stretched and rubbed her eyes.

It was nine-thirty and a knock on the door startled her. *Who can it be*? After another knock, she rushed across the room and opened the door, half expecting Lorenzo. Instead, Neve, with a closed expression dominated the doorway.

"Hi," Rita said.

Neve tilted her head slightly. "Can't you sleep? I believe Lorenzo told you we start early."

Rita felt her hackles rose at the inference she couldn't take care of herself. "Yes, Lorenzo told me. I wasn't tired and thought I'd try to get a head start by at least knowing how to turn the computer on."

"It's password protected," Neve replied.

"I know that now!"

"Lesson number one, I guess."

Rita's turned her attention back to the woman. "Sorry, what did you say?"

"May I come inside?" Neve shifted her lithe frame.

Rita waved her hand and Neve walked in as if she owned the place.

Idiot, Rita chastised herself. *She does*. She watched as Neve's sure hands entered a password, and the screen filled with a big top and numerous boxes in the shapes of circus performers. "Come here. I'll create a password for you and explain the rudiments of the system."

After Rita chose a password, she peered over Neve's wide shoulders watching fingers strike the keyboard with fluid keystrokes.

"Each performer represents that area of the circus," Neve explained. "You punch in say, *clowns*, and various boxes will fill the screen. You'll see everything from their paychecks to their required equipment, along with insurance info and anything related to their job." Neve tapped the screen. "You get the idea. This is the model for each section of the performers. Then, we have the icon for casual labor, which includes administration and sundries. The list, as you can see, is quite comprehensive. Running a circus is a bit like running a major corporation—it isn't easy."

Neve shot a sharp glance up and caught Rita's brown steady gaze.

Rita was suddenly tongue tied. "I never thought it would be." She pointed at the middle icon, which was a ringmaster. "What does that represent?"

"Oh, that's me." She selected the icon and a message popped up asking for a password.

"I take it that's out of bounds?"

Neve didn't answer immediately but when she did, her voice was quiet. "That holds personnel records and sensitive contract information. It's not something you need to worry about or know."

Well, she told me. "When will you begin to instruct me on the general workings?"

"Tomorrow morning. When we stop in Richmond, which is two hours into the trip, I suggest you stock up on certain provisions for your personal use, groceries, and the like. Of course, there are the basics here." She gestured toward the kitchen area. "However, personal choice is always wise, particularly when you're away from home. It counteracts some of the homesickness I hear. You can transfer to the administration bus in Richmond and we can go through things as we travel."

Rita looked surprised. "I thought I worked from here."

Neve let out a short laugh. "Hardly. This is for any work you choose to do after the normal work hours. The administration bus is the powerhouse around here and you'll understand when you go inside."

Rita watched as the woman's toned body gracefully arose from the computer chair. She inhaled the scent of almond and coconut, a pleasant, clean smell that reminded Rita of someone fresh out of the shower. Rita waved her hand in the direction of the computer. "Thank you for…this."

"You're welcome. Tomorrow I'll give you the keys to the cabinets and some other things." Neve hesitated before she held out her hand. "Welcome to Garmancelli circus, Rita Collins."

Rita felt her jaw slacken as she automatically reached out. Neve's hand was cool and her handshake firm.

After a brief *goodnight*, Neve was gone.

Rita stood rooted to the spot where her new boss had left her. "Wow. That was a surprise. At least she didn't call me *confounded*." A slight glow warmed her body as she considered the possibility that Neve Garmancelli wasn't, perhaps, a cold bitch.

†

Larry had been considerate, not making too much noise, when he arrived at five-fifteen the next morning. However, Rita had been up since four-thirty in anticipation of her first real working day. When she worked at the mill, her starting time had been seven so being up at six was only an hour difference.

Now, waiting in line to pay for her groceries at a supermarket in Richmond, Rita looked out the window and saw several of the circus vehicles in the parking lot. It made her smile that she was actually part of something new and exciting—for her at least.

A plump woman in front of Rita said in a loud voice, "That's good news those gypsies aren't staying around. Do you remember that last circus? Thieves, the lot of them."

The cashier merely nodded her head automatically and carried on with scanning the woman's items on the rotating belt.

"Well, my husband, Burt, had his watch stolen at one of those stalls. Shady, shifty characters the whole bunch." The woman sniffed and turned to Rita with an air of expectation. "Don't you agree, dear?"

Rita frowned. "I'm with that circus. Frankly, I'm glad that we aren't staying, if that's the opinion of folks around here."

The plump woman gasped her cheeks turning a mild purple. "Not everyone is a thief, I suppose."

"How would you know what the people are like? Do you personally know anyone from the circus? I very much doubt it. If you did, you might have a more informed opinion," Rita said.

"Well, really!" the other woman huffed. "It's worse than I thought! No manners, either." She stormed out with her bags.

Rita looked at the cashier, who gave her an impish grin. "About time someone stood their ground against old Gladys. She's so full of herself." The girl winked.

Five minutes later, Rita was carrying her bags toward the RV. After opening the door, she deposited her purchases on the counter top. She felt irrationally angry with the woman. She'd heard it all before, the low opinion of circus workers and carnies. But, this was the first time she'd ever defended anyone or anything except for Angel and Charlie. *Strange how being part of something made me champion the cause, even if I'm not quite sure if I fit in.* She placed the last of her groceries in the cabinet, and a knock at the door caught her attention.

It was Neve Garmancelli.

"Have you finished what you were doing?"

Rita nodded. "Yes, your timing is perfect."

There was slight twitch of the lips at that comment then Neve pushed back the bangs that fell across her eyes. "I think it's time we went through a few things, don't you."

"Good idea," Rita replied. "You're going to show me the hub of the circus, right?"

"*The hub.* I like that. Yes, that's exactly what I'm going to do." Neve dropped down to the ground from the step she was on and Rita followed her after locking her door.

†

Rita chastised herself on her lack of observation the previous day as she walked toward a bus that appeared even larger than the Greyhound she'd ridden on. A giant ad in rainbow colors sprawled across its side: *Here we come! The one, the only Garmancelli Circus!* Two satellite dishes and a mass of aerials attached to the roof of the bus were so obvious that Rita didn't know how she missed them.

Until she heard her name, Rita was unaware she'd stopped short of the steps leading into monster vehicle. Her attention turned to Neve, who stood in the doorway with her hands on her hips, rolling her eyes. Embarrassed, Rita walked the few yards to the steps and mounted them with a sheepish apology. If she'd thought the outside impressive, the inside was even more so.

Three monitors on sturdy tables with office chairs were on either side of the bus. It looked like a surveillance setup. A large desk with a computer along with what looked like audio equipment was further toward the back of the RV. As Rita ventured further inside, she saw a cubicle that contained a circular table with chairs hidden underneath. Four people could easily sit there. There were two more cubicles and Neve indicated Rita should look inside the first. It contained a desk, laptop, and a phone along with three four-drawer filing cabinets.

"This is your work space."

"Wow, I didn't expect an office environment as well." Rita couldn't hide her surprise or pleasure with the area that would be her office.

Neve pointed to the cubicle next to the one Rita would occupy. "I work there when I'm not wanted outside."

With a nod, Neve pointed Rita to an alcove.

On one side, there was a tiny kitchen, with a small refrigerator and microwave, and on the other side, a door marked *toilet*. The final stop on the tour of the RV was a half partition that separated the office area from the driver.

"Steven Wright is the main driver. Laura, his daughter, is the co-driver."

Rita felt quite in awe of the place. It must have cost a fortune to set up, not to mention what it cost in maintenance. "Who staffs the security cameras?"

For a second Neve appeared perplexed. Then it dawned on her what Rita meant. "It isn't security, as you mean it. The monitors link to various points in the circus's big top. That allows us to manage the show efficiently and see potential problems before they manifest and the public sees something they shouldn't." She shrugged. "Bad for business."

It was the most conversation she'd ever heard from Neve and Rita liked the tone of Neve's voice. Although initially she thought it harsh, now it held strength that automatically made a person want to trust the speaker.

"Dave Tamborelli and Stuart Carlin operate the console when the circus is running. You'll meet them later today."

"That's great. I take it that, otherwise, I'm on my own here most of the working day?"

Neve gave her a sharp glance. "Does that bother you?"

"Oh, no, it will be really interesting to work on the move, so to speak." Rita half smiled as she let her eyes moved to her new office space.

"I guess. We'd better get started then. First you need a pager and a cell phone." Neve walked to the large desk next to the consoles and unlocked a draw then pulled out a pager and phone. She passed them to Rita and along with a form. "You need to sign this verifying that you've received these items. If and when you leave our employ, you turn them in and we give you back this signed form as proof."

Rita took the two objects, brand new and still in their packaging. "Thank you." She bent and signed the form.

"When you set them up, we'll log the data on the computer and it will be available to others for updating. We generally use the pager during the performances." Neve placed the folded form in her pocket and they moved to Rita's office.

Neve pointed to the black leather, executive style chair behind the desk. "Take your seat."

Rita did so hesitantly. This was all so different to the way things were at the mill. *It's ultra modern in comparison.* "I can't wait to get started." She looked up and saw a shadow of a smile float over the thin lips of the woman standing over her.

Neve nodded. "That's all I wanted to hear. I'll get the external drive where I keep all the data that I've been working on. Be right back."

Rita watched the woman leave the area and gently rocked back on the chair as she fingered the laptop, which looked new. Then she whispered to the blank screen, "I think I'm going to like working here."

Seconds later, Neve appeared and placed the external drive on the desk.

"Lesson number two," Rita whispered.

Chapter Seven

Rita stood with her hands in the pockets of her long cardigan sweater and watched the happy faces of the people milling around the circus grounds. They looked very much as she, Charlie, and Dan had when they first saw the Garmancelli circus. It was at times like this, when families arrived, that she felt bereft. The past three months had been hectic while she tried to understand the way the circus worked and what was required of her. That gave her little time to reflect on what she'd left behind, but at moments like this, her heart felt the pang of missing Angel and Charlie.

The general accounting part of the job had been a breeze. However, there were the peripherals—various stalls selling candy and other sweet delights, fast food places, and a variety of booths selling 'merch' the circus themed souvenirs—for which she also was accountable, required a bit of learning. Within a week, she was in charge of ensuring that the concessionaires, some of them local to each town, accepted the circus's rules and paid the circus fifteen percent of their profits. Mixed into that, was the advertising and purchasing of everything under the sun. She was not, however responsible for equipment related to the acts for that was Neve's responsibility. Rita was thankful for that because she knew very little about trapeze wire, nets, and all other things circus.

Standing at the foot of her RV, she smiled. She saw the lights and heard the cheesy, but delightful music that followed a circus.

"Hey, you look cheerful."

Rita grinned at Dave Tamborelli, one of the console operators in the hub. Dave was a young man in his early twenties with a friendly smile for everyone. His buzz-cut hairstyle was so short it was impossible to make out the actual color—when Rita asked, he told her it was blonde. "Oh, I just love to watch people," Rita replied. "I guess for a few hours they can forget everything else in their worlds and just enjoy themselves."

Dave smiled. "That's the idea. Hey, have you seen the boss lady today?"

"Nope, she hasn't been around the bus while I've been here. She should be in the big top now; it's almost the finale." Rita knew that Neve normally turned up daily for a few minutes to check that everything was functioning.

"I thought that too, but Lorenzo is doing the stuff she does tonight. Oh, well, better go or Stu will be antsy all night." He winked and went on his way.

Rita watched him go, his long legs quickly taking him out of view. She frowned. "I wonder where she's been today." Then she shook her head. It wasn't any of her business.

Rita's thoughts turned to the past thirty days. For the most part, Neve had been helpful. However, it was clear from the first day that the woman who owned the circus didn't have a head for figures. It had made Rita smile a few times when she'd asked detailed questions about the accounts and Neve gave her a blank look. After a couple of days, Rita told her that she had enough information to get by and, if necessary, she'd ask. Since that time, she foraged as best she could through Silvestre's convoluted internal accounting files. Neve's uncle had complicated the numbers so much, that it must have been a nightmare for auditors. Rita decided early on that transparency was best, and she'd spent many a long hour at night working toward files that complied with standard accounting principles.

The sound of the final act's music accompanied Rita as she walked toward the stalls that littered either side of the two exits from the tent. She glanced at her watch and noted it was nine-forty. The Carmine high wire act, the final show of the evening, would last about thirty five minutes.

The *Incredible Carmines* were the circus's top act, and they knew it. Their demands, Rita thought, often were over the top but when she'd questioned one of their requests, Neve's response was cold and unequivocal. Anything the Carmines wanted, the Carmines could have. Since then, Rita approved every demand but privately kept a log of some of their requests. They just didn't sit right with her. To her, Danny Carmine bordered on creepy. At the first show Rita attended, she overheard him commenting about creaming a percentage off the top.

That had triggered something in her mind causing her to go over the concession figures from the last five years. Just that afternoon, she uncovered something odd in the accounts. She had yet to work it out enough to talk coherently about it to anyone and in particular, Neve. Rita was so absorbed with the anomaly of the books that she didn't see the tall figure next to her until a quiet, now familiar voice, spoke.

"Good evening, Rita, how are you doing tonight?"

Rita nearly jumped out of her skin. She sucked in a silent breath and gazed up at Neve. "Hi, we missed you today, at least…" Rita frowned at her choice of words. "Dave was looking for you earlier."

Neve didn't respond but cast her glance at the various vendors. "We seem to have more concessions here than last year. I've noticed that, since you've arrived, we appear to attract more local support."

Rita felt a glow begin to flood her body until Neve spoke again.

"Are you allowing them any special breaks?"

Rita's anger rose. "Don't you trust me? I'm doing exactly what you told me, and they're paying the rate you requested. I can show you, if you like."

Neve's eyebrows knitted together. "No need for that. It must be the feminine touch then."

That was the nearest to an apology the woman ever gave her. In the few weeks she had known Neve, Rita noticed she rarely apologized and, when she did, usually it was indirect. "Must be."

Neve continued to view the array of stalls and drew in a deep breath. "I guess I need to find out what Dave wants." Her eyes cast upwards to the clear night sky. "From the forecasts, we could have some squally weather over the next three days." Neve turned her glance to Rita. "I'll see you at the end of the evening, as usual, Rita."

Rita nodded. "Sounds like a plan to me."

Neve briskly walked away toward the bus.

Rita peered up at the sky before walking off in the opposite direction to check that the vendors were happy with the evening's take.

†

"Lorenzo, I don't have to explain myself to you," Neve replied.

Lorenzo gave his sister a look of impatience. "How can you say what you're implying without proof? I would have thought you'd be ecstatic. What is it, years, if ever, that you've actually seen a profit after a month on the road?"

Neve threaded her fingers and cracked her knuckles. "Of course, if I thought it was genuine, I'd be delighted, but—" She heard Lorenzo grinding his teeth.

"It's been three months, and we have funds in the bank. In that space of time, the bookings in most towns have doubled. And it's a recession, for God's sake. What do *you* think?"

"I think she's damn good at her job," Lorenzo shouted. "Rita's top-notch and honest. If you don't trust the numbers, why don't you ask *her* to explain it all to you?"

Neve glared at her brother but said nothing.

"Though, I'd be careful when you do, Neve. If she takes offense, you could end up doing the number crunching yourself again. And we definitely didn't make money with you at the financial helm," Lorenzo started walking toward the door of his sister's RV.

"Where are you going? I thought we could do it together."

Lorenzo shook his head. "Not a chance. I'm not the one wondering why we've come out in the black for the first time in years. I love you, but sometimes—" He left slamming the door behind him.

Silently, Neve watched him go. Then she thumbed through the quarterly financials Rita had prepared the day before. It looked good—too good. That was the problem. Her glance took in the details from the previous five years. Each year they had losses. In fact, after she'd taken over from her father twenty years earlier, the meager profits had dwindled within the first year. For a while, they broke even, but after outfitting the *hub*, they'd been in the red.

She walked to the tiny bar in the corner of her room, poured a decent scotch, drank it in one gulp, and then immediately poured another. "I just don't understand," she whispered. Wiping a hand over her forehead, she picked up the phone and dialed Rita's extension. "This is Neve. I need to see you now. And bring all the financials. I have some questions about the quarterly report you prepared. I'm in my RV." Neve walked back to her desk and picking up the report indicating a profitable enterprise, she shook her head. "I must be mad."

†

A short time later, there was a knock on her door. "Enter."

Rita came in, carrying several folders and her laptop. "Hi, how can I help?"

Neve eyed the woman. *She doesn't look like a con-woman. Hell, I should know. I've met a few.* "I'm concerned about the numbers."

A puzzled look covered Rita's face. "Okay, where shall I put these things?"

Neve nodded to the large, wooden coffee table.

Rita deposited her things on the coffee table and then looked at her boss. "Where shall we start? Do you have something specific in mind?"

Neve stared at Rita in silence. Since Rita had arrived, they had developed a reasonable business relationship but were hardly on friendly terms. Closeness created too many conflicts and it wasn't a good idea to be too familiar with direct employees. Lorenzo was the only one to whom she showed any warmth and that was because he was family. "Why is the circus suddenly making a profit?"

Rita appeared dumbstruck. "Because you are."

Neve sipped on her scotch but didn't take her eyes off the obviously surprised woman. "Rita, I've been in charge of this circus for over twenty years, and this is the first time that we've ever done that. Wouldn't that make you suspicious?"

The perplexed look on Rita's face told Neve its own story.

"Are you implying that I'm not doing the work correctly or I've botched the figures?"

"Have you?" Neve knew it was a legitimate question. Still, when she saw the set of Rita's body and the slight tremor in her voice, she knew she hit a nerve. Her blunt accusation normally wouldn't bother her, but something in Rita's steady brown gaze had her feeling another emotion—regret.

Rita nodded. "I'll go through everything with you, and you can tell me if I've missed something significant that will take you back into the red again. Presumably, you are more comfortable in that respect."

Neve felt her lips twitch almost into a smile at the brave retort. "Go for it."

Hours later, Rita tried to explain, for a third time, why the circus was genuinely making a profit. Rita glanced at the antique clock and groaned. “Look. It’s late. Perhaps we need to take this up again once we’ve had some sleep.”

Neve, at her computer, conceded the point. *It is late and perhaps Rita is right. Tomorrow I might understand.* She trailed her cursor over the icon for administration, then insurance. They’d gone over these areas in detail twice, but something hadn’t quite added up. She didn’t know why, and it frustrated her. “I agree, but before you go, can you just go over the insurance for me, one more time?”

Rita replied, “Sure. I checked the requirements for each performer, as you instructed. Each us insured to the max along with the circus liability insurance. The big top is on full replacement, along with the two reserve tents, and we have residual wear-and-tear on most everything else critical to the circus. The vehicles are fully insured. The equipment is on a wear-and-tear basis, although you replace at such frequent intervals that it’s unlikely you’ll ever have a failure.”

A tiny muscle in Neve’s cheek moved as she digested the information.

Rita continued, “All personnel are covered with private medical insurance per your instructions.”

Neve tapped the mouse and opened a spreadsheet her uncle had created for her to keep things simple. “Have insurance companies reduced their fees this year?”

“No. And it’s unlikely they would in your business. Your risks are too high, particularly with some of the performers and equipment. The circus will always pay the premium rate.” She paused for a moment. “I did change the insurance company you’ve been using for the last ten years.”

Neve’s head shot around and gave Rita a sharp glance. “Why?”

Rita pursed her lips. “In my professional opinion, they were unsuitable.”

“My uncle chose them specifically and found them to be reliable. We’ve been with them for years,” Neve growled.

"I'm sure he did—initially. I found that particular insurance company would have difficulty paying you off if, say, the big top burned down or one of the high profile acts was injured. They are only a C-rated company. That has always been that company's rating. They should never have been on a short list, never mind being the preferred company."

Neve swallowed hard. "Your figures for the quarter indicate that we'll be paying a third less annually than with the old company. How does this new insurance company rate?"

"Double A plus. In all good conscience, I couldn't place the business with anyone with a lower rating. It's your future and that of the others at stake. It would have been negligent of me," Rita replied.

"I want you to take a copy of this spreadsheet. When you've looked it over and checked the files, we need to talk again." Her jaw clenched as a disturbing thought began surfacing in her mind. She refused to acknowledge it.

"Of course. I'll get on it immediately," Rita replied.

Neve deposited the details onto a flash drive and handed it to Rita. Neve looked at the woman closely. "I'm sorry I doubted you."

"That's okay. It was perfectly understandable. I'm still the new guy here." Rita stooped to pick up her things.

Neve took the laptop before Rita could claim it. "I'll walk you back."

Rita smiled slightly. "Thanks. When the main lights go off, I'm often tripping over the odd rope or something."

"In that case, I'm going to have to get you one of those miners' lights on a hardhat to get you home safely."

Rita grinned. "Thanks, I'd appreciate that."

Neve merely nodded.

Chapter Eight

Neve stood up, walked around her cubicle, and, for the fifth time, checked for signs of Rita. Nothing. There wasn't a cheery good morning or the sound of Rita putting on the coffee. She slumped back into her chair.

Meanwhile, Laura Wright climbed aboard the bus and walked into the kitchenette. Her smile disappeared as she gazed at the empty coffee carafe. "Oh," she said.

Neve's head popped up over the partition wall. "Rita isn't here yet. I thought maybe you…

Laura jumped. "Oh, hi, Neve. I didn't know you'd be onboard this morning."

Both women turned when they heard the bus door open.

A disheveled looking Rita walked in juggling stacks of paper, four or five thick folders, and her laptop.

All the while, Neve could hear her muttering incoherently under breath. Neve held back a smile of amusement as she swiftly moved forward and took several folders from Rita's slipping grasp. "Here, let me help."

"Thanks. I thought I was going to drop them and have to re-file them again—just when I had them in the right order, too."

Laura grinned. "I'll make the coffee."

"I'm sorry I'm late, but I wanted to go over that spreadsheet you gave me, and suddenly the time disappeared, and…"

"Didn't you get any sleep last night?" Neve asked.

Rita blushed. "I felt it was important to look at the figures immediately. I never expected it to take as long as it did." She stifled a yawn. "We can go over them now, if you have the time."

Neve, completely taken aback by Rita's commitment, opened her mouth then closed it. *Yesterday I practically accused her of negligence and she stayed up all night*. Twinges of guilt caused Neve to persist. "You haven't had any sleep at all?"

Rita bowed head. "I might have cat napped around four this morning." Her gaze met Neve's eyes. "I think it's important for both of us to clear this, don't you?"

"Laura, you'd better make that coffee strong." Neve's phone rang and she headed toward her cubicle. "Give me a couple of minutes."

She strode behind the partition. "Neve here," she barked.

†

Laura and Rita stood silently for a second, and then Laura nudged Rita and winked.

"What was that for?" Rita asked in surprise.

"I see you and the boss are getting on like a house on fire. Good for you. Not many take the time to get to know Neve. That's probably because she won't let them or they don't care enough. I have a feeling you aren't in either category."

Rita was dumbstruck at the insinuation that she and Neve might actually be friends. "I, I…"

"Got to go." Laura grabbed her mug of coffee. "I have some final checks to do before we start." Laura smiled before heading to her domain at the front of the bus.

For a few seconds Rita stood there astonished by Laura's remark. *If only you knew that Neve thinks I'm incompetent, then you might revise your opinion.*

Still stunned, Rita poured two cups of coffee and brought them into her office space. Just as she settled in her chair, Neve arrived.

Rita pointed to the steaming cup on the desk. "That's for you."

"Thanks." Neve sank down in a chair and took a sip.

Rita allowed the silence to continue for a few moments and then pushed the spreadsheet toward Neve. "You wanted me to check this over for you."

Neve glanced at the document. "Yes."

"Will you promise to allow me to explain everything before you interrupt me?" Rita asked.

A frown drew Neve's eyebrows almost to the center of her forehead. "Is it that bad?"

Rita shrugged. "It depends on your point of view." Then she allowed her eyes to catch Neve's eyes. "I think in your case you're going to be upset."

Neve sat back in the chair. "I'm a big girl. I'm sure I can take it. I guess you'd better hit me with the bottom line."

Rita allowed a ghost of a smile. "Who produced the spreadsheet for you?"

"My uncle. I told you that. He felt that it would make it easier for me to understand the outgoings of the operation," Neve answered.

Rita nodded. "Did you ever challenge any of the data over the years?"

"No, why would I? I trusted him." Neve's stance stiffened.

Rita gave her boss a slight smile. "I figured that."

Neve's nostrils flared. "Rita, don't bullshit me. What is it?"

Rita squared her shoulders. "Your uncle had been siphoning funds from the circus for years. The figures he gave you are completely fabricated."

Neve replied, "Go on."

Rita began to explain. "The spreadsheet he gave you had figures at least twice, if not more, than the actual costs. The only real numbers are the salaries, probably because he knew that it would be foolish to tamper with those. He skimmed money off the top from the insurance firm. He had you underwrite the disposal of vehicles before their time and sold them for a colossal profit. From what I can discern, you didn't see any of that. He took a percentage from everything, Neve. From the minor to the major expense, he took a percentage. I had an idea a while back…" Rita's voice trailed off.

"You had an idea?"

Rita grimaced when she heard Neve growl and felt steel blue eyes boring into her body. "Yes, you once questioned me about why the number of vendors had been increasing. I found out that your uncle made them personally pay him a percentage of their takings in addition to the percentage you, as the circus, would take. That's why you struggled in this area. People didn't think it worthwhile."

"Why didn't you tell me at the time?" Neve asked.

Rita remained silent for a few moments, considering Neve's wooden features as she chose her next words carefully. "I guess because he was dead and, if that's all he did, then it was over. Why tarnish his memory for you."

Neve stood up unsteadily. "I need time to think."

Rita watched her boss retreat to her cubicle. She felt angry on Neve's behalf. *Why do people do that, betray trust. Especially family?* The weariness from lack of sleep began to take over. "God, I need a few hours sleep or a shower, preferably both."

Her eyes blurred over the notes she made and gathered them and placed them back in one of the folders. She'd give them to Neve and then it was up to her boss to decide what to do with the information. Not that there was much she could do, since her uncle was dead.

The sudden sound of the bus revving up had Rita sighing heavily. She hoped she'd make it to lunch when she'd transfer work to her home. And, she thought longingly, sleep.

†

Neve didn't know how long she sat in her chair. She was lost in the information Rita had given her. Bottom line: her uncle had been stealing her blind from day one. Why? She tried to find an answer but couldn't. She thought with bitterness about all those years she'd gone without any kind of salary. How she worked tirelessly abroad throughout the winter to bring back startup money so the circus could make it through another year. How he'd always gone on the vacation that she insisted he take. *God, what a damn fool I was. He was playing me the whole time.*

Her thoughts drifted to Rita. *I hardly know her and she tried to protect my uncle's image, even when I'd falsely accused her of wrongdoing. Why did she do that?* Another question vexed her. *How will this new information affect the circus?*

Neve stood and stretched her tense muscles before walking around her partition and peering into Rita's. She stood transfixed. Rita's head was slumped on the desk and she was snoring albeit quietly, but there was definitely a gentle snore. Neve felt a chuckle about to escape, but managed to contain it—just. Neve quietly advanced on the sleeping woman and looked at the information on the computer screen. There she saw a new color-coded spreadsheet that contained Rita's new numbers, her uncle's information, and the difference between them. The first few lines had her whistling at the value.

Rita's head shot up. "What, what is it?" She gazed at her boss.

Neve didn't look away or say anything. Instead, she reached down and gently pushed away the hair that had fallen over Rita's eyes. "You need to get some sleep."

"I feel better now, honestly. Catnaps work for me."

The two women exchanged slight smiles.

Neve didn't buy Rita's catnap routine and glanced at her watch. "It's close to eleven. I'll have Laura stop at the next diner. The least I can do is buy you lunch. And then you're going to get some rest. I'll have Larry stop as well. You can to transfer to your RV."

"After lunch I might get a second wind."

Another slight smile played at the edges of Neve's mouth. "You might. Although, it's more likely lunch will make you even more sleepy. We can catch up later, if you feel up to it." She pointed at Rita's computer screen. "I'd like to know what all that means in layman's terms."

Rita smiled. "You got it, boss."

Neve nodded. "Thank you."

†

Lunch was quiet. After the first ten minutes, even Laura had given up attempting to engage Rita and Neve in a conversation about the weather. Laura ate quickly, and then excused herself to check something with her father.

Neve waited until Laura left the diner before pointedly asking her accountant, "Okay, Rita, what does this mean to my circus, in words I can understand?"

Rita gave her boss a steady look. "I think you'll probably find that at the end of the season you'll be better off than you ever have been before. From what I saw in the records, each year, you needed more money to launch the new season. If the next couple of months continue as well as the last, you won't have that problem."

Neve swallowed hard at the news and felt her stomach do a somersault. She felt sick with shock. "How do you know this isn't a blip?"

Rita frowned and looked down before fidgeting with her coffee cup. "Obviously, I can't give you a cast-iron guarantee, and I know you have doubts about my competency. However, if you want me to arrange for a larger accounting firm to check the numbers and substantiate…"

Neve reached across the table, stilling Rita's agitated hand and squeezed it gently. "I trust you."

Rita's gaze flashed toward Neve. "I'm sorry all this has made you sad. It isn't easy when family lets you down."

Neve barely registered the words of sympathy. "No, it isn't."

They both fell silent.

The door to the diner opened and two roustabouts walked in. One of the men, whose wiry frame, long nose, and beady eyes would have done justice to a rat, nodded in their direction. The other with spiky blonde hair winked at Rita. The rat man's gaze never left them as they approached the two women.

"Boss, as instructed, the vehicles are here."

Neve removed her hand from Rita's, stood up, and gave the man a slight nod of acknowledgement. "Larry, Rita needs some rest. She's going to take a nap until you reach Farley."

Larry grinned. "No problem, Neve. Are you ready to go, Rita?"

Rita, Scraping back her chair, stood up. "I can go over the finer details later."

Neve's return look was long and measured. She then gave a quick nod. "Yeah, later is good." Neve watched Rita and Larry leave before turning to the man who had spoken earlier. "Craig, you can either travel with Larry or Laura. I'm going to drive myself. Lorenzo was too far ahead to make this stop." She reached into her plaid shirt pocket and pulled out a sealed envelope. "When you catch up with Lorenzo, I need you to give this to him."

Craig Williams frowned and took the offered envelope, and pocketed it. "You won't be following along with us?"

"No," Neve responded firmly. "I need to take care of something. Lorenzo will fill you in later." She cocked her head toward the parking lot. "You'd better go or they'll leave without you."

"Sure, boss, whatever you say. We'll see you later then?"

Neve replied, "Much later."

Neve stared at the bottles of ketchup and mustard on the table but didn't see them.

"What can I getchya, hon?" asked a waitress.

Neve answered, "Better judgment."

"Sorry, doll, didn't catch that." The waitress, dressed in pink waited with her pencil poised to take her order.

"Coffee, black. A lot of it. And I need a couple of sandwiches to take out. Chicken and beef with all the trimmings."

"You got it" The server walked away, snapping her gum.

Neve rocking on the back two legs of her chair, allowed the information of the morning take hold. Up until that moment, she'd kept it all together as she always had in the past—twenty plus years to be exact. She shook her head in disbelief as she thought of her sacrificed dreams and missed chances at love. *And for what? My uncle fleeced me. How could he have done such a thing? How could he watch me each year gradually become... What* have *I become?* One word hit her squarely. *Machine. I'm nothing more than a machine with only one purpose—to keep the circus going.*

Ten minutes later with thermos of coffee and sandwiches in tow, she left the diner. With long strides, she quickly moved reached her RV, climbed into the driver's seat, turned on the engine, and looked at the clock. Twelve-thirty.

"In twenty-four hours, I'll have all the answers I need."

She turned the RV in the opposite direction of the others. They headed north. She headed south.

Chapter Nine

Lorenzo ran up the few steps to Rita Collins' RV and rapped hard on the metallic surface. He jumped to the ground, agitatedly pacing back and forth, and waiting for her to answer. It was dark and he knew Rita had arrived, along with the bus, half an hour before. Inside Lorenzo's pocket was the letter Craig had given him from Neve. After reading Neve's note, he'd tried to call Neve on her cell with no luck. There was one person who might be able to give him some answers and he sprinted to Rita's trailer.

Rita eventually opened the door to the mobile home and blinked the sleep out of her eyes. "Is something wrong?"

Lorenzo stopped pacing and ran up the steps. "What the hell is going on, Rita?" With their faces only inches apart, he waved the note in front of her.

"I don't understand."

"Neve. She's gone! She said she needed to clear up some business and that I'm to take over until her return. God knows when that will be."

"How would I know what's going on, Lorenzo?" Rita asked. "Neve said nothing to me."

"Craig said you were the last one to see her. You had lunch together and that… Look, it isn't like her to go off like this."

"She does go off like this sometimes though. Right, Lorenzo? She leaves you in charge at least once a month. Maybe it's something to do with that."

Lorenzo shook his head. "That's different."

"Why?"

Lorenzo ground his teeth. "That's recreational. Even she needs time away from here. This is different. I know it."

"Did she say anything else in the letter?"

"Just not to worry." He focused on Rita. "Neve is the most predictable person I know. We rely on that. This isn't like her." He paused. "Are you sure she didn't tell you anything that might explain this?"

"Lorenzo, come inside. I'll make us coffee and tell you what I know."

"Thank you." Lorenzo flopped down dejectedly on the kitchen bench while Rita measured coffee.

"Perhaps she'll be back later tonight. It's only…" Rita glanced at the clock on the wall. "It's only seven. If, as you say, Neve is so predictable, she'll be back."

Lorenzo shook his head, pulling a hand through his dark hair causing the curly mass to spring forward then back into place. "Tell me what you know. Please, Rita."

†

Half an hour later, Rita and Lorenzo sat in silence.

Lorenzo said, "Why would he do such a thing to her? She's his flesh and blood. Me, I can understand; he didn't owe me anything. We weren't blood. But Neve was his niece, his beloved sister's only child. I don't understand any of this."

Rita remained silent.

"Neve kept this circus together when most would have been happy to let it sink without a trace," Lorenzo continued. "She's a true circus junkie. Me, ever since I was a teen I've wanted to get out of the circus business and do something normal."

"Why didn't you?" Rita asked.

Lorenzo looked past Rita's shoulder, recalling memories of earlier times. "Neve, I guess. Her mother died when she was three. Her father…our father…was devastated. He doted on Neve, you know. My mom, well, she was the nanny. And yes, like the old cliché, Neve's dad married my mom. She wasn't circus folk like Neve's mother, but she made our father happy."

He pulled out his wallet and showed Rita a well-worn photo of a young girl holding a baby. The girl had dark hair and she looked solemnly at the camera. "I came along when Neve was ten. Some kids would have been resentful, but not Neve. She looked out for me from day one. Or, so my dad used to say. He was so darn proud of her, even when she... Oh, well, that's not important now." He replaced the photo and put the wallet back into his pocket. "When the car accident took our parents' lives, I was eleven and Neve twenty-one."

Rita placed her hand on Lorenzo's outstretched hand. "I can understand that. My parents died in an accident, too, and I had to take responsibility for my younger sister." She paused. "It must have been hard for you both."

"I guess. Neve took charge right away of me and of the circus. I was angry that we'd lost our folks, and I wasn't the easiest person to live with. The things I used to do." Lorenzo lifted his head and made eye contact with Rita. "Now I wonder how she coped. I guess that's why she put so much trust in Silvestre. Over time, she gave up her own life to cope with me, my tantrums, and taking care of the rest of the circus performers. " "

"She probably doesn't see it that way, Lorenzo. She loves you and the circus. You can see that in everything she does."

"But at what cost, Rita? How can we ever repay her? We expect her to solve every problem, keep the performers happy, book the shows, and balance the books—" He stopped abruptly. "I've hardly been the most supportive brother over the years."

Rita stared hard at Lorenzo. "If you hated the circus so much, why didn't you leave?"

Lorenzo shrugged. "I guess I couldn't leave her to cope with this alone. She hasn't taken a vacation in over twenty years. She works all year round to keep the circus going, and now to find this has been happening under her nose and by someone she trusted implicitly." He shook his head. "I can't even imagine how betrayed she must feel." Lorenzo looked away.

"She'll be back."

"You sound so sure. I wish I felt the same." Lorenzo stood up and bit at his bottom lip. "I'd better see that everyone's arrived and that we're ready for the show tomorrow."

Rita came out from behind the table. "I can help, Lorenzo. I've been helping Neve with parts of her job." She briefly touched his arm. "Why don't we meet for breakfast and work it out. You could involve some of the older performers, like Clara and the brothers along with Jacamar. I think they'd appreciate it."

"Good idea. I'll arrange it." Lorenzo looked deeply into Rita's brown eyes and gave her a small smile. "Thank you, Rita, for being honest with me. At least now I know she had a good reason to leave." He nodded and left. He needed air.

†

Rita walked slowly over to the kitchen to brew her favorite tea. She recalled the feeling she'd had when Angel told her she was pregnant. Rita had disappeared for the whole day, needing time to think.

With a nod, Rita spoke quietly to the empty room. "Neve will be back. And when she returns, it will be for all the right reasons." Rita watched the tea leaves express their flavor into the warm water. *I wonder where Neve goes every month and what she does. Maybe she has a boyfriend. In a brooding kind of way, she's very attractive.*

†

Neve finally pulled the RV to a stop at midnight. She looked up and down the street that featured similarly built houses on either side. Once she turned off the engine, she reached for her address book on the seat next to her and glanced once more at the address. *Thirty-five. Green Acres Avenue.*

For several moments, she looked at the black front door. There was a porch light on, but nothing else. She noted it was pretty much the same, up and down the block, with the occasional flicker of a television screen from the front room. She figured it was family neighborhood. Most probably, the kids were in bed and at that hour probably their parents, too. Neve climbed out of the cab and walked up the driveway and onto the porch of the house with the number thirty-five. She hesitated for a few seconds, and then knocked. *I wonder if they still live here.* There was no sound from inside, so she tried again louder. Then she noticed a bell and pressed it determinedly.

A hall light went on, and she heard footsteps inside.

"Who is it?"

"Neve Garmancelli."

The door opened immediately and a woman about Neve's age stood there in a fleecy pink robe covered in stars, fluffy sheepskin slippers, and brunette hair mussed from sleep.

"Neve, what are you doing here?"

Neve shrugged. "I need to speak with you, Jane."

Jane Russo frowned before she opened the door and allowed her in. "Couldn't it have waited until the morning?"

"No. It can't." Neve walked into the house and stood in the entry hall. She took in the home's tidy appearance and comfortable, but inexpensive, furnishings.

Jane closed the door and headed toward an open doorway. "I'll make us some coffee. All I have is instant."

"Thanks." Neve followed the woman and noticed she'd put on a lot of weight since they'd last seen each other ten years ago.

Jane set two cups on the kitchen table.

Neve eyed Jane as she waited. "Can you guess why I'm here?"

"Silvestre."

"You never came to the funeral. Why not?" Neve took the cup of steaming instant coffee thrust toward her.

Jane shrugged and sat down heavily on one of the chairs at the kitchen table before she stared into her coffee cup. "It wasn't convenient." She looked up. "Though I'm surprised you care. You and I never did get along."

Neve expelled a breath. "True. I did at least expect to see Sasha there. He was her father, after all. Or was she too busy, too?"

"Leave Sasha out of this, Neve. Silvestre never deserved her. She's better off without him, dead or alive,"

"I'm sorry," Neve replied. "I never did understand why you hated him or the circus so much." Neve sat down opposite the woman and saw the impenetrable look on her face.

"Just tell me why you're here, Neve, and then leave."

Neve sighed. It had been a long day and it didn't look like it was going to get any shorter. "Did you know that Silvestre was stealing from the circus?"

A startled look came over Jane's face. "Don't tell me at last you found out your uncle's feet were made of clay. That must've been hard to take since you thought he walked on water."

Neve gritted her teeth. Even now, she hated to think that her uncle was as bad as he appeared. "Well, did you?"

Jane stood up and moved to pour hot water over a spoonful of the coffee granules. "No. But it doesn't surprise me. He craved money like a miser."

"Was that the reason you left him?" Jane swung around quickly. "No."

"Will you tell me why, please? It's important or I wouldn't ask."

"Sure, why not. After all this time, what does it matter?" Jane sank back into her chair. "He beat me. And at the end, he beat Sasha too. He drank a lot, especially when he was annoyed. And he was annoyed a lot." She looked at Neve defiantly. "I wasn't going to allow my little girl to be a punching bag. I left him and never looked back. Satisfied?"

"Why didn't you tell someone, anyone?" Neve asked.

Jane snorted. "Who would I have told? You? Give me some credit, Neve. Would you have believed me? We both know you wouldn't have."

Neve sat in stunned silence.

"For the record, we did tell someone, but I'd decided to leave before they could do anything to help."

"I'm sorry. If only I had known, I could have…" When Neve saw Jane's skeptical look she shut up.

Jane shook her head. "Ya know, I love it here. The small town peaceful life is wonderful. Sasha settled down quickly enough. She went to college, Neve, and is now an assistant bank manager. They wanted to promote her, but that would've meant moving up state. She decided her traveling days were over."

The two women sat in silence for a few moments.

"So how long had he been stealing from the circus…or, really, from *you*? You *are* the Garmancelli circus, after all. From the moment your dad died, you kept it running. Believe it or not, I admired you. You gave everything up for your father's dream.

Jane cocked her head and looked at Neve with curiosity. "What about your dreams, Neve? Did you ever try to make it work with that girl you lived with that last summer I was there?" Neve frowned at the questions. The first was easy to answer; the second not as much. She hadn't thought of Jennifer in a long time, ten years to be precise. "I had the same dream as my father, so it wasn't hard to do what I did…most of the time."

"And the girl?" Jane asked. "For the life of me, I can't remember her name. I do remember that she loved you. Worshiped you even."

"Jennifer," Neve breathed out the name. She thought of Jennifer's sparkling green eyes and a gentle, ready smile.

"No, I never did work it out with her. She left me and I haven't seen her since. Probably for the best."

Jane nodded. "Well, in your case, that's probably true. The circus was your real love. Jennifer couldn't compete with that, I doubt there's a woman on the planet that could, and if there is, you'd better snap her up fast."

Neve stood up stiffly. Jane's comment had punched the final hole in her confidence. Or was it arrogance or perhaps naiveté? Whatever it was, some place inside hurt like hell. "Thanks for the coffee, Jane. Sorry to have bothered you."

Jane walked with Neve toward the front door and then stopped. "You look tired. Why not stay the night. Tomorrow you can say hello to Sasha. You know, she never stopped loving you or Lorenzo. That was the hard part for her, leaving family behind."

Neve hesitated. She was bone weary for lots of reasons, and the offer was tempting. "Thanks, but I have my own transportation outside. I can sleep…"

"I insist," Jane said. "Besides, it will give the neighborhood kids a thrill. Do you still have one of those luxury units with 'Garmancelli Circus' plastered all over it?"

Neve smiled. "Yes."

"Okay, then, come on. I'll show you the guest room."

Jane pointed out the bathroom and gave Neve fresh towels. "I have to be up at seven. I work at the local vet's, and I have to be there by eight. Help yourself to whatever you can find in the kitchen."

Neve listlessly followed Jane to her room. Sometime later, staring up at the ceiling, she finally allowed the tears of sadness to fall. For her uncle, for Jane and Sasha, for Lorenzo, for the circus, and for all the people who depended on her. Then tears fell for Jennifer, who had offered her love and the promise of a future, which she had callously rejected so very long ago.

Chapter Ten

Rita stood just inside the entrance to the big top and watched, as she did most show nights, the spectacle of performers who loved their profession. Since Neve's disappearance a month earlier, she and Lorenzo, with the help of the troupe, had managed to keep the circus rolling and the public happy.

As a breeze began to flow gently but coolly through the canvas doorway, Rita wrapped her arms around her middle, tugging her jacket closer. Rita smiled as she heard Lorenzo introduce the final performance act. "Ladies and gentlemen, children of all ages, draw your attention skyward," he raised his white gloved hand upward, "and watch as the Carmine family dazzles and thrills you with their high wire act."

At first, Lorenzo had taken Neve's absence badly and then, after some gentle cajoling on her part, he took up the gauntlet, taking like a duck to water to the actual planning and understanding of what it took to keep the circus together. Only that day they'd had a quiet lunch together on the bus had he'd talked about it...

"I can't believe she kept all this together, Rita, especially with financial worries always threatening to shut us down. I love my sister very much but I kind of always felt she wasn't the warmest person in the world. Now, I understand, at least in part." Lorenzo bit into his ham and mustard sandwich.

Rita nodded. "Yeah, I guess she had to be totally focused because, I swear, anyone else would have given up and allowed the operation to go bust years ago."

Lorenzo nodded. "Our father was that type of man too. He only ever allowed his family to see the warm side of his nature." He shrugged. "I guess you can't be friends with everyone. Right?"

Rita felt the undercurrent in the man's tone. "Right. Have you had some personnel conflicts recently?"

"You could say that. Danny Carmine is talking about moving over to Lulu-Belle's next season." Lorenzo ate more of his lunch, as he touched the ringmaster icon on the computer screen.

Before answering, Rita thought about the Carmine family. It was true they were the headline act, but surely, there were others. Of all the performers at the circus, the Carmines insisted that everyone treat them like royalty. From what she could see in the accounts, Neve and Lorenzo met most of their demands. Danny Carmine, being the eldest of four brothers and a younger sister, headed his family troupe: Peter, John, Rafe, and Sally, all belonged to a family of circus performers, whose lineage in circus life spanned more than a century.

"Perhaps it's time for a change of act, Lorenzo. They've been here how long now…three or more years. Aren't they relatively young performers? Sally is around twenty-two isn't she?

Lorenzo shook his head and chuckled. "Neve would burst a blood vessel or two if she heard you say that, Rita. She battled hard to wrench them from the grips of Lulu-Belle five years ago."

Rita sipped on the herbal tea Clara gave her. The tea was now part of her daily routine that she enjoyed. "Tell me about Lulu-Belle. Is that just a theatrical title or is there really someone with that name running the show?"

"Oh, there is definitely a Lulu-Belle. In many ways, she's the opposite of Neve. That circus is financially wealthy because of a vast family fortune, made from oil, backing it. Lulu-Belle Christianson, is the only daughter of parents, who gave her everything money could buy. When she wanted a circus, she got one. The most interesting parts is that she actually loves it and is good at it. She was lucky that her two brothers kept the parents happy by taking over the family business. That allowed her to wander any place she wanted. She even took her *plaything*, as Neve calls it, abroad."

"They don't get along?"

Lorenzo laughed. "They did once, a long time ago. You could even say they were friendly at one time. Lulu got the bug of the circus life and once tried to be a partner with Neve. Obviously, my sister disagreed and things went sour. Months later, Lulu offered to buy us out and Neve adamantly refused to let her swallow us up like that. Since then, they've been arch enemies on the business front…particularly when it comes to the commodity of the big acts."

Rita scratched the side of her face as she contemplated this new information. From all she knew of Neve, that would have sparked the woman's intense drive. Possibly a large contributing factor in how she kept the business afloat so long. She refused to give up. "Have you recently heard from Neve?"

"Not since she called from our aunt's place the day after she left to say she needed a break and gave me her password for the computer. I always thought it odd."

Rita frowned "Odd that she called you? I don't think so. She'd have wanted you to know she was okay. She loves you."

"No, it's odd that she called from our aunt's home. The only aunt we have is Silvestre's ex-wife. She and Neve never really hit it off and for her to go there and stay, is definitely odd." He shut down the computer and stood. "Well, I guess we'd both better go do our stuff or the show won't go on."

Rita smiled. "Yeah, we can't have that, can we? Incidentally, for my two cents worth, I think she'll be back soon. It's in her blood and she's probably missing you like crazy." Her thoughts traveled to her own family, which reflected her own loneliness. She missed Angel and Charlie so much that it made her heart ache for them at times.

Lorenzo wrapped his arms around Rita and kissed her cheek. "Thanks, Rita. I couldn't keep this going without you."

As Lorenzo left the bus, Rita placed a hand to her cheek. It felt warm and the action had been nice. Then, she felt someone watching her and looked up.

Laura was grinning widely. She winked at Rita before turning back to her vehicle check.

With a shake of her head, Rita disappeared into her office area and carried on with the work at hand.

†

"I can't believe it. Stop the car!" a woman barked.

With the red SUV's tires screeching, the driver pulled the vehicle onto the shoulder of the road. "Is there a problem, Lulu?"

There was no immediate answer. Instead, the door to the passenger side quickly opened and the woman slid out of the vehicle's back seat. The woman, clad in expensively tailored black trousers and calfskin boots, took a breath of the clean early morning air and wrapped a lavender leather jacket around her emerald T-shirt to ward off the early morning chill.

"Is everything okay, Lulu?" The driver also climbed out of the vehicle.

Lulu turned her watery blue gaze to the anxious woman and gave her a small smile. "Yeah, sorry, Lilly. Call Stan and have him stop here. I think they're only a couple of miles behind us."

"Sure thing. What do I tell him? He's bound to ask."

Lulu turned her attention to the original reason she stopped, and then pointed in that direction. "When he gets here he'll understand."

Lilly nodded.

Lulu-Belle walked across the road and stared hard at the reason she stopped. She heard rumors recently but had dismissed them. Maybe I was been too hasty. With her boots scrunching the gravel beside the road, Lulu wondered if anyone heard her. There did not appear to be any movement in the bus, so she climbed the three small steps and rapped hard on the door. Her eyes scanned the windows for any sign that someone was inside. Another rap went unheeded. After a few moments, Lulu tried the door, which surprisingly opened with ease.

The stench of stale air, sweat, and rancid food assaulted her. Feeling queasy, she held her breath, stepped inside, and quickly shouted, "Neve, are you here?"

No answer.

Lulu surveyed the interior of the RV with horror. The sink overflowed with dirty dishes, and takeout cartons were everywhere. Amid the mess, several whiskey bottles, all empty, lay on the floor or on the table. Near the computer area, paper was scattered everywhere, and the drawers of the filing cabinet were ajar.

"What the hell! Has there been a break-in." Lulu took another step. "Neve, are you in here?" She heard a faint rustling sound from what she suspected was a bedroom and walked toward it. The door opened to reveal a bleary-eyed Neve who wore only boxer shorts and a stained sleeveless t-shirt. Her dark hair was so greasy it clung to her head like a helmet. Her nose wrinkled at the stench of stale body odor and booze.

Lulu took a step back and stared. "Why, Neve Garmancelli, as I live and breathe." She waved her hand in front of her nose.

Neve gave the impeccably dressed woman the once over. "Lulu-Belle Christianson. If you're here, I must be dead. And if I'm not what are you doing in my home?"

When the door to the RV opened, Neve put up her forearm to cover her eyes as the sun rays bounced off her face.

Stan, a wiry man with a flat nose that indicated he'd probably gone a few rounds in the ring entered the RV "Need any help, Lu?"

Lulu turned to the man and smiled. "No, everything's fine. I'll be out in a minute."

"Do you want…"

Lulu give Stan an arched eyebrow of censure.

Stan nodded and immediately left.

"You can go, too." Neve pushed Lulu toward the door. "I don't need you poking your nose in my affairs."

"You can forget that, Neve." Lulu stepped out of Neve's reach. "Did you know you didn't lock up? I'd say that was rather reckless."

"You're not my keeper."

Lulu gazed at the unkempt woman who once epitomized control and confidence. "Looks like you could use one." Lulu snorted and shook her head. "I see the rumors were true that you deserted your circus. I never believed it until now."

Neve shrugged and picked up a crumpled sweater from the floor and pulled it on over her thin t-shirt before dragging on a pair of equally worn denims. "Have you come here to gloat?"

"Hardly, Neve. I saw an old friend parked in an obscure spot and thought I'd check it out. I had the vague notion that you might need help."

"From you?" Neve laughed. "Hardly. I'm perfectly capable of looking after myself." Neve pushed past Lulu and walked into the main area.

Lulu drew in a shallow breath before following Neve who seemed oblivious to the hideous conditions around her. "I'd say you're doing a poor job in that area. If you want, we can have this place cleaned up and back in shape in a couple of hours. If not, I'll be on my way."

Neve turned. "You know where the door is."

Lulu nodded, walked toward the door, opened it, and saw another figure standing on the second step. "I told Stan I was only going to be a minute," Lulu said.

"Is it her?" a woman asked.

Before Lulu could answer, Neve shouted, "I'm not a fuckin' freak sideshow. Get your asshole workers out of here."

The woman stepped inside and swept past Lulu and sea green eyes widened. A hand covered her mouth then she gasped out. "Neve?" Neve's eyes closed and her body straightened. "Both of you get out! I don't need your charity or your help." Neve staggered to the only chair not buried in rubbish and slumped down.

Lulu looked alarmed as her friend, Jennifer Connelly, began to move slowly in Neve's direction. She placed a hand gently on Jennifer's forearm.

"It's okay, Belle."

Lulu's restraining hand reluctantly fell away and with a slight frown, watched as Jennifer moved in front of Neve and crouched down. "I'll be outside if you need me."

Jennifer turned and gave Lulu a sparkling smile. "Thank you."

†

When Lulu had left, Jennifer returned her gaze to Neve. "You look like hell, Neve. Anything I can do?"

"No."

"Okay, forthright as ever. That, at least, hasn't changed." Jennifer's eyes flickered over the mess. "Look, Lulu is just trying to help, Neve, and I think you need it. Why not let us at least clean up the place?"

"I don't need any help from you or from Lulu. Just get out of here, and leave me in peace." Neve's hand pushed unkempt hair out of her eyes.

Jennifer rocked back slightly on her haunches. Then, she gently touched Neve's cheek.

Neve's head jerked back. "Don't touch me."

Jennifer moved slightly away. "Sorry. Look, it's been a while. Maybe if you go have a shower, we can talk for old times' sake. Otherwise, I might be forced to annoy you by staying until you do." Jennifer stood.

"Will that get rid of you and *her*?

"Yes."

Neve stood. "Good. I'll be ten minutes."

†

Jennifer watched her go. Neve's perfect posture always fascinated her and still did. With a heavy sigh, she walked toward the door and let herself out.

Lulu turned. "Hi. Are we leaving?"

Jennifer shook her head. "Neve's having a shower and agreed to talk if we leave afterwards."

"Why bother, Jen? She's in a bad place right now. We aren't exactly the right people to help her. She isn't friendly and hasn't been for years…with me, in particular.

"I know, Belle, but I'd like to try. You don't have to wait. You can go and I'll catch up with you for breakfast at the planned stop." Jennifer moved within a hairsbreadth of an unhappy looking Lulu.

"Not a chance of that happening. She's unpredictable. I won't put you in that kind of danger."

Jennifer leaned forward and gently kissed Belle's lips. "Thank you, darling, but she won't hurt me."

Lulu rolled her eyes. "I'll stay." She turned to the drivers of the vehicles. "Come on, guys. We can at least clear away the rubbish before she throws us out."

Fifteen minutes later, with the aroma of coffee brewing and most of the surface debris removed, Neve walked out of her bedroom. She was in clean wheat colored sweater and black jeans. Her dark hair, still wet from her shower, was in a pony tail.

Jennifer nodded in approval and watched the woman she had once loved dearly enter the area and her pulse stirred at the sight. “Hey, we decided to give you a hand. Want some coffee?”

Neve glanced around. “Thanks.”

Jennifer, pouring the coffee, gave Neve a gentle smile. “Great. Here you go.”

Neve took the steaming cup. “Where’s Lulu-Belle?”

“She’s waiting outside,” Jennifer replied.

Neve looked out of the grimy window and saw her rival talking with two others. “I didn’t know you’d hooked up with her circus. When was that?”

Jennifer heard the hostility that was clear in the question. “About three years ago.”

Neve spun her head in Jennifer’s direction. “What did you do the other seven years?”

Jennifer sat down and contemplated her coffee. “I went home to my parents for a year. Then I decided to spend some time on the coast. For about two years, I did hair and saved like crazy. Then I bought into a salon franchise at the Carlton in Santa Raphael.” She paused. “That’s where I met Belle. She persuaded me that my talents were underutilized.”

“I’ll just bet she did.”

Jennifer looked into the cobalt eyes and knew what Neve was thinking, and shook her head. “What about you?”

Chapter Eleven

Neve hesitated. Part of her wanted to crawl into the shell she'd created since leaving her aunt's three weeks ago. The enormity of what her uncle had done to her life hit home, and overwhelmed her. However, Jennifer's gaze only held compassion, and she remembered that Jennifer had loved her once.

"My uncle was stealing me blind from day one. He made sure that the circus teetered on the brink of bankruptcy from the first year I took over." She smiled. "He took me for a ride and I let him."

Jennifer placed a hand on Neve's and smiled. "How did you find out?"

"He died six months ago. Initially, I was none the wiser; happily thinking a shoestring was holding the circus together as I had for twenty years. I blindly assumed finances were never going to be anything but borderline." Neve let out the breath she was holding. "Rita told me."

Jennifer asked, "Rita?"

"Yes, my new accountant. She showed me where my uncle had been siphoning off funds and generally ensuring that no profit was ever coming my way." She pounded her forehead with the heel of her hand. "I was a gullible idiot." That was her litany since learning the truth.

"You and your accountant must be on good terms."

Neve looked at Jennifer and creased her brow "What do you mean?"

Jennifer shrugged and a smile tugged at her mouth. "Not many would tell you that your uncle had been less than honest. From what I remember, you adored him. He was on the list of top three things you loved the most."

Neve considered the comment carefully. "What were the other two?"

"Lorenzo and the circus."

"Unfortunately, not in that order."

Silence hung in the air as Neve wondered if it were true. A chilling realization slowly surfaced. Jennifer was right—the circus always *had* come first. There always was one more emergency or one more problem that took up her time and energy. There really hadn't been time to think of anything or anyone else. The fragment of her personal life that she had allowed herself was on the fringes and cast aside when the circus needed her. Friends were practically nonexistent "You were right to leave me. I never deserved you."

Tears shimmered in Jennifer's eyes. "I know, but not because you didn't deserve me. It wasn't the right time for us."

Neve caught Jennifer's gaze and smiled for the first time in what seemed like a very long time. "What about now?"

Jennifer shrugged. "I've got to go, Neve." She smiled slightly. "Will you promise me one thing?"

Neve dropped her gaze and felt her gut roil at the rejection and the knowledge that there was no going back to what might have been. "What is it?"

"Take a good look at yourself in the mirror and ask yourself this question: What do *you* want out of life? When you have the answer, go for it. Don't let your uncle ruin the rest of your life. He's done enough damage to you already."

Neve didn't reply at first as thoughts of what was and what is rumbled in her mind. "I'll try, but only because you asked me."

Jennifer shook her head. "No, Neve, you don't understand. You have to do it for you and no one else. Today, make the change in your life that sets you up for the rest of it. It worked for me and I know it will work for you. You were always a shadow in the back of my mind and, even now, looking into your eyes, you could drag me in through sheer magnetism alone." She sighed. "Except that isn't what I want anymore. I'm certainly not what you need or ever really needed."

Neve looked up and saw the firm set of Jennifer's jaw. She knew the woman had moved on. "Good luck, Jennifer, and thanks."

Jennifer moved to the door but turned and rushed up to Neve who had just gotten up from her chair. She hugged her tightly. "Be happy, Neve. It's time for *you* now. Find some-one to love. It makes all the difference. You made me realize that." Jennifer kissed her cheek and left before Neve could reply.

Neve blinking at the gesture and her hand went to her cheek where the kiss seemed to have stung her. She moved to look outside and saw Jennifer walk toward Lulu-Belle. She sighed and turned to pour herself another cup of coffee. "It's time for *me* now, she says. Find someone to love." She shook her head. "Where the hell do I start?"

†

Jennifer, exiting the RV, saw Belle watch her as a tenta-tive smile crossed the older woman's face. She strode confi-dently toward Belle, whom she knew likely had paced the pavement as she waited outside for her. "Hey, you look pre-occupied."

Lulu, hands clenched at her sides. "Are we done here?"

Jennifer gave Belle a long, hard stare and then smiled. She reached out to take one of the clenched hands, unfolded it, and held it in her own. "Yes, we are."

Lulu asked, "Are you going to keep in contact with Neve, now that you've broken the ice?"

Jennifer glanced back at the RV and then at the pensive woman at her side. "No. Today, Belle, is the beginning of a new life for all of us." She paused. "I want to ask you a ques-tion."

Lulu nodded. "Go for it."

"Do you remember when we met and you asked me out? I said *no* because I hadn't gotten over someone I loved very much and didn't think it was fair to you."

Lulu rolled her eyes. "How could I forget? You've said no every time I've asked, which seemed monthly. Why?"

Jennifer grinned. "Will you go out with me on a date, Lulu-Belle Christianson?"

Lulu reached out and pulled Jennifer into her arms. "I would be delighted to go on a date with you, Jennifer Connelly". She looked at Jennifer with puzzled expression. "But why now? You've kept me at bay for three years."

"Because, I just realized that this is *our* time, Belle. I'm not going to waste any more of it."

Belle pulled Jennifer close. "I'll second that. Want to travel with me and have breakfast?"

"Try and stop me." Jennifer smiled. She placed a fleeting kiss on Belle's lips and hooking her arm into Lulu's before heading toward her vehicle and the beginning of their new future.

†

Lorenzo grinned as he checked the figures for the week. *According to Rita, it's another bumper profit.* That meant the circus had enough funds to close up for the winter and reopen without anyone having to scrape together money to begin a new season.

While dragging a hand through his curly hair, he couldn't stop a smug expression from crossing his face. He felt good, and the only thing that spoiled the moment was that Neve wasn't here to share it. *Neve deserves this and more.* He regretted that he wasn't more assertive in the early years when Neve categorically told him 'no' to his offer of help. *She said it was a bad enough mess for one of us, let alone two.* Neve owned the majority of the circus, so she insisted it was up to her. *Lorenzo,* she'd said, *you go off and enjoy the winter break. One of us should be fresh for the new season.* There was no further discussion and eventually, he stopped trying.

A knock on his door drew Lorenzo out of his memories. He said, “Enter”

An auburn head popped inside the door before the woman with a curvy yet athletic body stepped inside. “Hey, Lorenzo. Do ya have a few minutes to spare?”

Lorenzo smiled and motioned for her to come closer. “You’re welcome anytime, Sally. What can I do for you?” He watched as the lithe young woman sat on the couch. “Danny is making waves again.”

Lorenzo rubbed the stubble of half a day’s growth on his chin. “Anything specific?”

“He’s demanding we move to Lulu-Belle’s next season. He’s expecting a contract tomorrow. I’m sorry, Lorenzo.”

“To be honest, I’ve been expecting that,” Lorenzo replied. “What about your other brothers? Are they hell bent on leaving too?”Lorenzo stopped his pacing and looked intently at Sally. “Does your coming here now mean you aren’t on board with the move?”

“I’ve told Danny I don’t want to go. The others do what Danny says. Besides, the contract is for a boatload of money. Danny said *it is a million times more and that our career path is short and we need to make as much money as we can while we’re at the height of our success*. She brushed some invisible lint from her sweater. “I can’t blame him, really.”

Lorenzo nodded. “I don’t. You should think that way too, Sally. Do you have any idea how much they’re offering? Maybe we can match or better it.”

“I’m sorry, Lorenzo, I haven’t seen the exact amount.” She paused. “Danny was quick to point out that you can’t afford us. In fact, I’ve always wondered how the circus managed to keep my big brother happy. He was close to Silvestre, so he knew a lot about the finances. But Danny’s been out of sorts since your uncle’s passing.”

Sally continued. "I know we're not supposed to know that Neve works during the winter break to keep everything going, but word gets out. I've always admired her for that, and I think deep down that's why Danny's remained loyal. He knew how much your uncle loved your sister."

Lorenzo frowned heavily at her words.

Sally stood. "Look, you must be busy I'd better go."

Lorenzo stopped her with a gentle hold on her arm.

"Thanks for informing me, Sally. I'll miss you." His voice held a tinge of regret.

Sally smiled. "I'll miss you too. See you later in the big top." She made a quick exit.

Lorenzo watched Sally go, and stood in the same spot for a long time. He'd always liked Sally; too much, he often thought. *Why would a beautiful and talented young woman like her want a man at least sixteen years older?* He didn't have much to offer to any woman much less to a head turner like Sally. *Especially a part owner in a circus that, until recently, hadn't made a dime in profit.* No, he'd done the right thing by never tempting that fate, though he felt the loss keenly.

He pondered Sally's remarks about Danny and Silvestre. *Just how friendly had they been*?

He tapped the number nine on his cell and seconds later, it connected with Rita. "Hey, you got a minute? We need to talk." He replaced the phone in his pocket and sank into the couch, inhaling the faint scent of Sally's perfume. It was intoxicating.

†

Rita walked the length of the side show stalls for her final check before the public crammed the area. With a satisfied smile, she turned toward the big top and the cashier's booth.

"Rita, mein leibchen, how's business?" Carla boomed out as she walked up beside the accountant.

Rita smiled at Carla for a second then resumed surveying the grounds. "Good, I think. The house is three-quarters full for tonight and tomorrow. The sales for tomorrow are slow. But, what can we expect? It isn't the holidays."

Carla nodded. "Yah,Vednesdays vere never gut, even in vacation times." The smile left her face. "Und there's gossip that the Carmines vill be gone after the season ends."

It wasn't a question, yet Rita had the distinct feeling Carla was fishing. She could state confidently that it wasn't—yet. There'd been no official word from the head of the Carmine troupe, although Lorenzo had explained the situation to her. "Hadn't heard that, but I'm sure it's the buzz every year close to contract time."

"Yah," Carla agreed. "Yah. Vell, I must be off. Tonight I help the clowns. They have new sketch mit custard pies und I'm the star. Maybe they have extra pie I can eat." The woman laughed loudly, waved, and disappeared toward the clowns' changing tent.

Rita studied the sky that was a beautiful periwinkle soon to morph into a deep cobalt color. A smattering of stars glimmered; soon the heavens would fill with them. The half moon, on the rise, pale and solitary, would create its own natural beauty.

Rita continued her stroll past the cashier's booth and gave the woman behind the counter a small smile. "Hi, Lorraine, you'll be busy tonight. We've already sold three-quarters."

Lorraine, a middle-aged woman with a mop of curly orange hair and piercing brown eyes, smiled. "No prob, Rita, it'll mean my idle hands won't get bored."

"That they won't, Lorraine." Rita chuckled. "If you need help, call me. I'll be inside the big top watching from my usual spot." Rita sauntered in the direction of the big top. As she did, she turned to the area behind her and saw a mass of people streaming toward the booth. *And now it begins.*

She entered through a side curtain quietly and sat down on a chair put there especially for her. From her vantage point, Rita could see the main ring and watch the spectacle, which she enjoyed no matter how many times she'd seen it.

As the music began to swell, she wondered what Angel and Charlie were doing. When the season ended in a month, she'd be heading home. She hoped she could arrange to meet with Angel and her nephew for a few days. She left a text and a voice messages about when she was due home. Angel acknowledged the date but didn't mention getting together. There was time. Angel had never been much of a plan-ahead girl.

As she settled into her chair, she heard a sound behind her and turned to see what it was. Her eyes grew wide and she felt her mouth open to say something but no words came out.

"Hello, Rita. How are you?"

Rita blinked before she finally found her voice. "Neve…"

Neve raised her eyebrow slightly and nodded. "In the flesh. How have things been?"

Rita stood up so fast her chair almost toppled over. "Good, excellent, in fact. Lorenzo is going to be so happy you're back. He missed you. We all missed you."

Neve's expression was wry. "Then I'm glad I came back." Her eyes traveled to the main ring where Lorenzo was announcing the next act. "Do you mind if I watch the show from here?"

"No, of course not. Here, take the seat. I'll let you watch the show in peace." Rita turned to leave but saw the frown on Neve's face. "Is something wrong?"

"If you don't mind, I could do with the company."

Rita stopped in her tracks and gazed at Neve concentrating fully on her. She could see the dark shadows under those compelling eyes and that Neve looked desperately thin. "Sure, I love watching the show. Ever since you went away, I've been here in the background for every performance. Well, at least in the evening." She grinned. "I think I'm hooked on the circus."

Neve stared at the performers before her gaze turned to Rita. "I know exactly what you mean. Take a seat. I'll stand. I've been driving for hours."

Rita once again relaxed into her surroundings and the joy of the show. This time, however, she felt something else. It was a sensation of security and inner warmth. She never experienced this feeling before and wasn't sure why she did now. All she knew was that it felt good—damn good.

Chapter Twelve

Rita awoke the next morning feeling refreshed and ready for anything. Not that she ever woke up in a lethargic state or unhappy in her work—she didn't—but somehow today was different. The only answer that made any sense was that Neve had returned and the Garmancelli circus appeared to respond in a positive way…

The previous evening after the show, she'd had tears in her eyes when Lorenzo finally saw his sister. There had been whispers as the show had gone on that Neve was back, but until Lorenzo actually saw her, he wouldn't believe it and had soldiered on with the show and waited for it to end. As the public finally left the big top, Neve walked out of the shadows into the bright lights of the main ring and stood waiting for her brother to turn and acknowledge her. When he did, he walked over to her and pulled her off her feet and into a bear hug that would have crushed someone of a lesser stature.

Rita watched the reunion from her position, wiping away the few tears she had shed at the encounter. She knew that when she saw Angel and Charlie again she'd be an emotional wreck, too. About to leave, Lorenzo must have seen her move, and he shouted, "Rita, you can come out now. I promise not to get all teary eyed on you."

Up close, Rita saw what she had expected—the love they had for each other clearly expressed on their faces. "I think there's going to be a big celebration over late supper tonight."

Lorenzo grinned. "Is that okay with you, Neve? I know you never liked any fuss but…," he said looking deeply into his sister's eyes.

Neve appeared to consider his words carefully. "I think I can cope. Besides, I'm hungry. I haven't eaten all day. I wanted to get here before the show was finished."

Lorenzo bumped Neve's arm teasingly. "Did you enjoy actually watching the show and not having to work for once?"

"Little brother, you've done a marvelous job." Neve winked at him, and his cheeks flushed with pride.

Lorenzo rubbed his chin and then looked at Rita. "It isn't all my own work. Rita has been a rock. Without her I don't think you'd be too happy with me."

Neve glanced at Rita. "Thank you, Rita." She shrugged slightly. "It seems lately that's all I've been saying to you. I think you deserve a raise in salary."

Blushing at the compliments from both of her employers, Rita shook her head. "My salary is great. I hardly touch the bulk of it since you provide most things around here. And it wasn't just me. Clara, Mary-Lou, Jacamar, Leo and his brothers and just about everyone except…well, most, anyway had a hand in keeping everything going until you came back."

"Then I think I owe…most everyone a thank you as well." Neve gave Rita a steady look.

Rita frowned slightly and turned away from Neve's concentrated gaze. The Carmines would have to be Lorenzo's story to tell, and she hoped it would be sooner rather than later.

They disappeared off to the supper tent, and the evening turned out to be one of interest from Rita's point of view. She watched in fascination the interaction between Neve and her circus family. They were glad she was back, and their happiness made the atmosphere buzz with anticipation.

†

After quickly showering and having a simple breakfast of herbal tea and two slices of toast, dripping with her favorite marmalade, Rita exited her RV. In keeping with her early-morning routine, she began a walk around the sideshow stalls to check that everything was in order for the final day in this particular town. According to the planning schedule, they had three more weeks on the road and a final week in what Lorenzo called the *bustling metropolis* of Warrington.

Warrington, their last stop, had been a part of the circus's routine for almost thirty years and the show was always well received and profitable. The only venue where Silvestre acknowledged they made money. It was not enough money, but enough to ensure that Neve made the choice to continue to run the circus the next season. *Maybe Neve would make that choice now because it's what she wanted, rather than what she felt obligated to do.* Rita smiled at the thought.

The weather was turning as summer now lapsed into early autumn. The cooling breezes in the mornings ensured that a warm jacket was essential. Rita pulled her fleece-lined jacket closer before she dug her hands in her pockets and began walking down the line of stalls, checking each one with a critical eye. Reaching inside her top pocket, she pulled out a small notebook and pencil that she used to record any defects she might come across.

She'd undertaken the chore since starting at the circus. In the early weeks, she found that many of the stalls needed repair and updating. From what she could see, maintenance on them was lacking. Jack Randall, the circus carpenter who maintained and produced new props and sets, had been very happy to help with the upgrades. Over the months, he'd created new themes and applied fresh paintwork on over half of them. He promised that during the winter, after his month vacation, he'd ensure that the rest would be ready before they began the new season in the spring.

While checking the rifle range stall, Rita bent over the front bench causing her feet to dangle about a foot off the ground as she reached to unclip the security stays. A hand pushed on her back and Rita screamed as she swiveled and looked at the person who had snuck up on her.

"What do you want, Danny?" Rita fumbled with her balance and then finally landed back on the ground as she swung around to face the head of the Carmine family.

Danny Carmine had a trim lower body and powerful shoulders. His neck muscles bulged and reminded Rita of a body-builder. His sandy hair was cropped military style and his features, though handsome, had a weakness around the chin and lips that, since the day she met him, made her dislike the man. "I wanted to speak with you. Is that a crime?"

Rita glared at Danny. This wasn't his style. Normally, he demanded, like royalty, someone go to his RV to speak with him. "Can it wait? I'm busy."

Danny gave her a hard stare and then placed a strong hand on her arm. "No."

"Okay, what can I do for you?" Rita could have cheerfully turned her back and carried on her work, but she was loath to rile the man. He was important to the circus, and she wasn't going to be the one to offend him any more than he appeared to be now.

"How's the circus doing financially?"

She watched as Danny's arrogant gaze roamed her body before they stopped at her breasts pushing against the zipper of the jacket she wore. Rita shivered then shook her head at the man. "The financial situation of the circus isn't up for discussion. If you want that kind of information, ask Neve or Lorenzo."

"I'm asking you." Danny persisted by moving fractionally closer. "It's hardly a state secret. Besides, Silvestre and I had a deal. I think it's time you made good on it." His hand took Rita's arm and his finger trailed down the blue fabric of her jacket.

Rita glanced at the hand that was touching her wrist in an unpleasant way. His thumb was stroking the skin exposed below the jacket sleeve. "Any deal you had with the old accountant doesn't stand. It's as dead as he is. You could talk to the owners. I'm sure Neve, in particular, would be only too willing to listen to any deal you feel you've been losing out on. Now, if you'll excuse me, I have some work to do." She tried to turn away but the fingers that had been gently touching her skin now grew cruel and they closed around her thin wrist like a vice.

Danny Carmine gave Rita a twisted smile. "Not so fast, Rita. Rumor has it that you and Lorenzo are close. How close, I wonder?" He moved fast and caught Rita, then pulled her into his strong chest before claiming her lips in a wet, aggressive kiss.

The unexpected attack shocked Rita, making her submissive in Danny's arms for a few seconds before she began to twist and scream at his unwanted, amorous advances. By using his strength, Danny pushed her against the side of the stall and placed a hand over her mouth to stop the noise. His free hand roamed her body and unzipped her jacket to pull at her blouse and expose her breasts.

Shocked to the core and gasping for breath, Rita kicked out at him but his bulging thigh blocked her effort. She knew she had an effect when she heard his stifled grunt of pain.

Danny laughed in a wild pitch as he moved his hand to let his lips muffle any attempt for her to scream again. The canvas flap of the stall gave way, and he roughly pushed her to the ground. "You think I want to rape you? In your dreams, Rita. I want what I'm due in monetary value and if you don't comply, this is just a sample of what I can do to you. Believe me, next time you won't walk for a week. Besides, Lorenzo must be desperate. He certainly can't be mesmerized by your looks…you don't have any."

Rita felt her life swimming in front of her, praying someone—anyone—who would help her out of the nightmare. It was early, and most of the gophers would be having breakfast, which is where she would have gone with her notes to talk to the maintenance people. Right now, she didn't know what to do as she looked up at the smirking features of Danny Carmine. "What deal did you have with the last accountant?"

Danny nodded and moved off her. "That's better, Rita. I knew I'd get my point across. Fifty percent of the skim Silvestre was taking on the stalls."

"I don't understand. He gave you half of the vendor charge?'

"No, you stupid woman! Silvestre put that in the books. We then charged another percentage for the privilege. He was a charmer, old Silvestre. It never failed. Oh, and I want back pay for the past six months. You can pay me a visit at my place around noon today."

Rita scrambled up, her hands sweating so much she had to wipe the moisture off on her jeans. "I'm not sure that's possible."

"Make it possible." He moved aside and pointed in the direction of the main camping area.

†

Rita ran as fast as she could toward the safety of her RV. Before she got there, hands shot out and stopped her. Rita screamed.

"Hey, it's me, Neve. Rita, are you okay?"

Rita heard the voice and the concern in it, peripherally realizing that this wasn't Danny Carmine. Shaking from head to toe, Rita couldn't answer. Instead, she caught the concerned eyes of her boss and felt the tears begin to fall. "I…I can't explain…not now." She tugged violently at the hands that held her, and they dropped away as suddenly as they appeared.

"Okay, Rita. What's going on? You look terrified." Neve stared at her. "What's happened? Your clothes are…you look disheveled and that isn't like you."

Rita shook her head as she moved toward her home and the relative safety it held. “I need a shower.”

“Will you meet me for breakfast?” Neve’s features calm and unreadable as she tilted her head to one side and gazed at Rita..

“I can do that. I need to go.” Rita moved so fast she had her hand on her door handle before Neve could reply.

Neve caught up to her. “Rita, if someone has hurt you or done anything inappropriate, you’d tell me, wouldn’t you?”

Rita could see Neve’s eyes boring into her for an answer—she opened the door and shut it behind her without a word.

†

As Neve stood there in a state of confusion, she heard the door lock. *What the hell was that about*? Her gaze swung in the direction Rita had run from. *Okay, if she won’t tell me, then I have to find out myself.* Her long stride took her down the path Rita ran on.

The stalls were empty, as she would have expected at this time in the morning. Rita and a few of the maintenance people were the only ones who ever came this way during the morning. A sound caught her attention—a man’s voice cursing. Focusing on the sound, she walked toward the rifle range stall and looked over the counter but didn’t see anything. Neve, certain that the noise came from there, frowned. She heard a scuffling sound before a head appeared from behind the canvas flap at the back of the stall.

“Danny, what are you doing here?” Neve asked.

Danny Carmine gave her a hard stare then curled his upper lip, “What’s it got to do with you?”

Neve’s assessing gaze took in the twisted expression and shifty eyes. “Everything around here…you…the fixtures…and fittings are all my responsibility. I’m surprised you’ve forgotten that. I’ve only been away a month.”

"Who could have forgotten? That's all they talked about around here…it was getting boring. I want you to sack that accountant bitch, she's trouble." Danny snarled. His normally smooth, confident gait was now impaired as he limped toward Neve. When he stopped, he rubbed his thigh and then crossed his arms over his chest.

"Have you hurt yourself? Before you answer, know that it definitely is my concern. If you can't work, you're worthless to me."

Danny ground his teeth. "I fell over a guide rope and strained a muscle in my thigh. I'll be fine for the performances."

Neve nodded. "Before I sack someone for…what did you say again…*trouble*, I'm afraid you'll have to elaborate. Exactly how would my quiet and personable accountant be trouble and why to you? I had the distinct notion she wasn't part of your social crowd here. Then again, not many are."

"I don't need to explain. I want her gone."

His arrogant stance annoyed Neve, but she refused to allow it to show.

"If she isn't history by tomorrow then my family will be." Danny gave her a thin lipped smile.

"Can't do that, Danny. She's important to the business and I won't fire her without a really good reason. Do you have one?"

"Whatever, it's your choice. In the end, you will realize that the Carmine's are more important. I'll give you until tonight. If she isn't gone by morning, then we will be."

Neve wanted to deck the man but restraint her overrode her emotions. "What about our contract?"

Danny gave Neve a pitying look. "Read the small print, Neve. I'm sure you'll come to the right conclusion." He started to walk away with a definitely uncertain gait.

"If I find out that you're in any way responsible for Rita's distressed state, Danny, I'll personally tear the contract up and happily measure out my own circus brand of justice." She watched him turn back to face her, his features dark and threatening. "Remember one thing, Danny, I'm not like Rita. She might be innocent about some of things that go on in the circus world but I'm not.

Right now, you'd better watch your step because accidents can happen around here…fatal ones."

Danny stopped in his tracks. "Is that a threat?"

Neve shrugged and gave him a half smile. "All depends if you've done something wrong or not. You know we circus folk take care of our own."

"Did that bitch say I did something to her? She wasn't telling the truth. If anything, she asked for it." Danny smirked. "She isn't as innocent as you think. She and your brother are an item…if you didn't already know that."

Neve felt irked and slightly upset at his comment. Her overriding concern was that Danny had done something to Rita. In a roundabout way, he'd admitted it. Now, all she needed was for Rita to confirm her suspicions, and she'd nail the bastard to the highest point of the big top—personally. "What Rita and my brother do personally is exactly that, personal. It has nothing to do with me or you or anyone else." She fixed him with her eyes. "Do I make myself clear?"

Danny sneered. "Perfectly." He turned and walked slowly toward the Carmines' vehicles.

Neve wanted to be sick. She knew he definitely did something to Rita, and it didn't take much for her to guess what. After Rita confirmed the details, they could call the police and have that scum locked away. For years she'd put up with his petty requests and the disquieting things people said about him on a personal front. In the past, her uncle had always handled the situation and now, she had a good idea why. Danny Carmine and her uncle were out of the same mold—bad to the bone.

Her gaze switched toward Rita's RV, and she made a decision. Her legs moved at race speed to take her back where she came from.

Her hand hesitated for a few seconds before she knocked on her brother's door. Within a minute, the door swung open and Lorenzo peered at her in mild surprise.

"Hey, Sis, how's tricks?" He grinned, as he pushed a hand through his curly hair.

Neve looked at him and felt proud that he was her brother. He was the one stalwart in her life. She appreciated it and needed to tell him every now and again. "I need to speak to you about Rita."

Lorenzo frowned and moved to allow her to enter his RV.

Neve took a few steps inside and stopped.

"This doesn't look good. What about Rita?" Lorenzo asked.

"Are you and she an item?"

Lorenzo moved backwards looking slightly startled. "No, and, if we were, that isn't your business."

Neve shook her head and closed her eyes for a few brief moments. "I think Danny Carmine tried…may have raped her."

Lorenzo blinked several times seemingly at a loss for words. "Are you sure, Neve? When was this? Where is Rita? Have you called the police?"

"I'm not certain. My gut instinct tells me that *could* be the situation. He's certainly done something to her."

"Hell, Neve, you can't say that unless you're sure. Are you? How the hell did you come to this conclusion?"

Neve explained what had happened between her and Rita and with Danny and waited for Lorenzo to speak.

Lorenzo shook his head. "I want to kill the bastard. Sally said Danny and Silvestre were close and this proves it. Now, with Silvestre's death, his extra cash flow is gone and he's trying to shake down Rita. This is one hell of a mess, Neve. What are we going to do?"

Neve frowned. "We speak to Rita and find out the truth. She's the only one who can give us that."

Lorenzo with a subdued expression, nodded. "If that slime ball Danny Carmine has made any kind of move on her, so help me…"

Neve understood perfectly. "Stand in line, brother."

Chapter Thirteen

Rita scrubbed her skin so hard it looked red and raw when she'd finished. Her mind was set on removing any smell or trace of Danny Carmine. As she stepped out of the shower, she caught a glimpse of her body in the mirror. Tears begin again as she recalled the horrifying event in every sordid detail.

Why does he think he can do that to another person? That one question kept going through her mind. The only answer that came back: *He's sick.*

After vigorously toweling herself, Rita pulled on fresh undies, a shapeless sweater, and jogging pants. A few minutes later, she was filling the kettle in her kitchen area and hoping the herbal tea that usually soothed her would wipe away the taste of that man's vile kiss, his mental attack, and his threats. When the brew was complete, Rita sat down and drank from a small tea cup, allowing the tea's refreshing qualities to take over. For all of a few seconds it did until there was a rapping on the door, and she heard Neve's voice.

Oh, God, why had Neve been the one to see me? She'll ask twenty questions and more. When she didn't move or respond, Rita heard another voice—Lorenzo.

What does he want?

"Rita, it's Lorenzo and Neve. We need to speak with you. Please, open the door."

She knew there was nowhere to go, and Neve wasn't likely to give up; she knew at least that much of her boss's character. In a weak voice she replied, "Give me a minute, please."

Why she wanted that minute, she didn't know. Perhaps it was to compose her thoughts and steel features. She didn't want to talk to anyone. Her nerves were raw, and her confidence shattered in the space of a few minutes at the hands of—*him*. She drew in a deep breath and opened the door, staring into the eyes of her unwanted visitors.

Neve moved forward slightly. "We need to talk with you, Rita. Will you let us in?"

"Do I have a choice?"

Neve's voice was gentle. "Yes, you have choices, Rita. We want to help—if you'll allow us to."

Rita closed her eyes and considered her reply.

Neve had moved and half filled the doorway. "Please, Rita."

Neve's voice had dropped so low that only Rita heard it and that broke her resolve to ignore them. She moved toward the sofa and sank dejectedly into its depths

Lorenzo glanced at each woman before he pulled at his moustache and hesitatingly entered Rita's inner sanctum. "I'll get us something to drink. Do you mind if I make coffee, Rita?"

Rita gave Lorenzo a faint smile. His normal tone had her half believing that the last hour had been a figment of her imagination. His concerned expression said otherwise. "Go for it."

Lorenzo smiled and turned on the coffee machine.

Neve did not sit but towered over Rita with her face a blank mask.

"Have a seat, Neve," Rita said automatically. She watched Neve seemingly pondering the offer before finally sitting opposite her.

Neve bit her bottom lip. "Rita, did Danny Carmine make a pass at you or do something inappropriate?"

Neve's eyes pierced her with a considerate gaze, and Rita felt like she was under a microscope. Her mouth went dry, and she was unable to speak. Eventually she whispered, "What makes you think that?"

Neve sighed. "Because you looked…how can I put this delicately?" Neve frowned slightly and her left eyebrow drew down in concentration. "You looked disheveled, as if you'd been in some kind of altercation. You also flew toward your RV as if the devil was after you."

Rita looked away and then down. She wrung her hands and tried to compose herself. "I, uh, had an accident…I fell over…that's all."

"I don't believe you," Neve said.

Rita's eyes flared in anger. "Why not?"

Lorenzo joined them with a tray with the drinks. He sat down and placed the appropriate drink in front of the women. "Here you go. You both look like you could use it."

"Thank you," Rita whispered.

Neve acknowledged him with a nod of her head.

The silence in the room seemed to stretch forever. Finally, Lorenzo broke the ice and placed his cup on the coffee table. He looked at Rita with what looked like empathy. "Rita, Neve is worried about you. I'm worried about you. If you don't want to talk about what happened then that's fine. We'll understand."

Neve gave her brother a hard glance. "We need to know if there's a problem, Lorenzo. The kind of behavior we suspect is not tolerated."

Lorenzo turned to his sister. "Neve, if Rita doesn't want to talk to us, she has that right. Becoming angry isn't helping."

Neve jumped to her feet. "If it was me, I'd want that bastard hung, drawn and quartered," Neve snarled and strode to the end of the room and back.

Rita watched her boss's reaction. In a way, she felt divorced from the situation, as if they were talking about someone else—they weren't. "Why do you assume that anything happened between me and…Danny Carmine? We hardly speak."

Lorenzo's head moved upwards and his eyes narrowed at Rita's words.

With a rough voice, Neve said, "He admitted it."

Rita exhaled a harsh breath, dumbstruck at the supposed admission. *Why would anyone admit such a thing unless they didn't give a damn?* She summoned the strength she used against Danny's attack. "What did he say?"

Neve shook her head. "The details don't matter. Just suffice to know he's demanding you're out of the circus by tomorrow morning—or the Carmines will leave."

Lorenzo gasped in surprise. "You didn't tell me that, Neve. You aren't going to let that bastard blackmail us, are you?"

Neve growled. "You think I'd allow that?"

"No, of course not, but—" Lorenzo shook his head and took a large drink from his cup.

In a quiet, oddly calm voice, Rita interrupted the conversation between the siblings. "The Carmines are important to the circus. You need them. I don't want to be responsible for your losing what little you've gained over the past few months. I couldn't live with myself. I'll leave later today."

"That's ridiculous!" Lorenzo's eyes moved to his sister. "Tell her, Neve. It isn't an option."

Neve's gaze moved to that of her brother before she walked toward the door. "I have some thinking to do."

Rita and Lorenzo watched Neve leave.

"What just happened?" Lorenzo asked.

All Rita could think was that Neve knew she was right and that it would be best for the circus if she left. "Did you tell her that the Carmines are leaving for Lulu-Belle's next season?"

Lorenzo shook his head. "I thought we could discuss that today when she was settled in. This changes everything, though." He stood up with a perplexed expression on his face. "What the hell does she have to think about?"

"He threatened me, Lorenzo. He implied he'd rape me if I didn't do what he wanted. I was assessing the stalls, as I usually do, and he was there. He wants money. Apparently, he had a deal with your uncle, and he wants his share. Frankly, my leaving right now doesn't sound like such a bad thing." Rita's world, as she knew it, was suddenly coming to an abrupt stop.

Lorenzo closed his eyes briefly before sitting down next to Rita on the sofa and taking one of Rita's hands in his. "At least you aren't painting all men with the Danny Carmine brush, Rita. For that, I'm thankful. I'm so very sorry this happened to you, Rita. Do you want me to call the police? We can have him arrested within the hour."

Rita shook her head. "I don't want the police. Maybe that's a coward's way out, but I know it will be his word against mine. And, right now, all I want to do is forget it ever happened. As you both know, what he wants isn't going to happen…you'll never pay him off. Besides, Neve wants some time to think about…"

"Forget what Neve wants, Rita. It isn't about her *or* the circus. It's about you."

Lorenzo's tone, although not loud, sounded angry to Rita and she stared at him. "You know, you're better at this than she is."

Lorenzo gave Rita a smile and she responded with a tiny one in return. "I've had a lot of practice over the years. Neve isn't one for social chit chat, as you already know. I think I can count on one hand the number of times in the last couple of decades that I've actually seen her just enjoy life. Even so, she could have been more sympathetic."

Rita recalled Neve's initial reaction when she asked Rita about the event. Neve had been compassionate, with empathy reflected on her face. In a strange way, once Neve intercepted her after she'd gotten away from Danny, the situation hadn't seemed as serious. It had only been when she was alone that Carmine's threats overwhelmed her. She finally gave Lorenzo a smile. “Maybe if I have a week away and take the laptop, I could work from home…at least in part. By then, it should have all blown over, and we can get back to normal.”

Lorenzo frowned. “Is that really what you want, Rita? I can get rid of that bastard, if you want me to. All I need is one word from you. Neve’s probably up on the trapeze working out the problem.” He cocked his head and looked at Rita. “She does that, if you haven’t noticed.”

Rita had. Over the months, she had noticed that when Neve couldn’t solve a problem immediately, she disappeared and hung like a bat from the high trapeze. It was an astounding sight—breathtaking—but at the same time, it made Rita uncomfortable. The same thought always ran through her mind. *What if she falls*? Then, she’d chastise herself, knowing that Neve was as safe up there where she felt comfortable, as Rita would be having herbal tea while thinking out a strategy. “I had.”

†

A loud knocking on the door and shouting had Lorenzo standing up and opening the door of Rita’s RV. Jacamar stood there, his features ruddy and his breathing labored. “You’d better get over to Danny Carmine’s place. Neve’s gone berserk.”

Lorenzo blew out a breath. “So much for her just thinking about it. I should have known better. I’ll be right back, Rita.” He left and ran toward the three RVs that held the Carmine family.

†

When he got there, Lorenzo saw Danny Carmine slumped against the wheel of his Ford Explorer. His nose was bleeding and, from an initial glance, his arm looked out of place. His brother, John, was bending over him. Peter and

Rafe Carmine were holding Neve, who was struggling against their hold. Sally, standing in the doorway of her RV was staring at the scene with her mouth open.

Lorenzo, approached Neve."Let her go or you'll have me to contend with."

The two men looked at Lorenzo and then at Neve's angry expression.

Peter Carmine shook his head. "Not before we know why she did what she did. For God's sake, Lorenzo, she's broken his arm. How are we supposed to perform?"

"There isn't a performance…not here anyway. When I've finished telling people exactly the type of scum your brother is, he won't ever have a place in a reputable circus." Lorenzo announced.

Rafe Carmine, the youngest brother, shifted his glance from Lorenzo to his older brother. "Who is it this time?"

Sally walked down the steps and stood beside Rafe. "What do you mean by *who*, Rafe?"

Rafe dropped his hold on Neve and Peter reluctantly followed suit. "I'm sorry, Sally, but Danny seems to think that any girl is easy game and he doesn't understand the word *no.*"

Sally gasped. "What are you telling me?"

"That bastard you call big brother is a pervert and rapes women."

"No, no, he wouldn't do that," Sally wailed. "Who said this terrible thing?" Her eyes fixed on Danny and Lorenzo noticed he didn't make eye contact.

Lorenzo felt sorry for Sally. She obviously hadn't known about her brother's character flaw and he thanked God for that. Neve wasn't strictly correct. He hadn't raped Rita, but, in his opinion, the threat was just as serious. "I'm sorry, we can't break that confidence," he answered.

Sally tuned to her brothers. "It isn't true, is it?"

Peter shrugged and John, who looked like he was listening to the conversation, stepped forward. "Danny gets carried away…we always work it out." He turned to Lorenzo and Neve. "Your Uncle knew all about it and turned a blind eye. In fact, he paid off a few of the girls. So, you're as responsible as we are."

Neve screwed up her eyes and snorted. "I want him out of my circus by lunchtime. The rest of you can stay and carry on as normal until your contract expires. After that, you're on your own."

John nodded. "He needs medical attention. Then he can go home and recuperate. We'd like to stay on."

Sally held up her hands. "How can you casually say all these things and then go about business as normal? What about the poor woman who was attacked?"

Neve stepped in front of Sally. "That's not your concern. I'll take care of her."

"How? By doing the same thing your uncle did and buy her off?" Sally replied.

"No!" Neve replied explosively.

Sally looked at Danny and her lips twisted. "He should be punished by the authorities. If he's done this before, he needs help and he won't get that at home."

Danny snarled at Sally. "What do you know, bitch? You women are all the same. You lead us on, and when we take what you offer, you say *no*. No one is going to the authorities because women are all chicken." He nodded in Lorenzo and Neve's direction. "Who'd believe them anyway? It's my word against hers."

Neve moved forward and pushed at Danny's injured shoulder and laughed as he howled in pain. "If he ever comes within a mile of my circus or my people, I'll kill him."

"Let's go, Neve. Come on, he's not worth going to jail for on an assault charge." Lorenzo wished he never said those words when he saw a malicious smirk cross Danny Carmine's face. "Come on."

†

Lorenzo, walking quietly next to Neve, blew out a breath and shook his head. "I must remember that you think about things fast and react even faster."

Neve didn't reply as she flexed her fingers. "Ow."

Lorenzo stopped and took hold of his sister's hand—she pulled it away. "Stop and let me look at it to see if it is broken."

"Stop, it's fine."

"Have it your way. If it was me I'd get some ice on it."

"I'm not you."

Lorenzo rolled his eyes. "I'm not sure Rita will approve of what you did. She wanted to go home and let it all drop."

Neve stopped in her tracks and gave her a brother a hard stare. "I wouldn't have allowed that. You can't run from people like him or they win. I'm not like my uncle. He was as culpable as Carmine."

Lorenzo nodded. "Jane told you about him beating her and Sasha?"

Neve glared at her brother. "Ah, it was you she told. Why didn't you tell me? I could have…"

"Done what, Neve? Beat the tar out of him like you just did to Danny? Besides, they left before I could help. I confronted Silvestre and, as far as I know, he didn't attempt that kind of thing again. Though now, I'm not so sure."

They both glanced back to the Carmine vehicles.

"I've dropped the ball for years, Lorenzo. I need to make up for it, especially with Rita. She's so damned innocent. What must she be thinking about circus life?

Lorenzo placed a hand on her shoulder. "Trust me. Rita is stronger than she looks. Carmine only threatened rape if she didn't pay him a share of the stall percentage. She won't blame you or the circus. Maybe, going home for a week until he's gone might help."

Neve drew in a breath. “Are you and she seeing each other? This might change things if she now feels physically threatened by men.”

Lorenzo chuckled. “I already told you *no*. I’d be lucky for her to look at me that way. Who told you that?” He hesitated, “Nope, don’t answer. The gossipmongers around here have been having a field day because I kissed her once on the cheek. Laura read too much into it.”

Neve smiled.

†

Jacamar, having watched the altercations and listened intently to the conversations, knew the identity of the woman Danny had threatened—Rita Collins. He’d seen her worried and pale features after Lorenzo headed off to help his sister. Jacamar would have to have a chat with a few of the others—this was a circus matter and they dealt with things in house—the boss never should have been involved. He headed away from Lorenzo and Neve to the breakfast tent.

Chapter Fourteen

Sometimes life takes on a completely new perspective that you never figured could or would be part of your life. That's how Rita summed up her day. The trauma of the early morning had been difficult and when her bosses arrived, asking pertinent questions, it only added fuel to her feeling of being out of control. Going home was a good idea. However, would that mean that she was a coward, unable to face what had happened? Lorenzo was right and they should call the police. It was her responsibility to inform them. However, other than a possible bruise or two, Danny Carmine hadn't managed to inflict any physical injury. Her mental stability was another thing altogether, he instilled fear in her mind. All she really wanted was to forget it and go back to a normal life. This was merely a blip that helped her understand life better. "Yeah, right," Rita mumbled.

Rita glanced at the clock above the television and closed her eyes trying to blot out the images of the recent events. It was a quarter after ten and if she wanted to get back to normal, she needed to be at the hub and working. She swallowed down the bile that rose in her throat. The thought of leaving the safety of her *steel box* made her feel sick. It had now been over an hour since Lorenzo had left in a rush because of something Jacamar had said. The older man had given Rita a serious look and then shook his head before leaving with Lorenzo. No one had come by to check on her. She was disappointed Lorenzo, at least, hadn't done so. Although, deep down she wanted to see Neve again and explain her adamant protest refusing to press charges. Based on the grim expression and the anger that had exploded shortly thereafter, Neve wasn't happy with her decision and might not speak to her again. That consideration alone had the butterflies doing cartwheels in the pit of her stomach.

Yes, she needed to go back to work. Maybe allowing the more mundane tasks of the day to take over, clarity would surface, and she'd know what to do next. Angel had always told her that it was one of her interesting foibles—the colossal amount of time spent over making a decision. She was so unlike her sister, who ran full-tilt into any situation and gave it her all, no matter the consequences. She felt the tears prick as she thought of Angel and Charlie. How she wished she were with them in their small family home.

A strident knock had her jumping out of her skin as she walked shakily toward the door and opened it gingerly. Rita blinked back her surprise. "Neve."

Neve drew in a breath and gazed at Rita, "May I come in, Rita?"

Rita opened the door wider. Her gut was twisting as she turned away and walked to sit down heavily on a kitchen bench.

Neve followed and closed the door behind her. Rita now faced Neve and saw her hesitate a moment before she sat opposite her.

"I know I should be back at work. I'll get ready," Rita said.

"No. That isn't why I'm here. I wanted to make sure you're okay. Look, I know I was angry when I left, and I didn't say or do the right things when I was here the last time, but I'm here for you, Rita, whatever it takes."

"Thanks, that means a lot to me. I know you and Lorenzo want me to press charges, but I don't think I can." Rita clasped her fingers together so tightly that the knuckles were going white.

Neve nodded reaching out with her right hand and attempted to unclasp Rita's hands. Her lips twisted in pain. "Damn, that hurt."

The hiss of the comment made Rita direct her attention to the hands on the table and she saw the discoloration of Neve's fingers. Quickly, her gaze went to Neve's face and she saw the pain etched there. "What have you done?"

Neve frowned slightly then gave Rita a lop-sided grin. "The other guy came off worse."

Rita stood up, went around the table, and sat next to Neve. "Let me look." At the surprised expression on her boss's face, she insisted, "Please, Neve."

Neve reluctantly moved her hand and placed it in Rita's smaller hand.

At Rita gentle probing of fingertips Neve whistled."Hurts, huh?" Rita gave her a compassionate smile. "Was this why Jacamar came for Lorenzo earlier?"

Neve nodded. "I don't think it's as bad as it looks. Probably just bruised…it'll go down in time."

Rita heard the words but also the inflection and knew it was worse than Neve admitted. She stood and moved toward her bedroom to collect her coat and purse. "Let's go."

"Go? Go where?" Neve stood.

With a flick of her head, Rita gave her a small smile as she stopped. "I'm taking you to the hospital. I think you've broken something…maybe more than one *something*."

Neve's brow puckered. "I'd rather not. We can wait until tomorrow; if it isn't a lot better by then, we can go to the hospital in the next town.

"You're not telling me something, Neve. What is it?"

Neve gave a tight smile. "Are you hungry? I know you didn't have breakfast and frankly, I need sustenance."

Rita came to the only conclusion she could. "You said the 'other guy came off worse.' Was that Danny Carmine?"

"Yes," Neve responded.

Rita watched Neve's wide powerful shoulders ripple as they stretched her blue denim shirt. The sight pulled magnetically on Rita's senses, .and she wondered if the feeling that now hit the pit of her belly was an accumulation of all that she'd gone through today. "I'll have breakfast with you if you tell me what happened."

Neve appeared to consider the request. "Seems like a fair deal to me. There's a diner about two miles away. I think we both need to get away for a while." She looked down at her right hand. "Will you drive?"

A bubble of laughter floated upward and came out as a soft chuckle surprising Rita, as her lips tugged into a genuine smile. "As you've been injured protecting my honor, it's the least I can do."

"I wish I hadn't had to do that…"

Rita stopped Neve's apology by placing a gentle finger to Neve's lips. "Thank you."

A puzzled looked crossed Neve's face before a brief smile appeared. "You're welcome."

"Let's go, then. Funny, my appetite has just returned. Be right back." Rita looked around. "Darn it, I forgot my purse. I'll just be a minute." She walked toward her bedroom in search of her purse. When she returned, Neve reached inside her shirt pocket, and withdrew her keys.

†

Rita smiled as she saw Neve place her pen in her mouth, contemplating the financial information in front of her. Over the past three weeks since the episode with Carmine, she'd seen another side of Neve. The pen to mouth was an endearing trait, the kind you either loved or hated when you worked in close proximity every day. Since *the incident*, Rita had settled back into a normal routine because of Neve's patient attention.

"Rita, about the figures for the final take…" Neve had looked up. "Okay, why are you laughing at me? Have I left some of my breakfast on my face?"

Rita knew she was blushing. "No, not at all. I was just thinking about that pen."

"What pen?" Neve placed her pen back in her mouth.

"*That* pen." Rita pointed to the object sticking out of Neve's mouth.

Neve glanced down at the object and with a sheepish smile, pulled it out, and gave it an intense look. "Oh, I see. What has my poor pen done?"

Chuckling, Rita tilted her head to one side, regarding the pen and then the amused features of Neve. "Actually, I was thinking one day the pen might bite back and you'd have ink running down your lips."

"Ah, well, I haven't had that happen yet and, if it did, I'm sure it would amuse at least one of us," Neve placed the pen back in her mouth.

"I figured you'd look like a vampire."

Neve laughed as the pen slipped out. "What an imagination. Do I look the blood sucking type to you?"

"Well…I guess blue isn't the color of blood, unless you're royalty, that is." Rita laughed. She casually turned her attention to the private mail she had yet to open. One was from Angel, and she was desperate to read it and find out what was happening with her sister and nephew. *When did Angel ever send me a letter? She is a text queen. It must be important, or serious.* The second was an official one and that had more far-reaching aspects.

Neve grinned. "Hey, why don't we take a break for half an hour? I have some calls to make, and you can read your mail. I know they're burning a hole in your hand."

Rita smiled. "Thanks. Are you coming tonight to Clara's last poker night of the season?" Within the first couple of weeks of arriving at the circus, she had an invitation to Clara's poker evenings, usually once a week and normally on a Thursday. She'd miss those evenings with her circus family, as she called them. In two days' time, the final show of the season would go on and then the circus would be dormant for the winter.

"I'm not sure. It's a busy time right now. If I can, I will." Neve got up from the chair near Rita's desk and headed to her own cubicle.

Rita nodded and watched Neve leave before she looked down at the letters on her desk. "Should I have the bad news or the good first?" Unaware she spoke out loud, Rita was surprised when a head popped around her cubicle.

Neve winked. "Bad first, good later. Usually works for me." Then she was gone again.

Rita chuckled. Since that incident with Danny Carmine, their relationship took on a new level. Neve had become quite protective of her. Most mornings Neve would accompany her on her trip around the stalls; if she couldn't, she'd assign someone to go with her. She'd also bought several panic/attack pagers, linked to the computer system in the bus. Rita had one, as did several of the other women in vulnerable positions around the circus. The last few weeks had been, in an odd way, special, and she had to put it down to Neve opening up a little. Sometimes, they even spent the evening together having dinner or simply watching a movie. The first time that happened, it was surprising how much they had in common...

Rita smiled as Neve waved a DVD in front of her as she entered Rita's RV.

"I'm not sure if you'll like this type of movie. I confess that sci-fi is one of my favorites, and this is an old favorite of mine."

"Well, I'm partial to the odd fantasy movie myself. What is it?" Rita asked as she watched Neve walk confidently over to the player and drop it in, switching on the TV as she did. Then, she picked up a tray and moved toward a chair, Neve having taken the sofa.

"*Alien*. Have you seen it before?" Neve crossed her legs at the ankles and eyed the tray Rita had just placed on the coffee table between them.

"Yes, once. I was spooked when the thing came out of the chest the first time. I won't say that won't happen again this time. My dad wasn't very sympathetic when I shrieked the house down. He told me not to be a wuss. I was ten years old."

Neve caught Rita's gaze and smiled. "In that case, you'd better come share this couch. I promise to warn you when that's about to happen."

Rita chuckled. "Are you afraid I'll scare you with my screaming?"

"Nope, merely looking after my eardrums," Neve replied with a wink. "Hey, you've made popcorn, and do I smell apple cider?"

"You do. Why? Don't you like either?"

Neve laughed and shook her head. "Hardly, I love 'em both. Come on, this sofa can accommodate us both comfortably and, if you do get spooked, you can hide your head against my shoulder."

Rita held her breath for an instant and then grinned. "You have a deal."

Since then, Rita had found out that, in some ways, their lives mirrored each other's. When her parents died, she had to take care of Angel and Charlie, much as Neve had to do for Lorenzo and the circus—Neve's responsibilities outstripped hers because of the circus's magnitude.

When she'd asked Carla if Neve could come to one of the weekly poker sessions, the older woman had been delighted. Apparently, it was a big deal. Neve had never interacted in a frivolous, social way with circus personnel before. Neve, winning the first two sessions had been a surprise and made the older women at the poker table that evening out for her blood. Rita was surprised that Neve seemed to enjoy the time along with being there with the others. That showed Rita another facet of Neve that had once been private.

Shaking her head at her musings, Rita placed Angel's letter on the desk and slide the letter opener along the top of the official looking envelope. She closed her eyes for a second then unfolded the letter to read the contents. It sent a ripple through her stomach. She placed the letter in front of her and felt tears pricking her eyelids. It was far from the outcome she'd expected.

"It's finally over." Her words sounded heavy in the stillness around her.

Then she picked up her sister's letter, opened it, and read the contents. This time tears of happiness rolled down her cheeks. Angel's wedding coincided with Rita's going home. "Way to go, Angel."

Rita sat, taking in what the contents of the two letters meant for her life. For a few moments, she recalled the caring police woman, who gently helped her relive her nightmare of the Danny Carmine attack. She'd had the bruises on her body photographed, which had been embarrassing but essential. She expected to go to court and testify, but the letter indicated that wasn't necessary and confirmed that her ordeal was over.

†

Neve walked around the cubicle and settled into the chair opposite Rita, her curiosity piqued by the two short comments Rita had said aloud. "Everything okay?"

"Yeah, it is. Thanks for asking." Rita smiled with her gaze fixed on Neve's face.

"Excellent." Neve looked at Rita waiting for her to fill in the blanks.

Rita pushed an official letter across the desk. "I'd like you to read this."

Neve frowned. "Are you sure? If it's private…"

"Please, it's important."

"Okay." Neve picked up the letter and looked at the official letterhead. It was from the Merido County Police Department. "I didn't know you'd been to see them. Why didn't you say? I would have gone with you."

Rita looked down. Her hands were trembling. "Because you'd already done enough, and it was up to me to take responsibility, no matter how scared I felt at the time."

Neve picked up the letter and read the contents. She then placed it back on the desk and gave Rita a direct stare. "Are you okay with this?"

"Yes. He needs help and it was his first offense."

Neve almost retorted that, according to his brothers, it wasn't, but she left it alone. "He admitted he threatened you and physically molested you? I find that hard to believe. He obviously must have had some sense drummed into him."

Rita snorted softly. "More like punched." Her eyes traveled to Neve's right hand, encased in plaster. Neve looked down at her immobile hand. She'd broken three fingers and dislocated her thumb in that altercation. The cast would come off in two weeks' time. It was worth it. "I'm not sure about that. However, at least he has a record now and prospective employers will know about his temperament. It looks like he has to take anger management lessons for a while." Neve cocked her head and shrugged slightly. "He needs it."

"Yeah, well, I just wanted to ensure he doesn't do it again to someone else. Maybe Danny Carmine is truly sorry."

Neve shook her head. "If it makes you happy to think that way, Rita, go for it. I'm proud of you and I know Lorenzo will be too."

Rita smiled warmly. "Lorenzo's a lovely, caring man. I'm surprised he's still single, he never talks about girlfriends."

Neve laughed. "Who knows? When he gets back from the winter break in Vegas, he might bring someone home…maybe a showgirl." Neve watched for any sign of distress in Rita because of her words. She didn't see anything except a cheerful nod of agreement. "Otherwise, I suspect it will be the usual…lots of pretty women on his arm and anything else he can get. He says it's the closest thing to home, being in one place for the circus' hiatus. He calls Vegas the 'circus town of the western world'.

They both laughed.

"What about you? Where will you go this winter? It's going to be different for you, I assume?"

Neve considered the question for it was one that had been on her mind recently. "To be honest, I'm not sure. I've haven't had a vacation in over twenty years. I guess I have a lot of choices."

Rita smiled. "You can go anywhere in the world. Isn't there some place you'd like to go…dreamed of going?"

"Nope, this place is my life." Neve waved a hand around the bus.

"I guess we're going to have to work on finding you a new life in the winter."

Neve gave Rita an intense stare and then shrugged. "Yeah, I guess we are. What about you? You have six whole weeks of paid vacation before you come back to work."

Rita shook her head. "I still can't believe you've given me a contract of permanent employment, not to mention a generous increase in salary, complete with a benefits and profit sharing."

Neve's phone rang, she looked at the caller ID. "Hold that thought I need to take this but I'll be only a couple of minutes." Neve walked around to her cubicle.

Rita sitting alone again recalled when she received the contract...

"I can't accept this," Rita exclaimed as Neve stood beside her desk. It was late and the others had gone to late supper or home to bed leaving them alone on the bus.

Neve's eyebrows knitted. "I thought you liked working here. Before you say anything, I know the last few weeks have been difficult…traumatic…with what went on with Danny Carmine."

Rita looked at the contract that gave her a generous salary package, a third more than she was getting and a profit sharing scheme that would net her a bonus at the end of each season if they made a profit. The Carmine incident had shredded her confidence but, Neve, Lorenzo, and everyone else who knew about the incident—she supposed it would be everyone—were wonderful in their support. It was strange. In the space of five months, she'd come to look on the circus as family and not just a job. Now, with this contract, Neve invited her to stay and become a permanent part of the circus. It brought a lump to her throat just thinking about it—she had a new home.

She recalled how Neve watched her face as she waited for her answer.

"Okay, Rita, you don't have to do anything now. Take it home, think about it, and when you're ready to talk, call me."

That simple word *home* worked magic. At first, Rita had wondered how she would cope being away from Angel and especially from Charlie, but the circus people and in particular Neve had in the recent weeks proven that there was something more for her in life than the small town in which she'd been raised.

Rita picked up her pen, placed her signature in neat bold writing on the page, and dated it. She looked up into what looked like Neve's surprised, but delighted expression. "Thank you. There is no place I'd rather live and work."

"Earth to, Rita. Can you hear me?" Neve whispered in Rita's ear.

The close proximity of Neve had Rita's heartbeat increasing as she refocused on the question in hand. "I didn't know you'd come back, I'm sorry," Rita replied. "I was miles away. Angel's getting married in two weeks." Her fingers turned over the pretty invitation card in her hands. "I have a wedding to shop for and, hopefully, I can persuade Angel to allow Charlie to spend a little time with me. I miss him."

Neve frowned slightly. "Charlie means a lot to you, doesn't he?"

Rita smiled tenderly. "Yeah, he does. I was his second mother from the moment he was born. It was a bit of wrench to say goodbye when Angel found Trevor—Charlie's father—again."

"I suspect *a bit of a wrench* is a lukewarm phrase for what you felt. Is that why you took the job with the circus?"

Rita chuckled. "Charlie thinks I've run away to the circus. He thought it was cool."

"Is it…cool?" Neve had an amused expression tugging at her lips.

"Yes, as it happens, it is. He's going to ask twenty thousand questions when I do see him." Rita's smiled as she contemplated her nephew's constant thirst for knowledge.

"Oh, I imagine you'll have many stories to tell him. Besides, if you can't answer a question, you can always call me. What I don't know about this circus would fit on a postcard, I suspect."

Rita considered the offer then drew in a short breath. "Why don't you come home with me, at least for a couple of weeks, until the cast is off your hand? It will give you time to reflect on what you want to do for the rest of the winter." *Phew, I've said it. I hope she doesn't get mad.*

Neve leaned back in the chair with her eyebrows contracting, appearing to ponder the offer. "Now why would you want to be holed up with your boss for another two weeks? Don't you need a break from me?" Her lips relaxed into a small smile.

"I figure I owe you for your injury. Besides, have you ever stayed in a small town in a regular neighborhood and feel what it's like to live your life that way?" One thing Rita knew for sure, she didn't need a break from Neve—far from it. She had come to rely on their growing friendship.

"I haven't, and it would be different, I'd grant you that. As for your owing me, I think the shoe's on the other foot." Neve's gaze had become serious, as they traded steady looks.

"Okay, how about we agree to disagree on that point. However, if I asked you as a friend to stay and keep me company, what would you say? I'll show you my home town and keep you out of mischief until you have the cast off." Rita grinned. "Remember, I did promise to make sure you didn't do anything strenuous while you were injured. I take my role very seriously." Rita was sure Neve would roll her eyes and chuckle-she didn't.

Neve got up from her chair. "I think we need to get back to work."

Rita felt the disappointment in the pit of her stomach. She had hoped that they were becoming friends and that Neve might come home with her. What would be the harm in spending a couple of weeks together? "You're right, we should. I'm sorry for wasting your time."

Neve turned and stared at Rita. "You have never wasted my time, Rita, ever. Don't think that I'm not grateful you want to spend your free time with me. I am."

"I was presumptuous. You probably already have plans." Rita walked away from her desk and almost bumped into Neve, who hadn't moved.

Long arms snaked out and held Rita firmly but gently. "I'll come home with you, if you do something for me."

A burst of pleasure ran through Rita's body at the tone Neve used. It was part serious and part indulgent. "Name it."

Neve let out a deep chuckle and shook her head. "I'd be more careful in your choice of words, but, since you asked, I'd like you to teach me the basics of accounting so no one can ever do what my uncle did to me again."

Rita blinked as she tried to bury her happy bubbles, which wanted to explode at Neve's acceptance of her offer. "Of course, I can. It will be my pleasure." Rita felt herself responding positively to the hands that held her shoulders that seemed to burn into her skin.

Neve nodded and dropping her hands before moving away toward the central desk in the hub where they worked together. "Excellent, we can leave on Monday, if that's okay with you. I'd like to check that the main equipment is placed in storage and that the guys have a proper roster for the maintenance of the vehicles, including this one." Neve waved her hand around the bus.

"I'm not surprised. This vehicle alone costs a fortune to maintain with all the high-end equipment."

Neve looked around the bus and smiled in satisfaction. "Yes, but it's worth it. I made this one purchase against my uncle's advice. Now I know why he objected."

Rita nodded understanding perfectly what Neve meant—less money her uncle could swindle from her. "You do know that I'll never do anything like that, don't you."

Neve smiled and winked. "What, disagree with my choices of equipment? Oh, I'm sure you will and have already. Don't you remember that additional big top I proposed and you asked me to reconsider on the basis that it was an extremely costly, unnecessary addition."

Rita laughed softly. "Yeah, and I was right, but that wasn't what I meant."

"I know, and thank you. I have no doubts in that area at all. So, can you please tell me what the hell we spent an extra ten thousand dollars on last month under the administration column?"

Rita grinned peering at the figure on the spreadsheet. "Ah, well, it has something to do with not getting the additional big top…"

Chapter Fifteen

Rita's lips twitched slightly as she drove into the main street of Rochester. Several heads turned at the strange vehicle that entered the small town. Neve's large SUV, with the circus signage painted over every inch, definitely drew attention.

"So, this is Rita Collins' home town. How does it feel to be back?" Neve asked. Rita saw more heads turn as they drove further down the main street. "To use one of Charlie's expressions...*it's way weird!*" Rita laughed as she stopped at the traffic lights opposite her and Charlie's favorite soda fountain. It was also opposite Dan's garage, but she refused to look in that direction—Dan never missed a thing.

Neve smiled as she glanced across at Rita. "I'm with Charlie."

Rita shook her head. "You've been here before, Neve. Remember, this is where Lorenzo hired me."

"I hate to admit it, but small towns blur after a few years. Although, this one will now stick out in my memory as the birthplace of my friend, Rita Collins." Neve winked and then returned her attention to the buildings.

Rita was glad that Neve switched her attention elsewhere or she might have seen her blush at the words. As the signal turned to green, they drove on and Rita pointed to a medium-sized store. "My father used to own the hardware store. We had to sell it when my parents died."

"Must have been tough. Taking on a family business isn't for everyone."

"I'd have done it, but the store had a hefty mortgage, and with the death taxes and Angel just coming out of school…well, it was better to keep a roof over our heads. I could always get another job."

"Seems you and I are alike in more ways than we thought."

As they curved away from the main street, they headed down a tree-lined street that marked the beginning of a subdivision. A few minutes later, they rounded a bend and Rita slowly pulled the vehicle into a neat driveway. With a deep smile that carved grooves into Rita's cheeks, she glanced at Neve. "I'm glad you pay well…it means I could hire a handyman to keep the yard tidy. I had my neighbor, Lory, clean the house so we have fresh linens. Angel said she hasn't used the house for over five months and, as you know, I've been with you six months." The vehicle stopped, and Rita clambered out of the driver's seat, rushed up the five steps onto the porch, and simply twirled, taking in the fact that she was home again.

†

Neve felt a fresh wave of warmth flood through her as Rita's words floated by her. Since Rita's brush with Carmine, she'd taken on a protective role and, in doing so, had opened herself up to a previously unknown quantity in her life—a best friend. As she stared at the small, well-maintained property, she noticed it was like many others in the neighborhood and in many of the small towns, the circus visited. She wondered how people lived in a stationary box all their lives. With a smile, she whispered, "I'm glad I paid well, too." Neve watched the joyful expressions that floated across Rita's face. *Perhaps her words about loving the circus were just that—words. She certainly looks very happy to be here.*

Neve heard her name, opened the door, climbed out of the vehicle, and allowed her long legs to touch the graveled driveway. Moments later, she was standing beside Rita, "Looks like a nice place."

"Thank you. My dad was careful with money and didn't keep the place up properly. When Angel and I inherited it, and especially when Charlie came along, I made sure it was brought up to standards, or as much as I could afford." Rita placed her key in the door and opened it.

Neve sniffed the air, half expecting a stale smell of an unoccupied house to greet her. Instead, there was a fresh lavender smell mingled with…*baking*? She followed close behind, Rita into the small house and peered into the tiny living area just off the even smaller hallway. A wall separated the living room from the kitchen but the doorway was wide open. Neve saw Rita looking at something on the table and walked toward her. On the table in the kitchen sat a large cake with white swirling icing with the words *Welcome Home Rita*. Alongside the cake sat a loaf of bread. "Looks like you have a great neighbor."

Rita turned her head and tears were glistening in her eyes. She swiped at her eyes with the back of her hand before she picked up the folded paper besides the cake and Neve looked over her shoulder as they read it together.

Hi, Rita,

Thought you needed a proper homecoming. I had to go visit my eldest for the weekend. I'll catch up Monday. Glad you're back.

Love, Lory

Rita grinned. "You'll meet Lory...she always pops in when she gets back from visiting her family. I think you'll like her."

Neve chuckled. "If that cake tastes as good as it looks, then I'm going to be taking her back to the circus with us."

Rita smiled. "What would Clara say?"

Neve considered that and the fact that Clara was a rather large woman and one you didn't mess with. "I'm sure she'd love the competition." She winked and ran her finger along the edge of the icing and brought it to her lips.

"Hey, can't you wait until we unpack?"

Neve screwed up her lips. "Well..."

"Okay, let me cut you a slice. I must admit you were good this morning and didn't have a second muffin for breakfast."

"You give in too easily, Rita."

"Only to those I care about." Rita opened a drawer and withdrew a knife. "Right, here we go." Brandishing the knife theatrically, she cut a slice and placed it on a paper napkin before handing it to Neve.

Neve, for her part, had silently watched her cut the cake. Rita's admission of caring, even if she probably hadn't really meant it in quite the way Neve hoped, was nice to hear. She brought the cake to her lips and smacked them before taking a bite. "You do know me well. Welcome home, Rita."

Rita winked. "Put the kettle on, and I'll get our bags."

Neve was about to protest but realized it would be futile. Rita was as good as her word and ensured that there was no chance Neve would reinjure her hand. She glanced at the cast and growled in irritation. "Damn, I need a knitting needle."

†

Settled in, Neve smiled as she watched Rita begin preparing dinner. They decided that they were both tired from the journey and agreed that an early night after dinner sounded good. The more Neve observed Rita, the more her smile widened. The bedroom she had been allocated had been Angel's. Though the clothes and the very personal items were gone, there was lots of the sister's personality still stamped inside the room. As far as Neve could see, it was clear that Rita and her sister were definitely opposites. Rita's personality was down to earth like what she thought *the girl next door* might have. She noticed it in the RV and here too. On the other hand, Rita's sister looked like she enjoyed activities that were more frivolous such as dancing, going to bars, talking on the phone for hours, and hanging out with her friends. She grinned at the numerous out of date gossip magazines that were stacked on the dresser. *Yep, I don't she is very serious about much.* The room was a pastel pink and the furniture modern, inexpensive, white melamine. The bed was queen-sized and the bedding matched an oriental theme that ran throughout the posters and pictures on the walls.

Neve dragged her thoughts from the bedroom to the woman who had invited her to stay there. Rita had made a generous offer and one she hadn't expected. Of course, Lorenzo had insisted she tag along with him but she knew he really didn't want her along. His relieved expression, when told him she had a better offer made her laugh. However, he did raise his eyebrows a little when she'd told him where she was going for the first two weeks of her winter break. However, he agreed it was a wonderful way for her to relax before choosing where she actually wanted to go on vacation.

Now that she was at Rita's house, she was glad that she'd taken up the offer. She and Rita, as far removed personality-wise as any two people could be, got along very well. She enjoyed her accountant's quiet company. It made for a pleasant change from the more excitable people who usually surrounded her.

"Can I help with anything? I feel guilty."

Rita turned in Neve's direction and grinned. "Nope, it's all under control. However, when I'm ready, you can set the table."

"Good plan. Are you going to keep me guessing on what we're having for dinner?" Neve moved from her chair and settled her body easily against the doorjamb while she watched Rita work.

"Steak with lots of vegetables." Rita informed her with a smile.

"Darn it, Rita, you know I hate veggies."

"Right now you remind me of my nephew. He screws up his face at veggies too." Rita grinned and pulled open the oven door slightly.

Neve poked out her tongue playfully. "Are you implying I'm a child, by any chance?"

Rita looked up from the pie that was browning nicely the oven, shook her head, and glanced at Neve. "If the shoe fits. You can set the table. I think it's almost ready."

Neve nodded. "Where are the utensils?"

"In the drawer under the counter, second from the left. Don't forget we have that wonderful cake for dessert and I just made an apple pie." Neve's face light up and Rita shook her head in amusement as she checked the vegetables. An hour later, stuffed by the delicious meal and confectioneries, Neve leaned back and patted her stomach. "That was the best. Thanks, Rita."

Rita grinned as she raised the small glass of Jacob's Creek Pinot Noir that they had found in a liquor store in the last big city they passed before Rochester. It was smooth and complemented the meal perfectly. "You're welcome, Neve. This is nice, by the way." Rita held up her glass. "Are you a wine connoisseur along with your many other talents?"

"Not really, but I know what I like. The Australians can give us a run for their money, though there are some nice New Zealand wines coming through now. You know, that wouldn't be a bad kind of vacation…traveling to the Southern hemisphere and going on wine tours. What do you think?"

Rita smiled. "Yeah, I think that sounds wonderful. Maybe you should go to a travel agent and find out if they can tailor a package for you."

Neve frowned slightly as she considered Rita's words. "Maybe I will. Though it would be good to go..." A resounding knock on the door stopped Neve in midsentence.

Rita scowled. "I wonder who that can be."

"Only way to find out is if you open the door," Neve replied.

"Yeah, I'll be right back. Don't eat more than one more slice of cake, okay? You'll be sick." Rita stood up and left the kitchen.

†

Rita walked through the tiny hallway heading for the door. When she opened it, her eyes widened before they narrowed. "Dan, what are you doing here?" The sight of the man made her stomach churn.

"I noticed you came back. Thought you might want some *normal* company for a change. Lory has been talking about nothing but your return for the last couple of weeks."

"Thanks for coming, Dan, but you didn't need to. I'm fine." Rita hadn't expected Dan to approach her so soon.

"Looks like you got a company car as a perk. I thought this was a temporary job."

Rita's lips formed a tight line as she drew back her shoulders "That isn't any of your business."

"Aren't you going to ask me in?" Rita took in his bulky frame that always seemed to dwarf the doorway.

"I'm tired, Dan. I need to get some rest. I'll try to call you sometime."

Dan glared at her. "It's barely seven. Let me in so you can tell me what it's like to be part of the roving gypsy crowd."

Rita didn't like his tone that was less than complimentary about people she now considered her second family. Just about to reply, she stopped when she heard a voice from behind her speak.

"I take exception to being called a *gypsy*."

Rita turned when she heard the bristled pent-up anger in Neve's voice. Her stance was one she'd seen more than once before.

"Who the hell are you?" Dan moved a step closer.

Neve's lips twitched into a feral smile.

Rita placed her body between them. "This is my boss, Dan. She's staying with me for a couple of weeks. Go have a few beers with the guys, and I'll try and call you sometime while I'm here."

Dan's upper lip moved into a snarl. "You'd better call me." He moved his body slowly off the porch toward his Ford pickup truck.

Rita closed the door and turned to Neve, who had a closed expression on her face. "I'm sorry he said what he did about the gypsy thing."

Neve merely nodded. "I've heard worse. Look, I'm tired. Shall we wash the dishes and then call it a day?"

Rita felt exhausted—Dan's visit had taken the wind out of her sails. "I do have a dishwasher and will load it while you use the bathroom first."

Neve nodded, walked toward the bathroom, before turning back. "Don't accept second best, Rita. You're worth far more than that." Neve continued toward the bathroom, went inside, and shut the door.

Rita stood motionless. Dan's appearance had been unexpected and unwanted. His harsh words about the circus folk had rattled her and upset Neve even more. "Shit, I'm going have to tell him clearly that there is nothing between us. I hate confrontation." Then she walked toward the kitchen and dinner dishes that needed loading into the dishwasher.

†

The next morning had begun easily enough, both women rejuvenated from an early night. Over a congenial breakfast, Rita had persuaded Neve that a long walk in the park and surrounding area would help her get her bearings in case she wanted to explore alone.

Around midday, after a leisurely stroll, Rita suggested they walk up the mountain track to see the waterfall that was halfway up.

"Is this what you call a vacation, Rita?"

"What do you mean? I thought you liked the idea of a walk."

Neve laughed. "You should see the look on your face...it's priceless."

"Now you're laughing at me."

"Not at you. We've been walking since nine, and I've enjoyed every second, but how about we have lunch? We can go up the mountain this afternoon or another time." She reached out and touched Rita's hand. "We don't have to do everything the first morning."

Rita rolled her eyes and chuckled. "Sorry, I just wanted you to see all the beauty we have here. It's available at a big price."

Neve nodded. "Wonderful. You can tell me all about that price when we have lunch...any suggestions?"

"There are a couple of good cafés in town and there's a diner at the end of Main Street."

"Let's go. When I see the right place for lunch, I'll let you know. It's my treat, by the way."

Rita, not wanting Neve to pay, frowned then changed direction so they were heading toward Main Street.

†

Neve saw a nice-looking café in the center of the block. There were a couple of tables on the sidewalk and the inside seating didn't looked like the tables were jammed together with no space between them. "This one, I think."

"Good choice. Angel used to work the breakfast shift here during the summer. She'd have loved to work here full-time but the owners are like you...they close up for a long break after Christmas."

Café Europe, designed in the classical European tradition, had a nice ambiance. Photos and souvenirs of travels to Europe covered the walls. Bistro tables and chairs, along with the menu on a chalkboard, gave it that slightly authentic flavor. Rita and Neve sat at a table with a view of the street looking at their menu.

A few moments later, a stocky young woman with short blonde hair arrived. “Rita, this is a surprise. Angel said you’d be home for the wedding. This means you can come to the bachelorette party on Thursday. Angel has spoken to you, hasn’t she? She gets home Thursday morning, and next Friday night it’s back to the hotel for the big day on Saturday.”

Rita nodded at the chatty young woman. “Good to see you too, Rachel. I’ll be there. I wouldn’t miss it.”

Rachel grinned and then looked at Neve. “Are you ready to order?”

Neve felt amused at the intense stare Rachel gave her. In other circumstances, she might have thought the woman’s interest in her was sexual. But, in this case, she’d err on the side of caution and assume that it was nothing more than small town curiosity. “We need a few more minutes.”

“No problem. I’ll be back shortly.” Rachel wandered off to speak with a couple of other customers who had just arrived.

Rita viewed her menu with a smile tugging at her lips.

“What?” Neve asked.

“I think she was interested.” Rita announced. “The Mediterranean chicken looks good.”

Surprised, Neve put her menu on the table, flicked her finger at Rita’s menu, and pushed it down. “Interested? What do you mean?”

“Just because I come from a small town doesn’t mean that we don’t have our own tiny gay community. Rachel is out and proud, much to her parents’ mortification at times.” Rita casually returned her attention to her menu.

Neve, astounded by the reply, narrowed her eyes. Although she figured that Rita knew she was a lesbian—because of circus gossip—it had never come up. *Is that strange?* "I'm having a vacation here with you...with no extra ties...okay?"

Rita laughed. "Fine, but if you change your mind, I can arrange to give you her telephone number."

"I don't want her number." Neve felt disconcerted by the topic of discussion and didn't know why it upset her that Rita wanted to fix her up with the waitress.

"Are you sure? Hey, why don't you come to Angel's bachelorette party...you might change your mind about Rachel."

"No, I don't think so. That's just for family and friends. Besides, did you even know about it?" Neve's gaze captured Rita.

Rita put down her menu. "No, but that's Angel for you. She'll think it's a hoot to turn up out of the blue. Now, it won't be such a surprise."

"Thought so." *Selfish sister.*

Rachel returned. "Are you ready to order?"

Rita smiled. "I'll have the Mediterranean chicken with a side order of the vegetable of the day."

Neve frowned. She hadn't taken notice of the menu. "I'll have the same, without the side order. Oh, can you bring the wine list please?"

"Sure thing." Rachel grinned and walked off toward the counter area and returned moments later with the list. "According to the boss, we have one of the best wine cellars in the area."

"I'll let you know." Neve scanned the list.

"Do we want to be drinking at lunch? If we are going to walk up the mountain it might not be a good idea."

Neve chuckled. "As I said before, we don't have to do everything in one day. How about we table the waterfall for another day and take a picnic."

Rita beamed. "Wow, what a great idea."

Until their meal arrived, they talked generally about where some of the other circus performers went during winter break. When their meals arrived, Rita placed a hand over her mouth.

Neve's face filled with horror as she gazed at the plate piled high with the chicken, on a Turkish bread roll and accompanied by lots of salad. "I thought I said no side order of veggies for me?"

Rachel rolled her eyes. "The salad is part of the main meal. Enjoy."

Rita smirked. "Excuse me I'll be right back."

Neve shook her head and wondered why she didn't bother to read the menu. *Oh, yeah, I was thinking of the wine list...no, I was still trying to digest Rita's comment about hooking me up with Rachel.*

Rita grinned and retook her seat.

"Are you positive this is part of the meal?" She saw Rita nod. This will teach me not to look at the details of a menu properly."

"Oh, I don't know…it's an education, Neve. Try it you might like it." Rita picked up her fork and dug into her salad. "Hmm, this is so good. It's drizzled with balsamic vinegar and olive oil."

Neve sighed and let her fork pierce a few lettuce leaves and a cherry tomato before lifting it to her mouth. She chewed much like a child forced to eat something they didn't like.

"See, was that so bad?"

"I'll let you know when I'm done."

"I've been trying to educate you for weeks on the subject of vegetables. You do know they are good for you?"

Neve waved her fork half threateningly. "Vegetables and I are not on speaking terms. We prefer to avoid each other. Although, I keep telling you, threatening me with no dessert isn't fair."

Rita chuckled. "It was the only tool at my disposal. Besides, it hasn't been so bad, has it? You constantly remind me of Charlie, when he doesn't want to eat his vegetables."

"If I ever get to meet Charlie, he and I are going out for a burger without you."

Rita saw Rachel heading her way. She placed a large bowl of fries next to Neve with a wink.

Neve looked at Rita and a smile broke through the concentrated expression she had. "Why you devious...thank you."

"Any time. You're on vacation and I want you to be happy." Rita smiled and continued her meal.

Neve looked at the bent head and allowed a tender smile to cross her lips. "I am," she whispered. For the first time in a long time, she felt that she was happy, and it was all due to the generous nature of the woman opposite her.

Chapter Sixteen

Neve woke the next morning to the smell of bacon and eggs and the aroma teased her taste buds. In anticipation, she dragged herself out of bed, quickly showered, brushed her teeth, and made herself presentable. When she waltzed into the kitchen with a cheery *good morning*, she was glad she was dressed.

Rita smiled cheerfully and wished her a good morning, but there was someone else in the kitchen sitting at the table. She guessed that the middle-aged woman with velvet lines on her face and grey eyes that looked at her intently was Rita's neighbor, Lory.

"Morning." Neve moved to within a couple of inches of Rita. "Is there anything I can do?"

"Oh, no, it's all ready. Just take a seat. Neve, this is someone I know you want to meet." Rita grinned as she waved at the older woman. "Neve Garmancelli, meet my neighbor, Lory Parker."

Neve nodded and gave Lory a small smile. "Pleased to meet you, Lory. Just the lady I need to poach to join the circus."

Lory's cheeks reddened and she let out a chuckle. "Oh, dear me, no. I'm too old to run off to the circus."

"You're never too old, right, Rita?" Neve winked at Rita, who was shaking her head in what look like a warning.

"Breakfast is ready. Two eggs, bacon, and two hash browns okay for you, Neve?"

"Sure, do you want me to butter the toast?" Neve was about to stand but Rita waved her back down.

"I've got it under control. I never know where you put all this calorie-filled stuff. If I ate the amount you eat every day, I'd add on even more inches." Rita chuckled, as she placed hash browns and scrambled eggs in front of Lory, followed by Neve's plate. The ping of the toaster had her turn to smother the bread with butter. Then, she sat down herself with bacon, eggs, and toast.

"What do you think of Rochester, Neve?" Lory asked.

Neve chewed on her toast and cocked her head to one side. "I like it. There isn't the over commercialism that you see in most towns. I would think it's a good place for families."

Lory nodded. "Yes, but the work is limited these days. We are losing out to Johnstown and the even bigger cities further away. I remember when I was growing up…" She blushed slightly. "We used to have carnivals and there was always one traveling show or tradesman making their rounds in the summer. In the winter, for at least twenty years that I recall, there used to be a circus that made its home here. Of course, that was in the fifties and sixties. Things change." Lory sighed.

Rita glanced at Neve. "Maybe you could bring the circus here during the winter."

Neve grimaced slightly before she grinned. "Can you imagine Lorenzo's reaction if I mentioned he had to work over the winter too. My dad used to work in another circus during the winter. It was quite normal back then especially if you had a family and you wanted to make enough money to live on. Generally, these days, if you need to work as a circus performer, you have to move abroad in the winter."

"Rita said you owned the circus she works for. Have you ever been a performer?" Lory picked up a piece of the toast that dripped butter.

Neve chewed a corner of her toast as she narrowed her eyes, looked at Rita, and raised an eyebrow. *Gossiper. She's been taking lessons from Clara.* "Yes, it seems like a lifetime ago. I was a trapeze artist…a catcher back then. I still keep my hand in, so to speak, from time to time."

Rita looked up and stared at Neve. "I didn't know you were a catcher. I do know you love the trapeze. Was it part of your family's act?"

Neve stared right back at Rita, allowing a tiny, amused smile to curve her lips. "No, I joined one of the other family groups. By the time I was able to do what I did, my dad had already given up performing. Circus administration takes its pound of flesh."

Rita stopped eating and watched Neve. She asked, "Which family? I've seen you hanging like a monkey from the wire. I'll bet you were awesome."

Neve dug into her hash browns, exaggerating the chewing of her food as she collected her thoughts. "Top five in the world, for a while. The family isn't relevant…it was a long time ago now."

"The top five, Neve, wow! What happened that made you to give it up?"

Neve gave a tight smile. "We must be boring Lory…let's finish our breakfast."

Rita's face fell and changed the subject. "Lory, how was Jack? His youngest must be a teenager now."

"He's doing great …"

The rest of the meal passed in pleasant conversation.

After Lory left, Rita rinsed the dishes and Neve put them in the dishwasher.

As Neve put the last dish in the appropriate slot, she looked at Rita. Ever since the question about her short-lived career, their conversation was polite but stilted. If Lory hadn't been there, they might have had a long, silent breakfast. On reflection, she realized that, if a stranger hadn't been there, she might have opened up. She drew in a deep breath of courage. "In answer to your earlier question, I gave up being a performer to run the circus. My father died, and I had Lorenzo to consider. He was only fifteen and needed someone to be there. I don't need to tell you how that goes."

Rita turned and nodded. "Yeah, I know how that goes. I'm sorry if you think I was prying earlier. Would you like to do something today?"

Neve shrugged. "Do you mind if I just chill for a couple of hours on my own?"

Rita shook her head. "Of course, not. I'm sorry. I didn't mean to crowd your personal space. I was just trying to be a good hostess." Rita gave her a slight smile. "I didn't want you to get bored. Look, you tell me when you want to do something together and we will." Rita picked up a towel and wiped her hands.

Neve had the overwhelming need to take Rita in her arms and tell her that she was sorry for being a stupid bitch, but she didn't. "Thanks. Do you mind if I hook up my laptop to your landline?"

Rita ran her tongue over her teeth and her mouth opened slightly. "Go ahead though I warn you, it isn't as speedy as your network."

"I'll cope, thanks. Do you need me to do anything else?" Neve waited for the reply.

Rita swallowed. "No, go for it. I've got it all under control."

Neve hesitated for a second then placed the wet tea towel on the drainer before leaving for her room.

†

Rita felt tears bristling and refused to allow them to leak out. There was no reason for her to be upset. None at all. Her body disagreed. As the hours stretched to lunchtime, Rita was of two minds as to what to do. She could call Neve and ask if she wanted any lunch, or simply do her own thing? *It would be impolite not to ask.* A minute later, she knocked tentatively on the door to Angel's old room. "Neve, it's almost lunchtime and I wondered if you want anything."

There was no answer, not even a shuffle of a chair or movement of bed springs. Rita tried again with a slightly louder rap on the door—still no answer. Neve either was asleep, which she thought unusual, or she was deliberately ignoring her. She decided the latter was more likely. "Okay then, I've decided to go out for lunch. See you later." The silence had irked her.

In her bedroom, Rita looked at herself in the mirror. Her hair was in need of a cutting and her face was devoid of makeup. *Why would I to go to the trouble if all I'm going to do is clean the house?* Her plaid shirt was hardly glamorous and her black faded denims, rather than flatter, seemed to hug her wide hips, accentuating their enormity. If she had to choose words to describe herself, it would be *dowdy* and *fat*.

"Well, Rita Collins, Angel is going to come walking through that door as beautiful as ever, and you're going to be exactly as she remembered. The 'life- changing' event of the circus hasn't changed a thing." Deep down she knew it had inside.

After collecting her purse, she left her room and headed for the door. On impulse, she decided to leave a note for Neve, just in case she had been asleep—it was the polite thing to do. With determination in her step, she left the house. She knew exactly what she was going to do.

†

Neve awoke with a start and looked at her watch. "Damn, it's almost three!" Climbing off the bed, she shook her head and felt disorientated for a few seconds. "I must be getting old if I need a nap in the afternoon." She'd fallen asleep just before noon, after reading her emails and surfing the net for anything of interest in the circus world. She lay on the bed, thinking about her behavior with Rita, vowing to make amends, only to have her eyes close as she drifted off to sleep. "Rita will think I've deserted her."

Neve headed for the bathroom, washed her face, and combed her hair, which fell neatly into place around her angular face. Then, she felt and heard her stomach growl. *Yep, I'll take Rita out for a late lunch and apologize properly.*

Once Neve left the bathroom, she noticed the silence in the house. There wasn't even a radio on. She checked the living room and then the kitchen finding no sign of her friend. Neve looked out into the backyard and saw nothing but clothes on the line.

"She could be with her neighbor catching up, or shopping, or out for a walk. I did tell her I needed space…maybe she did too." The idea was depressing. Then she heard a key in the front door and her previously pensive expression turned to a smile. Her smile vanished immediately when a stranger walked in with a small overnight case.

"Hey, Rita, I'm home." Angel's smile froze as she stared at Neve. "Who are you?"

Cautious eyes captured each other before Neve broke the steady gaze and held out her uninjured hand. "I'm Neve Garmancelli. Rita wanted me to stay for a few days until my cast is removed." She lifted the offending limb to the woman.

Angel dropped her bag and took the hand cautiously before giving it a swift shake. "Hi, I'm Angel, Rita's sister." She peered expectantly around Neve's wide shoulders. "Where is she?"

Neve twisted her lips slightly and shook her head. "I fell asleep and when I woke up, she wasn't here. I don't think she'll be long."

"Okay, look, let me put my stuff away and then I could use a cup of coffee. It was a long bus ride."

"You don't have a car?" Neve was astonished that a woman as young as Angel wouldn't have a vehicle of her own.

Angel grinned. "Never learned to drive. Rita always wanted me to but…" She waved away the notion like a light summer breeze.

Neve followed Angel as she opened the door to her room and grimaced. "Sorry, that's my stuff. I'll move it out."

"No, that's fine. It's my fault. I didn't tell Rita I was staying over…I wanted it to be a surprise. Besides, I don't mind using Charlie's old room. It won't feel so lonely with him not being here. "Angel shut the door before opening another one.

Neve, remembering what Rita said about her sister and expected to dislike her. It sounded to her like Angel was selfish. After meeting her face-to-face, she found there might be redeeming qualities—she did have a gorgeous smile. "I'll make that coffee."

"Thanks, Neve. I'll be along in a minute."

†

An hour later, Rita stepped inside.

Angel quickly got out of her chair and ran across to her sister, hugging her hard. "It's wonderful to see you, Ri, and look at you, so glamorous. I never thought you'd ever change the hairstyle. It's perfect for you." Angel made Rita twirl. "The circus is wonderful for you, Ri. Look at you. That outfit flatters you in all the right places. Now, you're going to have to tell me all about it. Neve here won't spill any beans…she said it's your story to tell."

Rita shook her head. Her sister had never been one to let anyone else have a word in edgewise when she was on a roll. When Angel finally stopped talking, she hugged her little sister to her and kissed her cheek. "I've missed you, Angel. Where's Charlie?"

Angel grinned. "You can't bring an eight-year-old to a bachelorette party, especially if it's his mother's. You'll see him the day before the wedding and then I was hoping…well…that we could talk about that later. I was telling Neve about some of our family secrets."

"Do we have any?" Rita let go of her sister and looked across at Neve, who was staring at them with a closed expression.

"Not as many as my family, although you do have the odd bone rattling around," Neve said.

Rita grinned. "Let me put my packages away, and then I could really do with a cup of tea." She smiled broadly, left the two women alone, and walked toward her bedroom.

†

"I'll make it. I know how she likes it." Angel began to walk toward the kettle.

Neve was going to let her but decided against it. "No, let me. Believe it or not, I think I know better than you do these days."

Angel had a quizzical glance then she shrugged. "Okay. Right, I was telling you about our grandfather and his claim to a goldmine."

"Yes, you were." Neve filled the kettle and looked in the cupboard for the herbal tea Rita liked. She placed a spoonful of the tea in the special diffuser that was next to the package of tea.

A few minutes later, Rita appeared and sat down. "I don't know how you love to shop so much, Angel…I'm exhausted."

"That's because you're not used to it. I spent a lifetime here in Rochester window shopping and, now that I have the money," she laughed, "I still window shop. Trevor doesn't understand me. I guess Dad's frugal ways did make an impression, after all. He'd be so proud."

"Dad was always proud of you. I suspect it's because we never had any spare money available once Charlie was born."

Angel frowned. "Yeah, that's true. Trevor owes me big time for bringing up his son on a shoestring for eight years. Have you seen any of the girls since you've been back? I figure you have, since you didn't look that surprised that I was here. I told them not to tell."

"Well, Neve and I had lunch yesterday at the Europe."

"Don't tell me, Rach spilled the beans. You can always rely on her to let the cat out of the bag. Are you ready for my big night tomorrow?"

Rita chuckled. "Well, yeah. I wondered if it was okay if …"

Angel held up her hand. "I've already asked Neve, if that's what you were going to say, and she agreed. We've been having a great chat. Now it's your turn to tell me what you've been doing. Neve only said that you were friends and you had offered her a place to stay until she has her cast off. Exactly how did you do that anyway, Neve?"

Neve turned at that point and was glad she did, as she saw fear and uncertainty on Rita's face. "Oh, I collided with a stubborn object. Here you go, Rita. You'll feel better after this."

Rita smiled her thanks and let out a delighted sigh. "Oh, Neve, you're a lifesaver."

Angel grimaced. "You call that tea? It smells terrible."

The phone rang and Angel sprang up to answer it. Her voice dropped seductively, when she said, *Trevor*.

"Why don't we give her some privacy?" Neve said.

Rita smiled. "Good idea. All I want now is to put my feet up and enjoy my tea. Thank you, Neve. It's going to hit the spot. You know, I really didn't expect shopping to be such a hard task."

Neve laughed, as they sat on the couch after closing the kitchen door. "You look great, by the way." She waved her hand up and down Rita. "The hairstyle and the clothes are wonderful. What made you do it?"

Rita contemplated her tea. "You didn't seem interested in lunch, and I was at a loose end."

"I'm sorry, Rita. You'll never believe this because I don't myself, but I fell asleep. I didn't wake up until three and then Angel arrived. You must think me a terrible guest."

"No, not at all. I'm glad you were asleep. Well, not glad, but...you know what I mean."

"Yes, I do. I was going to ask if you wanted to go out for dinner...Angel too. I can go out on my own if you two want to catch up. It isn't a problem," Neve's stomach churned. She didn't want to spend the evening alone. She wanted to spend it with Rita.

Rita grinned. "As you've probably already found out within an hour of being in Angel's company, you will know everything she's done. My sister is a 'conversational monopolizer', if that is a proper expression. We are not alike in that respect."

"Well, I haven't heard that before but I think it covers your sister perfectly. You and she are not alike in looks, either. Which one of you is the *throw back*?" The expression around Rita's eyes told her that Rita was enjoying her herbal tea.

Rita laughed. "It has to be Angel. Our mom and dad both had dark coloring, as in hair and eyes. I'm a lot like my dad with dark hair and brown eyes. Some would say nondescript, really. Angel is exactly what her name says—she has the light touch about her. Mom used to say she was like a great aunt on her side. Angel was their favorite."

Neve heard the depreciating way that Rita talked about herself and shook her head. "You say that as if it doesn't matter that they had a favorite and showed it."

"It probably did when I was younger, but as you grow older, life teaches you that it isn't always fair and you need to make the most of what you have. I'm happy with who I am,"

"So why the makeover? Not that I'm complaining. When you get back to the circus looking as you do, you'll have trouble keeping the beaus at bay."

"Don't be silly, Neve. I'm not in your league."

Neve didn't reply immediately. "I don't have beaus, remember?"

Rita looked at her cup of tea. "True, but it means the same."

Neve gazed intently on Rita. "Does it?"

Rita started to reply but the door opened and Angel appeared.

"Sorry. Trevor wanted to make sure I arrived safely. He and Charlie were worried. As if, I believe that. They were probably playing some war game on the computer. Men. Who understands them?" She sank down in the sofa next to her sister.

"Not me." Neve chuckled.

Rita didn't say anything.

"Are you hungry, Angel? I was thinking of an early dinner and then you two can catch up." Neve smiled at the sisters. "What do you say?"

Angel grinned. "Sounds perfect to me. Let me take a shower and I'm all yours. Be back soon." She left the room with a wave.

Rita smiled as she watched her sister go.

"What are you smiling at?" Neve asked.

"*Soon* and a *shower* are not in Angel's repertoire. I can happily take as long as I want with this delicious tea. Thank you. I'm glad you made it because I needed it." Rita closed her eyes and drew her feet up under her legs.

Neve watched Rita relax. It was as if her whole body loosen up. "If you're tired we can table dinner and just have take-out. It's your call."

Rita blinked her eyes open. "Oh, please, no, I'd love to go out to dinner. Besides, I'm dressed for the part."

"That you are," Neve whispered. She settled into the opposite chair and watched quietly as Rita rested.

The silence went on for a few minutes, before Rita, with eyes still closed sighed. "This must be really boring for you after the hectic schedule you have with the circus."

Boring, no. Quiet and restful, yes. "Believe me, *restful* is exactly what I needed after the trauma of this year. I can't thank you enough for making it happen. In truth, from the first moment I met you, things changed."

Rita's eyes flashed open and she fixed her gaze on Neve. "I know and sometimes I wish…"

"If you were going to say you wish you'd never come to the circus or had never told me about my uncle, you'd be wrong. If there is one thing I've found out this year, you are one person I can trust."

Rita smiled and looked at her tea cup before placing it on the coffee table. "You'll think this is funny, but I feel the same way about you. I guess this really is what they call a friendship."

With her gaze transfixed on Rita, Neve didn't reply immediately. "Yes, I think you're right." She reached out her hand and held it out for Rita to take.

At an angle, Rita took the proffered hand and held it in a light hold. They stared into each other's eyes and didn't say anything. Then they heard the door of the bathroom open, and Rita moved suddenly and toppled forward. As she began to fall, Neve grasped her shoulders preventing her from falling. Their bodies were touching and their heads were close together.

Rita sucked in a breath. "Thank you."

Neve gave a crooked half smile. "Can't have us both injured can we?"

Rita shook her head and continued to gaze at Neve's face.

Neve, with her hands still loosely touching Rita's shoulders, maneuvered them so that they shared the sofa. She bent closer so she was about a hairsbreadth from Rita's lips.

The door to the living room sprang open and Angel walked in. "Hey, I'm ready. I'll bet you never expected I'd be that quick, Ri…"

Rita broke the contact and faced Angel, as her cheeks turned crimson. "No, I wouldn't. I was just telling Neve that you take an age."

Neve saw a curious expression appear on Angel's face. "I need to take a quick shower and change. I'll do my best to be as speedy." She strode out of the room, leaving the sisters alone.

†

Angel moved forward and placed a hand on Rita's arm. "Are you okay, Ri?"

Rita knitted her eyebrows together. "Yes, of course. Come on, Angel, have you brought pictures? I want to know how Charlie is doing."

Angel appeared to consider the request. "Sure, I have. He even chose them himself. He said you could 'see what a man he's becoming'."

Rita felt tears sting her eyes and was unsure of why. Was it the thought of Charlie growing up or what might have just happened between her and Neve. Either way, she was disconcerted, and her mind was throwing a million questions at her all at once. She had no answers.

Chapter Seventeen

Neve watched the two sisters interact. She only had a brother so it was interesting to watch them. They talked about everything under the sun, and it was impossible not to notice that the bond they shared went further than a mere formal family connection. She toyed with her glass of wine and pushed away the empty dessert plate—something called Total Chocolate Decadence—and heard Charlie's name mentioned again.

Charlie, it seemed, was the center of both of the sisters' worlds. Perhaps that was the focal point of how they functioned as a family. She half listened to Angel explaining how Charlie's father had been teaching his son to pitch, and it turned out that Charlie was far better than his dad acknowledging that Rita had taught him well. The sound of laughter, particularly from Rita, had Neve giving her closer inspection.

Laughter lines curved slightly at the corner of her lips and eyes. The sound of her laugh was melodic and natural. This was one of the things that she'd realized about Rita—the woman was exactly what she appeared to be and that had attracted Neve, especially recently.

A wry smile played on Neve's lips as she recalled a few hours earlier and that faint possibility that they might have kissed. *Or was it my fanciful imagination?* It was something she'd like to try with Rita. However, she didn't want to alienate someone she cared about by making unwanted advances. Their budding friendship was too new and important.

"Neve, how was the dangerous chocolate concoction?" Rita asked. "I hope we haven't been boring you with sister talk."

"Wonderful, the whole meal was great. The small talk is very informative." Neve leaned back in her chair and patted her flat stomach.

Rita smiled. "Really? I'm glad you think so. Richmond's City Council will, too. They want to promote the town and surrounding area for ecotourism. We have the luxury of being unspoiled with gourmet restaurants. Who better to sample the town's wares than a full-fledged business woman? Although, that could change. Business isn't exactly booming, and people have to move away for job security."

Neve gave Rita an intent look. "Like you."

"Yeah, like me. However, I was lucky. I found you." Rita smile warmly.

"I don't know about that. I think we were the lucky ones. You only have to ask Lorenzo, who thinks you're wonderful," Neve's gaze on Rita never faltered.

Angel chose that moment to enter the conversation. "Lorenzo? Who is Lorenzo? Are you holding out on me, Ri? What about poor Dan?"

Rita rolled her eyes heavenwards. "Don't talk about Dan and Lorenzo in the same breath. It would be like comparing the intelligence of a Neanderthal to Einstein."

Angel threw back her head and laughed so loudly others turned in their direction. "Oh, I don't know. Have the males of the species changed that much?"

Neve laughed along with Angel. *Rita is priceless.*

Rita shook her head. "Lorenzo is one of my bosses, and yes, I like him, but not romantically. Dan isn't in his league, although that's not why I don't want to go out with him. Let's drop it, Angel, please?"

Angel gave her sister an intense gaze and then smiled. "Sure. Okay, if Lorenzo isn't Rita's cup of tea, what about you, Neve? Does he ring your bells?"

"Angel!"

Neve laughed again and, as she did, she reached inside her jacket pocket, pulled out a wallet, and seconds later withdrew a photo. "This is Lorenzo…he was a skinny kid brother."

Angel groaned. "'Brother…I see." Angel looked at the picture of a kid about the same age as Charlie. A tender expression crossed her face as she looked at the boy with black, curly hair. "He's cute. Did he grow up to be cute too?"

Neve didn't reply and pushed another photo across to Angel. "Make your own call. This was taken a year ago."

Rita was looking at the photo of Lorenzo as a child that Angel had placed on the table.

Neve pulled out a few other pictures and placed them on the table. She looked up and caught Rita's intent gaze before her hand slid the photos across to her friend.

"My God, he's an Adonis. Don't tell me he's still single. Ri, what are you thinking by not being interested in him?"

A slight smile shimmered on Neve's lips as she turned her attention to Angel's outburst. "It's in the eye of the beholder, so the Bible says…at least, I think it does."

Rita rolled her eyes. "Angel, you're getting married next week. What would Trevor say?"

"Absolutely nothing. He'd say more if I *didn't* comment. He'll think you're crazy too."

"Why? Looks aren't everything. I go for personality," Rita countered.

"Lorenzo is a womanizer. He's currently in Vegas, chatting up anyone he thinks might be interesting. Do you want your sister involved with someone like that?" Strictly speaking, it wasn't the truth, but Angel didn't need to know that, and it did save Rita further embarrassment.

Rita looked at the photos Neve slid across to her. One was of a couple with a baby, the parents obviously proud and happy. The second was with a gangly teenage girl and a young boy, with the same man, but older, with a slightly younger woman.

"Well, of course not. My sister deserves only the best. Let's face it *finding the best* and *ending up on the shelf* go hand in glove these days. Probably always has." Angel gazed at the foyer of the restaurant. "Can you give me a minute? It's Sue." She scraped back her chair and left.

"Is this you?" Rita pointed to the photo of the couple with the baby.

There was a depreciating glance thrown at the photo and then Neve gave that trademark half smile. "Yes, apparently that was taken when I was two days old."

Rita looked at the second photo of Neve as a teenager. "If you don't mind my saying so, you haven't aged badly at all. I now see the young woman who was in you then."

"I don't mind at all. I was happy then. My uncle took that picture just before my father bought the circus. From then on, things changed. The dynamics of the family were never the same," Neve answered quietly.

Rita impulsively reached out and placed her hand over Neve's that was resting on the table. "Perhaps now is the time to be happy again," Rita said.

Neve felt a jolt run up her arm when Rita touched he hand and she glanced at Rita. The look on her face hinted that perhaps she too felt the connection. "Perhaps."

Angel arrived back at the table. "Guys, Sue and the other girls have asked if we want to join them for a drink and a game of pool."

"Are you any good at pool, Neve?" Rita asked.

Neve shook her head. "Wouldn't know one end of a pool cue from the other. Besides, I have this, remember?" waving the cast in front of Angel, who gave her a rueful grin in return. "What about you, Rita?"

"Me neither. I generally deferred the whole social, drinking, pool, clubs, etc, scene. At thirty-three, it still doesn't interest me."

"You're not that old yet, Ri. You can't say that until after next Sunday." Angel sat down reluctantly.

"Next Sunday, huh…another year older?" Neve asked.

"Oh, please, what's another year? It isn't my fortieth or anything significant."

"Every birthday is special, Rita," Neve whispered.

Rita quickly looked at Neve. "Yeah, I know but…"

"The drink sounds good, Angel. The pool, on the other hand, could be tricky." Neve turned to Angel and saw the look of relief.

Rita's eyebrows drew up. "Sure. I'm not a big drinker."

Angel laughed. "That's for sure. The most I've seen you drink is a couple of eggnogs at Christmas. I'll go tell Sue and the gang we're joining them."

"Go for it." Rita smiled brightly.

When Angel had left, Neve looked at the few plates that were still on the table. "I'll go pay. The place is busy. It might take a while to catch the waitress's eye for the bill." She pushing her chair back and headed for the cashier.

†

Left alone, Rita pondered what the rest of the evening would have in store for them before berating herself for acting like a stuffy accountant. *Why not just let it happen?* It was unfortunate that her long experience in being the sensible one made it difficult to cross the threshold to spontaneity.

Her mind then turned to what almost happened while Angel was taking her shower and getting ready to go out. *If Angel hadn't come in when she did would Neve have kissed me…would I have kissed her?* She couldn't deny the jolt she felt when she placed her hand over Neve's and that confused her. It was one thing to be empathic toward her boss and quite another to have stronger feelings. Feelings that were getting harder to deny. Somewhere from deep within, she knew the answer but refused to let it have a voice. "We are friends and that's all."

She looked up and saw Neve coming back to the table.

†

Angel couldn't stop laughing as they settled into the sofa at home and Rita made them warm drinks.

"You know, she'll get a complex if you don't stop laughing, Angel." Neve's lips were twitching into a smile.

"But, Neve, it was priceless. No one would ever have believed it unless they were there." Angel stifled her laughter as her sister walked in with three mugs in her hands.

"Oh, please, you're not still amused by this evening, Angel. It was a fluke," Rita offered nonchalantly, as she settled the drinks in front of the other two women before sliding easily onto the sofa next to Neve.

Angel shook her head as she reached for her drink. "Thanks, Ri, but let me tell you, Sue and the gang will be batting down your door for this winter's pool season. You beat the pants off one of our main rivals. I think you're a natural. What do you think, Neve?"

Neve picked up her steaming hot coffee and turned to Rita. "Thanks."

"You're welcome."

"Oh, don't go all closed ranks on me now. I'm right, aren't I, Neve?" Angel persisted.

"Yes, it looks that way to me." Neve winked in Rita's direction.

Rita smiled before she drank her tea. "What's on the agenda tomorrow, Angel?"

Angel appeared to contemplate the question. "I'm going to stay in bed until lunchtime. Then, I'm taking my favorite sister, who happens, of course, to be my only sister, out for lunch, my treat. I was then going to pamper myself for the afternoon until we go out on my bachelorette night."

Rita frowned slightly. There had been no mention of Neve going to lunch with them, and she didn't want her friend to think they were deliberately leaving her out.

"Now that works out well. I wish I could sleep that late. Rita is going to give me some lessons in accounting in the morning and then you two can go to lunch while I catch up on some emails and work." Neve sipped her drink and raised an eyebrow.

Rita blinked a couple of times. In the space of seconds, her day had pretty much been mapped out for her, and she wasn't entirely sure she approved. "That leaves me a few hours to do my thing in the afternoon then."

Angel grinned and got up. "I'm going to call Trevor before I hit the sack. Goodnight you two. Thanks it was a wonderful evening."

Neve frowned slightly. "I guess it's a good time to go to bed. Thank you for this evening, Rita. You do have a natural ability for sinking the pool balls. Goodnight."

"Yeah, goodnight." Rita answered sharper than she meant to but instead of apologizing, she returned to the contemplation of her empty tea cup. It wasn't going to tell her fortune this evening that was for sure—no tea leaves in the bottom.

Neve stood in the doorway. "You okay?"

Rita turned in Neve's direction. "Of course, why wouldn't I be."

Neve shrugged. "No reason. You just sound a little down."

"Don't be ridiculous, Neve. Go to bed. I'm fine."

Neve, walked back toward the sofa where Rita sat and took the opposite chair. She rested her elbows on her knees then put her chin on her cast encased hand. "You know, I'm always a bit dubious about the term *fine*. It has many connotations, at least *I* think so."

Rita caught her friend's gaze then let hers drop. "That's silly, Neve. Fine is fine. It means I'm okay."

"Look, take it from someone who says *fine* enough to knows it's a polite way of saying *I hate what's going on around me.* Please, tell me what's wrong. I might be able to help." Neve reached out and lifted Rita's chin. "Stranger things have been known to happen."

Rita swallowed hard and heaved a sigh. "You should have a different career."

"Yeah, everyone says that." Neve smiled.

A flicker of a smile ventured across Rita's lips. "I was just…I don't know how to explain."

Neve leaned forward and, with her good hand, reached out to clasp Rita's hand. "Tell me."

"I just felt that tomorrow, and probably the rest of my life, is all planned. I don't have a say…everything is mapped out for me." Rita shrugged. "Weird really, because I love to have plans and…it's ridiculous. Thank you for asking, though."

Neve remained silent for a few seconds and then let out a cynical chuckle. "You've obviously been around me too long. *Everything is mapped out* should be my line."

"No one plans your life, Neve. You're always in control."

"You think so? Let me tell you something, Rita. Since the day I was born, my parents set me on a path I did not choose. No one asked me what I wanted to do with my life…it was preordained…as a circus performer. Was that a good thing or a curse?" Neve shook her head. "Then there was the responsibility of the circus when my father died. He used my mother's money left in trust for me to buy the circus. There was no choice for me…I was bound to the circus. As they say, the rest is history. I've been paying for the privilege of owning a circus ever since. How does that compare with yours?"

Rita studied Neve as she digested her words. "As you know, I was the oldest. When Angel came, things changed. She became our parents' focal point. I was always an afterthought. It wasn't so bad because I loved Angel, too. Dad wanted help in the store from a financial point of view. I had an aptitude and was able to study accounting in college because it would serve that function for him. I worked at the hardware store until they died, and, you know, I probably would have continued on for years if they hadn't. Angel was pregnant with Charlie when it was time for the mortgage to be due. My only choice was to work at the Mill to ensure we would keep the roof over our heads. When Charlie was old enough, Angel went back to work, and we managed. When the Mill closed, well, that's history too. I came to work for your circus." Rita felt a glimmer of a smile hovering around her lips.

Neve squeezed the hands she gently held and nodded. "I guess we both are victims of our own types of moral upbringing. We help others before we consider ourselves."

Rita did smile then. "I never really looked at it that way. Thank you, Neve."

Neve chuckled. "Neither did I. Thank *you*, Rita."

Their eyes locked and, for a few seconds, Rita knew that they both felt the warmth of their friendship wash away some of the unfairness in their lives.

"I guess it's time for bed," Neve said.

The resonance of Neve's tone sang to Rita's blood as she felt it race through her veins. "Yeah, it's going to be another long day tomorrow. I hope you're ready for the rest of Angel's friends…they're an eclectic group."

Neve laughed, released Rita's hands, and stood. "I'm a little diverse myself. I'm sure I'll do all right. Sleep well, Rita." She dropped a swift kiss on top of Rita's head and left.

Rita murmured *goodnight* as she tentatively placed her fingers on the spot that Neve kissed. Her thoughts were chaotic. *It was only a simple, friendly gesture. Get over it. Neve didn't mean anything more than that. God, a part of me wants more than that. What's happening to me?* She closed her eyes and attempted to shake away the feelings that were growing exponentially each time she saw Neve. The more she thought about it, the more she thought of her trauma after the Danny Carmine incident. Perhaps that caused the shift in her emotions. *That has to be the answer. When have I ever been interested in a woman in that way before? Never.*

She took in a cleansing breath, stood, collected the empty mugs, walked absently toward the kitchen, and dropped them in the sink for the morning. They would wait. Then she checked the locks on the doors and the windows, as she'd always done, and wandered to her bedroom. Fifteen minutes later, lying in bed, Rita switched the light off and attempted to get some sleep. Sleep eluded her until she considered the only possibility that made sense. The truth—she had a crush on her boss. "I'll get over it." She yawned and closed her eyes.

Chapter Eighteen

Rita watched the five women around the table laughing and talking. Angel, of course, was the star of the evening and she took full advantage. Sue and Rachel, Angel's maid of honor and bridesmaid, respectively, flanked her. When Angel had approached her to be maid of honor, she'd been flattered but declined, since being center of that kind of attention wasn't for her. She had agreed to a speech and that made her as nervous as hell. Neve sat next to Rachel on one side and Lilly, who was six months pregnant, sat on the other side. Rachel, who'd been saving money since Angel moved in with Trevor, treated everyone to a great meal at Café Europe. She'd quipped that Angel leaving town had been great for her purse strings but crappy on her social life.

Rita zoned out of the conversations and contemplated her day. She and Neve ate breakfast and then commenced a three-hour session of basic accounting principles that focused on the circus and related business concerns, reflecting all the environments surrounding the circus background in which Neve was involved. Once Angel had finally risen, they went out for a leisurely lunch and after that, Rita had a couple of hours to herself. Neve had taken a coffee to her room to do whatever work she was going to do and didn't appear again until around five.

After her revelation the evening before, Rita found spending time with Neve wasn't as hard as she expected. In fact, it was nice. She would work through this new feeling—an automatic reaction to everything had happened in her life over the past six months. When everything went back to normal, she'd place her feelings for Neve in the friend department as it should be—or should it?

A paper napkin in the shape of a crude airplane floated past her nose and brought her out of her musings. “What was that for?”

Angel giggled. “You were asked a question but you were a million miles away.”

“I was? Oh, I’m sorry. What was the question?” Rita asked.

“Lilly and Jack are taking their first born to Italy next year to see his family there. We were discussing where in the world each one of us has been and now it’s your turn.”

Rita, disconcerted and embarrassed, said, “Oh. I’ve never left the US. In fact, up until recently, I’d never left the state.”

There was a quiet silence as Rita’s forlorn words traveled around the table.

Rachel boisterously interjected, “Me either, Rita. Except, I travel the world every day at work with all those posters and pictures…what more could I want?”

Angel chuckled, placed a hand on her friend’s shoulder, and mouthed *thanks*. “Neve, what about you?”

Neve placed sugar in her coffee and stirred it before she looked up and smiled. “Russia, Australia, and a little of Eastern Europe.”

“Wow, I bet you have stories to tell. That beats Rach’s posters any day of the week.” Angel winked at her friend, who poked out her tongue in return.

“Possibly not. I was working at the time, so I never actually had the time to see the sights. Inside the big top isn’t much different the world over.”

Rita noted the touch of regret in Neve’s voice and smiled at her.

Sue chose that moment to interrupt. “Changing the subject ladies, what do you think of Rita’s new image and my creative talents with these little hands?” She wriggled her fingers in the air.

Rachel laughed. "*Little* my ass, they'd make a blacksmith proud."

"Rach, that's mean." Sue pouted.

"I think Rita looks wonderful, but then, she always has."

The words brought the table conversation to a halt—not because of the words but because of who said them.

Rita tried desperately not to turn red and saw Angel looking at her with a strange expression.

"Well said, Neve. I agree," Angel said.

Rita gazed at her friend. Neve appeared to contemplate the tablecloth. Rita couldn't decide if Neve were being honest or just trying to bolster her ego. *It sounded genuine.*

Rachel leered teasingly in Rita's direction. "Yeah, you look gorgeous, girl. If I thought I had a chance, I'd be trying to date you myself."

Angel shook her head. "You'd have to fend off Dan for her attentions and you know what he thinks of you."

"He's an idiot. Just because he has a negative view of my lifestyle, doesn't mean that everybody else feels the same," Rachel spat.

Lilly groaned. "Sure, and don't we all know it? If it wasn't for the fact that we're all straight, you'd be hitting on us."

Rachel threw a kiss in Lilly's direction and winked. "Oh, I did that in fifth grade, remember? All those puckered lips and gropes in the cloakroom."

The table burst into laughter, and Rita was glad since it took the attention away from her for a few seconds.

"However, Rita, being older, hasn't had the benefit of my charms." Rachael remarked.

Angel scoffed. "Ri's got more sense than to have a romantic liaison with you, Rach. Isn't your middle name *womanizer*?"

"Oh, I'm hurt. Anyway," tapping her nose she continued, "my intuitive nose for all things lesbian didn't pick up that Rita would be interested. Unless she's changed in the last six months of being away…lot's of new experiences to try…right, Rita?" Rachel smiled gleefully as she peered over her coffee cup making direct contact with Rita's gaze.

Rita took the question in her stride and smiled. "No, Rach, I'm happy being your friend in a platonic way."

Rachel batted her eyelids. "You don't know what you're missing. What about you, Neve, care to try my charms?"

Rita hadn't mentioned that Neve was a lesbian, nor had Neve herself. She'd heard that others of the same lifestyle usually knew who else was of the same mind. *Had Rachel guessed?*

Neve shrugged. "I'm way too old for you, Rachel."

Rachel laughed. "Never say that, Neve." She winked at Neve and then her facial expression changed as she turned to the other women. "Guys, do you remember our art teacher in high school, Ms. Cransky?"

Sue and Lilly both nodded.

"Who wouldn't?" Angel said. "She was drop-dead gorgeous. I might have even changed sides myself back then if I'd had a chance. Not that she was gay. If I recall correctly; she had an engagement ring on her finger."

"Oh, that was a ruse to keep the men away. The *women*, on the other hand…" Rachel paused. "I met up with her in Johnstown a couple of months ago. Let's just say she's still gorgeous and her tongue action…"

Everyone around the table groaned.

"Way too much info, Rach. Are you seeing her again?" Angel asked.

Lilly, got up out of her seat as best she could for being pregnant. "Excuse me I need to use the ladies room."

Neve slid into the vacant seat next to Rita. "How are you doing?" she asked.

The conversation about Rachel and her conquest had Rita shaking her head before she answered Neve. "I forgot how raucous they can be."

"I guess that conversation is on a strictly personal, you-need-to-have been-there, scenario," Neve said.

Rita nodded. "Yes, and before you ask, she wasn't one of my teachers, so I wouldn't know if she was gorgeous or not. I think I had Mrs. Hardy, and she retired a year after I left." Rita chuckled as she recalled the older woman—*gorgeous* didn't quite come to mind.

Neve glanced at her watch—a quarter after twelve. "It's been a nice evening. Is anything more planned?"

Rita didn't reply immediately as she recalled what Angel told her over lunch. "I believe the girls want to check out a couple of the late bars."

"Would I be a party pooper if I said I'd rather go home to bed?"

"Nope, I was thinking the same. I mentioned to Angel at lunch that I wouldn't be up for a bar-hopping session." Rita smiled, as she cradled her cup of coffee laced with Baileys Irish Bristol Cream and sipped it in pleasure.

"Perhaps you and I can have a nightcap back at your place then," Neve said.

"Be careful, Rita, that sounds strangely like a 'would you like to come and see my etchings' type of comment," Rachel interrupted.

"Don't be crude, Rach. You know you don't stand a chance with either of them," Sue said.

"I wouldn't be so sure. If I actually allowed my charms to entice them, they might just welcome me." She winked at them both and smiled. "Only kidding, people. Right…is it Harry's bar next? I heard they have a great country western band on tonight."

"Sounds good to me," Angel said. Her eyes caught Rita's gaze. "Who's going to come?"

"Not for me, if that's okay, Angel." Rita smiled at her sister.

"Me neither. Apparently, I have etchings to show Rita." Neve smirked in Rachel's direction.

Lilly came back from the bathroom at that moment and smiled. "Now, I'm game for another hour and then Jack is coming for me. Sorry, girls."

"Don't worry, Angel. We promise you'll go out in style." Sue threw her arms around her friend.

"Always knew it would be the three stooges left standing." Angel laughed. "What are we waiting for, girls? The night is still young."

Neve and Rita said their respective goodnights, with Angel faithfully promising not to wake the neighborhood when she got home.

Rita watched the younger girls leave and smiled tenderly as she saw how happy her sister was. Since losing their parents, she'd only seen that expression of true happiness twice—when Charlie was born and when she introduced her to Trevor.

"You look lost in thought," Neve said.

"Oh, I'm sorry. I was just thinking…you know how it is," Rita replied.

Neve nodded. "I certainly do. Look, if you really want to go with them, I seriously don't mind going home alone."

Rita laughed. "I was serious when I said I wanted to go home. I'm afraid I really don't drink that much. What we've had during dinner is more than sufficient for me. If I have any more, I'll probably get drunk. My head already feels woozy after that Irish coffee."

Neve shook her head. "I see. Well, we can't have that, can we? Are you ready?"

"Sure." Rita stood and a few minutes later, they were walking amiably down the main street toward the turn for Rita's home.

†

As they walked, they enjoyed a companionable silence. In a surprise move, Neve linked her arm in Rita's arm. Their eyes locked and they continued on their way. As the house loomed closer, Neve hugged Rita a bit closer. "It's a beautiful night."

Rita smiled, looked heavenwards, and took in the canopy of stars on a midnight blue background. "It is a delightful night, and the forecast for rain tomorrow seems unlikely. I love this time of the year. I remember when I was young, going to Frobisher Hill, and wishing on the stars."

"Where's Frobisher Hill? Have we been there?"

Rita pointed in the direction of a hillock. "Nothing magnificent like Whittaker's Mountain, which we climbed earlier this week. But, it was easy to climb when I was eight years old, and it was closer to home. I haven't been there in years." She let out a long breath. "Somehow my dreams never seemed to be coming true."

Neve gazed at the hill. "Definitely easier than Whittaker's right? It looks like a great place for a young girl and her dreams. Are you cold?"

Rita's brow furrowed. "Cold? No. Why?"

"Because I think it's time you went back and did a little more dreaming." Neve tugged on Rita's arm. "Come on."

They headed in the direction of the hill.

Ten minutes later, they were atop the hill. Rita grinned happily before she closed her eyes. "I can feel the magic and see my dreams of long ago," she whispered.

Neve felt a sense of satisfaction seeing Rita's contented expression. *You need dreams, even if they never come true.* She settled her long body against the trunk of the only tree there and shifted her gaze from the stars to her friend with equal intensity. Then, she closed her own eyes and allowed some of her own dreams to float through her subconscious.

†

After a while, Rita opened her eyes and looked up at the darkening sky. Rain wasn't that far away now. She turned and glanced toward the tree where Neve had stood when they arrived and saw her friend totally devoid of any expression. All she saw was calm and that seemed totally out of character. She took the few steps to her friend and reached out to touch Neve's arm. "Hey, are you asleep?"

Neve's eyes flashed open and their gazes clung together with a backdrop of a star-filled sky and a lone tree. It was, in some ways, the simplest of perfect settings. With her good hand, Neve touched the fingers that were still on her arm. "No. Did you make a wish, along with those dreams of yours?"

Rita, startled by the question allowed a dreamy expression to cover her face. "Of course. Who wouldn't make a wish on such a beautiful night and with such great company?"

"Thank you. I did, too." Neve smiled warmly as their gazes continued to cling.

"Yeah?"

Neve chuckled. "Yeah. You think you have the monopoly on wishes?"

Rita laughed softly. "Nope, but some people don't always believe in wishes."

Neve moved to stand and their fingers entwined naturally. Neve chuckled. "But we know differently, right?"

"We most certainly do. Thank you for this, Neve. I needed it. Things are settling back into normal space again. Odd I know, but the fantasy occasionally makes reality that much easier to live with."

"You are most welcome, and thank you for allowing me into your home and experiencing things I've never had before. Let's go home to bed. I can feel a jaw- breaking yawn about to erupt."

"That, and in about ten minutes it's going to rain."

They headed down the hill laughing with their hands locked—neither apparently wanting to end their tactile rapport.

†

The rain caught them a few minutes from home and, laughing like children, they finally shut the door on the deluge and looked at each other.

"You look like a drowned rat." Rita chuckled as she stared at Neve's bedraggled appearance.

Raised eyebrows greeted the comment. "I think your friend, Sue would be royally disappointed if she saw you now—all her hard work in ruins."

"Oh, that's cruel, Neve." Rita smiled. "Besides, it was never going to last forever. A bit like Cinderella, except it's almost one, so I kept the magic for a little longer."

Neve moved her head to one side, closed the small distance between them, and reached out to thread the brown, tangled wet hair through her fingers. "You will always have magic. It's not about appearance but the soul." A finger pointed to her chest. "You have a beautiful soul, Rita Collins."

Words were stuck in her throat as Rita tried to come up with a quick response. She couldn't, for she was lost—so totally lost in the wave of feelings that wanted to wash away her staid outlook on life. "Thank you."

"You're welcome." Neve shrugged out of her wet jacket.

Rita stood still with her heart pounding. She knew it was up to her to make a move—Neve never would. She debated what to do. If she was wrong about how she felt, or if Neve didn't respond, she might lose the friendship. She dare not let that happen. Unrequited love was okay, she'd done without romantic love all these years and she could continue as long as Neve was in her life somewhere. With a deep intake of breath, she let out a yawn. "I'm going to lock up. I'll see you at breakfast."

Neve gave Rita an intense stare then smiled. "Sure you will. Good night, Rita."

"Good night, Neve."

Chapter Nineteen

Neve woke earlier than expected. She stretched her arms above her head in a pleasurable reworking of stiffening muscles. Normally she worked out in her tiny gym, a converted bedroom in her RV that held a multi-gym bench, complete with weights. Since breaking her hand on that loser Carmine, her weight training had ceased. Her upper body strength had always been important, so the hour she jogged before breakfast helped maintain her overall fitness. In the week she'd been staying with Rita, breakfast had taken on a completely new meaning and it had nothing to do with jogging.

Last night had been revealing in lots of ways and equally as baffling in others. Since returning to the circus after her brush with insanity—the only word she could think of that would describe her meltdown for a month—Neve had changed. Jennifer had been right; it was time for *her* now. She needed to do what *she* wanted, not what others asked of her, although she knew that would still happen. However, therein lay the big question: What did she want?

After climbing out of bed, Neve walked over to the mirror and looked intently at her reflection. She placed a finger at the corner of her eyes and tugged at the tiny lines that refused to disappear—crow's feet. It was a telling sign that time was marching on. Even if she didn't feel any older than twenty-five, her body had other ideas. Her overall physical figure was still good—almost perfect, in the sense that it hadn't changed that much over the years. Although, if she allowed Rita to pamper her with all the meals, she might have to revisit that conclusion. Her hands dragged through her hair and she saw the faint shift in color under the tresses—grey was beginning its onset. Otherwise, if she were really being critical, she'd say that generally, for her age, she was in good shape.

Her gaze caught a movement in the yard and she watched closely to see what it was. She saw two blackbirds vying for food scraps. Her thoughts shifted to Rita and what she thought was going on between them. Friendship was a wonderful plus to their working relationship and so easily forged. Though, it had been an interesting battle of wills to get to that point—mainly on her side—Rita had simply just been Rita. The more she learned about her friend, the more she liked the woman.

The kiss they'd almost shared the day before, or perhaps the day before that—time seemed to have no meaning when she was with Rita—was a surprise. The days seemed blur to the point that she really didn't know what day of the week it was. If Angel hadn't interrupted them, would they have kissed? Rachel's amusing chatter the night before had been revealing in its own way. Rita obviously had never had a liaison with a woman. And she wasn't that inclined to have a relationship with the man who wanted to court her. That left the question of Rita's sexuality up in the air. Neve pondered the question thoughtfully before whispering to a poster of a woman she'd never seen before on the wall, "I'm certain she isn't immune to me, and that has to be in my favor. But would that corrupt what we already have? Do I want to do that?" She shook her head, picked up her toiletry bag and headed for the bathroom. This morning she needed that jog to clear her scattered thoughts.

†

An hour later, having jogged her usual four miles, Neve arrived at the Collins' home and stopped, bent over and took in deep breaths gradually allowing her body to relax. Then she stood up with a fluid motion, her hair swinging in the light breeze. She bounded up the few steps to the porch and entered the house with the spare key Rita had given her.

There was noise from the kitchen. She moved in that direction and saw a rather pale and miserable Angel sitting, nursing her head. Rita, in a fleece nightgown, was turning the kettle on.

Angel looked up when the door opened. "You look positively too healthy for this time of the morning, Neve."

Neve glanced at Angel and allowed a faint smile to tug at her lips. "By any chance do you need a hangover cure? I can recommend a few."

Rita smiled at Neve as she shook her head in Angel's direction. "Angel arrived home about fifteen minutes ago. I think sleep might be a good cure, except she has a bus to catch at lunchtime. She promised Trevor and Charlie she'd be home by mid-afternoon."

"Oh, then it was a good night." Neve chuckled and walked over to Rita. "Do you have sugar, salt, warm water, and a little honey? Lemon would be good, too, if you have it."

"Yes," Rita replied and turned to the cupboards to select the items. "Did you have a good run?"

Neve grinned. "Yeah, it's a nice crisp morning for a jog. I've been allowing myself to indulge in your breakfasts way too much without making the effort in the exercise department."

Rita nodded. "Here you go."

A few minutes later, the concoction was set in front of Angel. "Drink this and don't gag on it. I won't leave until it's all gone." Neve stood beside the younger woman, who dutifully drank the horrible concoction almost retching a couple of times. "Trust me, Angel, it works. Now, I suggest you go to bed for a couple of hours. We'll get you up in time for you not to disappoint the men in your life."

Angel groaned. "Thanks." She stood, moved to Rita, and hugged her tightly. "Thanks for everything, Ri."

Rita hugged her back. “Go to bed, Angel.” She gently pushed her sister toward the door leading to the bedrooms before turning to Neve, “Thanks for helping her out. I never was much for hangover cures…not exactly in my repertoire.”

Neve sat down and nodded before she began to idly played with a fork on the table. “Why don’t you take the car and drive Angel home? That way you could stay the night and catch up with Charlie.”

“Neve, I can’t do that it would leave you all alone.”

Neve laughed. “I’m a big girl, Rita, or haven’t you noticed.” She waved her hand in an arc over her body.

A tinge of red stained Rita’s cheeks. “You know what I meant.”

Neve chuckled. “Would it make you happy if you could visit with Charlie earlier than planned?”

Rita nodded. “Oh, yes, I miss him dreadfully at times. How did you guess? I was hoping I didn’t make it too noticeable that I was pathetically yearning to see him.”

“Psychic.” Neve winked and settled back in her chair.

“For that you get the full works for breakfast. Are you hungry?” Rita smiled warmly and set about the task of making breakfast for them both.

“I’m famished. I could eat a horse. Do I have time to take a shower?”

“Go for it, but be back in fifteen.” Rita waved a spatula teasingly in Neve’s direction.

“Yes, ma’am.”

†

Angel slept for most of the hour and a half trip to Johnstown. Now, as Rita negotiated the main highway into the city, she wasn’t exactly sure where she was going and needed Angel’s navigation skills. Prodding her sister with her hand, she eventually had Angel groggily asking *what’s going on.*

"I'm not sure what intersection to take when we reach the end of Highway 11," Rita explained.

Angel frowned and then shook her head. "Take the sign for the football field. You go about a mile and then there's a sign for the City Hospital…take that and I'll navigate as we go."

"Sounds good to me. Weird, I've lived in this area all my life and have only been here about five times in thirty odd years." Rita followed the first sign Angel indicated and that led her to a turn-off into an industrial area.

"That's because you're not very adventurous." A grin crossed Angel's mouth, "Although, maybe you are beginning to be."

"What do you mean?"

"I like your friend, Neve. Doesn't it make it hard since she's the boss?" Angel opened her purse to withdraw a small tube of lipstick, pushed down the visor, looked in the mirror, and began to apply the color liberally.

Rita smiled slightly as she thought of Neve. It was hard leaving her behind to fend for herself. She remembered a grinning Neve telling her that it was only for a day and she'd be okay. "Not really. The environment of the circus is different to what I've been used to. We respect each other's professional skills set. The friendship is fairly new." Rita frowned wishing she hadn't said that.

"Really, what happened to forge that relationship?" Angel asked.

"Is this the turn?" Rita saw the sign indicating the turn for the hospital.

Angel gave a snort. "You'd have to be blind not to see that, Ri. Give, how did you become friends? Rach is convinced that Neve is a lesbian. Is she?"

Annoyed at the remark, Rita gave her sister a glare. "Does it matter?"

"Does what matter?" She pointed. "Take the next right. The lesbian part or why you're friends?" Angel asked.

"She's my friend. Anything else is just incidental. Her personal lifestyle isn't important to me. If that kind of thing had mattered…you and I wouldn't be having this conversation…we probably wouldn't even be talking."

Angel nodded. "Point taken. I know now that my becoming pregnant with Charlie and letting you take the brunt of the burden of keeping us together as a family was really selfish of me. Take the next right turn and then the first left. For the record, I think Neve is a good person. Is she coming to the wedding with you?"

Rita almost knocked down a traffic cone on the side of the road. "What do you mean?"

"Exactly what I said…if you want her to come, she's more than welcome. I told Trevor and his mom that if you wanted to bring someone, it was okay. After all, other than my close friends, his family far outweighs my guest list threefold." A small smile played on Angel lips.

"I'm sure Neve has other plans. She was going to leave on Friday."

"Ah, yes, but does she know she's invited? That could change everything. Your call, of course, but I think you'd enjoy having her there."

Rita reflected on the comment as Angel told her to take another left. It took them into an upscale neighborhood with expensive looking property. "Do you live here?"

Angel chuckled. "Yes, Trevor is a good doctor…no, an excellent one. That and his parents bought it for him when he graduated from medical school."

Rita was impressed but a little worried that her small town mentality might not fit in with Trevor's family. It was okay for Angel. Trevor loved her and that made all the difference, but she was just the small town sister. "I'll ask Neve when I get back."

Angel smirked. "Here we are, it's number two twelve."

As the car stopped, the front door of the house opened almost immediately and Charlie ran out toward the vehicle.

"Oh my, God, Angel, he's grown so much." Rita felt tears filling her eyes.

Angel grinned and placed a hand on Rita's arm. "I know and he's so going to be over the moon when he sees you."

Rita turned off the engine and opened the car door. Seconds later, a small tornado engulfed her in the hug.

A few minutes later Trevor, who had kissed Angel, was now smiling warmly at Rita. "Since he found out that you were coming to the wedding, Rita, he's been talking non-stop about you. I think he wants to go back with you."

Charlie looked at his dad and shook his head. "No, Dad. But maybe during school vacation I could." Charlie then moved to hug his mom.

Trevor held out his hand. "Good to see you again, Rita. I'd like to introduce you to my mom."

Rita looked at a woman of stout proportions who stood next to Trevor. She had the same coloring as her son and her facial expressions were similar.

"It's so wonderful to meet you, Rita. I think I know you already with what Angel, and particularly Charlie, say about you." She held out her arms and, slightly surprised, Rita went into them.

"Good to meet you too, Mrs. Arnold." Rita was happy with the warmth she felt from the older woman.

"Oh, my dear, please don't call me that. Kathy is good enough for me." After an intense stare at Rita, she smiled. "Thank you, my dear."

Rita was perplexed at the last words. "For what? I should be thanking you for taking my sister and Charlie into your heart so readily."

Kathy Arnold shook her head. "That's the point, Rita. Because of you, I have the luxury of these moments. Angel told me everything about what you sacrificed for her and Charlie. It's not something I will ever forget, nor will my son."

Rita smiled. "We love them, Kathy. As long as they are happy and safe, that's the only payment either of us will ever need."

Kathy was about to say something more when Trevor gave his mother a hug with one arm. "Let's go inside and I'll get the bags later. Besides, I'm hungry."

"Me too." Charlie took Rita's hand and dragged her toward the large house. "Gran made cake, Aunty Rita. It's like the one on my birthday."

†

Without Rita, Neve felt lost in the Collins' home for it wasn't the same without her friend. She was sitting at the kitchen table tapping her fingers wondering what to do. She finally decided to have lunch at the Café Europe. She knew it might not be a good choice as Rachel might be there but she was hungry and the food was good. "What the hell. Who cares if she tries to pick me up?"

An hour later, Neve sat at a table in the restaurant. Once she ordered her food and a drink, she sat looking at the people walking on the sidewalk until the man strutting in front of the garage directly across the street caught her attention. Her eyes narrowed as she noted something familiar about the large man. *Oh yeah, he's the one that came to Rita's house the first night we got here.* She frowned at the memory.

"Dan Flounder isn't your cup of tea, girl."

Neve glanced up in surprise as Rachel placed a beer on the table. "How certain are you of that?"

Rachel laughed. "Not absolutely certain, but ninety-nine percent sure. He's sweet on Rita and thinks he has a chance but he doesn't."

"He doesn't? What makes you say that?"

"Girlfriend, if you don't know that, I'm not going to burst your bubble. I'll bring your meal out in about ten minutes."

Neve frowned as Rachel moved away. *What does that mean?* Her eyes moved back to the thick-set man and she recalled the first time she'd seen him at the circus with Rita and Charlie. At the time, she thought they looked like the epitome of the Christian lifestyle or what she thought it should be—what her parents thought it should be. Just before he died, her father had begged her to give up her deviant ways. She had refused and they parted angrily and he died in a car crash a few hours later. Since then, she'd been unsure what to do with her personal life. Each time she came to a crossroads that pointed her to a solution, she evaded the opportunity.

Rachel appeared ten minutes later with her meal. "Here you go, Neve. The finest Mediterranean salad this side of the Atlantic. Enjoy."

Neve looked at the young woman and made a decision. "When does your shift finish, Rachel?"

"Six. Why?"

"Do you want to show me the sights that Rita doesn't even know about when you're done?"

"You don't need to ask twice. I'll see you in Freddy's bar at six-thirty. Oops, I almost forgot," she placed another plate in front of Neve, "here are your fries."

Neve looked at Rachel and frowned. "I didn't order fries."

Rachel grinned. "I had instructions that if you ever ate here again and had salad, I was to bring along the fries. I don't argue with a woman."

Surprised and touched at the same time, Neve let out a breath slowly. "Rita."

Rachel nodded and moved away to other customers.

Neve glanced at Dan Flounder and a disturbing pain in her chest took her breath away before she began eating her salad in a lackluster fashion.

†

"Oh come on, Neve, what will it hurt? I promise she's friendly and can be even more than that, if you want." Rachel said with a wink.

Neve, frowned before turning her attention to the young woman they were discussing. She was a small blonde, slim, and who kept licking her lips with her tongue as she danced. "Sorry, she's not my type. Why don't you dance with her?" Neve took a swig of her beer. *Coming here was a bad idea.*

Rachel groaned and shook her head. "What will it take, Neve…a certain brunette with a degree in caution?"

Neve scowled at Rachel's reference. Maybe it would be *take* Rita, but she wasn't going to tell Rachel that. Besides, she knew it was a lost cause. The sooner Friday came around the better, for them both. "I don't know what you mean."

"Yes, you do. Do you want my dime's worth on your chances with Rita Collins?" Rachel sipped her wine.

Neve stared at the Rachel wanting to slap the woman. *Isn't any subject off limits to her, for God's sake?* "I doubt I could stop you, so go for it."

"Glad you said that." Rachel chuckled, then placed her hand on Neve's and drew in a breath. "Rita has always been one of those people that you can depend on. So much so that they give up what the rest of us take for granted."

"And that is?"

"Fun, taking chances on romance, people, having friends…more than one, the whole rebellion thing. Rita has always done what other people expected of her. Her parents did and as much as I love her, Angel too. Dan Flounder is the only man in town who has ever taken notice of her. I know that's because she would be good for his business…a free accountant is nothing to sneeze at." Rachel glanced at Neve and gulped. "Take it easy, Neve. I've saved the best until last."

"Really, I highly doubt that." Neve ground her teeth as she waited for Rachel's finale.

"I think if you court her as you know you want to, she'll respond positively."

Neve raised an eyebrow.

Rachel grinned. "Look, I've seen the way she looks at you and you her. If there isn't romance in the air, then I'm taking vows of celibacy. That won't happen anytime soon."

Neve snorted. "Rita's not a lesbian…trust me. I'd know that."

Rachel shrugged. "Have it your way. You know, I think I might go dance with blondie…who knows, one of us might get laid tonight."

She watched Rachel leave the table and approach the blonde. Neve closed her eyes at the ridiculous notion that she and Rita could ever be an item. As tantalizing as the idea was, she knew it wasn't going to happen. She turned her attention to Rachel, who was now up close and personal with her dance partner.

"Wanna dance?"

Neve looked up at a woman taller than she was by a couple of inches, with a shaved head and tattooed forearms. She debated the question for a second or two, and then stood. "Sure." She followed the butch woman to the floor and they began gyrating to the music.

Chapter Twenty

Neve switched a curtain back and watched as the vehicle glide to a stop and, seconds later, Rita was climbing out onto the driveway. Neve felt that incredible bond they'd been developing click into place again. There was only one word for her current state of emotions—*happy*. She was delighted to have her friend back.

Neve hurried to the door, opened it, and walked onto the porch. She smiled warmly at Rita who was smiling back. "How was the trip and Charlie?"

Rita chuckled as she paused with one hand clutching an overnight bag and the other jingling the keys to the Jeep. "Wonderful. He's grown so much, Neve, I hardly recognized him."

"That's one thing you can guarantee with kids, they grow up. I've put the kettle on. I suspect you could use some tea." Neve grabbed the overnight bag and smiled as Rita moved toward the front door.

"Yep, that's true. Angel sends her regards and a big *thank you* for allowing me to use your Jeep," Rita laughed and shook her head as they stepped inside the house. "She slept all the way there."

The sound of the kettle whistling had Neve hurrying toward the kitchen. "You sit, and I'll bring the drinks."

Rita followed Neve into the kitchen. "You didn't have to do this. I can make my own tea. It isn't as if the trip was hours long, you know."

Neve didn't turn to face Rita. "I know I don't have to do it, but I wanted to. I missed you yesterday." She bit her lip for she hadn't meant to say that—it just slipped out.

"You did? I missed you too." Rita sat at the kitchen table as Neve finished off the tea. "Did you do anything last night or just chill in front of the TV?"

Neve bit the bottom of her lip again. "Oh, just this and that. What about you? Tell me about Charlie." Seconds later, she sat opposite Rita pouring the herbal tea into two cups.

"You're going to love Charlie, Neve. He's so full of questions. He was asking me about the circus: some things I could answer, others I'm leaving for you." Rita took a sip of her tea and smiled across at her friend. "This is so good, thanks."

"You're welcome. Charlie will have to write down his questions and I'll mail him the answers. Don't forget, I'm out of here on Friday." Neve felt the potency of her words sting.

Rita scrunched up her face. "Oh, yeah, we have the doctor's appointment Wednesday. The cast will come off and you'll be taking that well earned vacation."

Neve glanced down at her tea. The thought of leaving Rita behind changed the idea of a refreshing vacation to bitterness. "You could come with me…I mean take a vacation with me…a proper one. A beach in some place warm or maybe something more adventurous."

Rita sighed. "I've promised to take care of Charlie the week after next. Trevor's mom volunteered for the whole of the honeymoon, but I wanted…"

Neve saw the desperation in Rita's face and nodded. "Yeah, you've missed him. It's time for you and Charlie. I understand." Charlie ousting her wasn't the reaction she had been expecting. But knowing Rita, she should have. *I have to remember she has a life outside of the circus and me.*

"Oh, but you can meet Charlie, Neve. That is, if you don't mind attending the wedding with me."

Surprised at the invitation, Neve fixed her eyes on Rita. "You want me to go with you to the wedding?"

Rita grinned as she sipped her tea. "Of course, I'd love for you to come with me. You're my friend. Besides, Angel's friends, whom you met a few days ago, will be there. What do you say?"

Neve had reservations about going, but Rita's pleading was her undoing. "Okay, I guess I'm going to have to go buy something decent to wear. Jeans and a checked shirt aren't exactly the correct dress code for a wedding. Want to come with me to make sure I buy the right thing?"

"Of course, I will." Rita chuckled. "Don't forget, I'm no fashion guru."

Neve allowed the happy glow from her friend to invade her morose thoughts. *I don't want her to know that last night I had a one night stand. I'm going to have to have words with Rachel. It's bad enough that I feel lousy about it and guilty. Not that I should feel guilty. I just don't want Rita to know. Damn life can be complicated.*

A picture of the woman, Annie, she'd shared casual sex with the night before came to mind. She remembered turgid nipples, which she pulled until the woman moaned in pleasure, and the feel of the butch's fingers entering her, filling her up and taking away the frustration she was feeling. At the time, it had been satisfying and recalling the encounter made her squirm in the chair as her lower body reacted.

"Are you still with me? Rita placed a hand on Neve's arm. "You seem preoccupied?"

Neve moved her head slightly and gave Rita a tight smile. "I'm with you. I don't need a *fashion guru*, Rita. As long as you like the outfit, I know it will be perfect."

Rita grinned. "Sounds like a plan to me. How about I make us dinner and we can have a quiet night. We can shop tomorrow."

Neve returned the smile and nodded. "You're cooking works for me every time."

†

Most of the following week passed remarkably quietly. Rita found that talking, walking, and Neve's lessons on accounting were satisfying. The shopping trip for Neve's wedding outfit was easy. Neve's penchant for slacks and shirts quickly set the tone. They settled on a pale beige silk suit that shimmered in the light. It looked perfect and fit even better. Italian sling back shoes—more expensive than the outfit—were an indulgence that Neve said she deserved.

Before Neve's doctor appointment for the removal of her cast, they opted to go to Café Europe for lunch.

When they entered the restaurant, Rita smiled at Rachel who escorted them to their table. After she sat down, Rita saw Rachel place her hand on Neve's shoulder and whisper something in her ear. It wasn't anything to do with her, but she wondered if Rachel was making a pass at her friend. She couldn't blame her. If she weren't so chicken, Rita would too. The thought, though, sent a shiver of frustration down her back.

Once Neve sat, Rachel asked them what they wanted to drink. Neither Rita nor Neve wanted to give the wrong impression to Doctor Cameron by having alcohol on their breath, so they decided on club sodas. Rachel nodded and left to fetch their drinks.

As they sat in silence, perusing the menu, Rita felt a degree of tension coming from Neve. *It must have something to do with what Rachel whispered to her because prior to that, she was relaxed.* "Anything in particular you fancy?"

Neve glanced up and furrowed her brow. "Give me a minute, please."

Rita, surprised at the reply, bit her lip and didn't say anything more concentrating on the menu. Food wasn't at the top of her agenda. When Rachel arrived with their drinks, Rita placed her menu on the table.

"Do you ladies both know what you want?" Rachel winked at Neve.

Rita noticed Neve looking uncomfortable, which made her feel like a spare wheel. Something was going on, and it didn't look like she was going to be party to the information. Rita gazed at Rachel. "I'll have the Caesar salad with fries."

Neve frowned. "Chicken burger for me, no fries."

"You got it, ladies. It shouldn't be too long. I'll try to get your order ahead of that bus party that's just come in. I'll miss the old biddies when they stop that senior citizens tour." Rachel strode off and one of the old woman who looked to be about ninety slapped Rachel's ass as she walked past.

"I wonder why they're stopping the tour. It's been coming through here for years. I'll have to remember to ask Rachel." The silent void that settled between them made Rita feel anxious and she began to fold her napkin into different styles.

"Probably because there isn't much around here for them to do."

Startled and upset by the remark, Rita gave Neve a hard look. *So that's what she really thinks of my home town! She must be bored to death.* "You're probably right."

"Look, I need to use the bathroom. I'll be right back." Neve pushed back her chair and got up.

"Sure." Rita glanced at the posters that, according to Rachel, should make her feel as if she'd traveled the world. Her eyes took in a particularly wonderful day and night shot of the European continent from outer space. The contrast was remarkable, and the image, taken at night, glowed with dots of light in differing degrees of intensity. As she looked at other posters beside the front counter, she saw Neve talking animatedly with Rachel. Her stomach sank, and she felt positively sick to her stomach. *Why am I feeling like this?* She had no hold over Neve, and Rachel had no permanent relationship. *Why shouldn't Neve be friends, or more than friends, with Rachel? They have the same lifestyle.* A troubling thought surfaced: *So where does that leave me?*

A few minutes later, Neve arrived back at the table. "Ah, that's better. Right, I was thinking about what you said."

Rita frowned. "About what?"

"Why the bus tour isn't coming through anymore. I just asked Rachel…it seemed important to you," Neve replied.

"Oh, I see, and why isn't it coming through anymore?" Rita felt the dip in her stomach disappear, only to rise again—she was hungry. *Obviously, I'm making a mountain out of a mole hill. Or am I?* It certainly hadn't look like a conversation about senior citizens bus tours to her.

"Apparently, the guy who runs the business retired three months ago after a stroke. His son took over but didn't think the bus tour business was his style. He tried to sell it, with no luck, so he's closing up at the end of the autumn season," Neve explained.

Rita felt sorry for the senior citizens who relied on the service. It took them out of their retirement homes and often boring daily routines, allowing them to live a little.

"You look sad. Why?" Neve asked.

"Oh, it just seems a shame to me. Most of these people can't afford a proper vacation and rely on that type of service. I hope someone gives it a reprieve at the last minute. I know I would if I had the money."

When their food arrived, they both smiled. Saying in unison, "I'm starved," made them, laugh as they began their meal.

†

Doctor Lance Cameron went through a series of tests, flexing and un-flexing Neve's fingers after the cast came off. The pale skin looked out of place next to the darker shade that adorned the arm. "It looks pretty good to me, Ms. Garmancelli. Does your insurance allow physical therapy? I think a few sessions might aid the strengthening part of the recovery."

Neve said, "I have insurance, but I won't need physical therapy. I've had enough experience in the past to know if my hand has recovered. The strength part of it will just take time and exercise."

Doctor Cameron nodded. "Yes, it will. You can drive and eat and all the normal stuff, but don't be surprised if you feel some pain for a week or so…the muscles have had a long vacation."

"Thanks, Doctor, I figured that." Neve flexed her hand again and ignored the slight tingle of pain.

"Well, Ms. Garmancelli, good luck and whatever you did to break the hand, I'd make sure you don't try it again." Doctor Cameron smiled.

Neve grinned. "Don't worry, Doctor, I have no intention of that happening again."

"Nice to meet you, Ms. Garmancelli." He stood up and walked her to the door.

Two minutes later, Neve was standing at the reception counter, paying her bill with Rita hovering beside her.

Once they were outside, Rita tugged on Neve's sleeve. "What did he say?"

"Exactly what I thought he'd say. The break has healed, and I'm back to full working capacity."

Rita hugged Neve close. "Oh, that's great. I felt so guilty that it was because of me and…"

"Don't be. Carmine deserved that and more. Okay, I feel like driving. Where shall we go?" Neve hugged Rita closer then let her go.

Rita chuckled. "Hey, you've been out of the cast two minutes, so now you can drive? Okay. There's a lovely view of the town from Castor Drive. The drive won't tax you."

Neve stuck out her tongue. "You think I'm not up for it?"

"I didn't mean it like that. Darn, you're teasing me!" Rita exclaimed.

"Absolutely, ma'am. Come on, Rita, let's get the Jeep, and have that drive. We deserve it."

"No objection from me," Rita replied

†

The day, which had started out well for Rita, then deteriorated for a little while at lunch before miraculously bouncing back, was almost over. She and Neve had spent a couple of hours driving around the surrounding area before returning to the house for barbecued steaks, fries, and salad.

They both were tired as they sat on the porch watching the sun go down. "You know, the more I stay here, the larger I'm going to be." Neve placed her left hand on her full stomach as she reached for her bottle Corona before taking a swig.

Rita chuckled. "Me too. Walking around the stalls during the day seemed to help keep the weight down."

Neve grinned before a serious expression crossed her face. "Do you miss the circus, Rita?"

Rita didn't hesitate. "I do, very much. It's not worth my asking you the same question because I know the answer."

"I'm that obvious? Yeah, I guess I am. I've spent the whole of my life in the circus in one form or another. I feel like a fish out of water anywhere else. Although…." Neve took another drink of her beer.

"Although?" Rita turned to gaze at Neve's partially averted profile.

Neve seemed lost in thought. "Here, with you, I think it wouldn't be so bad."

Surprised by the reply, Rita was speechless.

"Does that surprise you? It shouldn't. We've forged a good friendship, I think, and to be honest, I've never had that before."

Rita instinctively reached out and took Neve's hand in hers. "That must be one of the most wonderful things anyone has said to me. I value our friendship, too, Neve."

Neve gazed intently into the serious eyes of Rita. Then her hand squeezed Rita's hand. "How tired are you?"

"Hmm, I guess I'm tired, but not so much that I couldn't do something else if you have an idea in mind." Rita grinned.

Neve's lips curved into a teasing grin. She took Rita's hand and hauled them both out of their seats and into a standing position. The unexpected action had Rita toppling toward her. Seconds later, Neve held Rita in her arms with their faces an inch apart. "Sorry about that."

Rita felt her heart thumping at Neve's closeness. Her throat was dry, but she managed to whisper, "Don't be sorry."

The throaty words floated between them and Neve lowered her head slightly, moving toward the lips that were so tantalizingly close…

"Rita?"

Both women broke apart as the gruff voice of Dan Flounder invaded their personal space.

Rita rapidly turned toward the man and frowned. "Dan, what are you doing here?"

Dan moved his bulky frame closer to the porch steps. "I came to take you out. You said you'd call and you didn't. Anyone would think you're avoiding me."

Rita rolled her eyes, lifted one shoulder, and looked at Neve who retook her seat. She stepped down onto the path blocking Dan's view of Neve. "It isn't convenient to go out with you, Dan. You should have called me first instead of just coming to my home."

Dan's upper lip curled. "I did call about three hours ago—no one answered."

"I have an answering machine and if you *did* call you didn't leave a message."

"Message? I don't leave messages on those confounded contraptions. I've told you that before. Just get your things and we'll go to Rick's bar for a couple of hours…you owe me that." Dan folded his arms across his broad chest with a smug expression on his face.

Rita wasn't one to cause friction but Dan's attitude was one of possession. He didn't own her—no one did. She was her own woman, free to choose what she did and whom she did it with. Dan Flounder didn't even come close to anyone she wanted to spend her leisure time with—quite the opposite. "Dan, I'm not interested. For the record, I owe you nothing, and why you think I do amazes me."

The big man's face flushed a dull red, as his eyes grew wider. "I'm your only chance for a man in this town, Rita. No one else is interested in a plain, mousy creature like you. Don't forget, I'm the one who paid big bucks for you and that kid to go to the circus. Stuff like that doesn't come cheap."

The words hurt Rita. No one who had a heart would expect them not to. However, it didn't break her resolve—it -strengthened it. "Then, according to you, I'm going to be an old maid. This isn't the only town around. I find your words, and you, offensive, Dan, and I don't want you around here anymore. Please leave. Oh, and if you tell me how much you paid for those tickets, I'll reimburse you immediately. I'll even included your ticket. Then, according to your way of thinking, I will owe you nothing."

Dan's spluttered incoherently as he moved menacingly forward.

Neve chose that moment to stand from her seated position. It elevated her to be able to look over both their heads. Her imposing stature was intimidating.

Rita heard Neve move and growl.

"The lady said to leave, blockhead. Do you understand that or are you as dumb as you look?"

Dan gazed at the towering woman with an expression of distaste. "Give your *dyke orders* to someone who cares. You and that Rachel Dixon, going around and flaunting your perverted way of life on the rest of us, is obscene and unnatural."

Rita was ashamed and embarrassed and her anger began to escalate. "That was uncalled for, Dan. I asked you to leave."

"Ah, that's it, isn't it? Not only have you gone on your travels with the circus, it's corrupted your morals too." He sneered at Rita and gave Neve a narrowed look. "You haven't heard the last of this. If you stay in this town much longer, you'll be sorry." He turned and kicked open the small picket fence, leaving the gate hanging from one hinge. He opened the door to his truck. "You owe me a hundred bucks."

Tears welled in Rita's eyes as she watched him leave. She turned back to Neve, whose stance was like an avenging angel with a grim, uncompromising expression. "I'm sorry about what he said, Neve. Not everyone thinks like that." Rita sat back down. A thought occurred to her. *How does he know Neve is gay?*

†

Neve was angry and wanted nothing more than to punch the idiot's lights out, much as she did to Danny Carmine. Not because of what he'd said to her—she heard all that before—it was old news. No, it was because he upset Rita and to her, that was more important. Her anger was simmering and barely under control, Neve got up and paced the porch area before she plunked back down heavily in the chair next to Rita "People like him aren't worth my time but what about you, Rita. Is he important to you and what you want in the future?" Even though she hoped she knew the answer, she had to ask. *Rita has more sense and taste than to want to be associated with that idiot.*

Rita remained silent for a moment. "Before he came, what were you going to suggest?"

Rita's evasive response wasn't lost on Neve. "I was actually going to suggest we go out for a couple of hours to a local bar. Now I'm not so sure that's a good idea."

"No, it's a great idea. I think it will be good for us both. Now that your hand is available, I know a great place where I can teach you how to play pool." Rita smiled and looked at the hands in question.

Although the words were in an upbeat mode, Neve felt that they weren't altogether true. "We can do that. We circus people are renowned for having time on our hands to practice the ancient art of bar games. It will be a great asset."

Rita giggled and stood. "I'll get my purse and be right back."

Neve nodded and watched Rita enter the house. The sooner she left, the better it would be for them both. "Maybe I'd better start looking for a new accountant." Rita evaded her question making her think that she just might want a future with the man.

"I'm back and I know just the place to go." Rita instinctively took Neve's arm and they walked down the three steps of the porch to the path and through the gate of the picket fence that was hanging askew.

"You don't owe that jerk a hundred dollars. Those tickets were free," Neve whispered.

Rita stared hard at Neve. "I don't understand."

"Sure you do. Remember, you've chastised me a million times about giving away special privileges on a whim?" Neve grinned, as she saw Rita open her mouth to speak then clamp it shut. "I guess you owe me instead."

Rita laughed. "If it's of any interest, I'd prefer to owe you than him any day of the week. I guess it's my round first."

Neve drew Rita close to her body. "Sounds perfect to me."

†

There were two bars in town that had pool tables. One was Rick's—predominately occupied by men with a mentality like Dan Flounder. The other was Last Stand, opened by Roy and April Alameter in the early seventies. They thought the name appropriate as Roy was a conscientious objector to the draft system back in the sixties. They'd originally intended to move on but, as with life in general, roots were set down and, suddenly a few years later, things weren't so clear. They'd semi-retired and their youngest son and his wife now ran the place in the evenings. Carl and Lucy Alameter were in their late thirties and tried everything from karaoke evenings, quizzes, and poker nights to keep the paying customers happy. It was working.

As Rita and Neve entered the establishment, it wasn't exactly full but busy. The bar meals were plain and a good value and that's all that mattered to most people.

"I like this place." Neve gazed around the traditional bar that had a large screen TV, pool table, and a few other machines like pinball around the place.

"You've just stepped through the door. How can you say that?" The place was noisy and Rita had to shout for Neve to hear her.

Neve shrugged and then winked, "It feels right."

"Ah, so to your way of thinking, if something feels right, everything will work out?" Rita reached the bar and immediately drew the attention of a bartender.

"Rita, haven't seen you here in ages. What have you been doing with yourself?" The buxom barmaid immediately pulled a pint of light beer from the pump. "What's your friend's drink?"

Rita smiled warmly at the bartender. "Neve, what do you want?"

Neve frowned that Rita knew someone here knew her well enough to remember what she drank. "Oh, I'll try what you're having."

Rita laughed. "No, you won't. She'll have one of your strong specialty beers, Marie. When I say strong, I mean *strong*."

Marie grinned. "Coming up…she's a girl after my own heart."

A few minutes later, they found a table that overlooked the pool table. Three couples waiting to play.

"I'll put our names down for a game." Neve headed for the chalk board.

Rita jumped up on the stool at the pub table and glanced around the bar.

When Neve returned, she took the seat opposite Rita. After a quick swallow of her beer, she let a surprised and satisfied smile cross her face. "I'm intrigued."

"Really? About what?"

"How do you know the bartender so well that she remembers your drink when you haven't been in town in months?"

Rita threw her head back and laughed. "Marie and I went to school together. I was the geek; she was the outrageous one. Neither of us were the sports type, but we managed to accidentally became locked in the girls' locker room when the others had left…we became friends. She's gone through two husbands, so far, and has three children that she adores. She works here for a little pocket money and the social aspect although I think it is more the latter than the money." Rita smiled and drank from her glass. "Angel thinks I didn't have a life outside of her and Charlie. I did, it just wasn't as ostentatious as hers."

Neve felt relieved for some unknown reason and then berated herself. *Why does everyone, me included, think that Rita doesn't have friends or is naive to the ways of the world*? "There you go then, another reason for me to like being here."

Rita shook her head. "You're teasing me, but that's okay. Neve, can I ask you something?"

Neve automatically nodded. "Sure, what do you want to know?"

"What did you do on those Fridays you'd take off and leave Lorenzo running the circus? I know I'm being nosey so if you don't want to answer, that's okay." Rita smiled, took a sip of her drink, and glanced at the pool players.

Neve drew in a silent breath. It would be so easy to lie. *Why should I?* Her heart was telling her that this question and her answer would be more important than anything else in their relationship. *Why?* "Sex."

Rita blinked rapidly and gave her full attention to Neve. "Sex? What do you mean?"

"Are you that naïve? Maybe you are. Do I need to spell it out for you?"

"No, no, of course not." Rita's cheeks began to get red. "I can understand that."

"You can? Then explain it to me." Neve regretted her caustic reply as soon as it left her mouth. She saw Rita shrink before her eyes. "Look, I'm sorry. You asked, I told. It's pretty sad really."

"I do understand, Neve, and it's nothing to be ashamed of."

"I'm not ashamed…well, maybe a little bit. How do you deal with your sexual urges, Ms. Accountant?" Neve took a teasing route and knew it worked when as she heard Rita's laugh.

"Oh, I've been saving them for the right person."

"Really? Wow. I hope whoever you give that particular gift to doesn't squander it. I know I wouldn't."

Rita grinned. "Drink your drink, Neve, and enjoy."

I am so enjoying myself.

†

A congenial hour later they ended up at the pool table and after several hilarious attempts at holding the cue properly, Neve gave in and allowed Rita to show her. The up close and personal tutoring had Rita catching her breath. Rita could smell the clean scent Neve exuded and the light breath that fanned her cheek as she placed her hands on Neve's to guide the cue forward.

"Thanks, now it's your turn, O' Master of the Cue Ball." Neve smiled as she retrieved her third beer and drank from the bottle.

Virtually closing her eyes rather than looking at the target, Rita pointed the stick, as she'd called it, at the ball.cue. Seconds later, the five ball slid into a side pocket. With a whoop, she screamed out her delight and several heads turned, all smiling at her obvious pleasure.

Rita laughed self consciously. With a wry smile, she tried to sink another but failed. "I guess I'm just good for fluky shots."

Half an hour later, they sat at their table.

"You enjoyed the game?" Neve asked.

"I did, even though I'm sure you let me win." Rita grinned and finished off her drink. "Do you want another?"

Neve nodded. "I'll get them."

"Nope, it's my treat." Rita slid off her stool and went to the bar.

"You played a good game, Neve. Want to have a match against me?"

Neve looked up and came face-to-face with the butch woman she'd had a fling with when Rita was away. "Annie, no thanks. I'm with someone."

Annie glanced toward the bar and Rita's back, then toward Neve again. "At least you remembered my name…that must be a good sign. I never figured Rita Collins for one of us. She's kept herself well hidden in the closet. What made her come out? You? Though I have to admit, you are one hell of a fuck."

"Hardly, and she isn't out of the closet. She wasn't in there in the first place. Look, I'm having a nice evening with a friend, so why don't you ask someone else to play?"

"I can do that, but if you change your mind…about anything…I'm game. Maybe Collins is too…a threesome can be awesome." Annie began to move away just as Rita returned.

Rita gave Annie a curt nod as she placed the drinks on the table.

Annie stopped moving away and gazed directly at Rita. "How're you doing, Rita? I heard Angel finally snared someone to be Charlie's father."

Rita ground her teeth. She remained calm, and, as she sat back down, she glared at the woman. "I'm good. I'll let Angel know you sent her your best when I see her in a couple of days."

Annie nodded. "You do that, Rita. Don't forget my offer, Neve." She blew Neve a kiss before her lanky frame moved away toward a table where three women sat near the door.

"Thanks for the drink." Neve raised the bottle of beer toward Rita.

Rita gave her a half-smile. "You're welcome. I guess the chances of us getting to the table again are remote. Have you seen all those names on the board?"

"Yeah I have. Look, Rita, about Annie."

"No, it's okay I get it—sex, right?"

Neve almost choked on her beer as she nodded.

Rita took a drink. The alcohol she'd consumed allowed her a sense of bravado. "Was she good? I've heard differing reports about her performance in bed."

This time Neve did choke. "You've heard differing reports? From whom?"

"Rachel, for one, and then there was Judy. Oh, and Annie's got a reputation at the nightclub for being the right girl, in the right place, at the right time, if that's what you're looking for."

"How do you know all this?"

Rita chuckled. "Gossip, mainly. Annie used to work at the Mill and people talk. About Rachel, well, Angel told me that. She was annoyed one night when Rachel left the club unexpectedly and didn't return. Apparently, Annie has a bed in her SUV. Is that right?"

Neve shook her head. "I really don't know…it was in a private booth at the club."

Rita looked directly into Neve's eyes and allowed their gazes to linger for a few moments. "Did you think that I wouldn't approve? Is that why you didn't tell me? I figured something was going on earlier, but I thought it might be you and Rachel."

"Would it have mattered if it had been Rachel?" Neve asked.

Rita mulled that over for a while then nodded. "Yeah, it would."

"Oh."

"What do you say we call it a night after this drink? I think we've had an interesting day all around don't you?"

"I'll go with that. Besides, tomorrow I need to shop for a wedding present for Angel and Trevor."

Rita let the other matter slide for a moment. "You don't need to do that. She's not expecting anything."

"Ah, but she'll get something anyway. What did you get them?"

Rita chuckled. "Nothing, yet. I was going to shop for something tomorrow too."

"Sounds like a plan then."

"Yes, it does."

Chapter Twenty-one

Neve collapsed on one of the beds in the twin hotel room she shared with Rita and flipped off her leather shoes. "Your brother-in-law seems to be is a nice man."

Rita shook her head at Neve's relaxed pose. A part of her wanted to do the exact same thing, except years of being slightly uptight about that kind of thing won the day—only by a whisker. "Yes, he is. What do you think of Charlie?" Rita dropped her small packages on the round table in the room, pulled out the chair, and sat down.

Neve moved to pull a pillow from under the quilt and propped herself up. "He's a handsome little guy. Who does he take after with all those questions? We're going to have to give the full tour of the circus when he comes to stay."

Rita listened to the words and thought they could have so many meanings. The one her heart wanted probably wasn't Neve's meaning, but she could dream. "Yeah, we will. I expect Angel will want to send him over to me for a short time during the summer break…if that's okay with you?"

Neve grinned. "No problem from me. Lorenzo will most likely have something to say."

Rita's eyes widened. "What will he say? Do you think it's a problem? What?"

"No, not like that." Neve chuckled. "He'll want to take Charlie under his wing. I think at one point he wanted to settle down and have a family. Who knows, he still might." Neve glanced at Rita. "Is that what you'd like one day Rita—to settle down and have a family?"

Rita considered the question carefully before replying. "I thought I did. I wanted pretty much what most people want.

Now…no, not really…at least the family part. The settling down with someone special is important still. I think most everyone wants that in their life at some point." Rita moved to pick up her packages and began opening them. "It's finding the right person to settle down with that's the tricky part."

"Maybe you already have, but don't know it yet."

"Perhaps." Rita turned with a smile to face her friend. "Okay, what are you going to do until Angel arrives in a couple of hours?"

Neve dragged herself up and looked at Rita. "I'm going to take advantage of a fully equipped gym and spend at least an hour in there. Want to join me?"

Rita chuckled. "It's tempting, but no. I'm going to relax a while, maybe watch TV."

"Sounds like the ideal scenario, especially as tomorrow will be a busy day for you. You should have seen your face when Angel told you that you'd have to sit at the main table." Neve walked over to her suitcase and withdrew a t-shirt and shorts.

"I'm still in shock. I know I should have prepared for that but I wanted to stay low-key. Anyway, I don't know why you're so cheerful since you get to sit next to me."

Neve glanced up with surprise on her face. "What do you mean? I'm not family?"

"Sorry, you're my guest and other than Angel's girlfriends and anyone they bring, that's the sum total of people on our side. Trevor's relatives and friends outnumber us ten to one, at least. Angel was never very good at figures when she said three to one," Rita picked up the complimentary notepad and pen and began pondering what she was going to say in a speech.

Neve headed for the bathroom. "You do know that fair's fair. If Lorenzo embarks on this scenario, you're going to have to accompany me at the main table."

Rita chuckled softly. "It's a deal, as long as I don't have to do a speech." Rita contemplated what she could possibly say to a room of eighty people. She heard Neve come out of the bathroom looked at her. "Go have that workout, and don't forget we're having an early dinner at six with Angel and Mrs. Arnold."

Neve walked over to Rita and placed her hands on Rita's shoulders. "Yes, Mom. Oh, and you'll come up with the right words for all the things you love about your sister—trust me."

Rita felt her breath catch in her throat at Neve's touch and found answering difficult. The release of her shoulders as Neve headed to the door had Rita glancing in her direction and wishing she hadn't—the lithe body encased in skimpy clothes caused her to suck in a breath. "Will you read it over when you get back and tell me what you think?"

Neve smiled. "I'd be happy to. See you in an hour."

Rita was alone in the room. She began to dwell on her escalating feelings for Neve. She sucked in a deep breath and shook her head. "No, I need to find the right words for that speech." She picked up the pen and thought what to say that would make Angel know how important she was in her life and how happy she was for her.

†

The wedding ceremony went off without a hitch. It was all that any young woman would want. *Angel epitomizes her name*, Rita thought as she gazed at her sister's beaming face. Angel clutched Trevor's hand as they sat at the main table of the reception. Rita's glance went to her nephew, who was talking animatedly with his grandmother. All-in-all, Angel's life was working out and that meant Charlie's would, too. Though occasionally life did throw the odd curve ball into the mix from time to time, she had no major doubts about their future.

On reflection, her life wasn't doing so badly either. She glanced discreetly at Neve, who was chatting with an older gentleman, introduced as Uncle Max, the oldest brother of Trevor's deceased father. Neve appeared confident and completely at ease, and she looked simply breathtaking in a pale beige silk suit that perfectly complemented her skin tone—not to mention that it clung in all the right places. She'd already caught more than one man's eye.

The sound of a voice asking for quiet silenced the room.

"We've decided to split the speeches into two parts. The bride's family is first." Ben, who was Trevor's best man, grinned first in Rita's direction and then winked at Charlie. "Fortunately, there's only two, and Charlie wanted to enjoy the meal and didn't want to wait."

Rita grinned at her nephew. *Oh, thank you, Charlie, the nerves were getting to me.*

"Therefore, with no further ado, Rita, Angel's sister, is first up." Ben smiled warmly in her direction.

Rita blushed. About to stand on shaky legs, she felt a hand enclose hers for a fraction of a second in reassurance and looked at Neve, who smiled reassuringly at her. It gave her that added encouragement she needed.

"I'm not exactly sure what you say at this kind of function, but a friend of mine," her eyes moved fractionally to Neve, who remained impassive, "well, she said there is only one thing to say—Angel, you've brought great joy to many people since you were born. Our parents would have been over the moon at this event and would have welcomed Trevor into the family with open arms. I welcome Trevor into the Collins family, and I know he'll make Angel very happy. As for Angel, you only have to look at her to see she's found the happiness most of us hope to achieve one day. Love transcends many barriers, and for Angel and Trevor, it was timing. When they first met, they had the right place but the wrong time. Now, they have the right time and the right place, with the right people here to show them that they all agree. What more could we want for anyone?" Turning to the bride and groom, she lifted her glass. "All the very best to you both for your future together."

There was instant applause as Rita sat down quickly and heaved a silent sigh of relief.

Trevor, who was on her right side, turned, and hugged her. "That was …thank you, Rita. Now I understand why Angel and Charlie love you as much as they do." He kissed her cheek and grinned as Ben announced it was Charlie's turn to speak. With pride, Trevor said, "That's my son."

Rita blinked back tears. "Yes, he is."

As she settled back and listened to Charlie, Neve touched her hand. "You were a real pro there. Are you sure you haven't done this before?"

Rita shuddered at the thought. "Nope." She turned her attention back to Charlie. Her heart swelled with pride as he stood there in a tuxedo that matched his dad's and made a speech. What she hadn't been prepared for were the final words of the speech…

"I want everyone to know that my Aunt Rita is my mom, too. I miss her when she's at work, but I know she has to go away. Now she's found a new family at the circus. I'm going to go there soon and check them out. Mom and Dad, I'm glad you got married. It means I can go to the circus sooner…isn't that right, Neve?"

All eyes of those who knew who Neve was turned in her direction.

Neve appeared discomfited at the question and nodded before she took a long drink from her wine glass.

Rita glanced at her friend and saw a definite red hue on Neve's cheeks—most unusual.

Applause and laughter followed Charlie's speech as the meal arrived.

"Well, that was interesting," Rita commented.

Neve looked down at her name plate and replied off-handedly, "Was it? How?"

Rita was quick to notice Neve's discomposure. "Charlie's speech. He indicated you said something along the lines of he could visit me at the circus earlier than the school holidays?"

"I didn't say that, exactly."

"No, what did you say?"

A waiter brought their meal.

"How about we discuss this later?" Neve muttered, "Much later—like never."

Distracted by something Trevor said, Rita ignored Neve's underlying reply Trevor dragged her into a discussion. She did manage to say a few words to Neve. "Eat up, Neve. Today I'm not keeping score on your lack of vegetables."

Neve smiled as a waiter placed a plate of king prawns covered in a creamy sauce in front of her.

The leisurely meal, along with surprisingly entertaining speeches by the best man, Trevor's Uncle Max, and Trevor, himself, ended the afternoon gathering. There was a respite for a couple of hours for people to change, if they wished, before moving onto the next venue—the hospital's Social Club. More than once in the last twenty-four hours, Angel insisted that the evening celebration was going to be *low key* and *fun*.

Rita drew in a satisfied breath. *Angel is happy, Charlie is happy, and that's all that matters.*

"You look faraway, is anything wrong?" Neve and Rita were the only two left at the main table after all the others had drifted off to speak with relatives or guests.

Rita turned to her friend with a deep smile that curved her full lips. "Nope, everything is quite the opposite."

Neve chuckled at the reply before taking a sip of wine. "Glad to hear it. I think Rachel has fallen badly. She's not taken her eyes off that woman in the far corner since she came in. Maybe we need to ask Angel to introduce them."

"Are you a matchmaker now, Neve? Lorenzo will certainly get a shock when the winter is over. By the way, do you plan to catch up with him in the next couple of months or do you both just do your own thing? The circumstances this year are a little different." Rita swirled the almost full glass of wine around in the large glass.

"I'm not a gambler, and he needs his space. We live in each other's pockets for too much of the year as it is." Neve changed the subject back to her original thoughts. "Going back to that woman, what do you think? Look, look now, and you're sure to see it, too." Rita glanced discreetly at Rachel, who was looking in the direction Neve indicated. Then she switched her view to the direction in which Rachel was looking. A young woman, possibly in her early thirties at the most, sat alone at a small table wedged close to the door. No one could call her beautiful. In fact, Rita would say she was pretty much like her—average—nothing to write home about. She turned to Neve with a frown. "She doesn't look like Rachel's type. Why do you think that? And she might not be gay."

"True, she might not be and that's what Rachel is trying, from a distance, to decide. I think I'm going to help her out." Neve stood and moved a few feet then looked back. "Are you coming?"

"Me? Oh, I don't know…it isn't any of our business, Neve."

Neve smiled and then winked. "I know, but it's a wedding, and things kind of get muddled at weddings. Anyone who attends is everyone's business." She headed in the direction of the unknown woman and Rita, who had stood automatically, wasn't sure what to do. Then she made a decision to go over to Rachel. Neve might have gotten it all wrong. People could be embarrassed, and she didn't want that at her sister's wedding.

As Neve moved to the stranger's table, Rita reached Rachel and Angel's other friends. She saw a disappointed expression on Rachel's face. Rita looked in the direction Rachel's eyes were looking and saw Neve talking to the woman.

"Hi, did you enjoy the wedding reception?" Rita asked conversationally. The others all gave big thumbs up and she even received a partial grin from Rachel.

"Is everyone staying for the evening's reception?" Rita knew they were, as they were all booked into the same hotel for the evening, but she asked anyway.

They all answered in the affirmative. Rita smiled and then allowed the conversation to lapse. Soon everyone was talking amongst themselves except for Rachel. Rita slid into a vacant chair next to Rachel and smiled at her friend. "You didn't bring anyone?"

Rachel shook her head. "Oh, you know me, Rita, footloose and fancy free. You never know who you might meet…" Her voice trailed off as her eyes distinctly traveled to the woman, who was now laughing at something Neve said.

"You should have told me that. I thought I'd be the only one alone here tonight and persuaded Neve to come."

"Yeah, and you made a bad call. She's left you alone to chat up another woman," Rachel's reply was caustic. "Sorry, Rita, I didn't mean to sound so…"

"Spiteful? She was right."

"What do you mean, she was right?"

Rita laughed and placed a hand on Rachel's forearm. "Neve said you were interested in the woman she's currently talking to. She's checking her out for you."

Rachel laughed so loudly that several people looked in their direction. "She's checking her out for me? Oh my God, was I that transparent?" Rachel dropped her head in a theatrical way so that it hit the tablecloth gently.

Rita grinned. Neve was turning out to be inexplicable in many ways—it was rather wonderful. Then she felt Rachel's hand clutching her arm so hard it hurt.

"Neve's heading this way with her."

Rita, with a half smile and a half grimace of pain, shook her head. "I'm sure she is." *She'd better be quick, or I'm going to lose the circulation in my arm.*

Neve sidled up to Rita's chair, placing her hand possessively on the arm. "Hey, guys, I'd like you to meet Charmaine Jacobs. She works with Trevor and is a surgeon." Neve winked at Rita. "If you want more details, you have to ask yourself."

Charmaine's face beamed a smile. "Hi. Neve said this was the table to get to know for tonight. She said it's where all the fun would be."

Rita had to stop herself from laughing when she saw Rachel's' jaw drop—the woman was smitten. "Well, I have to go. Here, take my seat, Charmaine. I look forward to seeing you all tonight."

Neve moved fractionally and then placed her arm around Rita's waist, indicating to Charmaine to sit. "Rachel will look after you. Won't you, Rach?"

Shock and surprise covered Rachel's face. "Yep, sure, no problem…the fun starts here."

Neve gently guided Rita way from the table and they headed back to the main table.

"Is she?" Rita finally spurted out.

"Is she what?"

Rolling her eyes, Rita asked, "Is she a lesbian?"

Neve, with what appeared to be a thoughtful look around the room, grinned. "Absolutely. She was getting bored and thought there was no chance of her finding like-minded people at a heterosexual wedding."

"She never said that?"

Neve grinned and then laughed. "Come on, let's go back to the hotel, and chill for a couple of hours." When Rita didn't move and her hands went to her wide hips, Neve relented. "Nope, she didn't. However, she is interested in women and, trust me, I know that kind of thing."

"Arrgh, you're a crazy person to know, Neve Garmancelli," Rita picked up her things and headed for the exit.

Neve placed a casual arm around Rita's shoulders. "Gotta keep 'em guessing."

Chapter Twenty-two

Worn out, Charlie's head nestled into Rita's shoulder. His parents were circulating, and his grandmother had disappeared an hour earlier and left Rita alone with her nephew. Not exactly alone, as Neve and the others she knew were all at the same table.

She glanced down at his tousled hair and smiled tenderly. She loved him like her own and leaving him again was going to be hard, particularly as Neve would be gone, too. Tomorrow afternoon she'd be heading home with Rachel, who had offered her a lift. It made sense, since Neve was heading in the *opposite direction. She kissed the top of his head.* He'd grown so much since I've been gone. She suspected that, as the months passed between visits, he'd no longer be as excited about her arrival. Kids liked their own space, and good old aunt Rita wasn't going to be a priority when his friends were around. He'd probably be like his mom and have friends coming out of the woodwork.

"I'm tired, Aunty Rita," Charlie mumbled and burrowed closer into her body.

"I know, darling. I promise I'll have your grandma take you to bed soon." Rita hugged him with a faint smile on her lips. Her eyes scanned the room looking for Trevor's mother, and she frowned when she didn't see the woman.

"Is there a problem, Rita?" Lilly Sparrow asked.

Rita shook her head and smiled at the pregnant woman who was sitting across from her. "Oh, no. I was just wondering where Mrs. Arnold had gone…she's supposed to be Charlie's caretaker this evening, and he wants to go to bed." She smiled at Angel's friend. "Where's Jack?"

Lilly giggled. "He's dancing with Rach. She crooks her finger, and away he goes. Men, who understands them? I sure don't."

"Me, neither." Neve sank down into the chair next to Rita. "Here you go, and yes, it has alcohol, and yes, I know you said you only wanted a juice, but this is a big day for you, too."

Rita rolled her eyes at her friend. "I get the message."

"Rita is looking for Mrs. Arnold. Charlie is exhausted and wants to go to bed. It's been a big day for him too," Lilly said. "I see Jack out on the dance floor jiving with Rachel. Even before I was pregnant, I couldn't do those moves."

Neve glanced at Charlie and then around the room. "Be right back."

Rita smiled before shaking her head. "Neve's very organized, and I can guess where she's gone."

A few minutes later, Neve returned, along with a very apologetic Mrs. Arnold.

"I'm so sorry, Rita. Would you believe there was someone here who works with Trevor whom I haven't seen in years? The poor man, he's a widower now." Her eyes rested on Charlie. "He looks all tuckered out. Let me take him home."

Rita felt embarrassed that Neve had interfered and began to offer her apologies. "No problem. Look, if you want to stay, I can always…"

"Good gracious, me. No! Ronnie and I have arranged to meet tomorrow for lunch. Besides, it always pays not to be too eager for a relationship, even at my age," Kathy Arnold winked.

"Shall I carry him?" Rita asked.

Neve bent down and easily picked up Charlie. "I've got him, Rita. Where are we going, Mrs. A?"

Rita had reluctantly relinquished Charlie and felt moderately angry at Neve's high- handed attitude as she watched Neve, Charlie, and Mrs. Arnold disappear out of the room.

"She's quite indomitable, isn't she?" Lilly remarked.

Rita was still watching the door, fully expecting them to return with Charlie. "Yeah, years of practice, Lilly."

"She's nice though…you could do a lot worse."

Rita, with her gaze fixed on the door, wasn't fully paying attention to Lilly until that second. *What the hell does she mean by that?* Rita turned to Lilly and gave her an intent look. "I could do a lot worse?"

Lilly fiddled with her orange juice glass and pursed her lips. "I mean as a friend."

The lame reply didn't wash with Rita. She drew in a breath and was about to challenge the retort when Rachel and Jack arrived at the table.

"Wow, I hadn't realized Jack was such a good dancer, Lil. You've been holding out on us." Rachel reached for her glass of wine and downed the remaining contents.

"Rach, you'll be drunk before ten if you carry on at that rate," Lilly admonished.

"I will not! What happened to Sue?" Rachel's eyes scanned the room and then spied her friend. "There she is. I'm going over there. See you guys later." She got up and almost sprinted across the room.

Lilly asked, "What's wrong with Rach? She looks like she's on drugs."

Rita shook her head and was about to speak when a deeper voice spoke. "She's upset because the woman of her dreams had to back out for this evening."

Rita looked up into Neve's strong profile. "Charlene?"

"Yep. Apparently, she offered to be on call for Trevor for the next couple of weeks, and there was an accident on the freeway and she had to leave." Neve sat beside Rita.

"How do you know all this? Are you suddenly her best buddy?" Rita knew her words were callous and her eyes averted Neve.

Neve narrowed her eyes. "Now, that was harsh. Actually, your new relative told me."

Rita gave Neve a puzzled expression.

"Mrs. A."

"Oh," Rita remarked.

Lilly commented, "Thank, God, for that. At least we can tell Rach she was stood up for a good reason."

Rita nodded and then smiled as she watched Jack whisper something in Lilly's ear. Lilly's smile almost lit up the room. Then they stood up and headed to the dance floor for a slow dance. As the couple left the table, Rita reached for her drink and took a sip. Surprised by the good taste, she took another. She wasn't going to allow her eyes to gaze at Neve. Her previous words were uncalled for and embarrassed her.

"Are we going to have one of those silent moments because it's a slow dance?"

Rita didn't answer immediately.

"Okay, if for some reason you think I've done something to offend you, please just tell me, and we can sort it out." Neve waited. "Because right now, Rita, the North Pole is warmer than the atmosphere at this table."

"You haven't!" Rita exclaimed.

Neve cocked her head to one side. "I haven't. Well, if it isn't me, what or who is it that has?"

Rita took another drink and then saw Neve's eyebrows rise. "What?"

Neve chuckled and touched Rita's warm cheek. "You don't usually drink that much so quickly. What's rattled you, Rita? Please tell me and maybe I can work it out for you."

"Like you did with Trevor's mother? I could have handled that."

"I know, but why should you if you had a friend who volunteered. Besides, it's more than Mrs. A and Charlie that has you defensive. What is it?"

The slightly higher pitch of Neve's voice had Rita recalling the numerous times she'd worked with woman that she used that particular tone. "It's nothing. It must be the excitement of the day."

"Pull the other one, Rita. I wasn't born yesterday. I'm your friend, right?"

"Yes."

"Then tell me what's bothering you, and we can work it out together."

Rita frowned and drew in a heavy breath that came out like a sigh. "They think you and I are together."

"That's perfectly true. We are together. You invited me, remember."

"No, not just that…I mean as a couple."

Neve picked up her own drink and gulped half of the beer down. "I guess from your expression, that's not a good thing."

"It's not about good or bad, it's about the truth."

"Novel, I'll give you that, Rita. Are you ashamed or horrified by what people might think our relationship is?" Neve drank more of her beer.

Rita followed suit. "What is this drink?"

"Singapore Sling. Is that a way for you not to answer my question?"

"No, I'm not ashamed of you or what I think about you or how you fit in my life."

"Good, because neither am I. Now, what difference does it make if people think what they do? Isn't it what *we* think that makes the most difference?"

Rita mulled over what Neve said and then gave her a small smile. "I'm sorry."

Neve nodded and gripped Rita's hand in a light hold, lacing their fingers together. "Never be sorry for other people, Rita. It's up to them what they think and how they act. All that matters to me is what you think."

Rita looked tentatively into Neve's eyes. "I think you are the best thing that has ever happened to me."

Neve smiled. "I think the same about you."

A slightly inebriated voice interrupted them. "Come on, guys, it's Culture Club. We all know this song, let's dance."

Neve shook her head as she looked across at Rachel. "Yes, we do. Rita. No excuses, let's go."

Rita felt her hand clasped in Neve's move upward and with it her unresisting body.

†

The evening moved on remarkably quickly as they danced, chatted, and had a good time. Around midnight, Rachel brightened up when Charlene arrived and sank down at their table, full of apologies.

Rita shook her head. "Please, no apologies. You were doing something wonderful. We, on the other hand, have been having fun and some of us more so than others."

A consensus of eyes turned to Rachel, who appeared to be gazing at the doctor in a trance.

Neve whispered, "She's smitten. Maybe there will be another celebration here soon."

Rita giggled and turned to Neve, wishing she hadn't as her heartbeat increased. She was certain it was louder than the music filling the room. Neve's face was inches from hers. As Rita looked closely, she could see the wrinkles around Neve's eyes, faint but there, nonetheless. Her dark hair had flecks of grey coming through, barely discernible unless you were up close—Rita was.

"I hate to tell you this, but people are looking in our direction."

The lips moving had Rita mesmerized until her mind deciphered what Neve said. Then, with a startled movement of her head, she broke the hypnotic attachment. "I think it must be my round." Rita slid out of her chair and hurriedly made for the bar.

†

Lilly moved fractionally and placed a hand on Neve's arm. "She's a lovely person. You won't let her down, will you?"

"I don't understand. Let her down?"

"We were talking the other night, Angel and the other girls, about how great it was that Rita finally found a good friend. Angel, in particular, has been worried about her. You can't always tell with Angel because she comes across all flighty, but she loves her sister and …well, we were glad when Rita turned up at home with you." Lilly placed a hand on her belly and scrunched up her face. "There he goes again with the kicks. Jack is sure he's going to be a pro football player when he grows up."

"And if it's a girl?"

"Oh, if it's a girl he'd be happier still. He coaches a female basketball team at the local high school. He isn't like a lot of the guys in town, allowing their macho image to take over with all that crap they spout." Turning her head slightly, she pointed at Sue on the dance floor with her boyfriend, Harry. "I have a feeling he's going to propose anytime soon."

"I'm sure Sue will be thrilled. Look, I'd better go help Rita with the drinks."

Lilly grinned. "Sure, see you in five."

†

Neve stood up and walked over to the bar thoughtfully. *Girly gossip, big time.* There was no point getting upset about it. She should have been aware there'd be speculation once Rachel spilled the beans on her sexuality. She slowed her pace slightly when she saw Rita's back at the bar conversing with a rotund man next to her.

Maybe it was a mistake to come here with Rita. After all, she might have met someone tonight. There seems to be plenty of single men here. There wasn't anyone available in the afternoon, but the evening was a different ball game. People of differing ages of both sexes packed the room. Neve scanned the room and saw at least three groups of single men together. She didn't know for sure that they were single, but they looked like damn wallflowers against the wall, so it wasn't such a great leap. Moving closer to Rita, Neve could hear some of the conversation her friend was having with the man next to her.

"I'm sorry but, no."

"Oh, come on, sweet thing, only one dance. I might not look nimble on my feet, but I can show you some great gyrating moves."

Neve rolled her eyes. "I'm sure you can," she whispered. She waited a few more seconds to hear Rita's next words.

"I'm with friends, and I've promised the next dance."

"Who said anything about the next dance? I was thinking of the slow ones where you get real close."

That does it. Neve moved in on the bar. "Rita, have you been served yet? The girls are getting thirsty."

Rita turned away from the man and the bar and smiled at Neve. "I'm just waiting for the cocktails."

The man turned at that moment, allowing Neve to take in his general appearance. He was overweight, his skin was an olive shade, his nose was stubby, and dark stubble covered his chin. The man's pale grey eyes didn't focus immediately and Neve assumed that was because he was drunk. He was better looking than Dan Flounder was and wore an expensive-looking deep blue suit, accompanied by a lilac shirt with the top button open with a loosened tie around his.

"Oh, you've got friends. Maybe we can all get together. I've got a couple of friends who need company, too." He waved vaguely in the direction of a corner of the room.

Neve bit down on her lip slightly, unsure if Rita wanted her to intervene—she hadn't been too happy the last time. "I'll take those drinks, shall I?" She reached across to take the beers and a couple of shot glasses.

"Will you please get rid of this jerk for me?"

Neve's smile beamed at Rita's whispered request. With a wink in her friend's direction, she turned to the man, who was half watching them and half with an eye elsewhere. Neve decided that was an almost impossible feat unless you were inebriated. "Thanks for the offer of company, but we've plenty already. Enjoy your evening."

"Oh, please, lovely ladies like you can never have too much company."

He sidled closer to Neve and she felt her hackles begin to rise. She could punch him, but that would be a little over the top. There was a much easier way but she didn't know if Rita understand. "I guess he doesn't take *no* for answer, darling." Neve discreetly winked at Rita before placing her arm around Rita's waist.

The man coughed slightly, staring intently at Neve's hand caressing Rita's waist and then frowned. "Ah, okay, I know when I'm beat."

At that moment, the bartender arrived with two more cocktails and Rita paid the bill.

"What can I get you?" the bartender asked the man. "A double whiskey."

With a grin, Neve placed the drinks on a tray and they walked back toward the table.

"Thank you."

Neve smiled. "My pleasure, although there might be a faint chance that people saw me put my arm around your waist, so there may be even more speculation."

Rita frowned. "Let 'em bite me."

Neve couldn't do anything else so she threw her head back and laughed. Lucky for her the drinks didn't end up on the floor. "Excellent reply."

†

The evening was almost over. The DJ was playing golden oldies, and everyone at their table had moved to the dance floor. Rita, alone at the table, fidgeted a few times on her seat and then looked at her empty glass. She didn't want a refill. Her eyes moved to Angel and Trevor, wrapped around each other like a second skin. She could see how happy they were and that, to her, was the most important part. Rachel and Charlene were dancing close, although she was sure Charlene was holding Rachel up. Lilly and Sue, with their respective partners, were equally engaged in the slower tempos.

"Hey, did you miss me?"

Rita swiftly looked up to see Neve towering over her. "Well, I knew you went to the bathroom, so I figured I wouldn't be alone for too long."

"You should never be alone."

Rita felt the muscles in her cheek flex at the quiet statement. Before she could reply, Neve softly said, "Dance with me."

It was an innocent enough request, but, for Rita, it felt like more and she wasn't sure if she could handle it. "It's the slow stuff…do you really want to dance with me?"

Neve remained standing and held out her hand. "I want to dance with you."

Rita swallowed hard. *What the hell? Everyone thinks we're together that way, anyway.* "Don't step on my toes."

Neve grinned. "Never."

They headed for the dance floor as the plaintive sounds of *Flying Without Wings* rang out of the speaker system.

Rita felt Neve's hand on her waist. It was a gentle touch but nothing particularly sexual—unlike earlier at the bar when it had sent tingles down her spine. Soon she relaxed as they danced to the song. Then the tempo changed and the lights went down. The DJ announced there would only be another couple of songs and then it was time to go home.

"Do you want to sit them out?"

Rita shook her head. "I'm enjoying myself. Do you?"

"Absolutely not. It feels good with you close to me."

Rita wasn't sure what to say. Instead, she allowed her body to make the decision as it molded closer to Neve's body. They went suddenly from relatively close to intertwined. It caused so many conflicting emotions in Rita she wasn't sure what to make of it—so she didn't.

"Hey, Ri, thank you for everything. I love you." Angel's voice came from far away when she was actually next to them on the floor. Glancing in her Angel's direction, she winked at her. *Crap, who gives a damn...this feels wonderful.*

"I love you, too, Angel. I'll see you when I bring Charlie back in a couple of weeks." The music changed, and Neve pulled her closer. Rita allowed Neve's warm body to encompass every sensation Rita was feeling.

"Pity you don't want to travel the world with me."

The words had Rita trying to work out if they were honest or were just the drink talking. She'd had more than her usual and that allowed her to relax more than normal—especially right now. "Maybe next year?"

"Maybe next year sounds like a plan to me."

Rita smiled and rested her head against Neve's shoulder. "Plans are what I do well."

Neve moved slightly, allowing them to look at each other. "Thank you for inviting me. I've had a wonderful day…especially now. It can't get any better."

Rita smiled up at Neve. "I agree."

As they looked at each other, Rita felt Neve pull her tenderly forward and their lips met in a natural motion. She felt an explosion of senses flood her consciousness like fireworks.

Moments later, they parted and Neve rested her chin on Rita's head. "Now, it's perfect."

Inside, Rita felt like a volcano about to erupt as she relived the sensation of Neve's kiss. With a sigh of happiness, Rita said, "Perfect."

Chapter Twenty-three

The taxi taking Neve, Rita, and Rachel back to the hotel was less than quiet. Rachel rambled nonstop about how wonderful Charlene was. Rita was half asleep, her head bobbing around as they hit bumps in the road. The only sounds from her were an occasional *huh* as she was jolted out of her sleep. Neve linked one hand with Rita's, who gently rested her head on Neve's shoulder. The soft snore shortly afterwards had Neve smiling.

When they arrived at the hotel, Neve gently shook Rita. "Hey, we're here."

There was a shuffling at Neve's side and she heard a slight groan. If Rachel hadn't been present, there would have been the distinct possibility that she'd have picked Rita up and carried her to her room. With her working on the high trapeze for all those years along with her workouts ever since it would have been a piece of cake.

Neve glanced at Rachel, who was trying to extricate herself from the taxi in a lady-like way. However, she ended up in a move that a contortionist would have been proud of, as her legs apparently decided to go in opposite directions. Neve, sighing and shaking her head in silent amusement, secured Rita by the arm and pulled her gently out onto the sidewalk in front of the hotel. "Stay there...I'll be right back." Then she gave the driver a shrug and disappeared around the vehicle to ensure Rachel didn't land on her ass in oncoming traffic. When she'd brought Rachel from the roadside to the sidewalk next to Rita, her friend had partially awakened.

"Rita, make sure Rach doesn't end up on the sidewalk ass first while I'll pay the driver."

Rita nodded and took hold of Rachel's arm.

A few minutes later, Neve took a second to look at the two women. It was all she could do not to laugh. Neither, she suspected, had her tolerance for alcohol indulgence. She drew in a deep breath, walked over to the two of them, took an arm of each, drill marched them into the hotel lobby, and into the elevator. Fortunately, there was only the concierge on duty, who gave Neve a sympathetic look.

Ten minutes later, Neve had Rachel safely tucked up in a blanket on top of the bed and then headed to the room she shared with Rita, who had gone ahead to their room.

The keycard allowed her entry into the room where she found Rita lying fast asleep on top of the bed. Neve whispered, "There I was thinking we might enjoy a nightcap and who knows, maybe something even more wonderful. Wishful thinking, Garmancelli." She grabbed a blanket, much as she'd done for Rachel, and wrapped it around Rita. However, in this instance, she added something else, bent her head, and kissed Rita's forehead. "Good night, Rita, sweet dreams."

Neve kicked off her shoes, which landed with a thud against one of the chairs in room and flipped open her laptop and turned it on. Moments later, she was reading her e-mail and saw one marked urgent. It was from a group of lawyers. The title let her know it wasn't spam. *A bequeath from your Uncle Silvestre Russo.* When she opened it, her eyes nearly bulged out of their sockets as she read the contents. She read the message several times before she checked the time—quarter after three. In a fluid motion, she found her cell phone and quickly dialed the number the e-mail indicated she could call, no matter what time of the day it was. Several rings later, she heard a woman's voice answer.

"Hello?"

"Hi, I have an urgent message that says I must speak with a Christian Chandler?"

"May I please ask who is calling?"

Neve glanced at Rita fast asleep on the bed. "Neve Garmancelli."

"Please hold the line, Ms. Garmancelli."

Neve listened to a Bob Marley song that was playing loudly in the background. *Fitting.* She also heard several voices and decided she must have called in the middle of a party. A few minutes later, a man's deep voice came on the line.

"Ms. Garmancelli, how good of you to call. I was beginning to wonder if we were going to be too late."

Neve frowned. "Too late for what exactly? You're e-mail wasn't that explicit, other than saying it was urgent and to call this number about my uncle. I'm sorry if I've spoiled your evening. I'm not even sure what time it is where you are."

"Mr. Russo was specific in the time frame of the bequest. Another few days…three to be precise, then I'm afraid you'd no longer be eligible. As to the other, it's Saturday, well, Sunday morning. We stay up late, or should that be early?"

"Uncle Silvestre left me a bequest? I don't understand. He's been dead almost a year and there was nothing mentioned earlier from the lawyers in New York."

There was a cough at the other end of the line. "Well, they wouldn't. I was Mr. Russo's lawyer in the Caribbean, where he had many interests."

"I see," Neve said. "Actually, no, I don't see. What exactly are you telling me?" Her voice rose slightly, and she glanced across at Rita who hadn't moved. She looked happy in her cocoon of sleep. It made Neve smile tenderly at her friend.

"I don't want to discuss this over the phone, Ms. Garmancelli. In fact, it is part of the will that you make the journey here to accept the bequest in person. It's a rather strange request. However, we will have to follow your uncle's wishes to the letter. Again, I stress the urgency. You must be here by tomorrow to accept the bequest and you must have the formalities with the taxes, etc., formalized by Wednesday."

Neve was frowning so hard that she thought her face would remain that way forever. "Is this an elaborate joke of my uncle's to have me travel to Jamaica, only to find he left me a hundred bucks?"

This time there was a definite clearing of the throat. "My dear, *no*. I'm sure if you pay us a visit, there will be no doubt in your mind that it was worth it. I'm afraid I can't say more, and perhaps I've said too much."

"Thanks, I think." Neve scratched the side of her face and puzzled over the situation for a few moments. *Well, I wasn't going any place special anyway*. Her glance once more settled on Rita and she nodded in reflection. "I'll take the next flight out. I'll need your address."

"My dear, Ms Garmancelli, let me know the flight number and I will have someone waiting for you when you arrive."

Neve felt disconcerted at the offer. *What has my uncle left me for this lawyer to be so solicitous, particularly at this hour*? "I'll check to see when the next flight is available and let you know. Goodbye, Mr. Chandler."

Neve disconnected and sucked in a deep breath. "This is weird. Why would Silvestre have a lawyer in the Caribbean and why after a year are we only finding out about it? I'd go, even if the bastard only left me a dollar, just to find out."

Her eyes settled on Rita. "I wish you were awake. You'd make more sense of this than I do. I'm going to have to tell you sooner or later that I value your opinion in my life—the whole of it—and I can't say I ever felt that way before." Her thoughts drifted to her liaisons after Jennifer—one-night stands. If she were honest with herself, her relationships, including the one with Jennifer, were one-sided. She had no inclination to share her life with anyone—not even Lorenzo. She gazed at the peaceful expression on Rita's face and felt that unusual tug on her heart. "You are so important, my friend. I hope you know that."

She pressed a few keys and pulled up the airline schedules for Jamaica.

†

Rita awoke to the sound of the alarm ringing insistently next to her ear, or so she thought. She groggily, opened first her left eye then the right before she screwed up her face as the light filtered through. There was a sharp pain behind her eyes.

"Oh my, God, what happened last night?"

She looked at her surroundings blearily, as her hand fumbled with the alarm clock buttons until the noise finally stopped. This didn't look like her family home and it certainly didn't have the comfortable ambiance of her RV at the circus. Then it dawned on her. "Angel's wedding."

Her glance strayed to the bed next to hers. It looked unused. "I'm pretty darned sure Neve came home with me." She sat up gingerly causing the headache to increase twofold. "I need one of Neve's magic cures." She listened intently for any sound from the bathroom—silence.

"Neve, are you up?" *Stupid question, of course she is.*

Rita frowned and then realized that she wasn't actually in bed, but on the top of the bed with a blanket covering her. She was fully clothed. "Oh crap, was I drunk? I must have been. I've never done this before. Neve's probably laughing her socks off. Although I recall Rach was in a worse condition…" The thought of Rachel brought its own connotations. "Maybe she stayed with Rach last night. I vaguely remember her taking Rach to her room, then nothing much after that." The idea made her feel sick. Although her hangover caused a slight attack of nausea, there was a definite shift in queasiness when she considered that Neve and Rach might have spent the night together.

"She kissed me." Rita placed a finger over her lips as the hazy recollection of Neve's kiss taunted her. "She said it was perfect. Surely, she wouldn't have gone off with Rach... Nope, I don't believe that."

As she climbed off the bed, she groaned at the throbbing in her head and slowly made it to the bathroom. She splashed cold water on her face in an effort to feel better. A sound of loud bells echoed in the white tiled bathroom. Rita screwed up her bleary eyes as she wondered if she was going to be fit for the brunch at eleven with Angel, the family and their close friends. The bells continued and finally Rita's brain connected the sound with the phone. She dashed out of the bathroom. Her eyes narrowing at the pain in her head, she reached for the phone. "Hello?"

"Rita, it's me, Neve."

Rita's eyes flew open in surprise. "Why are you calling me? Oh, no, don't tell me you're in the gym already." The mere idea of such a healthy activity made Rita feel like retching, and she had to hold onto her stomach.

There was a slight chuckle at the other end of the line. "Nothing so disgustingly healthy. I'm at the airport. I left you a note on the dresser."

"The airport? Why? I never saw a note."

"When I arrived back at the room, you'd fallen asleep. I checked my e-mail and there was an urgent message from some law firm in Jamaica. My uncle had dealings abroad and the lawyer needs to see me right away."

"You had to go immediately? Isn't that rather theatrical? Besides, how many lawyers do you know that are open all hours?" Rita asked.

"This one, apparently. I heard that Jamaicans were laid back." A soft laugh accompanied the comment. "This lawyer assures me it's necessary. I'm sorry for not being able to be there this morning, Rita, and explain this in person. Look, I expect to be back by the end of the week. How about I catch up with you then?"

Rita blew out a breath and felt her body sag. "I guess…you were leaving today anyway."

There was a marked silence for a few seconds. "That's true."

A hollow, metallic voice announcing flight details echoed in the background on the phone. "That's my flight. I have to go."

Rita nodded then realizing that Neve couldn't see her. "Sure. Remember, I have Charlie. Perhaps it's best if we catch up after your vacation. Why not make this part of it, as you'll be out of the country already."

"Right…yeah…Charlie. Okay. Look, I've left my keys to the car. You take it and use it. I can rent one when I get back."

"Thanks."

"Rita, are you okay? You sound…oh, I don't know…distant."

Rita allowed a faint smile to cross her lips as she replied, "I have a hangover. What I need right now is one of your magic cures."

"Ah, that explains it. Hey, talk to Rachel. I left a note on her table in her room about how to make a hangover cure. I thought she might need it when she woke up."

"Oh, you never thought I would? Or is it in the note I haven't read yet?"

"Sorry, no. I figured I'd be there to administer to you personally."

"Oh." Rita didn't know what else to say.

"I have to go, Rita. I'll call you when I get there."

"Have a safe trip, Neve."

Seconds later the connection went dead and Rita placed the receiver back on the cradle. Her smile grew wider, allowing the soft words Neve spoke to permeate her brain only to have the pain in her head discourage any more thought.

†

The flight, a little less than three hours to Jamaica, was routine with little turbulence. Neve hadn't eaten anything for breakfast. The only thing she purchased was orange juice to counter the effects of the alcohol she'd consumed the night before. The flight had given her time to contemplate her relationship with Rita. It was not far short of a miracle that their friendship lasted, as she recalled how they'd started. It certainly wasn't on friendly terms, at least not from her point of view. That hadn't deterred Rita. In fact, the woman had made it her goal to stick with it, and things couldn't have turned out better.

Somehow, against her usual temperament, she'd allowed Rita inside, and then the rest, as they say, is history. The small town, suburban lifestyle had been interesting and enjoyable. Rita's family and the friends she'd met had become part of her life now—at least that was the impression they gave. She allowed her smile to widen as she thought of inviting Rachel to stay at the circus for a week. Lorenzo, Jacamar and the rest of the gang would run rings around her, in a nice way. Rachel would love the experience, and it would give her an entirely new outlook on traveling the world, even if it were only state to state.

The bump and squeal of tires on the tarmac announced their arrival into Jamaica. From here on, she was in an unknown territory. "I wonder what you have up your sleeve for your final bow, Uncle," she whispered. The seat belt lights turned off, and they could move out of their seats and through to immigration.

Half an hour later, having only brought carry-on luggage, Neve walked out of the customs area and into the air-conditioned arrivals hall.

After glancing around, she couldn't see anyone waiting for her. With a shrug, she left to find a cab and book into a decent hotel. With long, determined strides, Neve walked toward a help counter and, as she did, she saw a huge man, both in height and breadth, walk through the outside doors waving a plaque. She could easily read her name on it.

The more she gazed at the large man, the more she felt completely bewildered. He was waving this god almighty large banner with her name on it and pushing forward until he reached the front of the glass partition between the hall and customs. Suddenly, the whole scene looked like a scenario from the clown routines at the circus. She chuckled softly and walked back the way she came. After making her way through the people standing around waiting for passengers, she tapped the man on the shoulder.

"Hi, I think you're here for me."

The man turned and stared at her. His eyes were the most remarkable brown she'd ever seen, a creamy chocolate shade, giving his dark complexion a softer look. "Neve Garmancelli?" he asked.

"Yep, that's me. Mr. Chandler sent you?" Neve grinned as she saw his infectious smile, showing the whitest teeth she'd seen on anyone, bar a TV commercial for tooth whitener.

"He did. Let me take your bags and we'll go see the boss."

Neve looked down at her overnight bag. "This is all I have. I figured I wouldn't be here long." The rest of her clothes were in a suitcase in the back of the Jeep. She knew Rita would look after them until she got back.

The man's eyes bulged at the comment. "Once you've seen my beautiful country, you won't want to leave." He grinned widely and took her bag. "Please, follow me. The car is on the forecourt through these doors." He tapped his nose. "I have friends in all the right places."

Neve wanted to answer but he was heading toward the door. With a shrug and a wry expression, she followed him.

†

Outside the restaurant, Rita rested her elbows on the dark, wooden table that she and the others were sitting at in the restaurant. She cast a quick glance backwards and saw Angel and Trevor laughing with Charlie. Rachel was still picking at her food, her hangover worse than hers. So much so, Rita would be the one driving them home later that day.

Harry, Sue's boyfriend, was going to drive Rachel's car back for her. Lilly and Jack were talking to Kathy Arnold intently. There were a few others whose names Rita couldn't even remember. She knew that was dreadful, but her attention was on one person—Neve. She turned back to the view of the river that ran through Johnstown and saw a resplendent paddle boat restored from the 1800's.

"Ri, are you okay?"

Rita dragged herself from her contemplation of the river to her sister, who had silently sidled up beside her. "Hey, I'm fine. I don't need to ask how you are."

"You don't, that's true. I know you said Neve was called away on urgent business but I thought she was on vacation, like you."

Rita nodded. "She is…this was personal."

Angel moved her head slightly. "Must be urgent because when I talked with her last night, she was going to attend today…unless, of course."

Rita immediately reacted to the comment. "What? Unless of course what, Angel?"

"Hey, don't get your panties in a wad. I just thought maybe you'd had a difference of opinion."

"About what?" Rita glared at her sister.

"That she's a lesbian and you're not. Maybe it might have come up after last night."

Rita clutched the handrail. "Angel, why does my being straight or Neve being a lesbian cause a problem? We're friends and work colleagues…okay…she's my boss. What exactly are you trying to say?"

Angel shrugged. "Hey, that's great. Look, all I was trying to say was, don't let something good go because you might be afraid."

"I'm not afraid!" Rita adamantly exclaimed.

Angel wrapped her arms around Rita. "Love comes in unexpected packages. If you feel that way, don't wait as long as I did to take a chance on what may be the real thing."

Rita was unsure about what was going on. "Angel, you and Trevor are different. Look at you…you're meant to be together."

"Yeah, we are, but it was so easily lost, Ri. Please don't let that happen to you. There's always been you, Charlie, and me in our family, and now we have Trevor and his family. We could always accommodate another and those Garmancelli's certainly are lookers." Angel winked then her tone turned serious. "I love and respect you. Charlie thinks that you're one of the wise people who gave baby Jesus a gift. Hey, don't look like that, he really does."

Rita shook her head. "Get to the point, Angel."

"If it's not a Dan Flounder in your bed but a Neve Garmancelli, we are happy for you. On a personal plus side, Neve is gorgeous in comparison. Don't tell my husband I said that."

Rita saw the wink accompanying the statement. "I love you, Angel, and I'm glad you found Trevor. He can take responsibility now for the wild imagination you seem to have."

Angel grinned. "I never doubted it. That's why I waited. I would have waited until the last breath I took in this life."

Rita shook her head. "You make love sound so simple and intrinsic."

"Because when the right person comes into your life, Ri, it is."

Angel hugged Rita and then kissed her cheek. "The life I have now, Ri, I owe to you. Charlie owes you big time, though he'll never really understand it until he's grown. And you, I want you to be as happy as I am at this moment."

Rita gazed into her sister's joyful face. There was no doubt that she genuinely meant every word. "Thank you. Come on, let's go back to the others or they'll think we've abandoned them."

Angel readily agreed as they linked arms and walked back to their family and friends.

Chapter Twenty-four

Rita watched Charlie playing with his old neighborhood buddies. She and Charlie had spent a great five days together. Tomorrow was their final full day before Angel and Trevor picked him up to take him home. That would leave her at loose ends for a week before going back to work. Not that she expected it to be that busy. After all, the circus wasn't due to start until the spring and that was still three months away. It gave her time to work on some new ideas for spreadsheets during the circus's hiatus.

Christmas was in a little over three weeks. Not that she was prepared—she wasn't. Somehow, the whole Christmas present and food foraging had passed her by. Normally, she was wondering where she could find the money to do justice to the Christmas feast, festivities, and presents. This year she knew she could do both but would probably only do the presents. Being alone for Christmas was a scary thought.

"Aunty Ri, Stewie is going to the circus on Sunday. I thought you said the circus was on holiday?" Charlie's inquisitive gaze caught Rita unaware in more ways than the question.

Rita gave him a smile of reassurance. "Honey, the circus I work for *is* on holiday but not all of them are. Where is it?"

Charlie nodded in understanding. "Forest Lake…do you think we can go? Stewie said they had lions and cool animals."

It wasn't somewhere she'd considered taking Charlie—to a rival circus—but then again, it could be a good insight into their competition, not that it was her business. *What the hell?* "I'll call Stewie's mom to find out where she bought the tickets. We'll have to go tomorrow or your parents will have to take you."

The boy nodded vigorously then rushed from the door where he'd been standing to give her a bear hug. When he left, Rita shook her head at the small, muddy imprints of his sneakers he'd left behind. "I've missed this." She chuckled, proceeding to find a mop and bucket to clean up the offending marks on her sparkling, wooden floor.

†

Neve sat at the hotel pool bar contemplating the marvelous view of the bay with its sea of baby blue and pristine beach. Several people were walking, carrying water sports equipment, or getting ready to swim. Because the beach was part of the hotel complex, it wasn't congested.

"Can I interest you in a refill, ma'am?" The cheerful bartender, in a garish, multi-colored shirt, grinned warmly at her as his hands rocked back and forth with a cocktail shaker.

Neve cocked her head to one side and briefly nodded at her almost empty glass.

"Same again?" he asked.

"Nope, I'll have whatever is in the shaker," Neve replied with a slight smile, her eyes taking in the view of half naked men and women, wearing the barest of swimwear and parading around the poolside. Sipping the remnants of her drink, she considered what was on offer. If nothing else, it was a feast of flesh to the eye. She had to admit that some of it was quite tasty. In the ten days she'd spent in Jamaica, her life had taken another turn. The crazy world she was living in had suddenly turned even crazier.

"There you go, ma'am." He placed a purplish colored drink, complete with umbrella and pineapple slices on either side of the glass, in front of Neve.

"Thanks, Jago." Neve took a sip and raised her eyebrows at the taste sensation it created in her mouth. "What do you call this concoction? It's good."

"Jamaican Forest Rush. Enjoy." He winked at her then moved along the bar to serve a couple who had just sat down.

Taking another sip, Neve returned to her earlier thoughts and the reason she was there…

"Ms. Garmancelli, how prompt of you. Elian tells me that you travel light, and he almost missed you."

Neve sat in the wicker chair offered. The room was unlike any lawyer's office she'd been in. It reminded her of a personal study—quite casual, with rattan chairs, a wooden table with a glass top. Books and papers were stacked in differing degrees of tidiness—or untidiness, depending on one's view point. "You said my uncle left me a bequest."

Mr. Chambers nodded. His jet black hair shimmered as the sun caught the sleek oil he used to keep it in place. His brown skin, the color of a burnt walnut, contrasted well with his unlikely, pale blue eyes. "Of course, of course."

Neve watched as the lawyer picked up several papers and then discarded them. His lack of order made her smile inwardly. Several shuffles later, he found what he was looking for. He gave her a wide smile, revealing white teeth that rivaled those of the driver, Elian.

"Here we are…I knew I'd put them on my desk. I'm retired now. For the most part, I see only the old clients left on the books. I rarely venture to the office anymore." He opened the documents and scanned them, before he looked up again at Neve and smiled. "Well, my dear, as I said, your uncle had interests in the Caribbean. Dating from…oh…twenty years ago."

Neve gasped. *That was around the time I took over the circus.* She swallowed hard. "Go on."

He nodded and spoke in a calm voice. "Your uncle was an astute businessman. He felt that property was an asset that would always benefit in the long term. There are several blocks of land, still undeveloped, and a hotel complex, along with three houses; one here, one in Bermuda, and one in St. Kitts. Needless to say, that's quite a portfolio."

Neve held up her hand and cleared her throat. "Are you telling me my uncle left me his estate here?"

"Yes, along with…let me see now…at the last bank statement three months ago…ah, yes, there it is. See for yourself. Five million dollars."

Neve felt the blood drain from her face as she shakily looked at the bank statement the lawyer handed her. Once she finally found her voice again, she looked at the man suspiciously. "I'm the only beneficiary?"

"Oh, yes, there is a private letter for you." He once more rummaged in a pile of papers before he withdrew a white envelope and gave it to her.

Sure enough, it was her uncle's handwriting. Neve rapidly broke the seal and withdrew the one page letter. It seemed short and to the point.

Neve,

I've robbed you blind and watched you work harder than any person I've ever met in my life before, and all for that damned circus.

Neve drew in a breath as she read more.

I won't waste time apologizing for what I did to you. Instead, I'm going to ensure that the investments I made with the sweat of your brow return where they should. I gave it almost a year before having Chambers contact you because I wanted you to find out for yourself what a flawed hero I was.

Neve felt her upper lip move into a snarling position. *Flawed hero, where the fuck does* hero *come into this.* Her eyes moved over the remaining words.

What I've left you, asset wise, is more than you would have ever earned from the circus. As it should be! Your inheritance from your mother was worth investing in something more than a dead loss. Your father was such a fool when it came to that circus and what he called his extended family. If

I hadn't done what I did...anyway, you can't change the past. Though I can't really compensate you for your loss of personal leisure time and the stress, you had to undergo each year keeping the business afloat it was necessary in the end, as I saw it. You might never thank me for this windfall, but you might consider I wasn't all bad.

Neve felt sure her teeth were grinding as she read the final paragraph.

As a final request, as I cannot in good faith bequest this under these circumstances, I'd appreciate it if you could find it in your heart to be generous to my daughter. Neither she nor Jane knew of my dealings here or at the circus.

You might not believe this, but I love and admire you for your fortitude. I'm so sorry your mother died when she did. She would have been proud of you.

With love,

Silvestre

Neve dropped the letter to the desk and shook her head in disbelief. In a hoarse voice, she asked the lawyer, "As an estimate, what do you think the whole portfolio is worth today?"

The lawyer looked slightly flustered at the request. Then he pulled at his clean shaven chin and announced, "Barring the undeveloped land, I'd say at today's market prices the properties are worth around eleven million."

"Can't you at least give a reasonable estimate for the undeveloped land?" Neve persisted.

Chambers looked slightly bewildered then he frowned. "About two years ago, your uncle was offered three million for two adjacent blocks he owns on the south side of the island."

"How much land *does* he own?"

"*Did,* my dear, *did*. You own it all now. There are seven plots in all." Chambers smiled warmly at her. "Now we need to go through the formalities of exchange. I've booked you a premier suite at the Laredo Hotel. I'll notify the manager that you will be in residence."

Neve shook her head. "I assume this is the hotel in the list of things I now own? If so, I want to see for myself as a guest, not as the owner, how the current staff works."

"Very wise, my dear. It's a five star, luxury complex, always full at the high season, and has good figures for the rest of the year. I'd recommend keeping the hotel for the time being until your accountants have verified the figures."

Neve felt her stomach double flip. "I think my accountant is going to have a fit with the extra work involved." The idea of Rita being there and seeing what she just inherited made her smile. Her friend would probably call it justice.

"I can recommend a good company that has been handling your uncle's assets, before and after his death. Very wisely, I might add."

"I'll see them, if you can arrange it. What happens next?"

Chambers stood and Neve followed as he held out his hand. Neve shook the proffered hand and then waited for the man to reply to her question.

"I'll have the papers ready tomorrow morning for you to sign and we can go to the government building as soon as I can make the arrangements."

That was ten days ago and now she owned the hotel and a substantial block of real estate. She'd also taken Rita's advice and used the days simply to chill. She needed it in order to take in the fact that she'd become wealthy overnight. The accountants she'd met over the past few days who received an extortionate fee seemed to be respectable. Thanks to Rita's lessons, she wasn't blind to their every statement. If Rita hadn't been spending vacation time with Charlie, she'd have called her and had her come here to talk to the people. As it was, she'd managed to ride the crest of the accountant wave and had the understanding that, barring the total collapse of the economy, the assets were in great shape.

A sultry voice spoke at her side and Neve glanced at the person, who slid into the seat next to her.

"Do you mind?"

Neve gave a small nod toward the vacant seat. Dark lens sunglasses allowed her to appraise the dusky-skinned woman who sat beside her. She'd seen her by the pool several times in the past couple of days, always in a thong that didn't leave much of her athletic frame to the imagination. Her brown hair braided close to her head in a style popular with lots of women on the Island.

Chocolate brown eyes turned to her. "Do you recommend the drink?" A slim finger with bright red nail polish pointed at her half empty cocktail.

"I do, one of Jago's specials. He calls it a Jamaican Forest Rush." Neve took in the lime green top that barely covered the woman's creamy, beige colored breasts.

"Thanks. I'm Claris Rolando, by the way." She gave a wide smile that showed small, neat teeth.

Neve pondered beginning a meaningful conversation with the woman. She was due to meet Chambers in an hour for a session of documentation finalization. "Neve Garmancelli."

Jago arrived and Claris ordered a drink and asked if Neve wanted a refill.

For a second Neve hesitated, then thought *what the hell* and accepted. As their drinks were being prepared in front of them, Jago began a conversation.

"You both interested in a good looking, young, and virile man to take you out on the town?" He grinned as his eyes flashed as his body, as well as his hands, shook all over as he made the cocktails.

Claris chuckled and shook her head. "Not my type," she whispered.

Neve didn't say anything but she now knew that the woman's offer of a drink had an extra dimension. She'd had a suspicion when the woman made eye contact, but she couldn't be sure. It was a holiday location and strangers sought other strangers just to pass the time of day.

"What about you, Neve?"

"Me either." Neve's eyes never left her drink.

Jago raised his eyebrows in a exaggerating fashion. "Oh, you girls these days." He poured the drinks from the shaker and placed them before the women. With a flash of a smile, he was gone to the other end of the bar.

"Do you think he was disappointed?" Brown eyes gazed directly into Neve's shaded features.

"I doubt it. He's a flirt. It's one of the characteristics of a great bartender in this kind of environment. Are you on vacation, Claris?" Neve really wasn't interested either way but asked anyway. The woman was good to look at and it passed the time.

Claris grinned. "Nope, I use the place for recreation. I'm a personal trainer in a gym at a rival hotel. You look like you work out." Her hand reached out and tentatively touched Neve's powerful muscles on her right forearm, "Especially your upper body. What about you, Neve what are you doing here?"

Neve sipped her drink, the alcohol sending a tingling message through her blood. *This has to be my last one or I'll be inebriated when I met the lawyer.* "Business and pleasure."

"Nice. You must have a great job to include both. Are you a travel consultant or something along those lines?"

Neve shook her head. "I run a circus."

Brown eyes widened in surprise. "Get out of here, you don't."

"I do."

Claris laughed. "Business and pleasure, you say. I didn't realize Jamaica had wild lions or tigers on the prowl. Are you out to catch one with a big net and put them in a cage for our pleasure?"

Neve was sure the woman didn't mean to sound disbelieving or shallow but somehow it came across that way. "I don't keep animals in cages for other people's pleasure. Thanks for the drink. I'm due at a business meeting shortly. Good to meet you, Claris." Before the woman could reply, Neve slid off her chair and waved at Jago to put the drinks on her tab. She left the poolside for her private bungalow.

When she opened the door, she looked around and not for the first time realized it was large enough to hold a family. There were three bedrooms, a kitchen, and a spacious living area. "I should have begged Rita to bring Charlie for the week, instead of letting her railroad me with *you need a personal break from work and people you work with* crap. I know she's only thinking of me and the fact I haven't had a vacation in twenty years but darn, I miss you, Rita." Suddenly it dawned on her what was missing. She needed to share this good fortune with someone, and right now, there wasn't one person who would be interested. They all had other commitments. The more she thought about it, the more she wondered if that was what her life would now be like—filled with voids. *Money can't buy love or friendship.*

†

Rita swung Neve's SUV into a large enough parking space in the area cordoned for the Lulu-Belle Circus. The tickets had been hard to get, the only ones available being the most expensive. Not that it mattered. Because they were for Charlie and she'd have paid twice as much.

Charlie's eyes blazed as he looked all around him, the brightness of the lighting shining in his eyes. "Wow, look at all the stalls and the lights, and listen to the music. Is your circus like this, Aunty Ri?"

"Yes, but not quite as large." There had to be at least double the number of stalls and the big top was twice the size, possibly more, of the main Garmancelli tent.

"Way cool." Charlie excitedly exclaimed, as they climbed out of the truck and he heard a lion roar.

Rita smiled. "Hmm, maybe my circus might not be as cool. There aren't any animals."

Charlie shook his head. "It will be better. You're there and so is Neve."

Rita felt the emotion of those words wash over her. Neve would have smiled at that comment. For a few seconds she wondered how her friend was doing. *Probably getting a tan and making new friends.* The latter thought, *making new friends*, made her stomach lurch. Taking Charlie by the hand, she led him toward the counter to check on their tickets.

Half an hour later, they sat with drinks, and Charlie had popcorn. They both gazed around the large tent for different reasons. The props were first rate and the equipment looked pristine. The atmosphere was definitely *festive.* Clowns and the acrobats amused the waiting audience, then the music changed and the lights went down. "Okay, Charlie, it's about to start. See, the ringmaster is arriving."

A large, rotund man in the gaudiest yet most spectacular outfit Rita had seen outside the cinema entered the main ring and the show began.

Two hours later, as they left to walk around the stalls, Rita asked Charlie what he thought.

"Awesome! I can't wait to tell my buddies at school." Charlie's eyes and tone said *incredulous*.

Rita nodded. "The Lulu-Belle circus certainly puts *spectacular* into the word *circus*." Then she asked, "What was your favorite part, the lion tamer or the elephants?"

Charlie grinned. "They were cool, Aunty Ri, but I want to be the guy that catches all those people way up in the air. That was awesome!"

Rita blinked at the response. She noticed he was engrossed with the trapeze artists, but she never expected him to say that was his favorite. "You want to work the high trapeze?"

The boy nodded. "Do you think Neve will let me try with her guys when I come to visit?"

Rita knew Neve would teach Charlie herself. This whole circus stuff and Neve seemed to be meshing together with her family, until she couldn't see where her old life ended and the circus began. It was almost surreal. "When we see Neve again, you can ask her yourself, after you've talked with your parents about it. Come on, Charlie, let's check out the stalls."

An hour later, tired and happy, Charlie hung onto her hand as they neared the SUV. Bending down, she pulled the child closer and whispered into his tousled hair, "I'll have you home and in bed in an hour."

As they approached the easy to spot SUV that displayed signage for the Garmancelli Circus, she wasn't surprised to see a couple looking it over. With a smile, she deposited Charlie in the backseat. After carefully clipping him into the seat belt, she moved to the driver's side. The couple hadn't moved—they seemed to be waiting.

"Hi, is there something I can do for you?" Rita wasn't exactly fearful but certainly aware that she was alone with Charlie and there didn't seem to be anyone else around, if there were a problem. The threat dissipated when the woman told the man to leave.

"Hi, I'm Jennifer Connelly. I hope you don't mind my asking, but is this Neve Garmancelli's vehicle?"

Green eyes and a gentle smile had Rita nodding—the woman was no threat. "Yes, do you know her?"

The woman nodded briefly. "She's not with you?"

Rita thought she heard disappointment in the tone. "No, I can pass a message on to her when I see her."

"Will you tell her *hi* for me? I just wanted to check that she was okay."

"I can have her contact you when she gets back from vacation. If you're a friend..." Rita stopped when the woman shook her head.

"No, *hi* will be enough." Her eyes strayed to Charlie, who looked like he was asleep in the car. "Did your boy enjoy the show?"

"He did. Would you believe he wants to be a trapeze artist?" Rita smiled and then saw a shadow pass over Jennifer eyes.

"That should please Neve. It is, after all, her discipline in the circus."

Rita wasn't sure what that meant at first then it dawned on her that this woman thought she was more than a friend to Neve. That obviously hit a chord in the woman. "Did you know Neve when she was working in the circus on the wire?"

Jennifer shook her head. "Not in her heyday...I knew her the last year when she only worked when necessary. I'm glad to see that she's finally realized that there's more to life than the circus."

"I'm not sure that's true. I did persuade her to see what suburbia was like for a couple of weeks." Rita didn't know why she told the woman who was a stranger that. Neve wouldn't be happy about her imparting personal information.

Jennifer smiled. "I'm glad. She needs someone who can make her see past the circus. I never could...in fact, I think I was an irritation."

Rita felt sorry for the woman. Her words seemed to echo a melancholy she sometimes felt with Neve. "I'm Rita Collins. I work for Neve." She thrust out her hand.

Jennifer's eyebrows rose at the knowledge. She shook Rita's hand. "Ah, right, that's why you have her vehicle?"

"Yes, she's abroad at the moment and left it with me for safe-keeping." Rita smiled slowly at the woman who looked perplexed.

"I thought you and Neve…stupid mistake. Look, sorry to have taken up your time, Rita. Your boy looks all in."

"He is. It's all the excitement. Look, I know you said to tell Neve *hi,* but is there anything else you want me to say to her?" Rita was sure the woman wanted to say more.

Another voice joined the mix. "There you are, Jen. Freddy tells me Garmancelli's here. Is that true?"

Rita watched as a woman the same height as Neve approached. Where Neve was dark, this woman was blonde. Rita wasn't sure of the color of her eyes in the dim light, but they glittered as she slung her arm possessively around Jennifer.

"Belle, this is, Rita. She works for Neve. Neve isn't here, so you can stop worrying that they are poaching the secret of your success." Jennifer's voice warmed considerably.

Rita saw Jennifer smile affectionately at the woman.

"I was never worried about the circus." She grinned at Jennifer then turned to Rita. "Hi, I guess the old reprobate has finally found someone she trusts. Jen used to tell me that the personal possessions of Garmancelli were out of bounds for everyone—even someone she professed to love." The woman gave Rita the once-over. "If you don't mind me saying, you don't look her type,."

Rita's hackles rose at the demeaning words about Neve. Or was it that she felt it a personal slight? Whatever it was, she wasn't happy. "I do mind, actually. What my relationship is with Neve, and hers with me, has nothing whatsoever to do with you, whoever you are. I need to go. Charlie is tired. Good night." Rita opened the door to the vehicle and was about to climb in when Jennifer placed a gentle hand on her arm.

"Belle didn't mean anything bad, Rita. In fact, she's probably in shock as much as I was. We saw Neve only a few months ago, drinking herself to death and the only thing that seemed to bring her out of it was the mention of one of her employees. We're glad you enjoyed the show. Have a safe trip home, Rita." Jennifer gave her an apologetic smile.

Rita fought hard not to ask who that employee was. Her curiosity won the day as she sat in the driver's seat and was about to start the ignition. "Jennifer. Who was the employee?"

Jennifer gave her an intense look and then nodded. Rita guessed it was more to herself than her. "Her new accountant. Can't remember the name, though. You work for her, you'll know, right?"

Rita was flabbergasted "I do. Thanks." She engaged the engine and moved the Jeep away from the two women. When she glanced at Charlie, she smiled. *He is in dreamland—what better place.*

†

Lulu gave Jennifer a shrewd glance. "She's the accountant, right?"

Jennifer turned to Lulu and rolled her eyes. "I honestly don't know, but I think she might be."

"Trust me, my love, she is. People like Garmancelli don't change their spots, they just caramelize them."

Jennifer frowned. "Huh?"

Lulu shrugged. "You know what I mean."

"Ah, that she *camouflages* them. Right?"

Lulu pulled Jen close and smiled as she dropped a tender kiss on her lips. "Exactly. One of the reasons I love you."

"Yeah, well, I hope you're right. She was a nice woman." Jennifer said.

"Hey, she has a kid, and Neve is still around. Maybe she's finally found out it's okay to love someone."

"Yeah."

Lulu looked at her partner and for a split second wondered.... *Don't go there, Lulu, girl, just don't.* She decided to take the bull by the horns. "If she's changed that much, would you want to try again with her?"

Jennifer gave Lulu her full attention. "There is no place I want to be but with you." She frowned. "I haven't convinced you of that yet, have I?"

Lulu gave a shamefaced expression. "Yeah, you have."

"Marry me."

Lulu felt her mouth open and then shut several times before she swallowed hard and simply gazed at Jennifer.

"Oh, the mighty Lulu-Belle Christianson is lost for words. That must be a first."

Lulu heard Jennifer chuckle and then she breathed several shallow breaths and dropped to her knee. "Will you marry me, Jennifer?"

There was delighted laugh from Jennifer as she dropped to her knees and faced Lulu. "Try and stop me."

Lulu drew in a deep breath, placed her hands around Jennifer's face. "I love you. I always have. I promise to make you happy."

"You do, you always have. I was just too foolish to realize it, that's all." Jennifer moved closer and they kissed long and passionately.

Lulu eventually cradled Jennifer into her shoulder. "Neve is going to be happy too, Jen. I'm sure that woman has something to do with it."

Jennifer looked deep into Lulu's eyes and nodded. "Right now, who gives a damn? Let's go home to bed."

Lulu laughed as she hauled Jen up from her kneeling position. "You never need to ask me that twice."

Arms around each other, they headed for their trailer.

Chapter Twenty-five

Neve looked at the expanse of beach from the patio of her bungalow, where she sat on one of the wicker lounge chairs. It was Christmas Eve. For a few seconds she allowed the peace and quiet to wash over her as she gazed over the tranquil scene. In the past three weeks, she'd ensured that all the legalities were complete on what she wanted to do with the windfall from her uncle. It had been a no-brainer.

With a sigh, she stood up and looked in the mirror. Her skin glowed with a deep brown tan, causing the whites of her eyes to flash whenever she moved them. From a health point of view, she looked good. A little overweight, but she could solve that in the gym. She smoothed her palms over the green cotton shirt, open at the neck. Her knee length khaki shorts had several pockets—mostly empty. She turned away from the mirror and walked a few paces toward the door where she picked up her sneakers, and sunglasses. Before she opened the door, she placed the dark lenses over her eyes. With her shoes in hand, she walked back to the patio and stepped off it into the sand below. It took her all of two minutes to reach the pool. When she did, she looked around and spied who she was looking for. With a wave of her hand, she headed in her direction.

"We can't keep meeting like this." Neve smiled warmly at the young woman lying on a lounge next to the pool.

"We can't? Why? Are you ashamed of me because your tan is better than mine?" A soft chuckle accompanied the comment.

"Nope. Never ashamed of you." Neve sat down next to the pretty blonde her gaze traveling toward the bar and the hotel beyond. "Do you want something from the bar?"

A grey gaze caught Neve's dark lenses as the woman leaned on one elbow and peered at her. "It's only eleven. Besides, I'm still getting over last night. You certainly know how to party, Neve."

Neve leaned closer "You haven't seen anything yet." She tickled the exposed skin of the woman's stomach and the blonde jumped. With a wicked grin, Neve stood and moved out of a retaliation reach. "I'll fetch you a drink on the way back. Don't burn."

Neve walked away from the pool and vaulted easily onto the seat at the pool bar. In the weeks she'd stayed there, it had become one of her favorite haunts.

"Ah, the beautiful, but mysterious Neve. What can I get you, darling?"

Neve shook her head and grinned at the man. "Jago, you're such a flirt."

Brown eyes flashed in her direction then to the young woman at the pool. "And you're not?"

Neve ignored the good-natured observation and looked at the row of bottles. "I'll have vodka in a long glass of orange juice, please. Oh, and you can send one over to the lady at the pool in say..." Neve checked her watch, "half an hour should do it."

"Ah, you wouldn't want to take it yourself?" Jago gave her a wide smile.

Neve winked and with drink in hand, she headed toward the main hotel. Her steps led her in the direction of the reception area. She waited as others in front of her as the desk staff cordially attended to their needs. Anonymity was one of the beauties of no one knowing she owned the place. She watched the interaction with the staff and guests as an outsider. In the weeks she resided there, the staff had been exemplary. Chambers had asked her several times to inform the manager of her status, but she refused. New Year's Day was going to be a completely new ball game for her, her family, and the employees.

A chirpy young woman with a bright, infectious smile looked at Neve. "Ms. Garmancelli, how may I help you?"

"The shower head in my bungalow is acting up. Do you think you could inform maintenance for me?"

"Absolutely, Ms. Garmancelli. I'm sorry it caused you problems."

Neve nodded and walked away. She looked down at her feet, which were still bare—her sandals were poolside. "What next? I'm going native." She chuckled as she headed back toward the door to the pool. The vibration of her phone stopped her in her tracks. With one hand, she fished it out of one of her pockets.

"Hi?"

"Hey, Sis, it's me."

Neve grinned as she heard the deep rich tone of her brother's voice on the line. "I know it's you. Why did you wait until Christmas Eve to call me? I've been leaving messages for two weeks. Anyone would think you didn't want to talk with me."

There was a laugh at the other end of the line.

"Not so, we've exchanged messages by email. Look, I can't explain right now, but I'll be there to spend New Year's Eve with you."

Neve frowned. "Why not Christmas? If it's money…"

"Nope, it's not money, Sis. When I get there, you'll understand. This inheritance Silvestre left you must be special to keep you there."

Neve noted her brother's interest. She knew he wasn't going to ask her directly, and she was glad. She wanted it to be a surprise. "I'll explain when you get here. Lorenzo, take care of yourself, and have a wonderful Christmas. I love you."

There was silence for a few seconds. "I love you too, Sis. Take care of yourself, enjoy Christmas, and I'll expect to see a tanned you when I get there."

His laughter at the last comment had Neve shaking her head. *Isn't he going to be surprised at my new look.* "Bye, Lorenzo."

Neve went on her way toward the pool then she changed her mind. She took a sip of her drink as her thoughts were miles away—literally. She glanced around, saw an empty sofa in the reception area, and plunked down on it and placed her drink on the wicker glass-topped table. She took out her cell, located a number, and pressed *connect*.

†

Rita paused in thought as Dave Tamborelli stood at her desk in the control room vehicle. It was snowing outside, and she and Dave were the only two working. Stuart, the other console operator, was going to be there for New Year's Eve and Day. Although the circus was in hibernation, so to speak, there was still the general administration to take care of by catching up on what the continual traveling from place to place wouldn't allow. Dave and Stuart maintained the hub during this time, replacing, renewing, and doing what needed doing for another grueling season.

"I think you should go, Rita. If you don't, the chances are that you won't get home. That drive is at least three hours, right?"

Rita nodded. "On a good day. More likely five today."

"They closed the airports in the nearest five cities an hour ago and put out a blizzard warning. You should have gone hours ago, Rita just take a look outside." Dave pointed to the snow building up on the windows.

"If it gets too bad, I'll stay overnight. It's not a big deal. I wasn't going anywhere this year." Her voice held a tinge of sadness.

"Really? I thought you had family."

Rita explained, "I do. However, I decided this year it was good for my sister and nephew to have a family Christmas with her new husband. It will be just the three of them."

Dave stroked the dark shadow that was forming on his chin before he grinned warmly. "My parents always said that Christmas was for family, the more the merrier," he shrugged, "but then my folks came from large families and the house always was bursting at the seams."

Rita could picture the scene in her mind and it made her loneliness of the moment increase. "You'll be stuck here, won't you?"

"Not twenty-four seven. The boss isn't that cruel. She has an arrangement with a local security firm that takes over the holiday evening shifts. I have a twelve-hour pass, from six pm Christmas Day until six the following morning. My mom makes sure I have the roast and trimmings waiting for me when I get there."

Rita smiled at the younger man. "Want a guest?"

Dave smiled. "Sure. I guess if you're not going to take my advice I'd better get back to work. Makes you wonder what the boss and Lorenzo are up to right now, doesn't it?" He ambled back to his console and the continuation of his computer maintenance checks.

Rita sucked on the top of her pen. It was a bad habit she'd picked up from Neve, but who was there to see her. "I wonder what you're doing too, Neve. Jamaica must be good for you, and I'm glad." As she looked down at the register of the assets she was checking, she recalled the message she received from that woman, Jennifer…

On the drive home after going to the circus with Charlie, Rita was irked. It wasn't much of a leap to consider that the woman, who was very pretty, had, or once had a relationship with Neve, and it probably was intimate.

"I can't go there. It wouldn't do anything but cause pain. Besides, when we've talked, all Neve's been is friendly with nothing personal at all. It's as if she's forgotten we kissed."

"Are you talking to yourself, Rita? If so, I definitely think it's time to go home." Dave had popped his head over the top of the barrier that made her office space a little more private.

Rita shook herself out of her wanderings and shrugged, slightly embarrassed at being caught talking to herself. "You're right, I should. I'll be gone in ten minutes. I just need to finish a couple more entries."

The man seemed happy with her explanation as he nodded his head and walked toward a bank of monitors that currently weren't working.

Rita closed the application on her computer and gazed out the window at the worsening weather. She'd be an idiot to try to travel in the current conditions. When she was working, her RV was at her disposal. During the work week, she stayed there and went home on the weekend to break up her week. Now, it looked like she was going to spend Christmas alone in a scenic, but almost deserted, RV park, where her vehicle was temporarily stationed, along with several of the other vehicles from the circus including Neve's.

She collected her belongings and put on her warm overcoat and gloves before walking over to Dave and giving him a hug. "Merry Christmas, Dave."

"You too, Rita. Take care out there. If you get in any difficulties, call me. The boss would kill me if anything happened to you." He grinned before he kissed her cheek.

Rita shook her head. "I'll see you in three days."

When Rita opened the door, an icy blast of snow blew immediately hit her face. *Whoa, no way will I make it home in this. I'll be lucky to get to the RV park. Lucky I have Neve's Jeep.* Her teeth began to chatter—the weather reports, for once, were right.

Her cell phone began to ring, but there was no way she was going to answer a call. Taking steps that pitched her five inches into the snow drifts, she made it to the Jeep and climbed inside. She shook some of the snow off and hoped that Neve didn't mind her using the monster as a metallic towel. The white scene in front of her looked the part for Christmas. She fished out her cell phone to see who had called and closed her eyes before tilting her head upwards. "Crap. Neve." Rita inserted the key in the ignition, selected four-wheel drive, and set the vehicle in motion. When she arrived at the relative comfort of the RV, she'd call her back.

†

Neve frowned, as the call didn't connect. "Damn." She pondered trying again, but overheard someone talking.

"Are we glad to get here! Just as the plane took off, we heard that they closed the airport. Worse weather we've had for twenty-five years."

Another person added, "Yeah, snow in Johnstown and surrounding areas is the worst in their history. Good for the skiers, though, especially this time of year."

Neve frowned. Maybe Rita was snowed in at home or work or worse..." The thought of her friend stuck in a snow drift alone had her heart beating fast. She decided to try the control vehicle since there was always someone there.

"Tamborelli."

"Dave, it's Neve."

"Hey, boss, Merry Christmas. What can I do for you?"

"Is Rita there?"

"Oh, you just missed her. I told her to go home or she'd never get there...not sure it was a good idea for her to leave in the first place though."

Neve's eyes widened at that remark. "Why?"

"Snowing hard here, boss. It'll take her at least five hours to make it to Rochester...if she's lucky."

Neve's anger escalated. "You let her go when you knew it was dangerous?"

"Hey, boss, it wasn't my fault. She kind of invited herself to my place for dinner and I said she could, but I think she was teasing. She's going to be alone this Christmas."

Neve sucked in a breath and glanced at her own tranquil panorama. "Why will she be alone?"

"She said something about her sister and nephew spending the first Christmas with a new husband, that sort of thing. Want me to call her on her cell and have her contact you?"

"I already did that…she's not answering. When did she leave exactly?"

"I'd say ten minutes ago."

Neve considered that and bit down gently on her inner lip. "Thanks. Have a good Christmas, Dave. I'll see you soon."

She disconnected the call and jumped up from the sofa. "I hope you haven't gone home, Rita. It sounds like the weather there is terrible."

Her bare feet quickly headed back to the poolside, and she saw the blonde head she was looking for.

"Hey, how's the tan coming?" Neve sat down on the empty lounge and toyed with her cell phone.

Grey eyes cast a look directly at Neve. "Something wrong?"

Neve frowned slightly. "Not really. Apparently, the weather is bad back in the Midwest. I've been trying to call a friend, but she's not answering."

The lithe body moved next to her and a small hand latched onto Neve's forearm. "I'm sure your friend is fine. Call her later. She might be out shopping. Remember, it's Christmas Eve."

"How could I forget that with you here?" Neve placed the phone back in her shorts pocket and waved at Jago at the bar. A few minutes later two drinks arrived. "Let's drink a toast."

The blonde took the drink and smiled warmly. "I'm game. A toast to whom?"

"To friends and loved ones, old and new. Wherever in the world they are right now, keep them safe."

"I'll drink to that."

†

Rita slammed hard on the brakes as a car ran a red light. It was fortunate for her that the wheels only spun her into a ditch and not into the oncoming traffic. She threw the gears into reverse and attempted to back out. All that happened were wheels spinning and going nowhere.

"That's all I need." She pulled her cell out and dialed Dave's number.

"Tamborelli."

"Dave, it's me, Rita."

"Ah, Rita…I've just been talking about you."

"Really? I need you to contact a tow truck for me. Some idiot went through a stop light and now I'm stuck in a ditch."

"Crap, that sucks, Rita. Are you okay? Where are you?"

Rita frowned while looking for a street name. "I'm fine. I can't make any names out. The snow has obscured almost everything."

"Is the satellite navigation on?"

Rita rolled her eyes. Of course, this being Neve's vehicle, she'd have all the toys; funny how she hadn't realized that. She pressed a button on the small screen—it lit up immediately. Moments later, she replied, "Corner of Eighth and Wabash."

"I know that area. I'll call you back when I find someone."

Rita nodded to herself as the call ended. She considered calling Neve but the battery was low and she didn't have the charger with her. She needed the phone in case Dave called her back or something else happened—like another car losing control and running into the Jeep. Neve was going to have to wait. Rita quickly pressed several keys and sent a text.

†

Neve hugged her knees up to her chin as she watched the swimmers in the pool—swimming had never been a pastime she'd enjoyed. With her thoughts firmly fixed on Rita and the snow. "Damn, I wish I wasn't so far away. We could have spent Christmas together." Her eyes located a blonde head coming up for air in the pool just as her phone vibrated. She quickly retrieved it from her pocket and saw she had a new message…

N, Mry Xmas. I will call latr. R

Neve smiled broadly.

"Hey, you look happy. Was that from your friend?"

Neve looked up, still smiling as she watched the woman towel her hair partially dry. "Yeah."

"Great. That will take that hound dog expression from your face. Want to join me for a swim?"

"As tempting as that offer is, no thank you. I want to go over a few papers. Want to have lunch with me around one. Neve stood and was face-to-face with the blonde.

"Neve, do you ever stop and just enjoy smelling the roses? Of course, I will have lunch with you."

Neve dropped a hand around the slim waist and hugged the woman tight. "Roses? What roses?" With a chuckle, Neve dropped a kiss on the wet skin of the woman's cheek and left with a wave of her hand.

†

It took two hours for Rita to reach her RV. She was freezing and the first thing she did after turning up the heat was to place the kettle on the stove—she needed her tea. Ten minutes later, having divested herself of her wet outer gear, she placed the boiling water in the pot and moved it to the table for it to steep.

Her stomach growled and she opened the refrigerator door. "Hmm, ham slices, butter, condiments and a bottle of red wine." She closed the refrigerator door and her glance fell on the snow that had half covered her windows. "I guess I'll have to go out again to buy something for dinner tomorrow. I'll go to that small market down the road." Rita closed her eyes and groaned. "Like the market is going to be open."

Then she remembered her low cell battery and plugged it into the phone charger. Later, she'd call Neve back and then Angel, so she could wish Charlie a goodnight—he'd always been so excited going to bed on Christmas Eve. She pulled her favorite cup and saucer out of the cupboard, poured the herbal tea, and contemplated spending Christmas day alone.

†

Neve laughed at a tired joke making the rounds of the dining room, as she pierced a forkful of fresh tuna. A tangy sauce accompanied it, and she relished the taste on her tongue.

The vibrating of her phone in her slacks pocket had her quickly retrieving it and pressing a button to connect.

"Hey, I thought you said that you weren't going to bring that thing with you tonight." The young woman from earlier in the day pointed to the cell phone. "Give it to me."

Neve scowled. "Leave it, Sash." Without warning, the woman wrenched it from her grip.

"Hi, Merry Christmas, whoever you are."

Neve attempted to take back the phone but the woman held firm.

Sasha held the phone up. "It's Rita. Everyone say Merry Christmas to Rita."

There was a vocal response of, "Merry Christmas."

"Rita says, 'Merry Christmas back. I suppose you want Neve.'"

Neve finally recovered the phone, and, with a narrowing of her eyes in annoyance, scraped back her chair and walked over to the patio, away from the others at the table.

"Hey, Rita. Sorry about that."

There was a soft chuckle at the end of the line. "Sounds like you're having a party or something."

"Nothing so decadent…that's later. We're having dinner. How are you doing? Is the weather really as bad as I've heard?"

"Yeah, I'm snowed in. I didn't make it to Rochester, so figured I'd stay in the RV. It has all the luxuries of home. I'm warm enough. I feel sorry for anyone out in the storm. They must be freezing."

Neve frowned. "This means you really are on your own for Christmas. Why aren't you with Angel and Charlie?"

"I decided it was a good experience for them to have Christmas alone. Kathy, Trevor's mom, is away visiting her sister and…"

Neve pulled at her bottom lip. "You decided to play the martyr, right?"

"I did no such thing. You would have done the same in my place." Rita switched topics. "What's the weather like there, anyway?"

Neve ruefully agreed with Rita's comment and smiled. "I wish I'd known about you being alone. You could have flown here before the airports shut down. Funny thing is, I thought of you the other day as I was strolling down the beach." *I think of you every day. I wonder what you'd make of that.*

"Yeah?"

Neve chuckled. "Yeah. It's beautiful and a balmy eighty-five degrees now. Sash is trying to compete with me on a tan."

There was a short silence then Rita asked, "Sash. Is that the person who just talked to me?"

"Yeah, that's Sash. She's had two glasses of wine with dinner already, and they've gone to her head. I'm going to have to make sure that she eats properly or she won't be much fun later at the party." Neve looked over her shoulder to the blonde-haired woman, who was laughing at something one of their table guests was saying.

"I'd better let you go then, or your dinner will get cold. I just wanted to wish you a Merry Christmas and let you know that the inventory you asked me to correlate is ninety percent complete. I'll probably do the rest from here tomorrow."

"You will not!" Neve turned her full attention to the phone call. "Look, Rita, I know it's not the best of circumstances but…"

Sasha appeared at Neve's side. "Neve, if you don't hurry you won't get to taste the crayfish."

Neve scowled. "I've got to go, Rita. Look, when the airports open, I want you to buy a ticket on the next flight out and join me. There's no discussion. Okay?" Neve desperately wanted to explain more, but Sash's constant pulling at the sleeve of her silk shirt didn't help.

"I'm not sure…"

Neve was annoyed at her predicament. "Just do it, Rita. I'm the boss, right?"

"Right…you're the boss."

Neve glared at the young woman next to her and shook her arm free. "Sash, go…I'm nearly done. Are you still there, Rita?"

"Yes." Neve could tell by Rita's cold tone that she wasn't happy.

Sasha moved so she was close to Neve's face, "I love you, Neve."

"Yeah, I love you too, Sash." Neve gently pushed the younger woman away before she returned to the awkward conversation with Rita.

"Merry Christmas, Rita. Call me, email, or text the flight number. All costs are on me. Pay for it through the admin account. I've got to go. That woman never gives me any peace."

"Goodnight."

The phone went dead.

Neve held the phone in her hand and looked down at it. "I have the distinct feeling I've just screwed up somehow."

Sasha's waving had her walking back to the table with a grim expression. That lasted for all of a few seconds when Sash smiled at her.

†

Rita looked at the phone in her hand for some time before placing it on the coffee table. Then she leaned back into the comforting fabric of her sofa and felt tears begin to fall. In the space of a few minutes, her fantasy world had exploded around her. Neve had found someone else and obviously had feelings for her. *She said* 'I love you' *to that woman named Sash.* Rita frowned. *Why does Neve want me there*? It didn't make sense. She recalled Neve's tone near the end of the call—irritated—it hurt. They might from time-to-time play at being friends, but in reality, she worked for Neve. End of story.

It was useless to kid herself about the kiss they shared at Angel's wedding. It was nothing more than the right place at the right time for the occasion. It didn't mean Neve's feelings went any deeper or that the kiss meant anything to her. Neve had a penchant for one-night stands meaning she wasn't monogamous. That was clear when she had sex with Annie. Rita grimaced. Neve's dalliance with Annie had hurt her deeply, but she couldn't say anything at the time for it wasn't as if they were dating. They were friends, and, more correctly, colleagues. Neve was the boss and had made that point clear when she demanded that she join her as soon as the airport opened.

Insecurities began to stampede through Rita's mind. She had no chance of capturing Neve's love. It was now plainly obvious that Neve satisfied her sexual appetites easily with random women. There was no way she wanted part of that—she wouldn't become a casual flirtation when Neve felt the need.

The tears that had fallen began to dry as she resurrected a wall she long ago built to protect her from cruel jibes in the romance department. All her life people compared her to Angel in looks. Once they saw her sister, her chance of romance was history. Only Dan Flounder had ever taken any real interest in her and that was more to do with her career choice than romance.

Her phone rang. Distraught, hurt and disappointed she allowed it to go to voice mail. Once she heard the beep that told her she had a voice message, she punched in the code and listened…

"Rita, it's me. Look, I'm sorry about our earlier call. I didn't want our conversation to end that way. Please, will you come here? I need your help. You're the only one I trust completely."

Rita closed her eyes and allowed Neve's voice and apology to wash over her.

"God, I hate voice mail. I really do wish you a Merry Christmas, and I miss you. Please make the trip, Rita. I promise you won't regret it."

The call ended.

Rita cradled the phone to her cheek, and allowed Neve's words to soothe her inner fears. Tears again began to fall when she allowed herself to accept the finality of the situation. "I'm really done for. She just apologizes and expects me to come running." She felt her lips twist wryly, "I will, because she needs me and I need her too…even if all we can ever be is friends."

She stood up, walked over to the small window, swung back the curtain, and watched the snow falling. All around her, she could see the glittering of multi-colored lights from other occupied RVs.

Chapter Twenty-six

Rita flew into Kingston as a tropical shower thundered all around her. She could faintly see people running around with umbrellas as the flight made its descent. It was quite remarkable the difference three hours made when you traveled by plane. She left behind a dark, snow covered terminal and seeing the sun peek through the rain clouds brightened her considerably.

Half an hour later, she was waiting at the baggage carousel. Since her brief and emotionally draining conversation with Neve on Christmas Eve, the only contact she'd had with her boss was the apologetic voice mail along will several emails involving her arrival in Jamaica. Because Rita's original flight was overbooked, the airline offered her a much earlier one. This all happened about eight-thirty in the morning and she had to rush to make sure she got to the airport on time. With all of the confusion and rush, she didn't have time to let Neve know about the changes. She'd expected to make a call during the flight, but the weather hadn't permitted it. Once the plane touched down, she pulled out her cell to phone Neve, but the number wouldn't connect—no international coverage.

"Great!" Rita exclaimed.

The woman next to her at baggage claim gave her a smile. "No signal?"

Rita returned a brief smile to the women who had kind features. "Something like that."

"If it helps, there's a courtesy phone in *arrivals* that connects to most of the main hotels."

"Thanks. That does help. You must have been here before." Rita glanced at the carousel, as it began to creak and groan under the weight of suitcases and other objects.

The woman's brunette hair, which was silver in places, moved from side to side as she shook her head vigorously. "No, my daughter arrived here ten days ago. She told me where to contact the hotel when I arrived, if she wasn't here to meet me. Being early, I suspect I'll have to do that."

"That's a good plan. I'm meeting my boss…at least I was. Like you, I'm earlier than planned. I'm not even sure how far away from the airport she is. I should have called her when we boarded. I just didn't think." *Yeah, right. You wanted to be independent and show up unaided.*

"My name is Jane Russo. I'm still amazed that I'm here, actually. It's all to do with an unexpected windfall," she said.

Rita smiled warmly. The woman looked positively glowing with excitement. "I wish I had that kind of luck. I'm afraid I'm here on business, and I doubt I'll be here longer than a few days." A distressing thought flickered away like a neon light inside her mind. *You'll want to be with Sash and not saddled with me, won't you, Neve? Or have you moved on in the past three days? Holiday romances can be that way.* Rita suddenly remembered her manners. "Sorry, I'm Rita Collins."

"Is it common for you to travel abroad? I've never been outside of the United States, unless you call Mexico City abroad." Jane chuckled.

"I've never been that far. To be honest, I'm a little nervous being in a strange country. Someone told me that as long as I stick to the main tourist routes and the hotel boundaries, I shouldn't come to any harm. Kind of scary, though." Rita shrugged as she spied a case that might be hers. "That looks like mine. It was nice to meet you, Jane. Have a great time."

"You, too, Rita. Take care of yourself, and don't work too hard."

Rita nodded, collected her bag, and, with a quick smile in Jane's direction, headed toward customs.

Fifteen minutes later, Rita frowned at each notice board she came to in search of information that could tell her which phone to use—she didn't have a clue. She was annoyed with herself. She should have been less proud and contacted Neve when the plane was about to take off. Rita, looking around decided to ask a small, wiry Jamaican who was cleaning the floor with an over-large broom, for information.

"Hi, could you tell me where the hotel courtesy phone is, please?"

The man gave her a strange glance from weak, sandy eyes and shrugged. Then he pointed to a column ten feet to her left.

With a smile of thanks, Rita headed toward the column and sure enough, she found a phone. She pulled out an information sheet with the hotel's name from her purse—Laredo. The hotel was in the upper five of the listings and she punched in number four as the listing directed.

"Hotel Laredo, how may I help you?"

"Hi, my name is Rita Collins, and I'm booked into your hotel. Do you have a shuttle from the airport?"

"Of course, ma'am. Let me check your reservation. I'll just be a moment."

Rita waited and within seconds, the person at the other end spoke again.

"Why, of course, you're a guest of Ms. Garmancelli. We'll have a car for you in ten minutes. Please wait in the VIP lounge next to the entrance. The hotel looks forward to being of further service, Ms. Collins."

Rita replaced the phone and then looked around for the VIP lounge. *Ten minutes to wait isn't too shabby. Neve must be staying at some swanky place.*

†

Neve awoke with a thumping headache and peered blearily toward the window through which the sun streamed. From the fronds of the tropical foliage outside her bedroom, she saw raindrops drip. "'I missed rain. Bummer."

With an effort, she climbed out of bed, felt the headache slam like a truck into her temples, and narrowed her eyes at the blinding pain. "I didn't drink that much last night." Her brow creased as she headed for the kitchen and withdrew a bottle of sparkling water from the fridge. The coarse feeling in the back of her throat felt like a file scraping. She lethargically headed for the shower and hoped that would cure the crushing pain.

Ten minutes later, she toweled her body dry but felt only a little better. "Crap, don't tell me I've caught a damn virus! Today of all days." She scowled heavily irritated by the turn of events. Flicking open the bathroom cabinet, she found some aspirin. Once she swallowed a couple of tablets, she went to the kitchen, where she drank another bottle of water. Although she knew that breakfast would help, she didn't feel much like food.

The wet towel still around her body wasn't going to help. With a heavy sigh, she found walking back to the bedroom a chore. Instead of getting dressed, she tossed the damp towel aside, sank back into the bed, and pulled up the covers. Neve closed her eyes hoping that another hour's sleep would help. Rita was going to call her when she boarded the flight, so there was enough time to catch the arrival.

A loud knocking on the bungalow door had Neve blinking rapidly. The headache, although still pounding, had none of its initial rage The persistent knocking was an annoyance and eventually she dragged herself out of bed, put on a multicolored wrap, stumbled to the door and opened it with a jerk. "Yes?"

"Hey, that's not a very nice welcome. Wow, you look like shit. I thought you said you never suffered from hangovers."

Neve groaned silently. This was all she needed now—Sash. "I think I'm coming down with a cold. Is there a problem?"

Sash moved Neve's hair with a carelessly hand and then pushed her gently backwards inside the bungalow. She placed her hand on Neve's forehead. "You've got a temp. Have you taken anything?"

Neve heard the genuine concern in Sash's voice. "Just a couple of aspirin. That seems to have calmed down the headache a little. My legs feel like rubber and my throat is scratchy." She sat down heavily on the sofa and closed her eyes.

Sash moved toward the kitchen. "Have you any tea here?"

At the mention of tea, Neve groaned. "Rita." After a moment, she opened her eyes. "I need to check my messages. I'm expecting someone today."

"Yeah, well, right now you need a doctor to make sure it isn't anything other than a cold. You can't be too careful, especially with all the bugs going around this time of year. I'll take care of everything else. You need to rest."

Neve struggled to stand, but her legs obstinately refused to function accordingly. "My accountant is due in today. I don't want her to arrive without a suitable welcome."

Sash nodded. "Mom arrived this morning, too. That's why I'm here. She's expecting to have lunch with us."

Neve closed her eyes and groaned softly. "I'm sorry, Sash. I'm in no fit state to meet your mom. Will you apologize for me?"

"Knowing my mom, she'll come here and check on you for herself. She loves taking care of people, which was the reason she wasn't here at Christmas—her commitment to the local shelter. I'm going to find that doctor, Neve. Go back to bed."

Neve didn't have the energy to argue. "Rita, Rita Collins. Sash, will you make sure she's not left hanging at the airport. Tell her I'll see her at dinner, and I'll explain why I need her here."

Sash gave Neve a steady glance and then nodded. "Sure I will." She moved and took Neve by the arm before leading her, unresisting, to the bedroom. "I'll be back soon…you get some rest."

Neve looked at Sash with a weak smile. "Thanks."

"No problem. I love you, Neve, and I don't like to see you sick." Sash kissed Neve's forehead, pushed her gently toward the bed, and quietly closed the bedroom door behind her as she left.

Neve slid deeper into the bed and closed her eyes. A few more hours sleep, and she'd be okay. Colds rarely ever last long with her.

†

Rita felt like a VIP as she entered the plush lobby of the Laredo. Even if she saved up for a year, Rita wouldn't be able to afford this kind of place. A bell-hop retrieved her bag, as she alighted from the hotel vehicle and took it inside. Rita smiled at the receptionist when she reached the front desk.

A young woman with an ebony complexion and a wide, infectious smile greeted her. "Hi, how may I be of service?"

"I have a reservation…Rita Collins."

The woman pressed a few keys into her computer console and grinned widely. "Ah yes, Ms. Garmancelli's guest. All the formalities were taken care of when you called us from the airport. We just need to check your passport and ask you to fill in the guest register card." The woman passed over a small white card embossed with the hotel's logo and several questions.

Rita took it with a smile and glanced at the contents—the logo's design seemed vaguely familiar. She fished in her purse, withdrew her passport, and handed it over. Within minutes, the procedure was complete.

"Here's your key, Ms. Collins. Have a wonderful stay."

Rita took the key and glanced around for her bag.

"Just follow Adam, Ms. Collins, he'll show you to your bungalow."

"Thank you." Rita looked at the young, spidery man who had crooked teeth and a friendly expression.

A few minutes later, she was walking back outside, down a small path flanked on either side by colorful foliage she'd only ever seen on TV. As they walked farther, she saw a small bank of five bungalows on the waterfront along with a glorious stretch of beach between the bungalows and the water.

Her eyes narrowed and her brow furrowed as she looked where Adam was taking her. *A bungalow? Neve must have gotten it wrong. I'm only going to be here for a few days.* A couple of minutes later, she was standing in the bungalow nearest the hotel that was several hundred yards away from the outer boundaries of the hotel grounds.

Rita tipped Adam, who left her in the luxurious surroundings. The first thing she did was go out onto the patio and marvel at the view. It was stupendous. "Now, I know why you didn't go anywhere else, Neve. This is exactly what you needed."

Delighted at being there, Rita walked back into the room. The only thing that was marring her enjoyment of her surrounding was the hurt and disappointment she felt at Neve not meeting her or at lease leaving her a message at the front desk. A complimentary basket of fruit and a bottle of a wine she particularly liked were on a table. Rita walked toward the kitchen, opened the refrigerator, and found it filled with bottled water, milk, eggs, butter, her favorite cheese, and a few other essentials. The cabinets held all the necessary utensils and pans, if she wanted to make her own breakfast.

Her traveling clothes quickly became oppressive. When she left home, she had needed the heavy wool suit, but now, after a few minutes in the humidity and temperature, she was roasting. She pulled off her jacket and could see and smell the perspiration on her white cotton shirt. She screwed up her face.

"Shower, change, and then find Neve."

†

Sasha Russo walked briskly toward the reception desk and requested a doctor—he would be there within the hour. It was a quarter after twelve. She would first check on her mom, then see if Neve's accountant had arrived, and make sure she was okay and settled in her room.

"Ms. Garmancelli asked me to check to see if her guest..." She raised her eyes in recollection. "...Ms Collins has arrived."

"Oh, I don't need to check. I booked her in this morning around ten."

"Thanks. Look, Ms. Garmancelli is under the weather. She asked me to arrange with you to hold her calls until she feels better. Could you do that, please?"

"Of course, Ms Russo. There have been several inquiries from Ms. Collins regarding Ms. Garmancelli."

Sasha frowned. "Oh, right...okay...which room is she in?"

"Bungalow one."

Sasha smiled slowly and nodded. "I'll deal with it. Thanks again."

As Sasha walked, she pondered why Neve would place an employee in one of the complex's most expensive bungalows. Then it came to her—Christmas Eve—that phone call—she'd been so idiotic. "Was it Rita on the phone?" she thought for a moment. "Yes, that's the name she used." *Couldn't be a coincidence...could it? Hmm, now the plot really does thicken.* Still mulling over Neve and her love life, Sasha came to her own bungalow and opened the door.

"Mom, Neve has a virus. I've called the doctor as a precaution. Do you mind if I ask Neve's accountant to..." Sasha stopped in midsentence as she saw her mother having what looked like tea with a stranger. "Hello," she said to the unknown woman.

Jane Russo looked over her shoulder. "Now we know why Neve wasn't here to meet you, Rita. This is my daughter, Sasha, Neve's cousin."

Sasha strolled over and watched as Rita Collins stood up to shake her hand. Sasha thought she was what some might call plain. *A tan would make her look less pale, and she could do with a wardrobe change.* She appraised Rita's outfit. Her white cotton top was more in line with going to the office than a resort. Along with that, she had on a faded green cotton skirt that obviously hadn't been in fashion for some time. It accentuated the flare of her hips and that wasn't a good thing. "Hi, Rita. It's good to meet you. We did speak not too long ago...well sort of."

"Yes, I believe we did on Christmas Eve."

Sasha nodded. "Yes, Neve told me to tell you to enjoy today and she'll see us at dinner. Though, given her condition, I'd be more inclined to say tomorrow rather than tonight. We'll see what the doctor says."

"If it's possible, I'd like to see Neve." Rita didn't sit back down.

Sasha ignored what she thought was a less-than-friendly gaze from the accountant and took the seat next to her mother before smiling at the accountant. "She's sleeping. It's not wise to wake her. Look, when I take the doctor in I'll see if she's up for a visit." She sniffed the air. "Is that herbal tea I smell? Any left for me?"

Jane Russo grinned at her daughter. "Yes, and you can thank Rita. She brought her tea with her."

"Cool, Rita." Sasha looked at the accountant and could see the doubt on her face. "I promise you that Neve has a cold or some kind of virus and is really sleeping." *I suspect that there is more than meets the eye here between Neve and this woman.* The last thing she wanted to do was anger the accountant or, more importantly, anger her cousin.

"Thank you. I guess I could spend some time exploring the place. I've never been out of the States before." Rita retook her seat and then brought the cup of now cooling tea up to her lips.

Sasha frowned. "Don't go out of the complex alone, Rita. It isn't as safe as it appears. Look, I'm going to take mom to the small market they have in the closest village after lunch. Want to join us?"

Rita appeared to hesitate before she spoke. "Yes, if it isn't an imposition."

Jane spoke up at that point. "Excellent idea, Sasha. Why don't we all have lunch together?"

Sasha nodded as her mother poured her a cup of tea. "We'll have lunch here. By then the doctor should have seen to Neve, and then we can go. Will that suit everyone?"

The two women nodded.

Sasha settled back in her chair and eyed the quiet accountant as she sipped her tea. Rita Collins was definitely not, what she expected. If she was in a personal relationship with Neve, she didn't measure up to the others Neve dated in the past. *But, people change over time. Maybe Neve has too.* When Neve was up and around again, Sasha would know for sure. If she didn't, Lorenzo was due tomorrow and she was sure he'd know the score. The thought of Lorenzo made her smile even more.

"You look happy, Sasha, want to share?" Jane asked.

Sasha winked at her mom. "Enzo is due tomorrow. It will be good to see him. Neve missed him at Christmas."

"Do you mean, Lorenzo?" Rita asked.

"Of course. Do you know him too? He couldn't make Christmas, which peeved Neve, but she had me. Enzo is wicked fun." Sasha grinned and watched Rita's face transform as she smiled back.

"Yes, he's a lovely man," Jane said.

†

The doctor arrived just as they were ending a light lunch and, much to Rita's annoyance, Sasha left with him to see Neve. *She's a pain in the butt, big time. Who gave her the right to be Neve's keeper?* If she wasn't Neve's cousin and obviously close to her, Rita would have socked the woman for her take-charge attitude. Truth told, she was sick with envy. Alone with Jane, she picked at the remains of her lunch. The more she thought of Neve being ill, the more her worry increased.

"You'd like to see Neve, wouldn't you?"

Rita glanced up from her plate and shrugged. "Am I that obvious? She's my boss, but also a friend. So, yes, I would."

"Tell you what. When Sash comes back, how about I divert her attention for fifteen minutes and you go check on Neve for yourself. She's actually close by in bungalow two. We're in four, and Lorenzo will be in three."

Rita's eyes opened wide. "She booked all the bungalows on that stretch of beach? That scoundrel of an uncle must have left her a fortune." She immediately wished she hadn't said anything as she saw a look of sadness clouded Jane's otherwise friendly expression. "I'm sorry. Of course, he was your husband."

"We were divorced for over ten years. It hardly registers any more that we were even married. If it wasn't for Sasha…well, that's a long story. I take it Neve hasn't given you any details of the will." Jane brushed a lock of graying hair out of her eyes.

Rita shook her head. "I'm a little puzzled about why I'm here, actually. Neve told me on Christmas Eve she needed me here to do some work, so here I am…she *is* the boss."

"You know, of course, that my ex-husband used to be her accountant?"

"Yes." Rita wondered where the conversation was going.

"He was a drunk, a womanizer, and lots of other unsavory things. Until you came along, what I didn't know, and neither did Neve, was that he stole from her, too. I think that was the hardest part for Neve to understand. She gave him free reign of her financial dealings, and he almost ruined her, though God knows why he'd do that to someone he said he loved."

"I know. She went off the rails for a while. Of course you knew that, since she went to see you."

Jane looked surprised at the comment. "Yes, she did. You really are her friend, aren't you? I don't know anyone that she's ever confided in about personal stuff." Jane looked at Rita. "Not even Lorenzo." Her gaze found a large window, and she watched the waves roll onto the sandy beach. "I've known her for a long time. She used to be such a happy-go-lucky soul. Her father never understood her, but he loved her and that was enough. His death had a devastating effect on Neve." Jane took a sip of her drink. "Just before I left my husband, Neve found someone with whom I thought she might have found happiness—that was years ago—she told me it hadn't worked out."

"We don't discuss her personal life…well…I mean her romantic associations."

Jane gave her an intense look. "Do you disapprove of her lifestyle?"

Rita shook her head and smiled. "No. Not at all. It's just that, for the most part, she keeps the past in the past."

"Don't you think it's strange how we met at the airport and have so many things in common? Who would have thought it?"

"Who, indeed?" Rita looked at her watch. The doctor had been with Neve for a while and that made her think maybe it was something more than a virus. The more she thought that, the more her stomach churned. *My lunch might decide to reappear.*

"Here comes Sasha, and she looks calm enough. My daughter, for the record, isn't that good with sick people."

Rita didn't answer. Her opinion of Sasha varied from bitch to downright obnoxious. However, she waited anxiously to hear what the woman had to say about Neve.

Sasha slid into the chair she'd vacated earlier. "According to the doctor, my cousin has a bona-fide, twenty-four hour virus. He says that if she stays in bed for the rest of the day and takes the meds he's given her, she'll be feeling one hundred percent better by the morning. Of course, after he'd gone, Neve told me I was being overly cautious." She flashed a big smile. "We can go to the market now, if you're both ready."

Rita itched to get out of her seat and see Neve, but waited for Jane to say something that would distract Sasha. Not that she needed that to happen. She was a free agent and could change her mind about going with them if she chooses. *Yeah, right*. The younger woman probably would chastise her like a school girl and she have meekly would have followed like a sheep.

"Sasha, will you indulge me please? I'm going to have another piece of that key-lime pie. It was wonderful." Jane said.

Sasha frowned slightly before standing. "Sure, I'll have some too. Do you want anything, Rita?"

"No, actually, I was going to my room to freshen up before we go out. I'll be fifteen minutes. Is that okay?"

"Yep, we'll wait." Sasha nodded and walked away.

"Give Neve my love, Rita." Jane smiled as she waved Rita to go.

Rita grinned at the woman's subtle maneuver of her daughter. "I will." She walked away from the alfresco eating area toward the bungalows and Neve.

†

A few minutes later, she was outside Neve's bungalow tentatively knocking on the door. She didn't wait for a reply. Instead, she tried the door—locked. "Did I think this was going to be that easy?" She then walked around the bungalow to the beachfront and hoped that Sasha wouldn't see her. She looked in the direction she came from and figured it wasn't likely. Rita walked onto the patio that led to the lounge area of the bungalow and peered inside the window. There wasn't any sign of life. Certain that each bungalow had a similar layout, she moved to her right. She found a window with curtains that a light breeze was moving. A looked inside the room gave her a view of a familiar figure lying in the bed.

Rita debated the foolhardiness of what she was about to do, then did it anyway, "Neve, are you awake?"

There wasn't an immediate response, so she edged closer to the window. If Neve didn't reply this time, she'd go back to the others. "Neve, it's me, Rita. I just wanted to see if you are okay."

A grumpy, croaky voice replied, "I'm not okay, but I'll be better if you come in and talk to me rather than shouting at me from outside my bedroom window. It makes the damn headache worse."

Rita debated what to do next. Neve, remarkably fast for someone who was sick, opened the patio door. With an apologetic glance, she walked the few steps back to the patio door and followed Neve inside.

Neve climbed back in bed.

"Hey, look, I'm sorry. I was worried about you."

Neve moved the covers and stared at Rita. "Thank you, but it's a virus, nothing more. I'll be up and about for dinner."

"The doctor said tomorrow," Rita, countered.

Neve's expression looked annoyed. "Ah, and you think I believe a word they say. I know my own body."

Rita moved closer to the bed and sat down on the edge. "I'm sure you do. Your cousin is very protective of you."

Neve's face puckered in concentration. "Hmm, well, I hope she picked you up from the airport. I told her to. At least, I think I did."

"Don't worry about that…I'm here, aren't I? "Rita decided she wasn't going to let Sasha monopolize their conversation while they were alone. "Other than the virus, you look terrific."

"It's the tan. Wait until you get one…then you'll look the same"

Rita highly doubted that. "I'm here for business, not to work on a tan."

Neve pursed her lips. "You'll have time for a tan."

"What exactly do you want me to do for you here?" Rita smoothed a crease out of the coverlet on the bed.

Neve didn't reply immediately. "I wish you'd told me that you were going to be alone at Christmas."

Rita laughed self-consciously. "Why? What purpose would it have served?"

"You could have come here, or I could have come home to be with you. No one should be alone at Christmas."

Rita stared at Neve. *She means it…really means it.* "Thank you, that means a lot to me. Seriously, Neve, I wouldn't have been alone if it hadn't been for the snow. It was just too treacherous to travel back to Rochester. I had an open invitation to join Sue and the other girls at her place. I think Angel worked on them to invite me." Her chuckle stuck in her throat.

"No one should have to *work on* an invitation for you."

"Yeah, well, be that as it may, that's what happened. You still haven't told me why I'm here. I figure that it must have something to do with your uncle's second will." Rita half smiled. Her heart was beating rapidly as she caught Neve's intense gaze.

"It does. I want to discuss it with you when I'm not stuck in bed with a god awful headache pounding away each time I speak."

Rita couldn't help but laugh.

"What are you laughing at?"

"You…at least what you said. It appears that you and being sick in the same sentence don't exactly fit. You're such a grouch. Look, Jane gave me an excuse to be here, but I have to go, my fifteen minutes are almost up. We're going to a market in a village. Your cousin invited me, and I have the distinct feeling she'd hunt me down if I'm late or if she knows I'm here bar me from seeing you again."

Neve frowned. "Hey, there isn't a time limit, Rita. You can stay as long as you want. Then again, I'm not much company right now. If Sasha goes over the top, you have my permission to take her down a peg or two…but gently. The kid means well."

Rita pondered that and grinned. Sasha was obviously important to Neve much like a kid sister and appeared to have a good understanding of her faults. "If she annoys me, I'll treat her like I do Charlie. Do you want company later? I can order dinner in…if you're paying. Have you seen the price of room service?"

Neve laughed. "Please don't make me laugh. It makes the horrible headache worse."

Rita moved forward and touched Neve's hand lying outside the bed clothes. "I'm sorry."

Neve squeezed Rita's hand and gazed directly into her eyes. "I'm glad you came. I've missed having you around."

Rita was unsure if it was the sincerity or the way Neve looked at her that made Rita's skin grow warm and her cheeks hot. "I've missed you too."

Neve smiled. "When you're done with the market, why don't you all come over and keep me company for a while. You can take my key…it's on the dresser…and let yourself in. If I'm sleeping, wake me, and don't let Sash browbeat you if she doesn't agree." Neve's eyes began to droop.

"Okay, sounds like a plan to me." She took the key and looked back at Neve who was losing the battle to stay awake. "Sleep well, Neve, it's the best thing for a virus."

"Thanks, and you take care out there."

Rita watched Neve's eyes shut. "I will." She headed for the door, opened it, and locked it behind her.

Chapter Twenty-seven

Rita, Jane, and Sasha sat in Neve's patio after their shopping trip. Neve was glad to see them for she hated being in bed not feeling good.

"You bought me a shawl? Get out of here, Sash. Do you think I'm an ancient relic or something?" Neve screwed up her face as Sasha draped a multi-colored shawl around her shoulders.

"Well, you look as white as a sheet even with that tan. I figure it's perfect for you."

Jane nodded. "For once, I agree with Sash. You really should have stayed in bed, Neve."

Neve turned to Rita, who was giving her an amused, almost tolerant, look. "I suppose you agree, too?"

Rita smiled. "Sorry, yes, I agree. Sasha told me Lorenzo is due tomorrow. You want to be fit when he gets here, don't you?"

Neve was about to say something and narrowed her eyes at Rita only to clamp her mouth shut and switch her attention to her cousin. "Did you check his flight time, Sash?"

"Yep, close to midnight, so technically it will be New Year's Eve when he arrives. I've arranged transportation. I'll go and get him, unless you want that privilege."

Neve, perceiving the slight pleading in her cousin's tone smiled. "Sure, go for it. I'll be up waiting when you get back."

"Do you drive yourself around, Sasha, or take the hotel vehicles?"

Sasha looked at Rita and shook her head. "Nope, in the evening or when we go to special places the hotel transport doesn't go to, we have a driver, Elian. Well, actually, Elian's the driver for my father's lawyer, Christian Chamber."

Rita nodded. "Your father must have been well thought of here."

Jane snorted and Sasha remained quiet.

"His money paid for that respect."

"No, *your* money paid for it, Neve," Jane said.

There was a deathly silence for a few minutes until Neve picked up her fruity tropical drink and tasted it. "This tastes better with vodka in it." The others all looked at her with differing degrees of agreement or disapproval. "Hey, it does." Neve wrinkled her nose and drank another mouthful. "It helps to sooth my throat." Her headache was now just a minor irritation, and the doctor had told her, if she slept and holed herself up for twenty-four hours, she'd be okay.

"Your face will stay like that if you keep scowling." Rita touched the frown line on Neve's forehead.

Neve exaggerated another scowl and grinned as her eyes captured Rita. "Not a good look, then?" Neve concentrated solely on Rita who stared directly back at her. She saw that faint twist of lips that preceded Rita's beautiful smile. She instinctively reached out and touched a finger to the small line that ran along the side of Rita's mouth. "You should smile more often."

"You'd better keep scowling, then," Rita replied.

Neve saw Sasha and Jane over Rita's shoulder. They were watching the exchange with differing expressions. Sasha looked less than happy with her brow furrowed and a petulant curl to her lips. Jane had an indulgent, amused look on her face. *They're family. They'll get used to it.* Neve decided that having Rita this close, was her New Year's gift to herself.

Jane cleared her throat. "I don't usually drink alcohol but this tastes marvelous to me."

Sasha turned her gaze away from the window. "I agree with Neve. Look, there's still time for a little more sun worship around the pool before the sun moves. Anyone else game?"

Neve shook her head. "I like the idea of being poolside, but you can keep the sun worship."

Sasha snorted as she stood up. "Says the woman who has one of the best tans here. Incidentally, you still haven't told me your secret yet."

Neve chuckled. "I have great skin."

"Well, I'd like to sample a little sun myself, especially after the weather we just left behind. Besides, I think Neve and Rita need a little time to discuss business. Isn't that right, Rita?" Jane moved her chair and slowly rose of it.

Rita looked confused but automatically nodded.

Neve smiled. "Sounds perfect. I'll send Rita along to work on her tan as soon as we've finished talking business." She held up her hand. "Now, don't give me a hard time on this, Sash."

"Who, me? I'm not your keeper. Besides, I wouldn't dare. Come on, Mom, the sun awaits us."

Neve sank deeper in her chair, closed her eyes, and groaned softly.

"Are you okay? I can leave if you're tired."

Neve opened her eyelids and shook her head. "Just glad to be alone."

Rita's brow puckered. "You're not alone. I'm here, or did that small point pass you by and you really are delirious?"

The soft, amused tone made Neve smile inwardly. Then a thought struck her. *Rita doesn't know how important she is in my life. Maybe never will, because, sure as hell, I'm out of my depth with my feelings. How do I approach her without scaring her away*? "I'd never forget your presence. I meant from a family perspective…nice to have around, but *great* when they decide to leave."

Rita chuckled. "I hope you never say that kind of thing to Lorenzo."

Neve glanced at Rita and winked. "I never get tired of being with the people I love." She smiled at Rita and her heart jumped at the smile she received. "Right, you probably want to know why I brought you here."

"Yes, please. You were rather vague."

"You wonder why? From the first moment I met you, my life keeps taking different twists, and I haven't a clue where or what will happen next." Neve stood up and tilted her head slightly. The headache was almost gone. "Be right back." She headed for the bedroom and was back in a couple of minutes.

"Take a look at the portfolio, and you'll understand why I'm vague."

Rita took the folder and opened it. "Is that a bad thing?"

"What's inside the folder, you mean? Oh, no, I doubt I could have done so well with the profits generated from the circus." Neve retook her seat and drank a little more of her fruit punch.

"No, I didn't meant that…oh, it doesn't matter. Let me look at this. Give me a few minutes."

Neve glanced at the bent head of her friend. A tender smile played on her lips as she realized how much she'd missed just having Rita in the room with her. *Life is strange.* "Take your time. I need to make a phone call, okay?"

"Sure."

Neve stood up and allowed herself a moment to take in the woman's presence before she moved away. Rita took things seriously—one of the qualities Neve loved about her. *Hmm,* love. *There's that word again.*

In a recess, Neve pressed a number on the cell and waited a few moments until Christian Chambers came on the line. "Hi, Christian, it's Neve Garmancelli. My stateside accountant is here. Can you set up a meeting for her to see you and the resident accountants tomorrow? Be warned: she's very methodical."

Neve listened for a moment. "I suspect as early as possible would suit her. She'll want to visit the properties as well as look at the numbers in detail. She paused to listen to his response. "I know it's going to be tough," she continued. "Is it doable in a day?" Neve felt the headache begin again and frowned. "Okay, I've not been there anyway. I'll have the relevant parties check them out after the New Year. I take it everything is set up for the announcement on New Year's Day?"

Neve smiled, and then turned so she could see Rita, who was still poring over the papers. She watched as the tip of her friend's tongue poked out through her lips. Rita was concentrating—it was something she'd seen often, particularly in the working environment. "I'm sorry, I didn't catch that," she said.

"Right. Thank you, Christian. I'll see you tomorrow. Call me with a time within the next hour, please." She ended the call and simply stood in the recess, tenderly watching Rita. She was unable to think of a time she'd ever done that with regard to anyone else. *Maybe Lorenzo, in that first year after our parents died. I must be getting old and emotional.* Neve returned to the patio and sat down. "What do you think?"

"I think, as much as I have an aversion to the man, he knew what he was doing with canny investments."

Neve smiled as she heard Rita's reluctance to praise her uncle. "I think the same. I've arranged for you to meet the accountants currently handling the affairs and the lawyer, Christian Chambers. He is a good man and I think the accountants are okay, although they fleece the living daylights out of you for expenses." Neve shrugged. "It's business, right?"

Rita's head came up sharply. "We'll see about that."

Neve chuckled. "Exactly why I brought you here. I know I can trust you implicitly."

"You can." Rita's expression was determined.

Neve rested her chin on her hands as her elbows balanced on the table and saw the determined expression on Rita's face. "What did you mean earlier about w*hat isn't so bad*?"

Rita shrugged. "Not relevant. You do know that this means you're a very wealthy woman. You don't have to work or at least not as hard as you do now."

Neve persisted. "What *isn't so bad*, Rita? I want to know."

Rita gave Neve an uncompromising look. "You should have sent me this file as soon as you knew. How long have you been sitting on it…a month?"

Neve rocked back on her chair and shook her head, silently chuckling. "Yeah, about that."

"I wonder about you at times, Neve!"

Neve simply sat and watched every line of Rita's body and her facial expressions. It was just so right.

"What have I said? You're just staring."

Neve smiled openly. "I'm sorry." Chagrined, she pulled the file Rita was reading forward. "He did pretty well for a fraud, didn't he? Taking it makes *me* feel like a fraud in some ways."

Rita reached across the table and touched the hand placed on the papers. "You're not a fraud! End of discussion on that point. He was astute…I'll give him that. Did he leave anything to his immediate family, Sasha, in particular?"

Neve shook her head. "No, he left that in my hands saying that if I felt benevolent I could do something for Sash. I suspect he thought I wouldn't bother. I was never on the best of terms with Jane."

Rita snorted and gave Neve a serious glance. "That's not a problem then. What have you left yourself?"

There was a loud burst of laughter, as Neve almost toppled out of her chair. "You think I'll give it all away?"

Rita nodded. "You worked your butt off for years to have enough money to keep the circus going when most would have quit. Please, tell me I'm wrong."

"You're just too good to be true, you know that. Well, I have you in my life now, so it won't happen…right?"

"Darned right, it won't. You'll have at least enough left to pay the power bills."

They both laughed, and Neve reached out and linked Rita's hand with hers. "If there's ever a time when I want to murder someone, you just have to say one word."

Rita gave her questioning gaze. "What word is that?"

Neve narrowed her eyes for a moment. "Rita."

"Me? How does that equate? Not that I don't find it flattering."

Neve moved her head so that her chin rose in an autocratic fashion. "That's for me to know and others to solve…if they dare."

"Oh, you spoil sport. When exactly do I meet the lawyer and accountants? The earlier the better, I think."

"Tomorrow and that's just what I said…" The sound of her cell had Neve retrieve it with an apologetic expression.

Moments later, the call ended. "Good timing," Neve said. "Nine thirty at the lawyer's office okay with you?"

"Perfect."

Neve grinned. "My thoughts, exactly. Now, I think you need a break. Have a sun worshipping session with the family, and we'll talk tomorrow."

Rita stood up and gazed at Neve. "Do you want me to bring you a sandwich or something later?"

Neve shook her head. "Right now, I'm going back to bed and will probably sleep the rest of the day away." At the disappointment in Rita's face, she relented slightly. "How about on your way to bed you drop in and say goodnight…I'd like that."

Rita beamed a smile. "I'd like that, too."

Neve watched Rita stand, move toward the edge of the patio, and take the steps down to the beach. She felt that odd sensation in the pit of her stomach at Rita's leaving, which once again caused a lonely void. Rita took her by surprise when she turned suddenly and locked gazes with her. Neve's eyebrows rose as she asked, "Is there something wrong?"

"Nope. Just a question. Do you have an all-over tan?"

Neve chuckled. "Want me to show you?" Her sultry reply brought a tinge of red to Rita's cheeks.

Rita shook her head. "Maybe, but not today. Bye, Neve, enjoy your rest."

With a wave of her hand, Rita continued toward the beach.

Neve watched her go and long after she disappeared from her line of sight, Rita's steps were visible on the virgin sand. With a faint smile, Neve turned back toward the main bungalow deep in thought.

†

Rita made her way slowly toward the pool area and Neve's relatives. The whole day had taken on a surreal feeling from initially being angry at Neve. Her emotions had swung from concern, to amusement, and to caring. In between, there was a huge dollop of need. She knew, that from the first moment she'd met the woman love for her began to grow. Her mind had refused to allow her to feel those early emotions until recently. Now, it was as if a dam had broken sweeping her along in a torrent of feelings that she was unsure how to handle. Not the least of which was that it was a woman she'd fallen for.

With the bungalows behind her, the pool came into view and Rita switched her angle and walked toward a tree. Its branches overhung the water and underneath one was a log, which she assumed others had used for contemplating life. She checked for creepy crawlies before gingerly sitting on the log. She peered out at the expanse of turquoise water with differing boats bobbing in her view.

She shaded her eyes from the direct sunlight that bounced off the glassy surface of the water. "I need sunglasses. Perhaps I should have borrowed Neve's sunglasses. She won't need them for a while." The thought of Neve in sunglasses caused Rita's stomach to flip. *She is too darned sexy in them.* She envisioned a naked Neve with an all over tan wearing sunglasses. She squirmed as the thought made her face heat up. "Darn, I'm such a coward. I should have said *yes I want to see the tan.*" The thought of Neve undressing in front of her sent a tingle to just about every place possible—particularly between her legs. She wondered how she was going to get through this particular episode without giving her feelings away.

Her sight drifted to a lone figure on a windsurfer, the sail billowing in the gentle breeze. Right now, she wished she were that person and the only thing she needed to control were the elements. *Why can't life be simple? Why did I have to fall for Neve, of all people? She's way out of my league. I know she trusts me with her business finances but with her heart...I doubt it very much.* A barrage of feelings crowded her thoughts. *Especially once everyone knows how wealthy she is...she'll be able to choose from a whole bevy of beautiful women.* She shook her head. *Money seems to bring them out in droves. I hardly think a mousey creature like me is going to hold her attention other than as a friend. Can I deal with that?* The last question drifted in her head like the breeze, but she was unable to formulate a satisfactory answer. One of the things she was glad for—Sasha was Neve's cousin. The jealousy that erupted after the Christmas phone call now slid back to simmer until the next person came along to disrupt Rita's fantasy that Neve might actually consider her romantically.

Life is such a circus. She exhaled at the thought.

†

"Mom, what do you think about Neve and her accountant?" Sasha lathered more suntan lotion on her bronzed skin.

"What's to think? Rita's a nice woman, and, apparently, your cousin trusts her with her money. I must say that after your father, I'm surprised she trusts anyone."

Sasha gave her mother a long suffering look. "Not about her finances, Mom, I mean about her love life."

Jane rose from her prone position on the patio chaise lounge and frowned. "Does Neve have a love life? You haven't mentioned anyone special since you've been here. Is she playing the field as wildly as she did ten years ago? I still can't believe she allowed that young woman, whatever her name was, to slip through her fingers."

Sasha shook her head. *Mom doesn't have a clue.* "Forget I even mentioned it. Hey, look, here comes Rita. I wonder if she'll join me in a drink that isn't healthy." Sasha waved to Rita as she came up from the beach onto the wooden patio that engulfed the pool.

"She might be like me. I think Rita is a serious kind of woman." Jane said.

"Business all taken care of?" Sasha asked with a friendly smile.

"Yes. I'm meeting the lawyer and accountants tomorrow morning," Rita sat on the lounger next to Jane. "I'm not really dressed for the poolside."

"Who cares? Are you game for one of Neve's favorite poolside cocktails?" Sasha moved her lithe body to stand next to Rita's seat. "I'm buying."

"Well, I don't know. I don't drink much."

Sasha waved the negative vibe away and grinned. "You'll never know it has alcohol in it. I promise."

Rita smiled tentatively before nodding. "Sure, Neve told me to enjoy myself."

"I'm sure she did. I'll be right back." Sasha winked and headed off to the bar.

Chapter Twenty-eight

Rita moved gingerly toward Neve's bungalow. It was a little after ten, and she'd left Sasha partying with friends. Jane left shortly after dinner, around nine and Rita wanted to do the same but mindful that Sasha would be on her own, she stayed. She and Sasha talked briefly, about where they both lived, and Rita sensed the young woman had deep waters. Her current frivolous nature was the opposite of a staid banker image. In a way, she felt that Sasha might well be a younger version of Neve and that immediately gave a positive spin on her feelings for Sasha. The unexpected conversation shortly before Rita left, however, still rattled her…

"Neve isn't just your boss, is she?"

The candid question seemed to hang in the jasmine-scented air. Rita wasn't sure exactly what Sasha was asking.

"Technically, she is, though I work for Lorenzo too. He hired me initially, although it's a moot point since he works for Neve as well," Rita felt her eyes drawn in by Sasha's direct gaze.

"No, I meant informally. I know the technical stuff that you do for the circus. Garmancelli circus is Neve. I was thinking that on a personal front she's something a little more."

Rita felt her cheeks grow warm at the inference. She really didn't want to discuss her private life—or Neve's—with Sasha. "We're friends, if that's what you mean."

Sasha grinned and placed a hand on Rita's shoulder. "Oh, I know that…hell, everyone can see that."

"Are you implying something, Sasha? What can everyone see?"

"Neve is a very…hmm, let me see now…she's sexy and has that smoldering quality, if you know what I mean. And…she's not without means. I'd say she's a good catch and you've caught her in your net. Although, I'd say you're a novice in the fishing department and you're not sure if you should throw the catch back."

The whole conversation was becoming way too personal and unrealistic for Rita. She frowned and shook her head, more to herself than to Sasha. "Are you implying that Neve and I are romantically involved? I can assure you…"

Sasha grinned. "Look, I'm sorry, Rita. I like you, and Neve does…hell, my mom does, too, and she doesn't take to people easily. Whatever you and Neve have, I'd try to hold on to it. She needs someone like you in her life."

Against her better judgment to ask Sasha, any more questions but she couldn't help herself. "Someone like me? Why would you say that? She has you and it appears you like to run her life."

With a chuckle, Sasha's eyes moved over the people sitting on the patio after dinner. "I'm sorry if I'm over the top about Neve. She's my favorite female cousin. This new *getting to know her again* is wonderful. I guess I don't want to share it, in case it disappears again."

Rita felt slightly guilty at her jealousy over Sasha's involvement with Neve. "I think you'll find that this time she's going to be around for as long as you need her. You mentioned she needs someone like me…what exactly do you mean?"

Sasha grinned. "Oh, you know, dependable, honest, and ordinary, I guess." She nodded her head in the direction of the patio. "Look, there are some of my friends. Come on, we'll have a great night."

"You go ahead. I need to get some sleep. I have a business meeting in the morning, and I was up at the crack of dawn today."

"Oh yeah, bummer. I'll introduce you to the guys tomorrow. Sleep well, Rita." Sasha gave her a smile and wandered off toward her friends.

Now, as Rita was about to knock on Neve's bungalow door, she pondered Sasha's description of her. In retrospect, it was factual and she had thought pretty much the same thing only hours earlier. She scolded herself. "This is foolish! I need to do what Neve needs me to do and that's taking care of her financials, nothing more." That resolve taken, Rita gently knocked on the door. There was no answer.

Reaching inside her pocket, she withdrew Neve's key and slowly placed it in the lock, hoping if Neve were asleep, she wouldn't disturb her. A few moments later, with the moon her only source of light, she quietly made her way to the bedroom. Opening the door a bit, she peered inside. Sure enough, Neve was fast asleep.

What she should have done was go. What she did though, was enter the room and stand over Neve, tenderly watching her steady breathing. It's a good sign. It reminded her of the times she'd done the same for Charlie when he was sick, or simply to drink in the love she had for the boy. On a different level, that was exactly what she was doing right now, for Neve.

Rita didn't know how long she stood there—she suspected only moments—but it felt like time had stopped. She broke her trance like state, untwisted the sheet, and gently placed it around Neve. On impulse, she bent and kissed the smooth skin of Neve's forehead.

"Sleep well, Neve." She silently left the room. She let herself out of the bungalow, locked the door, and slid the key under it.

Rita's footsteps back to her bungalow were slow and despondent—life simply wasn't fair.

†

Breakfast was a rushed affair. Neve awoke the next morning to a much better state of health. Her throat was slightly sore, but the headache had completely disappeared. When she'd gone back to bed after Rita left in the afternoon, she'd slept for several hours and hadn't awakened until she heard the click of her bungalow's lock and groggily got out of bed. She thought Rita had arrived, but it appeared she'd been and gone. She hoped that one day soon, they'd get it right or she'd engineer it, which was probably more likely. She smiled when she picked up the phone to call Rita.

"Hello."

Neve smiled when she heard the sleepy answer. "I didn't wake you up did I?"

"Oh, Neve, what time is it? I overslept. I'm so sorry. I'll be ready to go as soon as I can."

"Slow down, you have enough time to get ready. Grab yourself a protein bar and I'll see you in the lobby in a half hour. Okay?"

"I'll be there, Neve, you can count on me."

"I know. See you then." Neve chuckled as she poured herself a glass of orange juice. "And you can count on me, Rita," she whispered.

†

The drive to Christian Chambers' office had been low-key. Rita was concerned about Neve's health but Neve convinced her that the worst was over.

"The only headache I'm going to get today is if the numbers don't add up," Neve said.

"I'll do my best to not let that happen."

Now, seated in the office with two representatives from the accounting firm that had represented her uncle, Neve spoke confidently. "Gentlemen, this is, Ms Rita Collins. She is my personal accountant. She has a right to see everything you have." She gave them a stern look. "Nothing is out of bounds."

Neve felt Rita's eyes on her, but she didn't look at her friend. Instead, she looked steadily at the men in the room to assure them she was serious.

Neve spoke again. "Christian, can you arrange for us to see the three plots in Montego Bay and the one in Port Antonio?"

The lawyer beamed. "Of course. Do you want me to come with you?"

Neve shook her head. "No, I can mange that myself." She smiled at him. "I'd love to use the services of Elian if that isn't an imposition."

"He'd be delighted, as am I, that we can be of service. I think he's quite enjoying being useful. He loves his country and is overjoyed to show people around." Christian grinned, his white teeth gleaming.

"Great." Neve turned her attention to Rita. "How about you and the other members of your *fraternity*," she winked, "go through the details and I'll meet you back here at twelve. I know a great place…well, Elian does, for lunch. Sound like a deal?"

Rita nodded. "Yes."

The other two men quickly stood and waited for Rita to do the same. The first gallantly held the door for her, as the second man followed his colleague. Neve stopped him. "Make sure she has something available to eat. We didn't have time for breakfast. Oh, and she'll want hot water too."

The man nodded though his eyebrows rose at her last remark.

When he'd left, Neve turned her attention to her lawyer.

"Why hot water?" he asked.

Neve chuckled and allowed a tender expression to cross her features. "Rita works better when she has a running supply of hot water for her herbal tea."

Christian nodded. "I can understand that. For me, it's coffee. Of course, we have the best in the world."

Neve smiled indulgently. "Of course."

"Well, in that case, as breakfast wasn't on the menu at the hotel this morning, would you care to join me? I promise the blue mountain coffee is perfect."

"Thank you. I'd appreciate it, and we can discuss tomorrow's events in detail." Neve settled further down in her chair, fully expecting to have a tray brought in. She was surprised when the lawyer stood and picked up his white linen jacket.

"Elian knows the perfect place for breakfast."

†

For lunch, Elian took them to a small bistro, hidden down a street that most tourists would never want to enter. The giant proportions of Elian and the fact that his sister-in-law owned the place made the women feel safe.

The eatery gave both Neve and Rita a feeling for the people of Jamaica. Numerous locals trailed in and out for anything from pastries and sandwiches to a full meal. The table where they sat overlooked the street. Neve knew that the current levels of crime, both petty and major, hung like a cloud over the country. Though Jamaica was a popular destination, it made actually participating in local activities as innocent as eating lunch difficult because of the crowds. Neve glanced around as a young woman, barely out of puberty, grinned at them and waved a couple of well-used menus in their faces. Her black, curly head of hair bobbed about as she giggled and asked if they wanted a drink.

"Rita, what would you like? I can make a recommendation." Neve quickly ran her shaded gaze over the menu.

"I'll have what you're having, unless it's…"

Neve looked up and caught Rita's gaze and she grinned. "I know…hard liquor. Why, Rita, anyone would think I was an alcoholic."

"I didn't mean to imply that. Okay, I'll have…"

Neve's hand dropped onto Rita's as she fiddled with the menu.

"We'll both have a Sorrel, no rum," Neve said.

The young girl giggled some more and wandered back to the counter.

Rita gave Neve a sharp look and asked, "Sorrel? I've never heard of it."

Neve smiled and tapped her nose with her finger. "According to Elian, it's one of the best drinks at this time of year. Apparently, it's a delicious herbal drink with awesome medicinal values and also is an excellent thirst-quencher that's a highly nutritious natural source of vitamin C."

Unable to stop herself, Rita laughed and rocked back on her wicker chair. "Herbal and medicinal…what did that doctor give you yesterday, a medical book?"

"Oh, how cutting." Neve winked at Rita. "Seriously, it is and I want a clear head for our tour this afternoon. What's the verdict on my affairs here in Jamaica?"

Rita narrowed her eyes. "I wouldn't know. Are you having any affairs here?"

Neve gave a startled expression before she saw Rita's eyes glowing. "Oh, I'm working on it."

Rita chuckled softly and glanced at the menu. "I'm stuffed after the breakfast they gave me. Are they always so generous?"

"What did you have? I had, let me see now…cornmeal porridge, sourdough bread with butter…oh, and a couple of eggs. The coffee was superb." Neve smacked her lips as she mentally savored the taste of the strong coffee beans used in the drink.

"And you're still hungry?"

Neve grinned. "What did you have?"

"Okay, I had sweet potato pudding, a fried egg sandwich, and bush tea."

Neve rested her chin on her hand. "Bush tea?"

"Yeah, herbal tea…I'm going to buy some to take home."

"Oh, I can probably swing a case of the stuff in your direction if you're nice to me." Neve saw the girl approaching, precariously carrying their drinks on a tiny tray.

"I'm always nice to you!" Rita exclaimed. "Oh, that looks good."

Neve chuckled as she checked out the bright red concoction filled to the brim with ice. "It is." Her dark gaze swung to the girl. "Thanks, can you give us a few minutes, and then we'll order."

"Cook 'n curry," the girl answered and disappeared.

"Cook and curry?"

Neve raised her hands. "Search me. Incidentally, speaking of odd things…Christian was a little more informative about my uncle and his dealings here over breakfast."

"Really, what did he say?" Rita asked.

"Apparently, he came here on vacation twenty years ago and bought up a small block of land on the west coast. Christian was the lawyer he used to complete the deal, and the business relationship remained strong over the years. From the little Christian knows, my uncle came to stay on the Island for two weeks every year and usually purchased some land. He stayed in a seedy hotel in the middle of town."

Rita looked genuinely surprised. "He didn't spend the money on himself? Doesn't add up. He made you go through all that pain and worry and not spend the actual ill-gotten gains on himself."

Neve turned her head slightly, considering the comment. "I've wondered that, too. I asked Christian what he thought of Silvestre. He said he was a loner, stingy when he spent money on anything other than land. When he bought the hotel complex from the owner who was virtually bankrupt, he got it for a fraction of its real worth." Neve blew out a breath. "Once he owed the hotel, he conceded to stay in a small bungalow tucked away from the main visitor access. Christian admired his business acumen, but I have a feeling he didn't actually like my uncle, although he was too polite to say that. I guess I'll never really know the truth behind why he did what he did or what type of person he really was. He certainly wasn't the man I thought him to be."

"From the information I've seen so far, your affairs are doing very well. Let's forget what a devious person he was and accept that he left you a wonderful portfolio. I've arranged to spend the day with your accountants tomorrow going over the hotel complex in more detail. It is, after all, the largest asset of value on the list."

Neve grimaced then pouted. "It's New Year's Eve. I thought we could spend the day together or at least with the family."

Rita shook her head. "Neve, you brought me here to work. If I don't do this, the accountants here won't be back in the office for another three days."

"That's not a problem." The point considerably cheered Neve.

"Neve!"

"Rita, let's order and we can discuss this over lunch." Neve spied the server eyeing them again.

"I'll have the curried shrimp," said Rita.

"Hmm, sounds interesting. Escovitch fish for me. I hope they have red snapper." Neve waved toward the girl who came immediately and took their order with a smile.

The lunch ambled on for a couple of pleasant hours. At two o'clock, Neve stretched in her chair when she saw Elian give her a quick wave. "Unfortunately, we have to go. Although, what I'm going to show you will be almost as good as the food."

Rita laughed softly. “You know we didn’t discuss a darned thing about business, Neve. Are you taking this seriously…me seriously…as to why I’m here?”

Neve moved tilted her head slightly to one side. “I take everything you say to me seriously, Rita,” she shrugged, “except that part when you mentioned that you took Charlie to a circus other than ours.”

“I was kind of working by taking stock of the competition.” Rita glanced toward the young woman who had been cheerfully serving them through lunch.

“Hmm, I’m supposed to believe that? Incidentally, you never mentioned which circus you took Charlie to.” Neve’s attention turned to the girl who brought the bill. She pulled out several notes, paid the bill, and placed a generous tip on the table. “Let’s go or the family will think we’ve deserted them if we’re not back for dinner.” Neve chuckled as she heard Rita groan. “Hey, sun, sea, food, fun, and romance…it’s a vacation, Rita.”

“For you, perhaps.” Rita followed Neve toward the large man waiting by the limousine.

Once inside the car, Neve did become business-like and explained the packages of land she and Rita were going to see. She explained that on paper, they were spectacular investments…in the flesh, so to speak, they were even better.

†

Montego Bay was beautiful and Neve heard Rita suck in her breath at the sights. “This is where the rich and famous play from time to time, which is why there are so many modern and expensive-looking properties along the shoreline. I inherited two along this bay and one further up the mountainside. There’s the house, of course, but we haven’t time to visit that properly today.”

An hour later, Rita was still in awe at the beautiful plots. “Are you going to keep them?”

"Maybe. If they were yours, which would you chose if you had to?"

Rita shook her head. "I love the two by the sea…but this one…" she waved her hand at the half acre of land surrounded by trees, "…there are fabulous views of the bay, and you're close, but not too close, to the town. I like this one."

"Hmm, I figured you for one of the beachfront properties." Neve winked. "Okay, let's move. We have one more to see at Port Antonio, and it's on the way back to the hotel."

It was around six when they arrived at a piece of land that, at one time, had been part of a much larger property. Again, a tree line provided privacy, and there was a pond, or mini-lake, some might say, in the three-acre plot.

"I'd build a house just there." Neve moved behind Rita and pointed to a spot over her shoulder.

"I think you'd be right. This is marvelous. It has everything and I loved the quaint village we came through. I could live here." Rita turned suddenly.

Neve's arms casually went around Rita's shoulders to prevent them from colliding as they faced each other. She smiled slightly, feeling once again drawn to Rita—as she had for some time. *It would be so easy to kiss her like I did at the wedding reception, but...* There were always *buts* and she was getting tired of them. "Yes, I think so, too, and I'm glad you do. The gardens are done and all it needs is a home."

Rita moistened her lips with the tip of her tongue. "You sound wistful. Are you thinking of actually building here?"

Neve's body reacted to Rita's wet lips. Moving away was the only thing that prevented her from soundly kissing her. She began walking over to a small path. "Come on, let me show you something."

Rita ambled along beside Neve as they made their way down a small incline that led out from the trees down to the beach. To the left was a tiny boat ramp and to the right a small wooden hut that had seen better days but could be rejuvenated as a changing room.

"Along this side of the property the beach is part of the deal. It runs for about three hundred yards." Neve looked out toward the calm sea. When Rita didn't say anything, Neve looked around and saw her seated on the side of the boat ramp with her eyes taking in everything around her. Neve sat next to her. "Hard to take in, huh?"

Rita nodded, and then turned away from the panorama to look at Neve. "You know, I was just sitting here thinking that as much of a scum ball your uncle was, he did right by you in the end."

Neve considered the words. "He never needed to steal from me. He could have asked and I'd have given it to him. He was family…family do not betray family…it's a big thing in my book. Having so few relatives, the ones I do have, mean more to me in the big picture." Neve felt Rita reach across the few inches between them and take her hand, squeezing it gently.

"I know. Did he leave any explanation why he did what he did to you for all those years?"

"He left a letter, but it was vague. I think he thought he was doing the right thing by," Neve's hand waved over the general area, "leaving me this opportunity."

Rita gave Neve a sympathetic look. "Perhaps you have to look at it as a second chance for all of the family."

Neve breathed in deeply before she nodded. "I guess we'd better go."

Rita asked, "Which site does Sasha like best?"

Neve frowned slightly. "Wouldn't know. She hasn't seen any of them. In fact, they don't know about the plots, houses, or the hotel."

Rita's mouth gaped. "You haven't told them? What about Lorenzo?"

Neve shook her head. "I wanted to check everything out first. Hell, I could have ended up with tax problems and all kinds of minefields. As it turned out, I didn't."

"You are going to tell them, I presume?"

Neve laughed. “Yeah. You think I could keep this secret from Lorenzo?”

Rita laughed too. “Nope. At least you didn’t keep it secret from me.”

Neve shrugged and took her hand. “Let’s go, you must be famished.”

The amused expression Neve received as a reply had them both laughing as they headed back toward the car.

Chapter Twenty-nine

Rita left Neve and her family shortly after dinner, explaining she wanted a clear head for her meeting the next day.

Neve reluctantly capitulated on the condition that Rita didn't work all day.

Rita readily agreed and wished the three women good night.

Neve with an unfathomable expression watched her leave.

"I'm going to check out the flights to make sure they're on time. Elian is coming by in about an hour to take me to the airport. I'll see you both later." Sash stood up and speedily caught up with Rita as they turned a bend toward the bungalow area.

After they left, Jane smiled at her niece. "You like her, don't you?"

Neve's expression remained bland as she smiled at the older woman. "I suppose it would be useless of me to say something obscure at this point?" At Jane's nod, Neve smiled slightly. "Yes. Very much. I'd call her a breath of fresh air in the stagnant vacuum that used to be my life."

Jane chuckled. "Does she know you feel that way?"

"Nope, and not likely to…I don't want to jeopardize our friendship." Neve gazed intently at Jane.

"Telling someone who is close to you that you love them won't change that, Neve. It could help."

Taken by surprise at the observation, Neve bit the inside of her cheek and wished she hadn't—it hurt. Finally, she responded, "No, I'm not even sure she would think of me that way. We're good friends and I'm pretty sure that's all there is on her part."

"How will you know that for sure if you never take the first step?" Jane asked.

Neve pulled at her lower lip in concentration. "It's complicated."

Jane nodded. "Yes, of course it is. Has it anything to do with that girl you used to live with years ago?"

Neve gave Jane a puzzled look before she shook her head. "Jennifer? No."

"Well, that was a very positive *no*. What then? You're single. I assume she is, too. You both like each other. I can't see a problem."

Neve blew out a frustrated breath. "I don't know that she's interested in me in a romantic way. She's not a lesbian. Though, I think she could be on the fence. I don't want to rush her if she's not ready. There's the possibility that she might never be ready for that kind of relationship."

Jane placed a hand on Neve's shoulder and smiled compassionately. "Perhaps she needs help in finding out. I think you're the one to help her. To find true happiness, you have to take risks sometimes."

There were a few moments of complete silence between them. "Thank you, Jane."

The older woman smiled. "You're welcome. Now, Rita was telling me about a drink you both had at lunch. Care to join me?"

"A Sorrel. Sure. I'll order." Neve stood up and headed for the bar. She suddenly felt a lot lighter and more in control after her brief heart-to-heart with Jane. *Sometimes you do have to risk it all for happiness.*

"That looks good. Do you mind if I ask what it is?"

Neve glanced at the woman at her side as she placed the two drinks on a tray. The bar was very busy, and the servers were hustling between tables. Neve found it quicker to go directly to the bar than to wait for someone to bring them over. "Sorrel, with or without the rum…both are equally as nice for differing reasons."

"Good recommendation, I'll try one. I'm Susan Ashby. You don't know me, but I know your cousin, Sasha. I've seen you around the pool with her."

Neve smiled slightly. "Right, hi, Susan. Neve Garmancelli," She nodded at the tray. "You'll enjoy the drink." Her eyes took in the wheat colored hair, cut into the shape of the woman's angular features. She had small bud like lips, a perfectly proportioned nose, and vivid green eyes. Neve surmised she was probably around the same age as Sasha—in her mid- to late twenties.

"Thanks. Look, I was wondering if you might want to join me for a drink."

Neve almost dropped the tray she was holding at the forthright invitation. *Sash is playing matchmaker again.* "It's not a good time right now."

Neve watched as the woman gave a shrug, her smile drooping slightly at the rejection. "I'm leaving in a couple of days. Will you be going to the festival on the harbor tomorrow night?"

"Isn't everyone?" Neve replied.

Susan smiled slightly, giving her an elfin appearance. "Maybe we can catch up there or later, if you have company for the event."

Neve smiled slightly and not wanting to be a total heel shrugged. "Maybe." Then she looked pointedly at the drinks and walked back to her aunt.

Jane grinned as Neve sat down beside her. "I was going to send out a search party for you until I saw you talking. She's a very pretty girl. Isn't she someone I've seen with Sash?"

Neve rolled her eyes at the comment and took a large swallow of the aromatic drink that had a liberal measure of rum. She mellowed slightly. "Apparently so. I can't say I've noticed her before, but then Sasha has made so many friends here. I think she likes it."

Jane chuckled as she sipped her drink before she nodded. "I know. I have the distinct feeling if she could wangle a bank job here, she'd stay."

Neve's expression remained unmoved as she drank some more of her drink. "Would you mind if she did?"

"In one way, sure. She'll be a long way from home. In another way, no. I think it's time she spread her wings, even if it's just to move out of the house." Jane laughed as she, too, drank some more of the drink. "This is rather good. I'm glad Rita mentioned it."

"What about you? I know you said you loved living the quiet life in Ridgeway, but, if Sasha came here or any other place in the world would you go, too?"

Jane pursed her lips. "I love Ridgeway. It gave me a second chance at happiness. I have friends, a job I enjoy…that's where I want to be. Wherever Sasha goes, I can visit."

"I feel that way about the circus. But I'm aware that it doesn't appeal to everyone on a permanent basis."

Jane smiled. "Wherever you are, the person who loves you will follow. It's a journey of the heart."

Neve let out a short laugh. "That's rather poetic, Jane."

"Hey, just because Sasha thinks I'm past the romantic stage, doesn't mean I don't dream there is still someone out there for me."

They both laughed and enjoyed the rest of their drink. An hour later, Jane returned to her room—she'd see Lorenzo in the morning.

Neve watched her go and ordered another drink. It was refreshing and allowed her mind to traverse the obstacles she placed in front of her when it came to Rita and a romantic relationship. *I should just ask her out on a date and see what reaction I get.* The more she thought of it, the more it made sense. The scraping of the chair next to her that Jane had vacated had her glancing up.

"Hi, again. You were all alone, so I figured maybe you'd have time for that drink."

Neve was about to decline but nodded instead. "Sure, I've just ordered. Why not join me."

Susan Ashby grinned. "Thank you. Sasha tells me your brother is arriving this evening."

"Yes, Sasha wanted to be the first to greet him off the plane. It's been a while since they were together." At that moment, the waiter arrived with Neve's drink. "What would you like, Susan?"

"The house cocktail special, please." Susan smiled at the waiter, who grinned broadly and left.

Neve ran a finger around the rim of her drink. She decided that having pretty company was better than spending the next hour alone waiting for Sash and Lorenzo to arrive. After all, she wasn't cheating on Rita as she had in Rochester with Annie. That had been a mistake, but it didn't seem to bother Rita. It was just another reason she felt that Rita wasn't interested in her that way. *How the hell can I be cheating anyway? We aren't even a couple.* She rolled her eyes as she mused over her thoughts.

"You look pensive, Neve, and that's not allowed on vacation."

"It isn't? I'll have to remember that. Where do you go back to in a couple of days, Susan?" Neve sipped her drink while watching the woman.

"St. George, Alabama. I'm a high school English teacher. What about you?"

Neve considered the question carefully. "Actually, no place in particular is home. I'm what some call a free spirit."

Susan laughed and it made her nose twitch slightly, which was adorable. Under any other circumstance, she would have given the woman her undivided attention—not anymore. Rita had snared her heart and it wasn't attempting to break free, no matter what Rita thought in the end.

"You can't be a homeless person. This place costs a fortune. The only reason I could afford to be here was a special offer they had about twelve months ago. I booked immediately." Her eyes cast around the patio where they sat with a wonderful view of the sea, palm trees, and golden sands. "Don't you think it's romantic?"

Neve had thought so herself on several occasions and had hoped that Rita might just relax from her accountant mode to see what was on offer. *Hopefully, tomorrow evening I'll persuade her*. "Yes, I do." Neve niftily changed the subject as Susan's drink arrived. "What do you think of the hotel and the complex?"

"Oh, the only complaint I have is that I can't afford to stay here longer. Although, I've met people in a similar position to mine and, I hope we'll keep in touch in the future."

The words rang sincerely in Neve's ears. "What date do you go back to your teaching job?"

Susan smiled as she took a sip from her drink. "A week from today. If I'd had the cash at the time, I'd have booked a three-week stay. When do you go back to being that free spirit and all?"

Neve chuckled softly—Susan was nice. "All depends, but tentatively in two months time."

"That sounds mysterious. Depends on what, or is that a no-no question?"

"What time do you leave New Year's Day?" Neve asked.

Susan pulled a face. "I have an early flight around three in the morning, which means the festivities have to be curtailed early for me. I guess that's one of the reasons for the trip being so cheap. Sasha has already offered me the use of her shower and bungalow after mid-day tomorrow. Your cousin is a cool person."

"Yes, she is. I take it you've met her mom?" Neve's mind working overtime on what Susan had said.

"Jane? Sure. She's wonderful, just like my mom back home,"

"Yeah, just like mom." Neve's thoughts traveled to the few vague memories of her own mother. *Mom would have wanted me to be happy.*

"You don't really want me here, do you? There's someone else, isn't there?" Susan asked.

Neve quickly turned her gaze to the woman. She normally would have denied the question but Susan was right on the button. "You're good company. However, there is someone in my life I'd love to be with at this moment."

"I figured. Sasha said you were a free agent. I think otherwise. You've found someone important and that's rather wonderful. You can always tell, you know." Susan placed the half empty glass on the table and stood up.

"You haven't finished your drink." Neve was perplexed at the way the conversation turned.

"Do you still want my company?"

"Yes, I do. Sash and my brother are due anytime. Please stay, Susan."

Susan sat down and frowned. "Okay. I guess I just missed the boat on romance here, didn't I."

"With me? Yes," Neve replied. "One day soon you'll find the right person. I guarantee it."

Susan drained her drink and shrugged. "I've been telling myself that ever since I knew I was gay. I guess I'm one of those people who will always miss the boat."

"Hey, you haven't reached thirty yet. Trust me, Susan. I'm way past that sell-by date and I've fallen hard. It's difficult to comprehend: impossible yet euphoric at the same time. Don't give up on love. It comes in unique packages and at incredibly normal times." Neve spoke from the heart and admitted soul deep that she loved Rita—it was a quiet revelation, rather than a startling one.

"I wanted to have a one-night stand with you, Neve, but it's taken me almost two weeks to summon up the courage to ask you for a drink. I'm glad it did because it would have been a cheap fix for both of us."

Neve frowned slightly. "Yes, it would." She wondered if she'd have had the strength to deny a purely physical relationship with Susan. *Thankfully, I never needed to find out.*

Susan leaned over and kissed Neve on the cheek. "I hope you'll both be very happy."

Embarrassed at the show of affection, Neve felt her cheeks grow warmer. "Me too." Then she stumbled out of her chair as a familiar voice spoke behind her.

"I knew it…you're worse than me, Sis."

Unable to hide her elation, Neve grinned widely as she saw her brother. In seconds, she was at his side, where he gave her a bear hug and a kiss on the cheek. "I'll never be worse than you, you old reprobate." She felt his chest reverberate as he laughed.

"Reprobate, indeed. Not anymore. I have a surprise for you, Sis. Meet my wife." He moved with Neve still close to his side and looked directly at the two women opposite them. "Sally Garmancelli, meet your new sister-in-law, Neve."

Neve blew out a shocked breath.

"Hi, Neve." Sally gave Neve a half smile.

The sounds seemed to fade around them as Neve gave her new sister-in-law an intense look. Then she smiled, nodded her head and extracting herself from Lorenzo, moved the short distance between them and hugged Sally. "Welcome to the Garmancelli family, Sally."

The music, laughter and talking all came back suddenly as they sat down. "Why did you keep it a secret? I would have been happy to stop everything to see you married."

Lorenzo smiled, and the lines at the corner of his eyes crinkled. He pulled Sally close to his side and winked. "Because we had a quick chapel ceremony in Vegas. Would you believe this wench followed me and proposed? What was I to do? A gallant gentleman never turns a lady down. We've been married for over a month. I'm sorry, Sis."

Neve shook her head in disbelief. "No problem. We all have secrets. This one deserves a celebration." She waved over the waiter and ordered champagne.

"Hey, look, I'd better go and leave you to your celebration."

Neve looked at an awkward Susan Ashby and grinned. "Absolutely not, Susan. Right, I want to know everything." She winked at Sally. "You didn't dress up as Elvis, did you?"

They all burst out laughing as Lorenzo narrowed his eyes at his sister.

†

Two exhilarating and exhausting hours later, most headed for their respective bungalows, except Susan and Sasha, who decided to have another drink and disappeared into the bar.

"You know, there was only one thing missing here tonight, Sis." Lorenzo walked beside his sister with his arm around his sleepy wife.

Neve arched an eyebrow in his direction as the moonlight illuminated her face. "What's that?"

Lorenzo gave her a half smile. "Someone who makes you happy. That girl, Susan, seems like a nice person and she's interested in you, big time."

"She is nice, but not my type."

Lorenzo chuckled softly. He moved his arm to snuggle closer to Sally, who murmured something unintelligible as she turned her head into his shoulder.

"Do you have a type? I've often wondered."

Neve shrugged as they neared her bungalow. "You'd be surprised. I'm glad you're here, both of you. Sleep well." Neve hugged Lorenzo then Sally and opened her door.

“Goodnight, or should I say *morning*? Will you be up for breakfast?” Lorenzo asked.

Neve smiled. “Probably. I doubt you two will. Goodnight.”

†

Inside her bungalow, Neve kicked off her shoes and wandered to the patio. Neve leaned on the rails and took in the view of the moon’s reflection shimmering on the water. Her gaze drifted to Rita’s bungalow and she smiled. Into the slight warm breeze, she whispered, “Yeah, you’d be surprised who my type is.” She sighed and headed for bed.

Chapter Thirty

Satisfied she had all the information necessary, Rita leaned back on the chair in the accountants' office. In addition to the printouts, they also had given her an external drive with additional information. Now, she could keep her promise and meet with Neve for a late lunch. Yesterday had been special, but she wondered how long that would last. Neve was now independently wealthy and could employ someone more capable to organize her financial life. Her experience didn't cover some of the tax complexities Neve had inherited. Rita glanced up when she heard a knock on the door of the office she was using.

Carl Ryder, an associate partner of the firm, entered the room. "Ms. Collins, do you need anything else?"

"No thank you, Carl, I'm good. Could you arrange a taxi so I can go back to the hotel?"

"That won't be necessary since Ms. Garmancelli has already taken care of that. The car that brought you is waiting for you to leave."

Rita frowned. "The car has been here all morning?" *What a waste of money. I'll have to have words with Neve.* She stood up, picked up her laptop, and slung her satchel over her shoulder.

"Yes, she wanted you to have transportation whenever you needed it. Will you be back after the vacation break?" Carl asked. He was a little younger than she was, but highly competent. He could, she suspected, run rings around her in certain instances.

"I'll be going back to the States tomorrow, I expect. You're doing a fine job for Ms. Garmancelli. It was a pleasure to meet you and your associates, Carl." Rita smiled and held out a hand.

The young man took it. "Thank you, Ms. Collins. If you require anything else, please don't hesitate to contact me."

Rita nodded. "Goodbye and happy New Year, Carl."

"Happy New Year's to you, too, Ms. Collins."

Rita left the premises and snorted softy as the car, which had been at her disposal this morning outside the hotel, immediately crawled up to the curbside and the driver rushed out to open the door for her. "Neve, what will I do with you and your generosity?" With a smile, she climbed into the back seat and enjoyed the ride back to the hotel through the colorful streets and exotic palms. When she left for the accountants at eight that morning, she hadn't seen anyone she knew assuming that they were all in bed.

She took her eyes off the passing scenery and glanced at the small face of the watch Charlie gave her. She smiled softly. In monetary terms, it was inexpensive, but, in emotional terms, it was like receiving a Rolex. Her smile grew as she recalled his excitement on Christmas Eve and disappointment that she wasn't going to be there when he opened his presents. Over the internet, on webcam, they opened each other's present on Christmas Eve. She remembered swiping her hand across her eyes when she opened Charlie's gift and saw the stainless steel banded watch. *Charlie, thank you it was just what I needed.* Next year for sure they would be together next Christmas.

It was twelve-thirty, and she wondered what Neve was doing—what she'd been doing in Jamaica for the past month. One thing for sure, she looked good. The virus Neve had worried her but it seemed to have miraculously disappeared in twenty-four hours just as the doctor indicated it would. Neve was now wealthy and in a different social status than she was. There was no point in thinking that she might have a chance for anything more than friendship. Romance with Neve was nothing more than a dream not realized. The brief kiss they shared at the wedding had been just that—brief. At least they were friends and she could cope with that—she had no choice.

Rita took a deep breath and turned back to the scenes outside the car window. As they were passing by a street filled with shops, she saw something out of the corner of her eye. "Driver, do you think you could go back? I need to take a look in the dress shop back there."

The cheerful driver gave her a toothy grin and turned the car around "Whatever you need, Môn."

†

Sasha was sitting with Neve on the beach outside Neve's Bungalow. "Susan thinks you're hot. You could do worse, Neve."

Neve gave her cousin a hard stare before she let out a low growl. "Susan is a nice woman and deserves more. She isn't a sack of goods sold to the highest bidder, Sash. We might be lesbians, but we have the same feelings you heterosexuals do and as much pride in not wanting to be second best."

Sasha held up her hands. "I'm sorry. Look, you won't make a move on your accountant friend, so you might as well enjoy female company. All I meant was you could be with someone who actually feels the same way."

"Right, so you think that Rita is indifferent to me?" Neve felt her irritation growing at her younger cousin's comments.

"Me, what do I know? You seem to think that way. My mom said you were chicken." Sasha moved slightly to shade her face from the sun.

"You're mother said what?" Neve exclaimed angrily. She stood up suddenly causing the sand to stir and cover Sasha's legs.

Sasha scowled. "Did you have to do that, Neve?"

A male voice spoke. "What have you been doing, Neve, to upset our cousin? I leave you for a few hours and here you are in trouble again."

Neve felt her anger dissipate immediately as she heard her brother's voice. Her scowl turning into a smile. "Nothing that needs to concern you, Lorenzo. Where's Sally?"

Lorenzo shrugged. "She woke up this morning and was sick to her stomach. I told her to take it easy. It's probably all the excitement, champagne, and the traveling. We aren't having lunch for another hour or so, right?"

"When she's ready, we'll have lunch." Neve turned her attention to Sasha, who was meticulously picking each grain of sand from her legs. "Where's your mother? I want a word with her."

Sasha didn't look up. "She went shopping for something to wear tonight."

"Probably just as well. Lorenzo, how about a drink at the bar before lunch, assuming that's still permitted now that you're a married man?"

Lorenzo chuckled. "I thought you'd never ask. Are you coming too, Sash?"

Sasha gave a tentative smile then looked at Neve. "Later. Lunch is around two, then?"

"Yeah, two is good. See you later, Sasha." Lorenzo turned to his sister. "Okay, let's go, Sis. We have some catching up to do."

Neve grinned and hooked her arm through his as they headed toward the bar, "Yes, we do."

Ten minutes later, they settled into two enormous wicker chairs with a glass table between them that held two ice-cold local beers. Neve grinned at her brother.

Lorenzo tilted his head slightly. "Out with it. You're dying to tell me something."

Neve laughed as she twirled her glass in her hand before taking a drink. "I was just thinking about my little brother all grown up and married."

Lorenzo rolled his eyes. "Yeah, right, I'm thirty-nine. It was about time."

His softly spoken words accompanied a light in his eyes. Neve couldn't recall him ever looking so happy. "Yeah, and I'm very happy for you. She's a nice girl."

"Yes, she is. In that respect, we'll have a toast to my wife." He raised his glass and Neve followed. "To Sally."

Neve glanced around the hotel lobby noting that it was relatively quiet. She assumed that most of the hotel's guests were probably out on the beach, in the ocean or poolside. It was another glorious day.

"You and Sasha appeared to be having an altercation. Anything serious?"

Neve let a brief smile curve her lips. "No, nothing serious. She's been matchmaking,"

Lorenzo reached across the small divide of the table and placed a hand on Neve's hand. "She doesn't mean to interfere. You know she's always looked up to you...worshipped you, in fact. I can remember a time when there was this chubby five year old girl, who annoyed the living daylights out of you by following you everywhere."

Neve nodded as the memory of those times engulfed her. Then she chuckled. "Yeah. She scared the hell out of me when she tried to climb up the ladder to the high trapeze. I'll never forget the horror on Jane's face."

"Yep, a brave kid. I think she's still the same inside or she'd never have tried matchmaking for you. Incidentally, that woman last night...what was her name, now?"

"Susan," Neve supplied.

"Yeah. She did look interested and she appeared nice." Lorenzo took a long drink from his glass.

Neve shook her head. "As I told Sasha, I'm not interested. Besides, she leaves early New Year's Day. I've given up one-night stands." The one she'd had with Annie was her last. She turned over a new leaf in that respect. She needed to keep it especially if she had any chance of courting Rita.

Lorenzo was silent for a short time then smiled. "I'm glad. You deserve more. Incidentally, how can you afford to put us all up in these swanky bungalows? Sasha told me last night you'd booked a whole row. Did Silvestre finally do the right thing by you and leave you something worthwhile?"

Neve scratched the side of her nose and smiled. "Rita said almost the same thing. Yes, he did the right thing. You'll know more tonight, I promise."

Lorenzo smiled widely. "Rita, how is she? How did the trip to small town living go? The last I heard you were going to her sister's wedding."

Neve sucked in a slow, inaudible breath. "Rita's here, Lorenzo. Didn't Sasha tell you?"

Lorenzo began to glance around. "No, she didn't. Where was she last night?"

Neve laughed. "Working, at least she is today and needed an early night. I'm hoping she'll join us for lunch. She promised, although if she's engrossed, who knows."

"Oh, I can't believe it, Neve. This beautiful place and you have Rita working. It's New Year's Eve…shame on you."

His mild chastisement made Neve shake her head vigorously. "Trust me, I asked her to take the day off, but she wanted to ensure that the accountants who are looking after Silvestre's affairs are on the up-and-up." She grinned. "Very tenacious is our Rita."

Lorenzo stared at his sister.

"Now you're staring at me as if you want to say something and aren't sure you should. Spill it."

Neve had a quirky smile as she took a drink from her glass. "Oh, it's nothing. I'm glad she's here."

"I'm glad, too."

Neve's glance took in the reception desk and she felt herself smiling. "Well, look who just walked into the lobby."

Lorenzo turned to stare in the direction Neve pointed, stood, and in a few short strides was behind Rita.

Neve watched in fascination as her brother tapped on Rita's shoulder before she turned in surprise. Her expression changed to delight when she saw who it was. They hugged, and Rita kissed him on the cheek.

Seconds later, Rita smiled at Neve when their eyes met. Neve moved out of her chair and walked over to them. "Hey, did you have a good day?"

Rita nodded. "It just got better."

Neve's eyes narrowed slightly at the answer before smiling. "Here, let me take some of those bags for you."

Rita laughed. "No, it's okay. I need to go change. I'm not too late for lunch, am I?"

Neve shook her head. "Nope. I'd call it perfect timing."

Lorenzo nodded. "Hey, let me take the bags. I'm heading back that way myself to check on my…wife."

Rita switched her attention to Lorenzo. "You finally did it? Sally, I take it?"

Neve frowned. "Hey, how did you know?"

Rita chuckled. "I notice things on the ground level, Neve. It's what you pay me for."

Neve gave Rita a long, thoughtful gaze, and then nodded. "Sure I do. Go change and don't take forever. I'll come looking for you—both of you."

Rita nodded and gave Lorenzo a grin.

Watching them leave, Neve felt a lump of emotion forming in her throat. She went back to her warming beer and waited for the people she loved to return to her.

†

Lunch was a leisurely experience, with Rita watching the interaction of the family members. Neve obviously was enjoying herself now that Lorenzo was there—his happiness with his new life rubbing off on her friend. Neve was laughing and joking all through the meal.

Jane had taken Sally under her wing in a motherly way, especially since she was still a little peaky after her bout of sickness. Initially, Sasha was relatively quiet but suddenly thawed when Neve discreetly whispered something to her.

"Well, we're going to have a nap before the festivities tonight. What time are we meeting?" Lorenzo asked and took Sally's hand as they slid out of their chairs.

Neve's eyebrows rose in what Rita thought was a suggestive manner. "Eight."

"We'll see you then. We're going for a siesta." They waved and walked away toward the walkway that led to the bungalows.

"That sounds like a good idea to me too," Jane said.

"Yeah, I was out late last night and it will probably be later tonight. A decadent afternoon nap sounds like a good idea," Sasha said. Just as she was about to leave, Sasha looked directly at Neve. "Susan wanted to thank you for a good time last night, Neve. She said she hoped to see you before she leaves." Sasha left.

Rita's observation of Neve's body language had her wondering exactly who this Susan was. The lack of knowledge gnawed at her stomach hoping that the woman wasn't one of Neve's one-night stands. Rita clasped her fingers together tightly and gave Neve a forced smile. "If you need to go and see Susan, I don't mind."

Neve turned to her and Rita saw a glittering in her blue eyes that were not happy. "I don't need to go. I'm right where I want to be. Susan isn't important, you are."

Rita warmed at the possible nuance of Neve's words. "Okay then. I have all the details from the accountants. I thought they were very helpful. I've already booked a flight back for tomorrow just after lunch."

"You are not leaving!"

Rita thought she was going to fall off her chair at the explosive reply. She couldn't comprehend how Neve's mood could swing from calmness to anger in the space of a few seconds. Then she closed her eyes. *She doesn't want me to know about this Susan person.* "Neve, you brought me here for work related purposes. I've completed the task and can upload whatever you need onto your private area in the circus network when I get back. I'm not on vacation. This was purely business…right."

Neve ran a hand along her firm jaw line and Rita wondered if it felt as firm as it looked. She desperately wanted to touch Neve's face that had suddenly clouded over.

"If I asked you to stay for a couple of extra days, would you?"

Rita considered the question. Her lips had gone dry and licked them before looking squarely at Neve. "As a guest, you mean?"

"You'd be here as my friend. Will you?"

There was, Rita was sure, an element of pleading in the voice that asked the question. She'd be a fool to turn the offer down, but at the same time, it was becoming increasingly more difficult not to allow her feelings for Neve to show. If she allowed those kinds of feeling to erupt, her irrational jealousy over an unknown woman could ruin their friendship.

"Look, I know we're friends, and I want to keep it that way. How would it look if you gave me preferential treatment?"

"I don't give a damn about what other people think." Neve dropped her gaze. "Will you at least enjoy tonight as my guest, not my employee?"

Rita smiled slightly knowing that unshed tears were not far away. Disappointment flooded her at Neve's ease in the way she took the refusal. "Of course, I will. I'm not on the clock after five."

Neve smiled. "Can I stop the clock now and invite you for a walk down the beach? I don't want you to go home without at least touching your toes in the water."

Rita grinned. "I'd love that, thank you."

Neve stood and held out her hand. "Thank you."

They wandered off toward the path that led down to the beach, hand in hand.

†

The fireworks, lanterns, and general upbeat atmosphere at the harbor had a euphoric effect on both tourists and general populace alike. As the bell chimed out the old year and heralded in the new, kisses and hugs, shouts, laughter, and general merriment seemed to burst out on the scene.

Neve, for a brief moment, relished the kiss she shared with Rita. It reminded her of another kiss they'd shared at Angel's wedding. One she dearly wanted to experience again and again. It appeared that Rita didn't remember the kiss or chose to be selective about that memory as she'd never mentioned it or appeared to want to share leisure time with her. The whole situation was frustrating. Maybe they could work it out—she desperately wanted that to happen.

Half an hour after midnight, Neve's party went back to the hotel complex, where a dance was underway. They secured a vacant table just inside the balcony and Neve watched everyone as they sat down.

Jane was sitting next to Christian Chambers, whom she invited to celebrate with her family—she liked the old lawyer. Sasha had declined sitting with them wanting to remain with her new friends who were all going to a night club together. Lorenzo and Sally sat at the far end of the table engrossed in each other. Then she glanced at the table and didn't see Rita. Instead of joining them, she was standing at the balcony looking up at the stars.

"I'll arrange drinks and be right back." Neve grinned…no one was listening to her. Jane and Christian struck up a conversation at the beginning of the evening over dinner and hadn't stopped for breath since. Lorenzo and Sally were still staring into each other's eyes paying little attention to anything else. Her attention turned to the inside bar where a throng of people stood. The pool bar was also busy but the number of people around it was considerably less. She diverted her attention back to Rita, who now leaned on the railing of the balcony seemingly lost in a world of her own. The deep blue simple a-line dress she wore fit exactly right on Rita's generous breasts and her wide hips. Some might call her overweight, but to Neve, she was perfect.

Neve took a route to the pool bar that would bring her next to Rita. "Hey, I'm going to order drinks. Can I entice you into champagne?"

Rita didn't look at Neve but kept her eyes glued to the scene in front of her. "It's quite simply stunning, isn't it?"

Neve didn't change the direction of her gaze that remained fixed on Rita. "Yes, it is."

"I don't think so on the champagne, but thanks. I've had three glasses of wine already." Rita turned to face Neve with a smile. "Besides, I'm leaving tomorrow, remember? My flight is booked for two in the afternoon."

Neve nodded. "You still haven't decided to take me up on the offer of a few more days?"

"I'm sorry, Neve. It just wouldn't be fair to the rest of the people you employ. Favoritism never works, in my opinion."

Neve shrugged as she thought about a solution. "Problem solved. I'll give them all an extra few vacation days. Will you stay?"

Rita chuckled. "As usual, very generous and, incidentally, I need to speak with you about that."

Neve took Rita's hand. "Then stay and speak with me the day after tomorrow about that. Tomorrow is a genuine holiday so we can't talk about work at all." She felt a tremor through her fingers and she hoped that what she was feeling was igniting some responding connection in Rita.

"Neve, what will I do with you?"

"Anything you want, name it." Neve replied in a low throaty pitch. Rita's gaze remained glued to hers and Neve knew the emotional maelstrom she was feeling was working its way through her friend. *I know I'm not way off base about that.*

"Okay, I'll have a glass of champagne. Out of curiosity, when are you going to tell the others about your windfall?"

Neve raised her eyebrows and then winked. "When the champagne is on the table. Didn't you suspect as much when I invited Christian to join us?"

"Hmm, I wondered. I can see it in your eyes when you speak to him that you like him. Go order that drink…I'm dying to see the look in their eyes when they find out what you've been willed by your *wicked* uncle."

Neve chuckled and released Rita's hand. "You got it. Please, sit by me. I might need the support when they find out."

Rita laughed. "Sure, I'll be right by your side. Count on it."

"I do." Neve impulsively bent and kissed Rita's cheek before she left to order the drinks.

Fifteen minutes later, everyone, except for Jane, had a full champagne flute glasses in front of them and they all looked at Neve with expectant looks on their faces.

"Now that we've rung in the New Year, I have something I want to tell you."

"Well, don't keep us waiting, Sis. Out with it."

"Impatient as always, Lorenzo?" Neve looked at everyone then smiled. "Ah, here comes the person I've been waiting for."

A middle-aged man with short, receding black hair and with a serious expression, walked up to the table.

"You requested that you needed to see the manager immediately, Ms. Garmancelli. How may I help?" The manager had a quiet lilt to his voice with the Jamaican influence in accent but it wasn't as pronounced as in some of the locals. It was more in keeping with the lawyer, whose voice held a more cultured tone.

"Please take a seat, Mr. Robinson. You need to hear this too."

Puzzled, the man did as requested.

Lorenzo placed a glass in front of the man and started to fill it with champagne.

"Oh, I can't do that. I'm on duty," the manager protested.

Neve frowned. "Is that because you don't drink, you hate champagne, or is it part of your contract?"

The man allowed his serious expression to drop slightly and smiled. "The latter."

"Fill the glass up, Lorenzo."

Mr. Robinson, along with several others at the table, looked at Neve with puzzled expressions.

"All except for Mr. Robinson, are aware that my uncle died and left a second will. Please, bear with me." She looked directly at the hotel manager. "My uncle, Mr. Robinson, was Silvestre Russo."

The hotel manager's eyes widened.

"Ah, I thought that might hold your attention. To get straight to the point, he left me this hotel complex, several plots of land, and three houses…oh, and a pot of money, too. I think that deserves a toast, if nothing else." She raised her glass and the others followed automatically with stunned looks on their faces.

"You own this place, Neve?" Lorenzo asked.

Neve grinned. "I do. Mr. Chambers here has been helping me in the past month to organize transfers and check out the financial situation. Rita came to ensure everything is in order." Neve glanced at Rita and winked.

Lorenzo shook his head. "Why you sneaky pair…neither of you let on."

Neve glanced at Jane, who was simply staring at the fruit juice she was drinking. "Are you okay, Jane? You look as white as a sheet," she asked.

"I didn't know he had any money. Not like this anyway." Her hand moved to circle the vicinity. "He was always so frugal at home."

"We can talk about that later. Mr. Robinson, I wanted to tell you personally that I'm impressed with how well you run things here. Your staff and general maintenance of my hotel are excellent. Mr. Chambers here has some papers for you and the rest of the staff. Can you take care of that, Christian?"

Christian stood up with a smile. "It will be a pleasure." He waited for the stunned manager to stand and follow him back to the manager's office.

"Are you changing their contract of employment?" Rita asked.

"In a way, yes. My uncle was a stingy man." Neve looked at Jane. "He paid the staff a basic wage, which isn't much here. I'm ensuring that excellent staff receives their true rewards."

"You're giving them a pay raise?"

"Yes, along with basic health benefits." She smiled at her brother. "Lorenzo, I have something for you." She slipped an envelope across the table. "You, too, Jane. I also have an envelope for Sasha, when she wakes in the morning. I doubt we'll see her for the rest of the evening."

Neve sat back in her chair with a smug expression as she watched her brother and Jane open the envelopes.

Jane was the first to speak. "I can't take this, Neve, we aren't even related."

Neve grinned. "Of all the people who should benefit from my uncle's will, you are the most deserving, Jane. I wish I'd known all those years ago what he was putting you through…anyway, the past is in the past, right?"

The older woman nodded.

"I figured a beach house on St. Kitts, with a ten percent stake in this place, would help. The house is now yours to do with, as you like. You can sell it, live in it, or rent it. The shares are a nest egg, and if you'd rather sell them, I have right of first refusal."

Jane nodded as tears streamed down her cheeks.

Then Neve turned her attention to her brother who was staring at her with a fixed gaze.

"I think you've actually stopped him in his tracks, Neve." Sally said.

Lorenzo shook his head and cleared his throat. "You've given us a house in Montego Bay and ten percent of this place, along with a million dollars. Neve, you can't do this."

"I've already done it. The same stipulation applies to you concerning the hotel shares…I have right of first refusal if you sell. I'm hoping you both don't." Neve smiled and when she saw Lorenzo's expression, she fought to keep her tears from falling.

"Thank you."

"You're welcome."

Seconds later, Lorenzo was out of his chair and dragging Neve into a fierce hug.

"I love you, Lorenzo. You deserve this for sticking with me through the years. I know it hasn't been easy or the perfect choice for you."

Lorenzo didn't speak. He simply shook his head before returning to his seat where Sally gave him a big hug.

Satisfied at her dealings of the evening, Neve took up her glass and drained the contents before refilling it. "You know, I think tonight of all nights is a great night to get drunk."

An hour later, the party broke up, leaving Neve and Rita alone at the table.

"Have you had enough or are you going to consume another bottle?"

Neve shook her head. "No more for me. What did you think of tonight?"

Rita held up her hands and laughed. "I've come to expect the unexpected from you, but tonight, Neve, yes, tonight, you out did yourself. You made a great deal of people happy. May I ask what Sasha is getting?"

Neve smiled and leaned in next to Rita's ear. "She gets the house in Bermuda, a million dollars, and ten percent of this place."

Rita simply shook her head.

"You don't think that's enough?"

"You have got to be kidding me! Neve, do you have anything left?" Rita asked.

Neve considered Rita's words carefully. "You know I do."

"Good point. You know something…I'm glad you're my boss and my friend. You are one fine woman, Neve Garmancelli."

Neve grinned. "Does that mean if I asked you to go to bed with me, you'd agree?"

Rita blinked rapidly. "What's in it for me?"

The light banter in Rita's voice invaded the numbing sensation of the alcohol she'd consumed and Neve moved in closer. "You get me."

Rita took Neve's hand and pulled her up. "Come on, Ms. Generosity, I think it's time you went to bed—alone."

Neve grinned. "Spoilsport."

"I know, but you wouldn't expect anything else from me."

They headed toward the bungalows while the voice of Bob Marley ran all around them.

†

Neve grumbled all the way to the bungalow. When they reached Rita's, she gave her a long intense stare. "If you won't go to bed with me, how about you dance with me on the beach? We'd be all alone, no one to watch and if they did, who gives a damn. Besides, they are playing our song."

Rita laughed. Under normal circumstances, even alcohol didn't faze Neve. Tonight however, she appeared to be inebriated. It was probably a mix of the night's euphoria and the drinks. In its own way, her apparent drunkenness had endearing tendencies. "Neve, by the time we hit the beach, *our song,* as you call it, will be over."

"Details, details. Please, for me. You won't stay longer or share my bed and now, not even a tiny dance. What's the point in being generous if you're not appreciated?" Neve stuck out her lower lip.

"I'm sure the others who have benefited from your generosity will be annoyed if they couldn't help you out." Rita grasped Neve's hand and led her a little closer to the path that would take her the short distance to her bungalow.

Neve stubbornly didn't move. "I don't want any of them in my bed. Anyway, you benefited."

Rita puzzled over that last statement. "Please, Neve, come on let's get you to bed."

"You don't understand, do you?"

"Okay, what do you mean?" Rita went along with the game. Neve was going to be annoyed that her self control had disappeared when she woke up in the morning.

Neve threw back her head and laughed. "You get me."

It was a simple enough explanation. Rita's heart was pounding. *Oh, I wish that were true, Neve, I really do*. "I give in. One dance on the beach and then to bed for you, my friend."

Neve beamed a smile that almost had Rita faltering in her steps. As they walked onto the strip of beach that was part of the private area of Rita's bungalow, they slid off their shoes and Neve held out her arms.

With a shake of her head and a mental sigh of happiness, Rita moved, allowing Neve to wrap her in her strong arms. Faint strains of a melody filtered through, and the two women moved in harmony to the gentle rhythms. Neve's head seemed to get lower with every beat of the music until, after the second song from the resident band, it touched Rita's shoulder.

"Hey, are you going to sleep on me?"

There was no reply for a few heartbeats. "I don't want to miss a second."

Rita quirked an eyebrow at Neve's statement and smiled. "How about going to bed now, Neve? It's well after three."

Neve looked into Rita's eyes. "You're like a will o' the wisp. As soon as I turn my back, you're gone. Please, don't leave me, Rita."

Rita felt tears forming at the words. People who allowed drink to overtake them were sometimes childlike—in Neve's case, it was rare—she'd never seen it before. However, tonight she deserved to let go. She stared into the trusting eyes of her friend and a feeling of complete love almost overwhelm her. "I won't. I promise. Not while you need me. Come on, I'll stay with you until you fall asleep."

"Perfect. Can I sleep here?"

Rita was about to answer *no* but shrugged. "Yes, you can."

Ten minutes later, they were back in Rita's bungalow with Neve fully clothed and sprawled on the bed. Rita watched as Neve slept before leaving to go sleep on the sofa bed. Rita bent and placed a tender kiss on Neve's forehead. "I'm so proud to have you as a friend. If that's all we will ever be, then I have more than most in this life. I love you, Neve, sleep well." She silently slipped out of the bedroom and walked to the balcony to think.

Chapter Thirty-one

Neve awoke with ten steel drums practicing in her head. She had a headache—a big one. After gradually opening her eyes and looking around, she noticed that the room seemed familiar and yet not. Gingerly moving her body, she headed in what she thought was the direction to the bathroom. It was where it should be but there wasn't anything personal in the bathroom. She didn't see cosmetics or her favorite toothbrush. All that was there were the requisite hotel sundries. After what seemed like minutes, Neve grumbled, "This isn't my room."

As her headache hit another pinnacle in her temple, she scowled and crossed to the kitchen area. She took a bottle of spring water out of the refrigerator while gazing at the contents. "I've gone and lost it this time." She unscrewed the bottle cap and took a long swig of the water. Her eyes closed in immense pleasure at the cool sensation running down her throat. With her bottle in hand, she stood in the small kitchenette and thought back to the night before. It was difficult to think about with the drums in her head. "I'm really going to have to give up the booze."

Neve ambled over to window to look out at the balcony. It dawned on her. "Rita!" Her eyes darting to inside the room to look at the clock—it was one-thirty. "She's gone."

The words echoed flatly in the room. Neve searched every flat surface she could find, looking for a note or any evidence that Rita had been there. She saw a piece of paper, folded in two and stuck to the side of the fridge under a magnet advertising a local nightclub. After quickly grabbing the paper, she greedily read the contents…

Neve,

I had to catch my flight. Sorry I didn't wake you, but you needed the sleep. This reminds me of when you left me at the hotel after Angel's wedding. At least you know the correct hangover cures. I'll email you when I get back home. Enjoy the rest of your vacation.

Rita

Neve's legs felt unsteady as she stumbled to the sofa and sank into it. "We are like ships that pass in the night, never quite meeting. I'm such a damned idiot! I should have told you outright *I love you* instead of being awkward." She dropped her head into her hands and felt the tears begin to flow, allowing the sorrow of Rita's departure and her own inadequacies to take over.

†

Rita closed the computer and looked outside of the bus. It was late February and almost everyone, barring Neve, Lorenzo, and Sally, had arrived back at the circus. It had been good to see the circus family again. It allowed her to stop dwelling on fantasies and live in the real world. The weeks since she'd been back home had been a mixture of emotions. There was the pain of not physically seeing Neve, and the relief of thinking that what she didn't know wouldn't hurt her. Since last seeing Neve, jealousy constantly preyed on Rita's mind as she thought of the many conquests Neve probably had made while in Jamaica. In the working environment, she could cope, but outside was a completely different ball game—her mind worked overtime.

Since arriving home, Neve and she had been in contact every day. Other than the first awkward conversation when Neve apologized profusely for her behavior that last night in Jamaica, their daily calls and emails were routine. Most of their conversations were business related, except for one particular project Neve had needed her opinion on—plans for a new house she wanted to build on the Jamaican plot of land they both loved.

They skirted the closer personal relationship issues and that irked Rita, but her mind kept telling her that it wasn't to be. *Maybe I should've taken up Neve's offer of going to bed that last night. Perhaps the pain of wanting her might be quenched, and I can move on.* Instead, she fantasized about what it would have been like and that's when jealousy eroded her common sense.

Dave Tamborelli appeared at her desk sporting a new hairstyle. He'd forgone his usual razor cut and let his blonde hair grow. "Rita, has the boss mentioned when she or Lorenzo are getting back? We need to go through the safety checklist before the end of the week. We won't get the certificate from the safety board if we don't."

Rita let out an exasperated breath. "Sorry, Dave, I don't know. I know she said was returning to the States sometime this week, but she wasn't specific. I'll call her cell if you need her." She steepled her fingers and gave him an apologetic look.

Dave ran his hand through his hair. "If we don't get the safety certificate, we're screwed for the next three months. Why aren't they here? They normally arrive a week before any of the others."

"Priorities change, Dave. Look, let me try contacting them both." That appeased the young man. Neve had been vague about her return date and Rita speculated that she was enjoying her leisure time more and thinking about the circus less.

There was a general commotion outside the bus, and Rita stood to look out of the tiny window. An expensive looking rig that she'd never seen before—and certainly had never authorized payment for—was maneuvering into a spot normally taken by Neve's rig. The Garmancelli circus logo all over the exterior sparked a thought to drift through her mind.

The Hotel Laredo's logo was an inverted circus logo. She *knew* it was familiar when she saw it at the hotel. Rita walked the few feet to the open door to see what was happening.

When the monster vehicle stopped, a large crowd drew around the bus that was bigger than the control bus. Just as it came to a stop, another vehicle of similar proportions came along and within a few minutes was alongside its twin. The Garmancelli logo was on this one, too, but in a subtly different shade.

"What the hell is going on? Who organized these?" Rita walked down the few steps to the first vehicle. A man was climbing out of the driver's cab with a clipboard in his hand—she didn't recognize him.

"I'm looking for a Ms. Garmancelli?"

People who had gathered there allowed Rita to move through as she approached the man. "I'm afraid she isn't here. Can I help you?"

The man gave her a thoughtful look from deep set, brown eyes and transferred his gaze back to the paperwork. "Mr. Garmancelli?"

Rita shook her head. "They haven't arrived yet. I'm the circus accountant. I'm not sure that…"

A vehicle sped into view and squealed to a stop just in front of the bus.

Rita gasped as Neve nonchalantly stepped out and came over to the man. "Sorry, got caught up in traffic. Give me the forms, please. I'm Neve Garmancelli." She displayed her driver's license as identification. A few minutes later, after Neve signed the documents, the two men who had driven the rigs, took the car that Neve arrived in and left.

Rita stood silently watching Neve take the keys and several folders before she began fielding questions from Jacamar, Dave, and several others.

Rita, puzzled and hurt that Neve hadn't included her in the decision of buying such expensive assets for the circus, shrugged. *Guess that says it all.* She proceeded to go back to her desk in the control center. The joy her heart had felt at seeing Neve erased by her mind's practicality—at least for the moment.

†

Half an hour later, Neve entered the bus. Dave was waiting and immediately stopped her and told her about the safety issue. Rita could hear her tell Dave that she'd handle it and to arrange the official check for tomorrow. He appeared happy and went away.

Rita held her breath as she waited for Neve to drop her head over the screen and say hello—she didn't. Instead, she heard the sound of the coffee machine filling the carafe. Annoyed and curious, Rita stood up from behind her desk and walked over to the entrance of her office space.

"Welcome back. Those look expensive." Rita motioned to the vehicles outside.

Neve shrugged and gave a smile that showed off her tanned features, with her white teeth the perfect backdrop. "Thanks. It's good to be back. I figured that circumstances dictated we need something more in assets."

The glib reply and the lack of Neve's usual buoyancy had Rita taken aback. *What's going on here?* "Really? You didn't figure that you might at least tell me these *assets*, as you call them, were coming?"

"No, I didn't. It was a surprise." Neve sipped on her coffee and looked pointedly at Rita. "Anything wrong with that?"

"I hate financial surprises. As your accountant, I would have expected you to inform me of the impending arrival. Just how much did they cost?" Rita knew her voice sounded bitter but was unable to stop it. She let telling Neve how she felt until it was too late. She over thought the situation and didn't acted swiftly enough—Neve had moved on. It was the story of her life.

"That's none of your concern now. In fact, I need to discuss with you a change in personnel. Lorenzo, as normal, will do the interviews but you might want some input."

Rita almost choked on the words that stuck in her throat until she finally found her voice. "Me? Why? Who are you replacing?"

"Your original position, actually." Neve placed her empty coffee cup on the counter.

When she realized that Neve avoided looking at her heart sank. "You're letting me go? Why?" Rita grabbed onto a chair tightly—the world as she knew was collapsing.

Neve shook her head. "That's a technicality…not exactly."

At Neve's obvious disregard for her feelings, Rita sucked in a breath. "A technicality? Exactly what's going on, Neve?" Shock was numbing every other sensation she had.

Neve smiled slowly. "I swear things have never worked out exactly how I've planned them since I've met you, Rita. We need to talk about this and lots of other things. Will you trust me?" Neve raised her eyebrows. "Unfortunately, Dave has brought up a problem that requires my immediate attention. When I get back, I promise you'll have my undivided attention and all the explanation you need. I'll catch up with you in a couple of hours."

Rita watched as Neve moved to within an inch of her. She steadied her shaking body thinking that Neve was going to reach out and touch her. Instead, she thrust her hands in the pocket of her coat, turned, and left the bus.

Rita felt numb—Neve shot her in the back. *I don't know if I will ever recover. What did I do?* "She's letting me go, and she calls that a *technicality*!" Her words echoed around the empty bus.

†

Neve stood outside the control bus and drew back her shoulders, hoping to stem the quivering in her stomach. She knew Rita could take that the comments she made a couple of hours earlier several ways. She hoped her friend would trust her and wait for the explanation. In fact, once inside and face-to-face with Rita earlier, she wanted to pull her into her arms and profess her love. Instead, circus business, as usual took priority. She didn't want to blurt a quick *I love you*, before turning away to handle circus problems. No, she wanted to tell Rita how she felt at the right time and in the right place. She hoped that was now. Drawing on her normal self-confidence, she entered the bus. It was relatively silent, except for quiet voices floating from Rita's office space.

The closer she got, the more familiar she found the second voice. When she was within a foot of the screen that surrounded Rita's area, she realized who it was—Jen.

"Neve, you've come back at last. Rita here was telling me you were due anytime." Jennifer Connelly peered over the edge of the screen.

"Jen, what are you doing here?" Neve smiled warmly at the woman with whom she had once shared a year of her life.

Jennifer moved from her position and walked around the screen to stand with her arms folded. "You have to ask me that? I've heard lots of interesting gossip about you recently, Neve. I thought I'd check up."

Neve grinned. "Of course. Circus gossip. Not everything you hear is true, Jen. You should know that."

Jennifer laughed. "Yes, I should. By the way, how cool is it, you becoming an aunt."

Neve took a moment to glance over Jennifer's shoulder and down to Rita's bent head. *Hmm, this isn't going as I planned.* "Yeah, could be. It's supposed to be a secret. What brings you here, other than that, Jen?"

"I'm going out for lunch. I'll be back later." Rita stood, grabbed her things, and rushed away.

Neve's annoyance was palpable at the sound of the door crashing shut. She looked at Jennifer. "You were saying?"

Jennifer shrugged. "Danny Carmine is the real reason I'm here. What do you know that you have selectively forgotten to tell his current employer?"

"Oh, Lulu doesn't come begging for my help, she sends you to do her dirty work. Typical." Neve lounged against a desk and narrowed her eyes.

Jennifer scowled. "She did nothing of the sort. In fact, she doesn't even know I'm here."

"She won't like that. Why *are* you here?"

"I couldn't believe that you'd allow someone with a criminal record and with that type of history to come over to us without a warning."

Neve shrugged. "You poached the Carmines from my circus when I was at a low point; therefore, why would I bother to inform you of something that is up to your diligence to find out."

"Semantics, Neve. You know we can't possibly employ him. That means we have to let the others go, too." Her tone softened. "Although Sally isn't an issue anymore, is she? Lorenzo finally did the right thing." Jennifer grinned.

Neve threw up her hands. "How is it that you and Rita knew about this before I did? You haven't been in Lorenzo's life for ten years. I don't get it."

"You never will, Neve, because you keep stuff too close to the vest. You're like Lulu—you and she might be twins."

"Over my dead body."

"Yeah, she would say the same. Exactly why are you and Lulu at loggerheads? I never did find out, and Lulu won't say or can't remember."

Neve frowned before letting out a soft chuckle, "Darned if I can remember either. It was something…or nothing…probably the latter."

Jennifer smiled. "Most probably. You're a fool, you know."

"How so?"

Jennifer tilted her head to one side then answered. "The woman who left. Rita. You like her, don't you…actually more than like her?"

"Who I like or care for has nothing to do with you."

"It's true, isn't it? I have the feeling that you're in a quandary and might lose something that's important to you. I know all about that—been there done that."

"She's my accountant, end of story."

"Yeah, and she runs around in your personal vehicle and her kid wants to be just like you on the high trapeze. Give me the benefit of some intelligence. You're more than her employer…hell…you look at her as if you could devour her."

Neve seemed to shrink inside herself at Jennifer's words. "Charlie wants to be like me?"

Jennifer smiled. "Apparently so. The lions and tigers were great, but the high trapeze caught his eye."

"I knew that Rita went to Lulu's circus. She never said… I never let her finish." Neve answered herself. "How do you know all this about Rita and Charlie? Have you met?"

Jennifer nodded. "We had a brief conversation. Maybe it's time you told her what you think and how you feel."

Neve blinked rapidly. "Darn it, Jen, I feel defenseless when she's near. But at the same time fearless…as if I can do anything as long as she's there. You could call it an ironic quandary. How do you tell someone that she means everything to you and not scare her away? I really don't know if what I want is anything Rita can accept."

Jennifer smiled and shook her head. "Tell her you love her."

Neve's eyes flew open. "Oh, I don't think I can do that if she doesn't …well, I don't want her to leave me. I can do the friendship thing, if that's all she wants. I've been working on that for a few months now. I was hoping my absence might make her grow to love me or, at least, miss me."

"I thought that once myself a long time ago, but it really doesn't work."

The plaintive words echoed deep inside Neve. "Yeah, I know. Right now, it's tearing me apart. What did you do?" Neve's eyes catching Jennifer's and she wished she hadn't. "It was me, wasn't it?"

Jennifer nodded. "It was a long time ago. Besides, I love Lulu, and believe me, I'm glad you didn't want me because she really is the love of my life. I think Rita might be that for you, Neve. Have you ever felt this strongly for anyone? No, forget that. I'd rather not go there. The real question, Neve, is would you give up everything for that someone?"

Neve didn't hesitate. "In a heartbeat. I'd find a way to be with her no matter what. There isn't a place on this planet far enough away."

"Then you need to tell her." Jennifer placed her arms around Neve and gave her a brief kiss on the lips.

At that moment, the door to bus opened, and Rita stood halfway inside the doorway with her mouth open.

"I'm sorry." Rita shut the door and was gone.

Neve raised her head and looked to the metal roof. "My timing sucks! It always has."

Jennifer shook her head. "I guess now you find out exactly what's going on inside her head. I have my own theory."

"Care to elaborate?"

"Nope, it's all up to you and her. Take care of yourself and Rita, Neve. Don't be a stranger. Lulu admires you…she really does."

Neve drew up her eyebrows at the comment. "We'll arrange dinner sometime, when our paths cross again."

"Deal." Jennifer turned away.

Neve clasped her arm gently. "I'm sorry for not understanding before. I never deserved you. In the end, it worked out for the best, didn't it?"

Jennifer grinned. "Yes, now go and be happy."

Neve rushed out after Rita

.

Chapter Thirty-two

"Rita, please open the door. I'm not leaving here until you do. We need to talk about this." Neve rapped on the door several more times. She'd been doing this for more than fifteen minutes and was causing quite a stir as her performers and technicians avidly watched the unfolding events.

In a fit of temper, Neve growled and glared at everyone. "Haven't you all got work to do?"

A shuffle of several feet had them heading off, but some remained at a distance. She was making a spectacle of herself and didn't blame their curiosity or Rita's refusal to let her in. Her original plan had gone out the window when Jen arrived—actually before that—when Dave mentioned the safety certification. As it was, her plans now looked like they were beyond recovery.

She sat down on the steps in front of the door, knowing that at least Rita couldn't leave without stepping on or over her. She pulled her black cashmere overcoat up around her neck. After the tropical paradise where she'd spent the best part of two months, the cold was a shock to her system.

A low, gravelly voice interrupted her thoughts. "I thought you might need this, boss."

Neve looked at the steaming cup of coffee Jacamar was thrusting into her hands. His dwarf-like features hadn't changed since they were last together, and his eyes, often dark pools of unfathomable thoughts, were kind. "Thanks, Jacamar. How have you and the family been?"

"We're all good, boss. I don't need to ask how your vacation went. You look like a million dollars." He grinned as he touched the wisps of a few days beard on his chin.

"Yeah, that would be about right. Did you know that Lorenzo and Sally Carmine married?" Neve fully expected him to say what all the others had.

"I'd heard a rumor and didn't believe it, probably won't until I see the boy myself."

Neve gave the man a half smile. "At least I'm not the only one who didn't actually know."

There was a marked silence for a few seconds then Jacamar bent his head slightly. "She's a good one. Rita, that is. I hope she stays with you." He shrugged and then headed back to where he came from.

Neve looked at the man whose short legs moved faster than she expected. He was gone from view within seconds. Taking a drink of the hot coffee, she again sighed heavily. After placing the cup on the step, she stood. "I hope she stays, too." Her hand reached for the door again and was about to rap on it when it opened.

Startled at the unexpected event, Neve was lost for words. She took in the swollen red eyes and the grim determination on Rita's face and she knew she'd made a hell of a mess. She wanted desperately to reach out, soothe her friend, and tell her that things were not as they seemed.

"I don't need to speak with you, Neve. Not now…not ever again. I'll be gone in an hour or less and you can bring onboard whomever you want as your new accountant and good luck to them. Please leave now. You're making a fool out of me." Rita was about to shut the door when Neve placed her expensive leather boot in the way.

Rita attempted to slam the door, hard. The resulting wail of pain from Neve had Rita's eyes fly open.

"For God's sake, Neve, why did you do that?"

Neve felt tears of pain spring to her eyes, but she gritted her teeth and stared at Rita. "If I hadn't, the likelihood of your ever speaking to me again would be minimal."

"It still is." Rita began to shut the door again.

This time Neve placed a hand on the door. "I'm begging you to speak with me, Rita. Please."

Rita peered closely into Neve's face, took her hand from the door, and walked inside the RV.

Neve, breathing in deeply, followed slowly behind. The pain in her foot was worse than she expected. Neve closed the door behind her and stood at the threshold of what could be the beginning of a new relationship with Rita. Things could go either good or bad.

"You wanted to explain." Rita sank down on the bench in the kitchen and wrapped her fingers around her cup of tea.

Rita's flat expression had Neve feeling the pain she was sure she had senselessly inflicted. Biting her bottom lip, she tried to find the right words. Then she realized that it was simple and she felt quite light headed at the prospect. "I love you."

There was no immediate response.

Neve ran a hand through her air musing up the style. "Did you hear what I said, Rita?"

Rita looked up; her eyes appeared haunted and hollow. "Sure, is that supposed to make me forget that you treat me like someone you can walk all over one minute and then say something nice the next, with everything else fading into a black abyss? It doesn't!"

"I know. I'm an idiot and I know I could do so many things better. You…you break every single rule in my head on what I want to say and do. I'm not even sure that what I said makes you happy, sad, or downright sick. All I know is that I love you." Neve felt the throbbing of her left foot and wished she could take off her boot and look at the damage. She didn't dare. Rita would probably think she was trying to pull out a sympathy card or worse—blame her for the injury.

"Why are you letting me go? What did I do wrong? All these months we've talked, and you never once mentioned you weren't satisfied with my work?" Rita's eyes never left her cup of tea.

Neve sucked in a breath. She hoped to be having a different conversation with Rita. The fact that she'd said *I love you* should have warranted some emotional remark, not the monotone questions Rita was asking. "I'm not. At least...I was right when I said it was a technicality and to trust me."

Rita looked up with an expression of bewilderment. "You're not? But you said…" Her tone shifted abruptly. "What the hell kind of *technicality* is it that includes hiring a new accountant?"

That's better: anger. At last, an emotion. Neve half smiled. "I figured that as my partner you'd have more things to do than mundane accounting. You'd need an assistant. I said it all wrong, didn't I?"

Rita stood up facing Neve. "Partner?"

Neve shrugged, her hand once more running her fingers through her hair—this time it shook. "I want to share my life with you, Rita…all my life…the business, the personal, the good times, and the bad ones. I also figure that you might not want a sexual relationship, although I was hoping, over time, you might consider it. I know you're somewhat attracted to me. Though right now, I suspect I might have blown that theory out of the water…and you probably want to get as far away from me as possible."

Rita stood silently with her eyes moving over Neve's face before she reached out and took one of Neve's shaking hands. "You're shaking."

Self consciously Neve laughed. "Yeah, can you believe it? I can bawl the hell out of the circus employees and make grown men cry, but you…you can make *me* cry…will make me cry if you leave me. I'm not perfect, Rita. I do things wrong all the time. My social skills need work, but I want to say one thing before you make your mind up about me. I do love you with all my heart. I promise I'll take care of you."

"I'm not sure it will work, Neve."

Neve frowned. She felt slightly more confident than she had since Rita still held her hand. "Is it the fact that I'm not a man?"

"No!"

"Thank, God, for that. It's the one thing I can't actually change." She shrugged. "And for the record, I wouldn't want to. All the rest can be worked on with help." Neve let out a brief laugh. "I want you to be happy, Rita. I want you to be happy with me. We can take as long as you like to get to know each other on a more personal level…I want to do that. Do you think you could consider taking me on…faults and all?"

Rita stared at Neve and then lifted her free hand to touch the worry lines on Neve's forehead. "I never thought you would ever see me seriously as anything more than your accountant and friend. To actually love me, that was like reaching for the moon…especially now that you're a rich woman you can have any girl you want."

Neve understood the last part. "Rita, I want you, not a string of strangers who want me for my money. I can give it all away and I will if it means you will stay with me."

"It's not that simple, Neve."

"How can I fix it to make it simple…for you to love me?"

Rita shook her head and turned away. "I already do love you, which is why it isn't simple. I don't want to be another notch on your belt or someone you profess to love this year and next it's someone else. I'm not sure I even want to put myself through loving you and then losing you."

Neve was shocked at Rita's disclosures. She moved quickly and flinched at the pain in her foot before she stood face-to-face with Rita. "For the record, I haven't slept with another woman since that day you came back to Rochester after taking your sister home. I was an idiot, selfish, and, God only knows what else you must have thought of me when you found out about that one-night stand." She paused. "Did you mean what you just said?"

"What?"

"That you love me, what else?"

Rita nodded. "Yes, though you exasperate me in lots of ways I don't understand, I do love you."

"Then it's already too late for you."

Rita looked at Neve's smiling face with puzzled expression. "Why are you laughing at me? Do you think what I feel is funny."

Neve placed her hands on Rita's shoulders. "No, you said you weren't sure about putting yourself through loving me and then losing me. But don't you see, Rita? We're both already doing the loving, and hurting like hell without the benefits. Don't we deserve a chance to see if it can work between us?"

Rita licked her lips and the action had Neve's gaze concentrating on the slight tongue action—it was making her wet. "Please?"

"Do you really love me?"

Neve nodded and looked deep into Rita's luminous brown eyes. "Tell me what I can do to convince you?"

Rita didn't flinch from the intense gaze and smiled. "Kiss me."

Neve grinned and lowered her head until their lips touched. They lost themselves in a gentle exploration of each other's lips until that wasn't enough, and they allowed their tongues to lock. Sometime later, they came up for breath. Neve rested her forehead on Rita's and tried to calm her shaking body. "I don't know what I'd do without you in my life now, Rita. You are my life. I love you so much."

Rita tentatively explored Neve's face with her fingers. "I thought I was going to die when you said you wanted another accountant. I've been counting the days for you to get back and kicking myself that I didn't accept your offer."

Neve smiled and then felt small kisses placed on her jaw, lips, and then all over her face feverishly. She lost herself in the sensations that were both wonderful and new. She'd never anticipated that. "Which offer was that? I think I mentioned at least a couple." Neve grinned as she saw Rita blush.

"I figured you were too drunk to remember *that* offer." Rita admitted as she allowed her fingers to tease Neve's lips.

Neve kissed the fingers tracing her mouth. "I never forget an offer like that. Besides, if you'd accepted, I would probably have found an excuse not to go through with it."

Rita's eyes flew open. "You would've? Why?"

"Because when you and I make love for the first time I want to be sober and remember every damned second, with nothing to addle my brain cells." Neve drew in a satisfied breath as she held Rita closer. "Want to sit and talk for a while?"

"I think that's a good idea, my legs feel like jelly. It isn't often my dreams and wishes come true at the same moment."

Neve smiled and snatched another kiss as they walked over to the more comfortable sofa. "Let me take off this coat." She quickly threw the expensive coat onto the kitchen bench and then sank down next to Rita, pulling her tenderly into her arms. "Now, that's better. Do you know how long I've just wanted to be this close to you and know that you're mine?"

Rita giggled. "I'm yours? Wow, you don't waste time in staking your claim, do you?"

Neve felt slightly embarrassed. "Sorry, I didn't mean to be so possessive, but you've been like the eternal will-o'-the-wisp since the moment I knew I loved you. I don't want to let you go now, just in case."

"Just in case of what?" Rita moved to snuggle into Neve's broad shoulder.

Neve kissed the top of Rita's head. "You might decide to change your mind. I know I'm asking a lot, and you might not be comfortable with making love to a woman. I'm willing to wait…although I'm hoping…" Rita's finger stopped her in mid-sentence.

"You decide." Rita began to kiss Neve passionately.

Sometime later, they drew apart, their clothes in disarray as they searched feverishly to contact skin.

"You look positively ravishing, my dear Ms. Collins." Neve teased as she traced a finger over the exposed lacy bra, stopping to begin taunting the nipple that responded immediately to her touch.

Rita chuckled. Her eyes caught Neve's—their passionate responses to each other were clear. "You've been in Jamaica too long, Neve. They sent back a pirate."

"Oh, I like that idea." Neve bent her head and her tongue trailed a line of moisture along Rita's shoulder to the valley between her breasts. "Can we ignore everyone for the next few days while I make you mine, you *wench*."

Rita wrapped her arms tightly around Neve's waist as she leaned into the caresses. Then her pager went off. "Darn, I arranged a meeting with outside contractors at three."

"Break it." Neve's tongue slid under the lacy bra, pulling Rita's left nipple into her mouth.

"Oh, my God, do you know what you're doing to me?"

Neve gave Rita a heady stare. "I certainly hope I do." Then, she pulled away and solicitously pulled the edges of Rita's blouse around her. "That's to prevent temptation."

Rita grinned and moved to rearrange Neve's sweater that had moved up her body. With a groan, she took another kiss. "I'll cancel that meeting."

Neve laughed. "I'm sure we can muster up enough professionalism to get through a few more hours. After that, dinner in my new abode, and yes, I'll explain all about it."

Rita stood and began to do up the buttons opened by Neve's questing fingers. "Yes, it needs explaining."

Neve stood up too and flinched at the pain in her foot.

"What's wrong?"

"I didn't think you'd shut the door with quite as much force as you did."

"Neve, you should have said. Let me look." Rita knelt down to quickly separate Neve from the offending leather boot.

Ten minutes later, with an aloe compress wrapped around Neve's foot to stop a bruise from forming, they left Rita's RV together in harmony.

†

Rita wasn't sure how she managed to have a fruitful meeting without rushing off to find Neve, who had diplomatically decided to do a round of the performers and check the equipment. It was probably just as well, under the circumstances, or they would surely have ended up in bed. That idea both frightened and excited her at the same time. *Am I going to be good enough to keep Neve interested sexually?* She glanced down at her ample breasts, which, even now several hours later, tingled in anticipation of Neve's touch. However, as she glanced down at her figure, which she'd never been comfortable with, she wondered. Tending toward overweight, she'd hardly had the incentive to diet—until now. If someone didn't like what she was or more importantly, *who* she was, weren't worth bothering with was her usual retort. Now, she wasn't so sure.

"Hey, what's the frown for? Didn't the meeting go well? If they upset you I'll personally ensure they never work with circus folk again."

Rita almost jumped in her chair, caught off guard at the unexpected arrival of her boss, friend, and soon-to-be-lover. "No, the meeting was good. Can you do that?" she tilted her head to one side.

Neve laughed. "I have absolutely no idea, but it's worth a try if they upset you."

"I was thinking about you actually. Us to be exact," Rita let a tentative smile curl her lips as Neve moved around the screen and sat down in the chair opposite her.

"By the look on your face I need to be worried. No, better yet, what have I done wrong or not done or…"

"Neve, stop it. It isn't you. It's me. I'm worrying about stuff before it actually happens so let's forget it. What have you been doing?" Rita attempted to move the conversation to something that didn't concern them on a personal level.

Neve gave Rita an intent look and then with a slight inclination of her head, she smiled "I've been organizing a wedding celebration for tomorrow."

Rita paused for a split second, wondering if… *No, it would never happen.* "Lorenzo and Sally, right?"

"Of course. They need the proper initiation into married life of the circus. Besides, I'm just sanctioning the money they've already spent setting it up. They'd pretty much done most of the organizing. It's tradition in the circus, at least in mine."

Rita chuckled. "I wondered what Clara meant this morning when she said they needed another twenty-four hours for the cake had to be just so. Hey, what do I know? I figured it was for the clowns act or something."

"Well, you got that right, darling…it was something. Are you ready to leave?"

Rita felt her heart somersault at the endearment Neve used. It had seemed so natural for her. "Are we going somewhere?"

Neve shook her head and narrowed her eyes. "It is six-fifteen and even the techs have gone for dinner. I figured you'd need at least half an hour to shower and change and then dinner is in a very special place at seven-thirty. Are you done here?"

Rita looked into Neve's eyes and saw the same thing she always saw when she looked into them—probably always had. This was her friend, someone she could trust, love, and she certainly did both. "Okay, I'll drop by your new place when I'm done." She closed the lid on her laptop.

Neve leaned forward. "Spoil sport. I thought you'd let me help scrub your back."

Rita felt the heat rise in her cheeks as she placed her hands automatically to them.

"I was only teasing. See you around seven." Neve stood up then hesitated.

"How's the foot?" Rita asked.

Neve grinned and moved in on Rita before kissing her. "Wonderful, see you around seven."

Rita, her lips still numb with the sensation of Neve's kiss, watched her move lithely away as she left the bus. Then she let out a slow breath. "I bet she wonders why she ever said she loved me. I'm so darned gauche at times." With determination, Rita headed for her RV. *What the heck am I going to wear*?

†

Neve cursed as the water began to boil over on the vegetables on the stove. She glanced at the glass door of the oven where the chicken at least was behaving—she hoped. Tonight, for the first time in God knew how long, she cooked a meal. The table preparations had been a piece of cake, but the cooking, well, she wasn't going to do this that often…unless Rita asked. That was another thing altogether.

A knock at the door had Neve's eyes darting to the stove once more. Satisfied, she turned down the gas enough to not burn the RV down, quickly walked over to the door, and opened it.

"Hey, you made great time…in fact, it's exactly seven." Neve grinned and moved to allow Rita in.

Rita smiled. "We're having dinner here?"

"Hey, don't sound so surprised. I'll have you know I've done this before," Neve chuckled as she stared intently at Rita. She then took her in her arms and began a passionate, yet gentle, exploration of her lips.

When they came up for air, Rita was breathless. "When?"

"A one-track mind. I'll have to remember that. Well, actually, I think it was at summer school, but only once. My roommate decided it was safer to have takeout than for me to cook." Neve wrapped her arms a little tighter around Rita.

"You were that bad?"

"Hey, no…let's just say we'd have needed extra fire insurance. I love you, and it's wonderful that I can say that." Neve smiled.

For several minutes they lost themselves in the sensual exploration of lips, face, and neck.

"Something is burning," Rita said.

"Darn it!" Neve left Rita's side to look at the food. The water that the vegetables were simmering in had evaporated and the chicken was starting to barbeque.

Rita laughed as she walked over to Neve. "Give me that." She took the oven mitts from Neve's grateful hands.

"Saving the day again, I see."

"Self-preservation. Sit down, and I'll see if we can salvage this." Rita took off her jacket and gave it to Neve.

Neve smiled. "Another reason why I love you. By the way, I could talk all night about why I do." She walked over to a door and opened it before depositing the coat on a hook inside.

"For now, put on some music. I'll have a glass of white wine." Rita pulled open the oven door inspecting the chicken.

"Are we celebrating something?" Neve teased.

"Yeah, your cooking me dinner. You do know I might get used to this."

Neve groaned. "Please don't, or I'll become the best customer of the local take-out…do you like Chinese?"

Rita laughed. "Yes, but wine and music for starters."

Neve felt the heavy burden of her inability to cook simply drop away as she uncorked a bottle of a Pinot Gris, and then moved to the IPod station and selected a variety of soft romantic music.

"Here's your wine. Is it a take-out night?"

"Not quite, but I hope you like your chicken with a slightly charcoal taste. The veggies might have that taste too." Rita grinned as she took the offered glass. "A couple of glasses of wine and we won't know."

"You might not, but I will. I promise you, one day I'll cook us a decent meal that you don't need the help of wine to disguise." Neve stared at her glass of wine.

Rita moved slightly, stood inches from Neve, and reached up with her free hand to touch the pout that formed on Neve's lips. "Wine doesn't always disguise, it can enhance flavors. Besides, it wouldn't matter if this meal tasted of sawdust, I'd still love it."

Neve frowned and then shrugged. "You would, why?"

Rita smiled then pressed her lips to Neve's cheek. "Because you made it for me."

Lost in the sensation of Rita's lips, Neve felt the trembling of her inner core at the touch. "I love you."

"And I love you. Come on, let's have dinner and then you can take me on the grand tour of your fine new establishment."

Neve nodded. "Now *that* I can do."

†

With the right spices and herbs, the dinner turned out to be rather delicious. Neve snuggled next to Rita after she gave her the grand tour of the new RV. It was about the size of the control bus but had six extensions that slid out to form extra space or beds. There was one small area in particular Neve had added hoping it would get the reaction she wanted from Rita.

"Now, my very special area." Neve winked at Rita's astonished expression. "I'm hoping you're going to love this." She opened the door to a room that was big enough to hold two medium-sized chairs. There was a marble bench with lots of cabinets above. "Go inside and see what you think."

Rita, frowning slightly, moved inside, her movements clearly indicating she was checking out every inch. Then, she looked at Neve as she neared the numerous cabinet spaces.

"Go ahead, open them." Neve lounged against the doorway with a smile flickering over her lips.

Seconds later, Rita turned, her eyes as wide as saucers, and with a hand to her mouth she gasped. "It's beautiful."

Neve grinned widely and pointed to a large cabinet on the wall. "Try that one."

Rita did so and then shook her head. There were two shelves, one filled with a consignment of bush tea and the other of blue mountain coffee.

"I figured that when it got too much for us individually or together we could hide away in here and chill. Great thinking space, don't you think? I had the solar light panels fitted for best use of sunlight. That particular window has a special sensor that shows images of terrains in different climate situations. It's kind of like a digital photo frame but larger. You can program your own pictures into the memory. I had this one put in so you could get an idea of what it was like." Neve pressed a button and Whittaker Hill came into view with a full moon glowing above. "Do you like it?"

Rita turned to Neve and simply stared at her. Then she moved closer and wrapped her arms around Neve's neck. "I don't know what I did to deserve you. I love this place and the fact that you thought about me and involved me touches my heart. In one simple gesture, you've cleared every single barrier I'd been placing in my head about how there was no way you could be serious about me. This," Rita waved her hand around the compact room, "proves you mean every single word."

Neve shrugged slightly and then bent to kiss Rita and allowed the kiss to linger and smolder passionately. "That's good enough. Come on, let's have that coffee and tea, and chill."

†

With Rita leaning against her chest, Neve wondered if she could hear her heart beat increasing as the smaller fingers circled her belly. "Are you sleepy?"

Rita murmured something but it wasn't audible.

She kissed Rita and leaned closer. "I think you are. Tell you what, how about we meet for breakfast. Then I need you to go with me to the city. Jacamar and Clara have some business and need our expertise.

Rita's head moved slightly. "Clara never said she was in any financial trouble. Do you know what it's about?"

Neve narrowed her eyes slightly and ignored the question. "We're due there at nine-thirty. I figure if we have breakfast around seven, then we'll easily make it time for the appointment."

Rita was about to reply but her lips were smothered with small kisses before Neve pulled away. "Sounds like a plan. Breakfast at my place…I insist."

Neve chuckled. "Okay. By the way, I'm taking you to a swanky lunch so dress for the occasion and don't tell me you have to be back here because I'm the boss and I need you with me."

Rita laughed softly. "Well…as you're the boss."

"Come here." Neve moved over a pliant, willing body and lost herself in the quiet exploration before she reluctantly pulled away.

When they broke apart, Rita's eyes, glazed over in passion, searched Neve's face before she took in an anxious breath. "I forgot to tell you that I'd met your friend Jennifer before."

Neve gazed into Rita's eyes and smiled before placing a gentle finger to lips that were full from kissing passionately. "Yeah, she mentioned it. Why didn't you tell me?"

Rita pulled away slightly and shrugged. "To be honest, I'd forgotten and then well, it just didn't cross my mind until she turned up here today."

The quiet desolation in the voice had Neve thinking fast. She moved to turn Rita so they faced each other. "I was hoping that we could leave this explanation for another day, but, on reflection, better to get rid of the old baggage early. I lived with Jennifer for a year, and we were lovers for about two."

"Neve, you don't have to explain about your past."

"I think I do. You can explain about yours afterwards if you want to, okay?" Neve half smiled as she stroked a finger down Rita's cheek and felt her react by moving into the caress.

"I don't have a past…well, not like yours."

"Oh. No pressure then. I'd best air that dirty laundry and then you can see who you really do love and if you want to change your mind." Neve shrugged and then felt Rita's lips on hers.

"It's not going to happen, but you're right, why not get it over with now." Rita snuggled back into Neve's chest.

"I met Jennifer when she came to work for the circus. It must be thirteen years ago now. She worked in make-up and she was good…better than good. Anyway, to make a long story short, we got together. It was something I felt she wanted rather than me. I was a rolling stone and enjoyed my freedom. When Jen said she loved me, I guess I was flattered. She was nineteen and I was a woman in my mid-thirties who should have known better. Still, I allowed it to happen and for a while, it was nice. It was good to have someone in my bed at night and someone to talk with. We did talk a lot. Somewhere along the line, I just took her for granted and eventually she became another part of the circus that required my attention when I had the time. It broke her heart when I admitted that the circus meant more to me than she did and that I didn't love her…not deeply. She deserved better."

Rita felt a wave of sympathy for Jennifer wash over her. "She's still your friend, so you must have kept in touch."

"No, she left one summer's night over ten years ago, and I didn't see her again until I went off the rails last year. It was a coincidence. She was traveling in the area, saw my vehicle, and stopped to check on me. I'm glad she did. She made me see sense. Otherwise, who knows where I'd be now or if I even would be alive?"

Rita's eyes flew open in horror as she clutched Neve's hand. "I'm glad she did. Strangely enough, when we first met, I liked her. She has gentle eyes."

"After she left me years ago, I decided that no woman was ever going to be allowed that close to me again. Why inflict that kind of pain on someone? To be honest, for a few weeks I missed her company. Then I found how easy it was just to have a sexual fix when we reached appropriate towns. I never figured myself for settling down…until now."

Rita stared into Neve's eyes and they locked gazes intently. "I'm glad you've decided to try again with me. Do you really want to settle down, Neve? We can have separate lives and still…well, you know."

Neve chuckled and kissed Rita tenderly. "Oh, trust me. You won't get rid of me so easily. Besides, I love you, and that makes all the difference. This time the only person who will end up with a broken heart is me, if you decide you don't want me."

"It's never going to happen then." Rita kissed Neve slowly at first then with mounting passion deepened the kiss.

Minutes later, they both moved apart breathlessly. "I guess that's my cue to escort you home."

Rita felt her lips curve into a tender smile. "You could ask me to stay."

Neve returned the smile. "I know I could, but right now I want you to digest today and what it will mean to the rest of your life and if you really do want this kind of commitment."

Rita blushed and then self-consciously shook her head. "It...does it make a difference that I'm inexperienced?"

"Right now for me, yes. I want the moment to be just right for you."

"You won't keep me waiting too long for the right moment, will you?"

Neve stood gently, bringing Rita up with her. They leaned against each other and Neve gave her a brief kiss. "Count on that moment being very soon." They again lost themselves in feverish kisses and traveling hands. Neve broke away first. "Right home to bed for you, and we'll meet up at your place at seven."

Rita allowed Neve to wrap her coat around her body as they left.

Chapter Thirty-three

When Neve knocked on the door, Rita turned down the flames on the grill before opening the door.

As soon as Neve stepped inside, she took Rita in her arms and thoroughly kissed her good morning.

"Oh, I could get used to this." Rita sighed happily before they broke the embrace and grinned at each other.

"Me, too. You'd best get used to it because from today and for the rest of your life, that's what you have in store. Do you think you can deal with that?"

Rita tilted her head to one side and gave Neve a teasing smile. "I sure can. Want to give me another sample just to be absolutely certain?"

Five minutes later, they moved out of arm's length. The aroma of the cooking breakfast was beginning to seep into their brains.

"I don't want you to do what I did last night." Neve grinned before removing her overcoat and Rita whistled at her clothes.

"Wow, what time did you get up to dress like that? You look like a million dollars." Rita gasped as she checked out Neve's expensively tailored suit. It was made of a dark crimson cloth that looked too good to touch. Under the vest, she wore a pristine, white silk shirt and on her feet were black, leather, highly polished shoes. She'd even taken the time to put on a little make-up, which was unusual. Antique diamond earrings adorned her ears, and a simple gold bracelet was on her wrist.

"Do you think I look presentable?" Neve's eyes never left Rita's face.

"Presentable isn't the word I'd use. You have me thinking about what I'm going to wear. I figured we have breakfast and then I'd take a quick shower and change. I don't want to go out with the smell of cooking in my hair or on my clothes." Rita frowned slightly. In light of Neve's sleek appearance, what to wear became a conundrum for her. A protest from the small stove had her quickly retrieving the sizzling bacon from the grill pan, "Take a seat. We're just about done. How many eggs?"

"Two, please. I need the sustenance. Good plan, by the way, on the shower and change thing. I should have insisted we eat out and not had you go to all this trouble."

"It isn't any trouble." Rita quickly broke three eggs that were cooking as the toast popped up.

Five minutes later, they sat opposite each other eating breakfast.

"What time do Lorenzo and Sally arrive today?" Rita bit into a piece of bacon.

"Oh, I'm not sure, but we'll be ready when they do. Have you heard from Angel recently?"

Rita grinned. "I have. She was telling me about Charlie's new school. Apparently he loves it."

"Speaking of Charlie, you've forgotten to tell me something else." Neve grinned as she munched on her breakfast.

"I have? What?"

Neve sipped her coffee and with a trace of a smile lurking around her eyes. "A circus visit, something about a possible career. Ring any bells?"

Rita thought for a moment and then remembered, "Oh, Neve, I totally forgot. So much has been happening around me that I feel like I'm losing it. Charlie wants to be a flying trapeze artist and not only that, he wants to do exactly what you did. I kind of said you might teach him one day…parents' approval pending, of course."

"Of course. And if his parents approve, I'll certainly teach him." Neve chuckled as they finished their breakfast quicker than normal. That gave Rita extra time to change.

Rita left Neve to finish her coffee and a round of toast while she headed for the shower. Ten minutes later, she toweled dry her hair then looked in the mirror. "Oh, God, who am I kidding? Even if I had a makeover I'd never look like Neve does at seven in the morning. Okay…hair first, then clothes…I can do this."

Fifteen minutes later, standing in her underwear perusing the small closet she pouted at her reflection in the mirror. "Nothing is as grand as what Neve is wearing. Then again, Neve can afford to have good clothes." She, on the other hand, needed to make sensible choices when it came to clothes. Her hand reached for her newest work suit. She'd purchased it only a month before and it looked good. It was certainly the most expensive she'd ever bought in her life for work purposes. It was next to the dress she'd worn for Angel's wedding. The dress had looked good on her, but hardly seemed appropriate for a day in the city. "Choices, choices." A voice from the other side of the door made her jump.

"Rita, how are you doing? Its eight-fifteen, and I can see Jacamar pacing beside the car," Neve said.

Rita, in exasperation, opened the door with a jerk. "I need help in what to wear. Please?"

Neve's eyes roamed over Rita's curves and smiled. "Well, I'd go with placing an overcoat on at this minute and to hell with other people. You look perfect to me…maybe even slightly overdressed."

Rita glanced down at her attire—or lack thereof—and blushed. "Neve, that isn't helping."

Neve chuckled then relented. "Okay, what do you have?" She walked into the small bedroom and looked at the array of clothes. "Nope, that isn't right, not that either." Her fingers slid through the clothes, and then she pulled something out. "Perfect. You looked perfect in this at Angel's wedding…it took my breath away." Neve handed Rita the dress she'd been looking at a few moments before.

Rita accepted the dress and clutched it to her. "You thought I looked *perfect*?"

Neve smiled and then bent her head to snatch a quick kiss. "I did. Now get dressed, and we'll be off. I'll give you another ten minutes. In the meantime, I'll cool Jacamar's heels. Meet you outside, okay?"

Rita nodded. "Okay."

Neve was half in and half out of the doorway when she turned back. "Whatever you wear or don't wear is perfect with me."

Rita didn't reply. She was still thunderstruck by what Neve had said about the dress. Then she quickly applied her make-up and dressed.

†

Jacamar looked at his boss. "Everything okay? We're running late. You do remember that the appointment is at nine-thirty don't you?"

Neve winked at the small man. "It's under control. We'll be there in time."

Clara chose that moment to turn up. "I'm not late, am I?"

"Nope, Rita isn't ready yet. She won't be more than another couple of minutes," Neve answered quietly, then gave Clara a bright smile.

The large woman moved closer to Neve and wrapped her arms around her, "Thank goodness. That isn't my prerogative, now is it, to be late?"

Neve laughed. "No, it isn't."

The door to the RV opened, and Rita stepped out. Neve sucked in a deep breath. "Perfect." She smiled at Rita and helped her into the vehicle.

"Let's go. We have an appointment to keep."

†

Neve parked her vehicle in one of the few parking spaces available in the County Courthouse parking lot and they all started to get out.

"Rita, can you wait a moment? I need to ask you something."

Rita smiled. "Sure."

Neve spoke to Jacamar and Clara. "Guys, we'll meet you in a few minutes. Room six, second floor, right?"

Jacamar nodded and began to leave. Clara gave Neve a quick look, and then agreed.

"See you both shortly." Clara gave Rita a brief smile while climbing out of the Jeep to join Jacamar.

Neve and Rita watched them slowly make their way toward the building.

"So, what can I do for you?" Rita asked with a grin.

Neve didn't answer immediately. Instead, she tapped her fingers on the steering wheel.

"Hey, you're scaring me. Is there anything wrong?" Rita placed her hand on the fingers and felt them shaking. "There's something wrong, isn't there? Please tell me, Neve."

Then Neve sucked in a deep breath. "I've brought you here under false pretenses."

"Oh, is that all. I thought you were sick or someone was dying. I kind of figured that dressing up and bringing along Jacamar and Clara might be a ruse for you to marry me or something." Rita chuckled, and then her smile froze on her face.

"You guessed? Wow, you're in the right place, living with me at a circus: you read minds." The nervous tension that had been flowing through Neve eased a little as she faced Rita. Then her stomach did a double flip at Rita's startled expression. "You were joking, weren't you?"

Rita nodded slowly. "You want to make this official? But how do you know that we're compatible? I mean, we've never even slept together. I could be a total failure in bed."

Neve smiled and then took the hand that remained on her fingers. She brought it up to her lips and kissed the fingers tenderly. "You could never be a failure in my eyes. Besides, sex is just one of many things in a committed relationship. I know we work well together, are good friends, and you certainly respond to my touch, as I do to yours. I figure we have a head start, don't you think?" Neve wriggled her eyebrows and saw the glimmer of a smile appear on Rita's still shocked expression.

"Why like this, in secret, and in such a hurry?" Rita asked.

Neve dropped her head slightly. "Because I didn't want you to think that I wasn't as committed as you. I love you, and I meant every word. I want to share my life with you, and in this state, we can make it legal." She paused. "Did I mention that I loved you?"

This time Rita laughed. "You mentioned it." She rubbed her forehead gently.

"What do you think? Will you consider having a civil ceremony? I promise to love, care for, and keep you for the rest of your life—if you'll have me." Neve held her breath as she waited.

"I promise to love, care for, and keep you for the rest of your life, Neve…if you'll have *me*."

Neve's grin was so wide she was sure her face would split as she pulled Rita into her arms and kissed her repeatedly. "We should go, or they might think we've changed our minds."

"Yes. Let's go."

†

The music in the smaller of the three circus tents was getting louder, or so Rita thought. She watched with a bemused expression as her friends, colleagues and loved ones had a good time—no, a great time.

The whole day had been a kaleidoscope of magical events that culminated in a double celebration of two Garmancelli family marriages: Lorenzo and Sally, Neve and herself.

Her brain simply buzzed with excitement. She thought back to a mere twenty-four hours ago when she had thought that, in all likelihood, her time with the circus, and, more importantly, her association with Neve was over. Now, they were married. She glanced over at Neve, who was twirling around a makeshift dance floor with Charlie. He, Angel and Trevor, waiting with Lorenzo, Sally, Jacamar, and Clara in the County Registrar's office had made the day even more special.

"Hey, Ri, what are you doing here alone?" Angel caught her sister off guard.

"I'm not alone. The place is filled." Rita smiled as she initiated a hug of her younger sibling.

Angel chuckled. "I knew she would make you happy. I'm glad you realized that, too."

Rita gave her sister a long, intense stare before she smiled. "She does make me happy. What I want to know is how you knew to be there today?"

Angel giggled and looked at Neve and her son on the dance floor. "She called us a couple of days after New Years and asked if Trevor could get any time off work and when would be most convenient. We eventually decided on today since he has the next couple of days off."

"You knew almost a month ago?" Rita was in shock.

"Rita, how else do you think we'd be there? Well, actually, no, we didn't know exactly why until a week ago and then Neve had to explain that she hadn't asked you and that it was all hush-hush. I'm glad you accepted though…she really does love you, Ri. She simply glows when she talks about you."

Neve arrived back at Rita's side and slung a casual arm of possession around her shoulders. "Hey, Charlie is sure a lively character. Are you going to let me train him for the flying trapeze?"

Angels' face fell a mile as she shook her head. "No, sorry. I know you're probably one of the best teachers in the world, but he gets to make that decision when he's sixteen."

Neve chuckled. "Too late by then…you need to begin training at his age now."

Rita felt Neve's fingers gently tracing a circular pattern on her shoulder and she lost herself in the sensual touch.

"Are you tired, darling? We seem to have lost you."

Rita shook her head as Angel and Neve looked at her. "No, I'm good. I was just thinking that's all."

"Thinking is good, doing is much better." Neve dropped her head for a quick kiss.

Rita felt her cheeks go warm at the public show of affection. It was all so new and exciting, and Neve's sudden display of love was in contrast to her usual character.

Angel cleared her throat. "Excuse me I need to find Trevor and I see that Charlie is much too fascinated with the man who swallowed swords." She moved away and then turned back, "this is so exciting I love you both."

"Think about letting him start training." Neve laughed heartily and pulled Rita in close. "What do you think?"

"What do I think?"

"Yes, about all this." Neve's hand did a circular pattern over the floor area. "The people…the festivities in general."

"It's wonderful, but it was happening anyway right…for Lorenzo and Sally?" Rita looked into Neve's eyes and saw a shimmering of lights on the surface. It mesmerized her as it always had.

"Well, of course, your family wouldn't be here, and there wouldn't be two cakes, and if you hadn't been here, I wouldn't...otherwise. I guess, yes, it was happening anyway."

Rita sucked in a deep breath. "What do you mean you wouldn't have been here if I weren't?"

"I'd have been hot on your trail, working out how to win your love."

Rita frowned before smiling affectionately and reaching up to touch Neve's cheek. "When can we get out of here? I want to show you, in detail, exactly how much love you did win."

This time Neve seemed to struggle for breath at the offer. Then she took Rita's hand, and, with a tender, sideways look at the people they loved, they walked to the side exit of the tent. "Let's go right now. If we want, we can come back...this party will go on all night."

Rita smiled and squeezed the hand that held hers, "Oh, I think you'll be way too busy teaching me about the pleasures of lovemaking to venture back here tonight."

Neve chuckled and snatched a tender kiss. "Have I unleashed a lustful woman?"

"I hope so."

Hand in hand they walked to Neve's new RV.

†

As the door to the RV shut behind them, neither woman lost any time falling into the other's arms. Their kisses were feverish and ardent. Neve was the first to pull away slightly, and smile tenderly when Rita pouted. Placing a finger to Rita's lips, she gently traced over the warm, wet surface, and then dropped her head to steal a kiss. This time it was barely a whisper of a caress. "I want this to be perfect, Rita. I know we haven't done much of the courtship side of getting to know one another, so I figured we could do that now. I have flowers, champagne, and chocolates—whatever you want."

Rita blinked rapidly. “You want to court me now?” Her gaze moved to the table in the kitchen that held the most gorgeous flowers she’d seen, an ice bucket with champagne, a gold box filled with bonbons, and numerous covered dishes.

Neve chuckled. “Yeah, I figure you’re worth waiting for. And you deserve to have me court you properly. Besides, I don’t want to do anything that might spoil this.”

“Oh.”

Neve leaned in and kissed Rita again. This time the kiss was lingering, and the moans that passed between them told their own story of shared passion.

When they broke for air, Rita had flushed cheeks and her breathing was a bit irregular. “You want to court me, you say?”

Neve, too, was breathing raggedly. She nodded faintly then drew Rita closer as their lips locked again. This time tongues followed. Time seemed to stand still, as they remained locked in a sexually charged embrace. Rita moved slightly and peeled back the collar of Neve’s shirt, She allowed her lips to move to the collarbone, which she kissed slowly, and then allowed her tongue to trace moisture from the top of the collarbone to the valley of Neve’s small breasts. Neve’s throaty moan had Rita deftly unbutton more of Neve’s shirt to expose her cream colored, lacy bra that opened at the front. Seconds later, Neve’s breasts were exposed, and Rita moved dexterously over first the right and then the left, trailing kisses over every inch of bare flesh. One of her hands moved out of Neve’s bear-like hug, traveled upward, and moved over Neve’s breast. It fit her hand perfectly.

Neve’s groan became more guttural, especially when Rita rolled one of Neve’s nipples between her fingers and tugged gently. Rita’s mouth moved to the other exposed nipple and sucked it into her mouth. As she did, Neve’s body ground itself against hers like a second skin.

Neve's head rocked back as the question hovered teasingly in the air. She opened her mouth to speak, but could only articulate a deep moan of pleasure when her breasts were under sensual attack. Her hands seemed to react much better than her brain, as they slid down over Rita's dress to caress the magnificent curves of her bottom.

This elicited a sound of pleasure from Rita, who moved her head away from Neve's breasts to look up into her face, placing tiny kisses from the collarbone up her neck and jaw, eventually finding Neve's lips. "You still want to court me?"

"No."

The single word seemed to say it all. Rita grinned. "Glad you said that. Let's go to bed."

Neve exhaled an agonized breath and tugged Rita toward the bedroom.

Before they reached the bedroom door, various items of clothing dropped along the way. Deep, passionate kisses and feverish hands seemed to have overtaken them—slow and patient clearly not on the menu.

Neve gently disengaged their lips and moved a fraction to open the door to the bedroom. Then with a flair for the theatrical, she picked Rita up in her arms and carried her the short distance to the king-sized bed.

"I love you, Rita." Neve's lips covered Rita's full ones.

After finally coming up for air, the last vestiges of their clothes became new piles on the floor. Neve, lying on top of Rita, caught her breath as her gaze captured the ample breasts, with taunt nipples, in her line of vision. She pulled her mouth away and smiled at Rita. "I want this to be the best time you've ever had, Rita. If we need to go slow and easy, we still can. I wouldn't want you to hate your first time or be disillusioned in any way."

Rita smiled lovingly. "I'd never hate anything you did to me, except for one thing."

Neve's expression held a worried look as she asked, "What's that?"

Rita chuckled and gently pulled Neve's head closer. "If you stop."

With a gasp, Neve captured Rita's lips and then began a dance of sensual pleasure over her skin until she reached the valley of her large breasts. With a moan Neve licked, sucked, and tasted first one breast and then the other, her tongue teasing the nipples into hard points.

Rita began to grind her body closer to Neve's, her strong thighs gently easing her legs open. Neve's hand trailed down Rita's stomach and stroked the flare of her hips, before traveling to the dark triangle of hair at the apex of her legs.

"I'm wet," Rita's voice had an awed tone as she gazed into Neve's darkening eyes.

"It's normal, my darling. Trust me."

Rita nodded, her eyes closing in passion.

Neve's fingers traced circular patterns between Rita's legs, concentrating on the thick bundle of nerves that quivered and cried out for more. Neve placed her fingers next to Rita's moist opening, "I love you, Rita."

Neve's fingers entered her wife and the muscled walls seemed to contract and relax in perfect rhythm with her fingers. Then she felt Rita's body move upwards, arching into her hand. As Rita began her release, she moaned Neve's name. Neve pumped harder, the spasm of Rita's orgasm took control.

Neve didn't immediately remove her fingers. When she felt Rita relax, she gently slid them out and moved to gaze into her lover's face. "How do you feel?"

Rita didn't dare open her eyes. Finally, she replied softly as she kissed Neve's forehead. "Can we stay in bed for the next month…year…forever?"

Neve chuckled and pulled Rita close to her body. "I take it you enjoyed making love with me?"

Rita moved to gaze directly into Neve's eyes. "Oh, yes."

Neve chuckled softly and then kissed Rita, slowly and passionately. "In that case, my love, let me show you one more time."

"You sure you don't want me to..." She drew in a deep breath as Neve's lips replaced her fingers. Rita dropped back on the pillows, lost all over again in a maelstrom of passion and glorious lovemaking.

Epilogue

Rita could hear riotous laughter in the garden below the bedroom. It brought a smile of love and tenderness to her face. "I wonder what Charlie is up to now." She crawled out of bed and looked out to the scene below. Sure enough, Charlie was there with Neve who looked like a drowned rat.

"Hey, what's going on, you two?" Rita called down to them. Two faces looked up both with differing expressions of guilt.

"Wasn't my fault, Aunty Ri, Neve was too close to the pool when she tried to catch the ball." Charley looked down at his bare feet, and, as he did, he threw a discreet look in Neve's direction.

Neve was standing, dripping wet in shorts and t-shirt. The view for Rita was nothing short of tempting. The thin material clearly outlined Neve's small breasts along with protruding nipples.

"Is that true, Neve?" Rita was unable to prevent her voice from catching—Neve's dark intense gaze captured her.

"Probably. He has a great arm. Anyway sleepyhead, I'm taking Charlie into town for breakfast, want to join us? Don't forget that Elian is taking Charlie and a couple of his nephews on a fishing trip in an hour. I said we'd meet him at the jetty."

Rita considered the offer and then shook her head. "I promised to visit Jane this morning. She's becoming quite nervous about the weekend."

Neve frowned then nodded. "Okay, I need to see Christian about some legal stuff. Will you meet me for lunch?"

Rita grinned. "Try and stop me. The usual place?"

"Oh, yes. Come on, Charlie, let's find the fishing gear." They headed off to the boat shed at the end of the garden.

Rita watched them go and smiled before she stretched and looked at the time—quarter after nine. She'd promised to meet Jane at ten. Jane and Christian Chambers were getting married Saturday, and Sasha was due there tomorrow.

Jamaica, almost a year later, had the most glorious memories she could think of. Glorious memories were in the making for Jane Russo as well. On Friday evening, the whole family, including a six-month pregnant Angel and Trevor, would be there to celebrate. It was going to be wonderful. Lorenzo and Sally, with baby Carlo, were going to stay for a few days at the house before going to their place in Montego Bay for a short winter break. At least it would be shorter than the usual Garmancelli vacation time.

Neve had done a wonderful thing for her new home town of Rochester and arranged for the smaller of her circus tents to be erected there over the winter period. During the three-month stay, the younger and retired circus performers would entertain the locals and become a draw for the desperate town. The local council had been astounded when Neve had talked to them about the proposal and members immediately became cooperative. The circus had been open about a month, and already there was a general buzz of excitement from townspeople about the increase in tourist traffic. Rachel, along with Carla and Jacamar, received the prestigious title of Personal Representative for the Circus. Their friends were delighted with the opportunity. The operation was still in its early days, but she and Neve both felt positive about the situation. Neve noted that it would give the younger performers the chance to shine without being in the shadow of bigger names. Yes, things were working out perfectly. With a spring in her step, Rita walked into the bathroom and began to dress for her visit.

†

Neve lounged on the blanket she'd placed on the sand in their private cove, yards from the house they'd built on the Port Antonio plot of land. It had been a labor of love as far as she and Rita were concerned. Shortly after their civil ceremony, they returned to Jamaica for a three-week honeymoon. In that time, they had hired builders to build their dream home. Completed only a month earlier, they spent the first week alone, enjoying the experience before Charlie arrived for a vacation.

Neve leaned back on the blanket and closed her eyes behind the sunglasses she wore. Her mind began to wander over the past year and Rita's influence in her life. The feeling of being in love had taken her completely by surprise. She knew it was wonderful, but over the time they'd spent getting to know each other sexually and mentally, she realized the extent of how much she needed Rita in her life. It would kill her to lose what they had. Her love for Rita grew stronger each day. Sometimes she wondered if Rita knew how much she meant to her life. "Have I actually ever told her?"

There was movement on the blanket and Neve opened her eyes to see Rita flop down next to her, wearing a skimpy T-shirt and bikini briefs. "I hope you didn't visit my aunt wearing those?"

"You don't approve of my attire?" Rita quipped as she placed a wicker picnic basket near their feet.

Neve leaned up on her elbows and tweaked her finger for Rita to come closer. She did, and Neve captured willing lips and explored them intimately before they finally drew away for breath. "I approve, but only if it's for me when we're alone."

"Spoilsport." Rita grinned snatching a quick kiss of her own. "What time is Charlie due back?"

Rita's light tone had Neve smiling. "Elian is taking him to meet the family, and he's staying overnight. I didn't think you'd mind, and he was all for it."

"I'm good. Elian will look after him." Rita traced a finger on Neve's thigh.

"Thought you might say that. This means we can do whatever you want for the rest of the day. Any suggestions?" Neve's heart jumped at every stroke of Rita's fingers on her bare flesh.

"Oh, yeah." Rita exhaled, moving slowly to pin Neve on the blanket. "You looked as sexy as hell this morning…you knew it, didn't you?"

Neve chuckled and removed her sunglasses. She traced the line of Rita's smile. "My darling, whatever do you mean?" Still laughing, she slowly lifted the t-shirt Rita wore. "You remembered the suntan lotion, I hope."

Rita, snared by Neve's smoldering expression, nodded.

"Good, I wouldn't want you to have sunburn like last time." Neve's fingers expertly removed the t-shirt and she felt herself drowning in the creamy flesh of Rita's breasts. Her lips, slowly following her eyes, pulled a nipple into her mouth, "Oh, darling, you shouldn't have…coconut is my favorite."

Rita giggled and couldn't stop as they rolled off the blanket. "You are way too confident, Neve Garmancelli."

Neve tossed her head and looked at the sea, then back to Rita, "Only because I love you. I do, more and more every day."

Rita smiled and bent her head to kiss Neve's lips tenderly. "Good. It works double for me. Guess we're stuck with each other."

"I wouldn't want it any other way."

"Me, either. I think you're way overdressed. I want to try out a new position. It has to do with your legs spread and me up close and personal between them."

Neve growled sensually. "That's not new."

Rita smiled as she pulled down Neve's shorts and expertly positioned herself exactly where she wanted to be "It always will be to me. Every time we make love is new. Do you object?"

Neve groaned as Rita's tongue teased her clit. "What's to object?" They lost all clarity of thought and speech as the passion of the moment and the love they shared encompassed them.

About The Author

JM Dragon

Born in England, JM Dragon is now a New Zealand citizen, living in the beautiful Canterbury countryside. JM Dragon loves to garden, travel and has a love of her animals. Sharing her life with her family, two cats, two alpacas, and over forty Bantam chickens of differing breeds, she's found a totally different focus in her life than when she lived in England.

Her writing is a long cherished release for the characters that invade her mind on many an occasion. Always having written stories from a childhood on, she found the Internet a place she could share her creative world with other readers. Having stumbled across venues on the net for her writing, she found new subjects to explore. She currently loves the creative, readership and friendship genre she has comfortably taken residence in for the last twelve years.

A keen reader of sci-fi, crime/mystery, classic, and romance, of course, JM Dragon is here to stay and loves to experiment with storylines—who knows what story genre she will tease us with next.

E-Books, Print, Free e**B**ooks

Visit our website for more publications available online.

www.affinityebooks.com

Published by Affinity E-Book Press NZ Ltd
Canterbury, New Zealand
Registered Company 2517228

2562790R00207

Printed in Great Britain
by Amazon.co.uk, Ltd.,
Marston Gate.